Miss Austen Investigates

A Fortune Most Fatal

By the same author

Miss Austen Investigates

Miss Austen Investigates

A Fortune
Most Fatal

JESSICA BULL

MICHAEL JOSEPH

PENGUIN MICHAEL JOSEPH

UK | USA | Canada | Ireland | Australia
India | New Zealand | South Africa

Penguin Michael Joseph is part of the Penguin Random House group of companies
whose addresses can be found at global.penguinrandomhouse.com

Penguin Random House UK
One Embassy Gardens, 8 Viaduct Gardens, London SW11 7BW

penguin.co.uk

Penguin
Random House
UK

First published 2025

001

Set in 12.25/18pt Adobe Caslon Pro
Typeset by Jouve (UK), Milton Keynes
Printed and bound in Great Britain by Clays Ltd, Elcograf S.p.A.

The authorized representative in the EEA is Penguin Random House Ireland,
Morrison Chambers, 32 Nassau Street, Dublin D02 YH68

A CIP catalogue record for this book is available from the British Library

HARDBACK ISBN: 978-0-241-64211-5
TRADE PAPERBACK ISBN: 978-0-241-64212-2

Penguin Random House is committed to a sustainable future
for our business, our readers and our planet. This book is made from
Forest Stewardship Council® certified paper

MIX
Paper | Supporting
responsible forestry
FSC
www.fsc.org   FSC® C018179

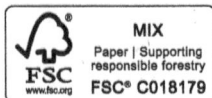

For my mum, dad, and sister, Kelly:

'There are few people whom I really love,
and still fewer of whom I think well.'

– Jane Austen, 1813

If sufficient variety of company will not befall a young lady in her own village, she must seek it abroad. The author, therefore, humbly presents the finest society in all of East Kent:

At Rowling Manor:

Mr Edward 'Neddy' Austen, later Knight (b. 1767): third son of the Reverend Mr George Austen (b. 1731) and his wife, Cassandra Austen, née Leigh (b. 1739). Adopted by his distant cousins, the Knights of Godmersham Park

Mrs Elizabeth Austen, née Bridges (b. 1773): Neddy's wife, daughter of Sir Brook Bridges, third baronet (b. 1733, d. 1791)

Miss Frances-Catherine 'Fanny' (b. 1793), Master Edward 'Ted' (b. 1794) and Master George-Thomas 'Little Georgy' (b. 1795) Austen, later Knight: the progeny of Neddy and Elizabeth

Conker (b. 1793): their dog

Miss Jane Austen (b. 1775): Neddy's sister, a young lady of little experience and no consequence

At Godmersham Park and nearby Crundale Parsonage:

Mrs Catherine Knight, née Knatchbull (b. 1753): Neddy's adoptive mother, widow of Thomas Knight II (b. 1735, d. 1794)

Princess Eleanor (b. circa 1775–80): Mrs Knight's
   enigmatic house guest
The Reverend Mr Samuel Blackall (b. 1762): Mrs
   Knight's clergyman, Kent's foremost exorcist

At Goodnestone House (pronounced 'Gunston'):
Sir Brook-William Bridges, fourth baronet (b. 1761):
   Elizabeth's eldest brother, owner of the
   Goodnestone estate
Miss Henrietta Bridges (b. 1768): Elizabeth's elder,
   unmarried sister, owner of a maudlin collection
   of sheet music
Mr Brook-Edward Bridges (b. 1779): Elizabeth's
   younger, unmarried brother. What a shame so
   many brothers lie, or rather stand, between him
   and the magnificent Goodnestone House

Chapter One

Kent, England, 8 June 1797

In the dimly lit dining room of the Bull and George inn, Dartford, Jane wrings her hands and paces. It takes thirteen steps to travel the narrow space between trestle tables, pushed up against bow-fronted windows, to the inglenook fireplace at the rear of the smoke-filled room. The distance is not enough to dispel the nervous energy from her limbs, forcing her to turn and begin again. Bunches of dried hops, suspended from worm-eaten beams, brush her forehead as she passes. The crisp flowers snap against her bonnet, dispensing flecks of broken petals onto the shoulders of her tawny pelisse. 'I can hardly believe this has happened.' She presses her forehead to the smeared glass.

Outside, the moonlit highway is deserted. Her stomach clenches at the thought of her father and brother forced out into this wilderness. All but the most intrepid of travellers take care to conclude their journeys by sunset. Highwaymen are known to work this stretch of road.

'Please, try to remain calm.' Mrs Austen sits on a hardbacked bench, beneath the window, her woollen cloak gathered tight around her narrow shoulders. Unlike her daughter, she has removed her bonnet, and balances it on her knee while she worries the ribbon with her fingers.

'Calm?' Jane's voice is shrill. 'My sisters are gone, Mother. Stolen. Abducted. They could be anywhere by now. Who knows what disreputable hands they may fall into? You heard the landlord. The post-chaise is on its way to Gravesend, its passengers bound for a ship to the West Indies. They'll be lost for ever, ruined!'

Mrs Austen purses her lips. 'Must you be so melodramatic, Jane? Your father and Neddy gave chase on horseback as soon as we realized the mistake. They're sure to catch up with the other party within a few miles. You'll have your manuscript back forthwith.'

Jane rests her hand at the base of her throat and swallows. *The Sisters* is her latest composition. Like everything else in her writing box, it is destined to cross the Atlantic, should her father and brother not retrieve it in time. 'Good Lord, what if the coachman mistakes Neddy and Papa for robbers and fires his pistol? They'll be killed!'

'Stop being ridiculous. Sit down at once and take a sip of brandy.' Mrs Austen swills her drink in its tin cup. 'It's rather good. Reminds me of what your cousin Eliza used to send us from France.'

'Dark days are coming,' cries a ragged old man from across the room, causing Jane and her mother to startle violently. He is the inn's only other patron. Hitherto he has sat quietly, warming his ancient bones beside the dwindling fire, a clay pipe clenched between his teeth. 'Judgement must be nigh if an honest soul can't pass a journey in peace. I thought to come by road, as the sea is turning against all who would sail on her. A cutter went down off the coast of Harty not five nights since.'

Jane squeezes her eyes shut, trying to block out the old man's ramblings. The foul stench of tobacco clogs her throat, threatening to choke her. 'I should have known to take better care of my writing box. What was I thinking, letting it be strapped onto the roof of the coach when it could have been inside with me? Then it would never have been confused with the other passengers' luggage.'

'The crew was up to no good, I expect.' The old man scratches his steel-grey beard and continues his nonsensical monologue. 'No one sails this way in a storm. Not unless they're trying to escape paying their dues. God alone knows what the skipper saw in those waves to make him attempt such a sharp turn without so much as readying the sails. Unless it was his own fate crashing towards him.'

Mrs Austen swivels her spare frame towards her daughter.

'Jane, I know your writing is important to you. Increasingly so during the last year, ever since your disappointment over –'

Jane balls her fists at her side. 'If you so much as say his name, Mother, I swear I'll combust on the spot.' Why must Jane's parents insist on reading any slight alteration to her mood as some aching regret over the loss of her former suitor? She knows she did the right thing in refusing Mr Lefroy's lacklustre proposal, especially in the face of such violent objections from his relations. To marry without the blessing of his great-uncle and patron would have been to the detriment of both their futures, no matter how fond of each other they were. It is only natural she should wish that circumstances had been different – or that they might become so in time. Ever since Tom's departure, she has tried her utmost to perform her duties to God and her family, and to seek solace in her compositions. It is not her fault her heartbeat occasionally trips over itself when she passes a fair-haired stranger in the street at the unlikely possibility it *might* be him.

'As I was saying, I know your work is important to you, but I shall not pay for a separate stagecoach ticket for your writing box. It should have been perfectly safe on the roof with your trunk and the rest of our luggage.' Mrs Austen folds her arms against her flat chest.

'But it wasn't, was it? Because while we were busy re-acquainting ourselves with Neddy, all my belongings were redirected to the West Indies. You don't understand. Everything I hold dear is locked away in that box. It's not just *The Sisters*. My only copies of *Catherine* and *First Impressions* are in there too.'

The old man grips the handle of his hazel walking stick with his gnarled hand and beats the tip against the stone hearth. 'Tossed and turned like it was no more than a toy. Mast broke first. Snapped in two like a blade of straw. We could hear the sailors' screams. But we can't do nothing, not when the sea decides she's going to make you hers.'

Mrs Austen angles her knees towards the window, proffering her back to the inn's noisy patron. 'Even if the very worst happens, and we fail to recover your luggage, you can always redraft those compositions. They're your creations, born out of your own head. You've spent so long locked away in your dressing room hunched over them that every word must be etched onto your memory by now. And if you were forced to rewrite them, they'd probably turn out even better.'

'Rewrite them?' Jane splutters, indignant at her mother's casual dismissal of her achievements. She has spent the last eighteen months labouring over each word, deliberating every sentence, writing and rewriting every paragraph of her compositions until the drafts are as near perfect as earthly hands can make them. *Catherine* and *First Impressions* are full-length novels. Both are longer, more serious and, dare she say it, far superior to anything she attempted in her youth. Her previous works were girlish trifles, mere skits to pass her time and amuse her family. She has only recently commenced work on *The Sisters*, but she hopes it will be her most accomplished delineation of human nature yet. 'Where would I find the time for that, given I'm committed to playing nursery maid to Neddy's brood all summer?'

Mrs Austen narrows her eyes. 'That was your choice, Jane. You volunteered to go to Rowling in Cassandra's place.'

'How could I not?' Jane bites back tears as she turns her face to the window. Mrs Austen is reflected in the glass, blinking into her lap.

A full moon has not yet passed since Cassandra's fiancé's ship returned to Falmouth and, rather than carrying her beloved Mr Fowle safely home, brought the news of his tragic demise. Poor Mr Fowle. He'd only just reached San Domingo when he was struck down with yellow fever. All these months Jane's sister had been excitedly sewing her trousseau and recording her mother's receipts in a household book of her very own, while his lifeless body had been drifting in the waves after burial at sea. In an instant, the knowledge washed away Cassandra's sunny temperament, her natural optimism sunk for ever beneath the burden of her grief.

And so Jane volunteered to go to Rowling to assist Neddy's wife, Elizabeth, in the safe delivery of their fourth child. Cassandra was present for the birth of all three of their older children. Before the news of the tragedy broke,

Elizabeth wrote to say she dearly hoped Cassandra would join her again, as she'd be lost without her help. Alas, this time she will have to find her way with only Jane to guide her. Stricken Cassandra remains in Hampshire with their eldest brother, James – the pair of them equally inconsolable in their grief. Mr Fowle was not only Cassandra's fiancé but James's best friend and a firm favourite with the entire Austen family. James's wife promised to take good care of him and Cassandra while Jane's parents escorted her as far as Dartford to meet Neddy. Mary Lloyd, or rather Mrs James Austen (it's been several months since the wedding but Jane still has to correct herself), is also expecting. Given her condition, Jane hopes Mary will remember to preserve herself too.

To Jane, Mr Fowle was already more of an honorary brother than merely another of the many schoolboys who grew up alongside her at Steventon Rectory. She pictures his smiling countenance when, as a boy, he patiently taught her and Cassandra how to swing a cricket bat and catch their brother's merciless throws without breaking all their fingers. An aching lump forms in her throat at the thought of that same handsome face tossed asunder until it was destroyed by the Caribbean Sea.

Everyone congratulates Jane on her selflessness in offering to attend her sister-in-law. They do not know she is going because she cannot bear to look upon Cassandra's agony. Her sister's sobs are a dagger to her own heart. If

Cassandra can be undone by love, then what chance has the more easily dejected Jane? Only a fool would risk indulging in hopes of lasting happiness after witnessing first-hand the agony of having one's expectations so cruelly dashed.

The old man takes a rasping breath, recalling Jane from her reflections. 'Every one of those poor souls perished that night. All the crew drowned. Must have been twenty men at least, on board a ship like that. If the skipper had lived, he'd be up in front of a justice by now – with a noose around his neck.'

The sorry tale further reinforces Jane's melancholy over the fate of Mr Fowle. She tips her head towards the chunky oak beam across the fireplace and mutters under her breath, 'I do wish he'd desist from that racket.'

'Quite.' Mrs Austen wriggles in her seat. 'His prophecies of doom are hardly helping matters.'

The front door swings open and a blast of cool air rushes in, extinguishing the fire and casting the old man into darkness. Neddy strides towards Jane. His golden curls flow over the collar of his blue velvet frock coat and his genial face beams in the darkness. 'We have it!' He grasps a mahogany box to his chest as if it weighed no more than a sheet of paper. 'The coachman was most apologetic about the confusion. Father and the innkeeper have your trunk, but I thought you'd want this straight away.' He slams the box onto the table.

Relief floods through Jane as she digs around in her

pocket for the tiny brass key. As she unlocks the lid and flips it open, the box is transformed into a green leather-topped writing slope. She hooks a finger into a brass pull and lifts away a section to reveal a cubbyhole. Inside, safe and sound, is *The Sisters*; the first sketches of the Misses Dashwood are contained within their letters to each other. Letters that Jane has lovingly composed as the start of her new story. Her shoulders fall away from her ears and her entire body turns limp.

Losing her writing box, and all the work contained within it, would have made an ominous start to her journey. Given Jane has never before ventured as far from home as East Kent, and has never travelled anywhere without Cassandra beside her, she is already full of trepidation as to how she will navigate the days and weeks ahead. She can lay claim to no natural inclination to be present at the birth of her newest niece or nephew, and being entrusted with the safety of her sister-in-law throughout her delivery is a daunting prospect. As agonizing as it was to witness Cassandra's suffering, being separated from her beloved sister is bound to bring its own torment. But surely Jane can withstand any trial, so long as she has her characters by her side.

Chapter Two

Queen Anne's lace billows in the breeze as Jane rattles through the Kent countryside in Neddy's phaeton. From her exposed position on the raised seats of the open carriage, the Garden of England is laid out before her. She had offered to take the mail coach from Dartford, so that Neddy would not have to retrieve her himself, but neither her father nor her brother would hear of her travelling unchaperoned. Given her inexperience as a lone traveller, they were probably right to err on the side of caution. On account of her family's protectiveness, she'll be stranded in Kent until such time as one of her male relations deigns to collect her.

The newly commissioned Captain Henry Austen volunteered to do the honours. Having graduated from St John's College, Oxford, Henry was meant to be preparing for ordination. However, with the war continuing to rage across Europe and the West Indies, and the French threatening to send another invasion force across the Channel at any moment, he secured a position as acting paymaster with the Oxfordshire militia instead. It is certainly more lucrative than a curacy. He expects to be granted leave in mid-August, a month after Elizabeth's baby is due. His regiment is stationed in East Anglia and he writes that he is most eager to visit his Kent relations before continuing home to Hampshire. But, as reliability has never been Henry's strong point, Jane hesitates to set too much store by his promise.

As they squeeze through the country lanes, encased on both sides by towering hedgerows, Jane reflects on the slight disparity of the countryside to that of her native Hampshire. The flat terrain enlarges the blue sky above them, and the white conical tips of oast houses peek over verdant slopes at almost every juncture. Every few miles, a farmer's daughter stands at the roadside with punnets of freshly picked strawberries or cherries for sale. Jane has already sampled both, delighting in the sweet yet sharp flavour of the newly ripened fruit. 'Your conveyance is very smart,' she says, searching for a way to engage Neddy in conversation. Despite his bonhomie, Jane is acutely aware of the distance between them. It was not so noticeable when her parents were present, but since she and Neddy set out alone, she cannot help but feel awkward and unsure of herself. He does not seem to grasp half her jokes, and she is too timid to tease him as she would her other brothers.

Neddy grins, well satisfied with the compliment. 'Beth

would prefer a closed carriage. While I admit such a vehicle might be more dignified for a family, a phaeton is made for speed. Perhaps I'll indulge her with a barouche next year, if my returns are as anticipated. I'll need to employ a dedicated coachman, mind, and purchase another pair of coach horses. It's difficult to find a truly well-matched team. Sixty guineas, this pair cost me. But as soon as I saw them, I simply *had* to have them.'

'I'm sure you did.' Jane smiles, holding tight to the crown of her straw hat to prevent it from blowing away. The elegant mares lift their dainty hoofs in unison, swishing their plaited tails. She does not mention that since Parliament introduced a new tax on carriages to fund the war effort, Mr Austen has been forced to sell his vehicle, leaving the family reliant on the kindness of their neighbours whenever they are in need of transport. Neddy was raised in a different world from her: there is no point in drawing comparisons.

Jane was only three years old when Mr and Mrs Knight called at Steventon Rectory while surveying their various estates as part of their bridal tour. The anticipation of their arrival is imprinted on her mind due to the uncharacteristically stern warning she and all the children had received from Mr Austen to be on their best behaviour throughout the duration of his cousin and benefactor's visit. It was Mr Knight's father who, having grown vastly rich by doing no more than outliving several of his wealthy but childless relations, gave the newly married Mr Austen the livings of

Steventon and Deane. The combined tithes yield an income of just over two hundred pounds per year, affording Jane's family the tenuous purchase on respectability they have enjoyed for the last three decades.

When the dazzling duo eventually arrived in a coach and six, all the children became giddy with excitement. Mr Knight smelt of lemon bonbons, which he handed out freely, and his handsome bride, almost twenty years his junior, wore an enormous wide-brimmed hat adorned with ostrich feathers. Jane's parents were no doubt relieved when, as they prepared to leave, the couple revealed themselves to be so charmed by the family that they invited one of the older boys to join them on their journey. James was busy preparing to go up to Oxford. Georgy, with his various afflictions, was never a consideration. Henry was already proving far too much of a handful to be trusted with the responsibility of representing his entire family. That left eleven-year-old Neddy, generally lauded as the Austens' prettiest and most affable child.

Indeed, Neddy did such a good job of making himself amiable that, once the Knights had completed their tour and returned to their magnificent home of Godmersham Park in Kent, they regularly invited their young favourite to join them for extended periods. Jane's mother explained that, as the Knights had not yet been blessed with children of their own, it was only charitable to let them borrow Neddy from time to time. Within four years, Mr Knight must have concluded that his union would remain childless, leaving him in want of nothing except an heir. So he asked if he could borrow Neddy for good.

The Godmersham coachman rode all the way with the message, along with a sleek bay pony tethered to his horse. At first, Mr Austen baulked at the notion of surrendering his son for adoption. It was Mrs Austen, with her eminent pragmatism, who had the foresight to counsel her husband: 'I think, my dear, you had better oblige your cousins, and let the child go.' Jane stood at the door of the rectory, with her remaining siblings, and tried desperately not to cry as Neddy mounted his new pony and called his adieus. From the moment Neddy went to live with the Knights, they raised him in the style of one anticipated to be a gentleman of great fortune. True to their word, Neddy is now heir to Mr Knight's widow, whose combined estates Mrs Austen estimates are worth eight thousand pounds a year, and his wife, Elizabeth, is the daughter of a baronet.

It proved a shrewd decision for the prospects of the wider Austen family too. Despite the generosity of Mr Austen's patron and his enthusiastic attempts to supplement his income by farming his glebe lands and running a school for boys, Jane's father complains his annual deposits to his banker never quite exceed his withdrawals. Not having to provide a portion for Neddy has afforded Mr Austen more liberty to secure the rest of his children's futures. James and Henry were content to claim their free places as descendants of a founder of St John's College, both with a view to following their father into holy orders, but Frank resolved to become a naval officer. And as Frank was determined to win his fortune at sea, so, too, was the youngest Austen boy, Charles, who had always idolized his most audacious elder brother. Since Mr Austen had no connections at the Admiralty who could offer the boys a place on board a ship, he paid the fifty pounds per year necessary to send each of them to the Royal Naval Academy in Portsmouth. It would have been impossible for him to be so supportive of his sons' ambitions if he'd been liable for launching the career of yet another.

Most significantly, Neddy's adoption provides a guarantee of future comfort. He may not yet be in possession of his fortune, but the family have already learnt to count on it. The expectation of his wealth, combined with his good nature, gives Jane's father the peace of mind that his wife and daughters, not to mention his most vulnerable child, Georgy, will continue to be provided for even after he is no more. For Georgy, who suffers from fits and is mute, will never be able to make his own way in the world and, as young ladies of the middling sort, Jane and Cassandra's only option for advancement is to marry well.

For a while after Neddy's removal from Steventon, Jane did wonder if she and the rest of the Austen children might also be adopted by their wealthier relations. By rights, her uncle, James Leigh-Perrot, should have been her first choice as he, too, had no offspring and a great propensity for inheriting legacies. However, Jane always suspected she'd be happier with her more frivolous late aunt, Philadelphia Hancock. While Aunt Phila's chaotic approach to economy meant that any money her husband, Mr Hancock, earned as a surgeon for the East India Company never stretched far, she had a knack for winning friends of extraordinary generosity. Several years after her marriage, while Aunt Phila was living in Bengal, she became a particular favourite of the great Warren Hastings. When Jane's cousin Eliza was born, less than a year later, Mr Hastings magnanimously agreed to stand as godfather and even bestowed a personal fortune of ten thousand pounds on her. How different Jane's life might have been if she was a woman of independent means. For a start, she would have been able to marry Tom.

Neddy disturbs her reverie by waving his hat enthusiastically at a shepherd leaning on his crook in the distance. 'We'll be at Rowling in no time.' The historic manor, where Neddy currently resides, is part of Elizabeth's family's larger estate of Goodnestone (which the Bridges family pronounce 'Gunston', their claim to the land being so well established that they may dispense with any extra syllables). 'These are my fields. The house came with a hundred acres, but I took an additional two hundred from Sir William on Lady Day. Luckily for me, the baronet has little interest in agriculture. He's very happy to lease it all on the promise of a good return.'

As Jane gazes appreciatively at the newly shorn sheep, gambolling about in what looks like their stockings and shifts, she wonders if Neddy's enthusiasm for proving his credentials as a tenant farmer is aimed at reassuring Mrs Knight that he is prepared for the enormous responsibility she will one day bequeath him. It strikes her that he might have expected to inherit a portion of his adoptive father's wealth immediately after he died, rather than having to wait for his widow's demise. The deeds to any one of her three largest estates (Steventon and Chawton in Hampshire, or Godmersham in Kent) would have made him a significant landowner: all three will put him on a par with a duke. 'How wonderful. Father will ask me to recount every detail, so you must tell me everything you can.'

'My flock are of a different breed from those in Steventon, darker in the face and without the horns. I don't suppose you noticed? Canterbury wool is the finest in the world. I could command a pretty penny for their fleeces on the Continent, if not for the execrable tax on exports.'

'I had no idea I was among such discerning company. May I beg an introduction to each of your ewes? Tell them I'm most eager to make their acquaintance.'

Neddy laughs over the creak of the whirring wheels. 'I'm so glad you're here. Beth and the children were delighted when you offered to come.'

'And I'm so pleased to be here.' Jane dips her chin to her chest, attempting to protect her countenance from becoming any further wind-chafed and sunburnt than it already is. The toes of her half-boots peep out from beneath the hem of her dress. In the harsh sunlight, the toes are scuffed and the leather is worn. She wishes she'd remembered to ask the new maid to blacken them before she left. Sally, the previous maidservant, would have done it without being asked. Unfortunately, Sally has jilted the Austens in favour of marriage and a home of her own, and the stout girl-of-all-work Jane's mother hired to replace her seems offended when asked to do any.

Neddy cracks the whip above the mares' hinds. 'I'll take them up to a gallop, shall I? See if we can go as fast as when I used to wrap you in a sheet and tug you down the rectory stairs.'

The motion throws Jane's body backwards. She grabs Neddy's elbow, and half screams, half laughs as she is reminded of his rumbustious play. Too many years have elapsed since the siblings spent any real time together and she has missed him dearly. It will be gratifying to spend a few weeks getting to know him and his young family better. Perhaps she will be able to close the gulf between them and, by the end of the summer, Neddy will be as familiar to her as any of her brothers. More selfishly, with her own room in Neddy's comfortable home, and without the distraction of her usual domestic duties, she should be able to make good progress with *The Sisters*.

Rowling Manor sits in its own manicured parkland, at the end of a long, serpentine drive. Handsome redbrick chimney

stacks protrude from the slate roof, glinting in the afternoon sunshine, and pale pink roses ramble across the façade,
perfuming the air with their sweet floral scent. There is an
extra wing, large enough to accommodate a cook, a manservant and two housemaids, as well as a separate coach house
and stables. In his letters, Neddy described it as a 'good-
sized family home'. Jane is obliged to agree: it is delightfully
cavernous.

The carriage draws to a halt and Elizabeth pokes her
head from behind the glossy black front door. At four-and-
twenty, Jane's sister-in-law is only three years older than
herself, but the fine lines around her dark eyes reveal she
has aged in the short time since she married. She is slen-
der, with a long neck that gives her the appearance of an
overly curious swan. In her high-waisted morning gown,
you'd hardly know she was expecting, until she turns to the
side and her bump protrudes so far it's a wonder she has
not delivered already. 'Edward, where have you been? I was
expecting you home yesterday. It doesn't take four nights to
get to Dartford and back.'

'Well, I'm here now, darling. Don't fret.' Neddy leaps
down, offering Jane his hand as soon as the soles of his
top boots hit the gravel. Jane clasps it and does her best to
descend gracefully under the scrutiny of her sister-in-law.
Elizabeth attended a frightfully expensive school for young
ladies in London, which she boasts keeps a retired coach
expressly for the purpose of instructing its pupils on how

to alight while revealing no more than the regulatory inch of stocking above the ankle.

'Jane.' Elizabeth offers her cheek. Jane kisses the air beside it. A toddler straddles Elizabeth's hip, eyeing Jane warily. Another two golden-haired infants peep out from behind their mother's skirts, while a pair of young women in matching grey dresses hover behind them.

'That's not Aunt Cassy.' The eldest child, a girl of four, fails to hide her disappointment as she stage-whispers to her mother. The little boy beside her glares at Jane with a decidedly hostile air. Only Conker, Neddy's brown-and-white-spotted spaniel, betrays any authentic enthusiasm for her arrival. The dog wags his docked tail frantically, and leaps straight upwards, so high he's like a marionette tugged by an invisible string.

'Don't be shy, Fanny, Ted. We told you it was Aunt *Jane* who was coming this time. We did tell them, didn't we? I'm sure Aunt Cassy will be with us again soon.' Neddy hoists both children up, with his strong arms, presenting each in turn. They smell of cooked milk and their ringlets are as soft as the fluffy down of a newly hatched chick. Jane tries to kiss them without sustaining an injury as they wriggle and kick to be released. Once Neddy has deposited them safely on the ground, he takes the toddler from Elizabeth. 'And what do you think of our Georgy? Is he as stout as his namesake yet?'

'Me, Itty Dordy?' the child lisps.

'That's right, you're Little Georgy.' Jane laughs. 'But Papa's right. You'll be as big as your uncle Georgy in no time.' She reaches out, stroking Georgy's rosy cheeks. The little boy gurgles and squashes his neck until it disappears into rolls of fat. She is relieved to find one of the children does not bear her any ill-humour for being the wrong aunt.

Elizabeth's features relax as she watches her husband cradle one child while the other two hang off his legs. 'Come along, let's get you settled.' She rests a cool hand on the small of Jane's back. 'We've put you in the green bedroom, overlooking the pond. We'll have a quiet family dinner tonight, but I have lots planned for the rest of your visit. Kent society is extremely lively, and I've made a list of all the families I absolutely must introduce you to.'

'But you mustn't fuss,' replies Jane. 'I'm here to help you, not give you more work to do.'

Elizabeth blinks at her. 'Help *me?*'

'Yes. You know, with your . . .' Jane gestures towards Elizabeth's swollen figure '. . . confinement. I'll feed and bathe the children, take care of any mending, run your errands. Do whatever Cassy usually does.'

Elizabeth flicks her hand at the two young women following them into the house. 'We have servants for that sort of thing, Jane. This is Susan and Susan.'

'Both Susan?' asks Jane. The taller replies with a shrug, while the shorter, younger girl simply stares at Jane.

Elizabeth continues: 'And as for my "confinement", I'm

not Anne Boleyn. You don't have to shut me away, smothered in tapestries. There are another six weeks until the baby is due. That gives us plenty of time to get you established.'

'Established?' Jane steps over the threshold into the grand entrance hall. A gentle flame flickers in the fireplace despite the mild summer's day. She releases the heavy lace band tied beneath her chin to remove her bergère hat. Beneath it, her chestnut curls are damp and slick against her forehead.

'Yes, established. Among our set.' Elizabeth takes Jane's hat, handing it to the taller maid as if it were a dirty rag. 'You are sister to the heir of Godmersham. There are plenty of eligible bachelors hereabouts who will be most eager for an introduction.'

Jane swallows the horrible suspicion that she has walked into a trap. It would seem she has arrived in Kent under the expectation she came to secure her future in the only way a respectable lady can. 'But I was hoping for a quiet summer, with you and the children. And perhaps a little time for my writing. I've brought *Catherine* and *First Impressions* to read to you in the evenings.'

'First what?' Elizabeth stares at her blankly.

'*First Impressions*. It's my latest composition. And I'm hoping to make great progress with my new one, *The Sisters*, while I'm here.'

'I hoped you'd have grown out of your freaks and fancies by now.' Elizabeth rests a hand on her hip. 'Well, I'm sorry but you won't have time for any of that nonsense.'

'But I . . .' Jane searches for a rebuttal but the words have dried on her tongue. Even her mother is not as dismissive of her literary ambitions. She dare not explain to Elizabeth that, rather than banishing such thoughts from her mind, she is more determined than ever to see her work in print.

'This is your chance to be well settled. We dine with the finest society in all of East Kent,' Elizabeth continues, heedless of the wound she has inflicted. Jane is beginning to wonder if Neddy's extra night of travel was an excuse to escape Elizabeth's henpecking. 'As for listening to you read, Neddy prefers cards and I'm worn out by the time the children are in bed.'

'It's no use.' Neddy rests a hand flat against the exposed oak beams as he tugs off his boots. 'Once my dear wife has her heart set on a course of action, I can tell you from experience it's far easier to submit than resist.'

Elizabeth beams, as if her husband has paid her the great-est compliment. 'I expect you'll want to change your dress.' She runs her eyes over Jane's tired apparel, indicating she had better tidy herself before daring to appear at her dinner table. 'Not to worry if you haven't brought much. I've laid out some of my old gowns from before I was married. I expect fashions will have changed entirely before I'm able to wear them again. Waistlines will be up around our earlobes, if we're not vigilant.'

'There's really no need.' Jane wriggles out of her dusty pelisse, hot and slick with perspiration all of a sudden. She tries to hang it on a row of hooks near the door, but the younger Susan blocks her path and grapples it out of her hands before she reaches it. There are never enough hours in the day to devote to her writing. She will not squander a moment of her precious free time in being introduced to Elizabeth's idea of diverting company. 'You mustn't go to any trouble for me. I'm not in the least in want of society. In fact, I'm not in the mood to entertain any suitors at present.'

'It's no trouble. I'd do the same for any of my own sisters. And we're aware you've been down in the dumps since your disappointment with that young Irish fellow.'

'Are you, now?' Jane grips the newel post, wondering how the news of her ill-fated liaison has made it all the way to the ears of her sister-in-law. 'Tell me, was the story circulated in the *Kentish Gazette*?'

'Don't be facetious. Your mother wrote and told us. I understand it was a blow, but you can't let one bad hand put you out of the game for good.'

Jane should have known. Elizabeth used the exact turn of phrase as Mrs Austen, who customarily refers to Jane's failed love affair as her 'disappointment' – as if it was comparable to a cold supper when she was expecting roast beef. *I know it's a disappointment, dear, when you were expecting more. But never mind, do tuck in.*

'Really, you've wasted enough time moping about in Steventon,' Elizabeth continues. 'You're a young lady, Jane, not at all unpleasant-looking, and with plenty of charms to recommend you. So I'm told, anyway. It's time for you to get out there, before it's too late.'

Evidently Mrs Austen has tasked Elizabeth with finding Jane a husband while she is here. Jane has every mind to demand to be taken to the nearest coaching inn. When she parted from her perfidious parents, they were on their way to Deptford in hopes of being present for the launch of Frank's new ship, the *Triton*. After many unsuccessful applications to the Admiralty, he has finally been made first lieutenant on board a new 32-gun frigate by his former shipmate, Captain Gore. If Jane hurries, she'll be able to catch up with them and insist on being taken home to Hampshire. But then she would have to face Cassandra's pain. Her spirit collapses at the prospect. Perhaps she could stow away on board the *Triton* instead? Captain Gore may need a scribe, and Jane has an inclination naval life would suit her. No, it's no good. Frank is proving merciless in his quest for promotion. He would likely have her flogged as an interloper.

As anticipated, Jane is well and truly stranded. She closes her eyes and inhales a very deep breath. 'Out where, exactly?'

'Into the world, of course.' Elizabeth tilts her head to the side. 'And if you really want to help, it's Mrs Knight we could use your assistance with.'

'Why? Is she ill?' Whenever Mr and Mrs Austen make polite enquiries as to when Neddy might expect to receive his full inheritance, thereby being required to change his surname to 'Knight' to assume the squireship of Chawton, he assures them his benefactress is in excellent health. While Jane would never wish Mrs Knight ill, she is conscious that too long a wait for his independence could leave her brother bitter and frustrated, like a midshipman who has passed his lieutenant's examination but cannot find a commission as an officer.

Elizabeth glances at her husband. 'Have you not apprised your family of the situation?'

Neddy's easy features grow stern. 'I was hoping it might have blown over by the time I returned, and I wouldn't need to.'

'Blown over?' Elizabeth splutters. 'Well, it hasn't. Nor is it likely to, unless you instruct your father to petition Mrs Knight on your behalf. I swear that harpy will swindle you out of your entire fortune.'

Jane flinches at Elizabeth's turn of phrase. Surely her most genteel sister-in-law cannot be referring to Mrs Knight in such vulgar terms. 'Who will swindle Neddy out of his entire fortune?'

'No one,' Neddy replies, stepping closer to his wife. 'Must we address this now? Things are hardly so dire.' Behind him, the taller housemaid ushers the children out of the entrance hall while the smaller girl meanders in an ill-disguised attempt to catch the gossip.

'They will be, if you don't resolve them.' Elizabeth jabs a finger at her husband's chest. 'Mrs Knight has acquired a new favourite.'

'A *favourite?*' Jane draws a sharp breath. Could Mrs Knight, having found it so easy to avail herself of a son, dispense with him as readily? If she decides, at this late stage, to favour another – a relative from her own branch of the family, say – his prospects would be ruined. More than that, the cushion that Jane's parents rely upon to protect them in their old age would be rudely snatched away. Neddy is not alone among her brothers in being willing to support his wider family, but he may yet prove the only one who can afford to. 'But Mr Knight stated that she should bequeath everything to you, Neddy. He made a promise. His widow wouldn't allow herself to be swayed from her late husband's intentions. Would she?'

Elizabeth places a hand to her forehead as if she is about to swoon. 'What good is a promise, unless it's set down in law? The estate is hers to dispose of as she likes. If your brother doesn't act soon, Jane, Mrs Knight could name her new pet as the next mistress of Godmersham Park.'

Neddy's ears are pink. He's clearly mortified at his wife's candour. 'You're being hysterical. It will never come to that.'

'Then why won't she expel that little hussy?'

'Because the poor girl is apparently destitute.'

'Poor girl?' Elizabeth touches a hand to her distended belly and bends from the waist, as if suffering a sudden pang. 'That wretch should be taken to the nearest bridewell and given the rope's end. That would get the truth out of her.'

Jane squirms at being caught in the clutches of another's

domestic dispute. She's not accustomed to it. Her parents rarely argue, and James seems perfectly content to let Mary lead him by the nose. 'Who is this young woman?'

'She's no one. I'll handle the matter.' Neddy places an arm around his wife, trying to placate her. 'Stop this talk at once. Think of the baby. It can't be good for the little fellow.'

'I *am* thinking of the baby. I'm thinking of all your children. They're the ones who will be destitute. You must do something, Edward. Or would you see us penniless before reminding your mother of her obligations towards you?'

Jane presses her temples, her head throbbing with confusion. 'Is she a niece? A cousin on her side?'

Elizabeth takes short breaths, clearly finding it an effort. 'No relation at all. Mrs Knight, in her infinite generosity, has invited a foreign princess to reside in her home.'

'A princess?' Jane looks to Neddy, but he is too busy trying to lead Elizabeth to a wooden bench to meet her eye. This story is ridiculous. Has the pressure of carrying so many of Neddy's children in such quick succession unmoored Elizabeth from her senses? 'Surely, a princess would have no need to impose on Mrs Knight's hospitality.'

'Ah, but rather conveniently, this particular princess is estranged from her noble family. She hasn't a friend in the world – apart from Mrs Knight. And your brother, who would happily give her the bread from his own children's mouths!'

'That's enough,' Neddy snaps, startling Jane. She cannot

remember him raising his voice so in all the time they lived together at Steventon Rectory. 'My dear, you're obviously in distress. Let me help you upstairs to bed.' He turns to Jane, his manner softening as Elizabeth continues to labour for breath beside him. 'Fetch her some tea, will you?'

Jane nods as she watches the pair climb the Charles II staircase. Every few steps, Elizabeth pauses to lean on the elaborately carved balustrades and rails against her husband's inactivity. Jane is overcome with a terrible sinking sensation as she realizes her time in Kent will not be the relaxing sojourn she had in mind. In fleeing Cassandra's devastation, she has walked straight into Neddy's. If the situation is as Elizabeth insists, then her sister-in-law is right to be alarmed. Neddy has devoted himself to pleasing his adoptive mother; it would be most cruel of her to cast him aside for another at this late stage. What can Mrs Knight be thinking, letting herself become prey to a likely fortune-hunter? And what can Jane possibly do to extract her from the vixen's clutches?

Chapter Three

The next morning, Jane wakes from her fitful sleep with a determination to find her brother alone and wring the truth of Mrs Knight's disaffection from him. She dare not ask Elizabeth for any more details in fear of, once again, despoiling their domestic harmony. After the scene in the entrance hall, her hosts decided to forgo a formal dinner in favour of retiring early, presumably to bicker in private. The taller Susan brought Jane a supper of toasted cheese, which she ate in the nursery with only the children and the maid for company.

Through her enquiries, Jane has discovered this Susan was baptized Kitty and is the upper servant owing to her age and experience. Her younger colleague is named Alice and holds a terrible grudge against Kitty for stealing the seniority when she has served the family the longest. According to Kitty, there was once a Susan who worked at Goodnestone when Elizabeth was a child, and since then Jane's sister-in-law has found it easier to refer to all her maid-servants as 'Susan'. Prior to this, Jane did not have much faith in her own ability to manage a large household – but she's quite sure that even she could memorize the Christian names of all who slept under her roof.

When Jane locates her brother, she finds he has shut himself away in his study. She rattles the handle to confirm he has turned the key to keep out intruders, an action that would be inconceivable in Steventon. No matter how pre-occupied her father was, he would never bar his wife or any of his children from entering his library.

'Ned?' she calls softly, not wanting to alert the rest of the house.

'Not now, Jane. I'm busy,' comes his gruff reply.

As it is Sunday, she knows he cannot be working. Even her father puts aside his ledgers to remember the Sabbath. Her brother is clearly avoiding her. She experiences a pang for him. It must be a terrible humiliation to have invited Jane to enjoy his good fortune at the very moment it is in question. Neddy does not emerge until it is time to squash his family into his phaeton and drive the short distance to attend service at Holy Cross, the handsome flint church on the Goodnestone estate. With all the time it takes to ensure the horses are properly tethered, and for Elizabeth to adequately attire herself and her children for the draughty ride, Jane suspects it might have been quicker to walk. As, indeed, the Susans and the rest of the household do, to arrive before the family despite setting off after they had begun to fill the carriage.

Throughout the journey Jane is discomforted by Neddy's sullen manner. Gone is her genial brother in favour of a stern patriarch who reprimands his children for fussing and tuts and sighs at his wife's pointed remarks about the risk to their health represented by an open carriage.

Upon entering Holy Cross, Elizabeth introduces Jane to the first three baronets of Goodnestone and their lady wives, who are all interred in the family vault. While Elizabeth's father lived to enjoy his dotage, her mother died suddenly a fortnight after the birth of her eleventh living child, presumably satisfied that she had delivered on her end of their bargain and had earned a place in the Kingdom of Eternal Rest. In this realm, a woman's work, even within the marriage bed, is never done. After Jane has been seated in the front pew for several awkward moments, under the scrutiny of the small congregation of farmers and estate workers, Elizabeth remembers to acquaint her with the fourth and only living baronet, Sir William, and her sister, Henrietta.

'And did you travel through Town on your way here, Miss Austen?' asks Sir William. The gravity of his demeanour and silver hairs at his temple place him at a generation older than Elizabeth, while Henrietta, despite approaching thirty years of age, is similar in air and form to her younger sister. Jane attributes her relative preservation to her lack of maternal cares.

'No, sir. We were eager to reach our destination, and therefore took the roads to the south, passing through Croydon.' It occurs to Jane that since Neddy will not divulge any more details about Mrs Knight's house guest, she might probe his wife's family for their estimation of her. Especially as Elizabeth is occupied in quieting her children, while Neddy, who has placed himself at the furthest end of the pew from Jane, is equally studious in ignoring them.

'Croydon?' Sir William splutters, looking appalled. 'But that must have been a very disagreeable route to follow.'

'Would you recommend passing through Town?' Jane asks. She must admit she had been disappointed not to drive through London. A trip to the theatre would have cheered her immensely. But, as her father liked to remind her throughout their journey, Parliament's efforts to fund the war, combined with the recent bouts of civil unrest, have made touring dangerous and expensive. It seemed churlish of Jane to complain too loudly about a lack of entertainment when elsewhere in the Kingdom of Great Britain people are rioting for want of bread.

'Absolutely not. The metropolis must be avoided at all costs.' Sir William echoes Mr Austen's refrain.

Jane pictures the map of south-east England, trying to work out how she might have arrived at Kent from Hampshire without passing through either Surrey or London. She had no hand in the matter, of course. Her father and Neddy managed the details of their journey between them. 'Then which route would you suggest?'

'I would not, Miss Austen. I would recommend staying at home.'

'Oh ...' Jane rebukes herself for having so offended the baronet that he rather wishes she had not left her native Hampshire. He will be of no use to her investigation unless she can win his confidence. Their interaction is observed by Henrietta – who watches Jane with the same mistrusting dark eyes as Elizabeth. Henrietta has clearly grown accustomed to being the only unmarried sister in the family and, despite the undesirability of the position, is loath to have it snatched away by another. She need not fret. Jane is able to suffer through her time as an unnecessary appendage only because she knows it is temporary.

'I do not understand young people's obsession with continually being upon the move.' Sir William shakes his head. 'I was most looking forward to having my younger brother safely returned from Oxford. Now he informs me he plans to spend the summer with a friend, all the way up in the Scottish Highlands. Added to that, my wife has decided to visit her relations in Merseyside. I warned her not to go, that the roads to the north are fraught with danger, and the air around Liverpool is very bad, but she would not listen.'

Henrietta pats her brother's hand. 'She'll be regretting that now, William.'

'Oh dear,' says Jane. 'I do hope she hasn't come to any calamity.'

'Calamity?' Sir William creases his brow. 'No, she writes to say she's been invited to return next year.'

Jane wonders if Lady Bridges is willing to risk touring because she knows her husband is determined to remain at home. She resolves to use his concerns over the safety of England's roads to obtain his opinion of Mrs Knight's house guest. 'Indeed, these are perilous times to be abroad, what with the continued insurrections destroying the peace in our towns and cities, and the Fleet daring mutiny at Spithead and the Nore ... But I must say, Mrs Knight is extraordinarily generous in providing hospitality to a stranger merely to save her from the inconvenience of further travel. Wouldn't you agree?'

'I do, but then to think how the princess has been so violently abused ... I can understand why she would take pity on her. For a person of rank to be robbed of their status and property is an affront to the rightful order.'

Elizabeth leans forward in her seat to hiss at her brother – a not inconsiderable feat for a woman in her condition. 'I've told you several times, William. That wretch is *not* a princess. Don't you dare go around hailing her as such.'

Jane bristles. She did not think Elizabeth was listening and she does not want to cause a fracas in the family pew.

Sir William's eyebrows pull down in consternation. 'But Dr Wilmot insisted she was.'

'Since when do you pay any mind to Dr Wilmot?' Elizabeth is trying to whisper, but her sharp voice is audible throughout the nave. 'Have you reduced your meat intake yet? You'll never rid yourself of the gout if you don't.'

'Never mind my gout.' Sir William waves a hand, dismissing her concerns for his health. 'How else do you account for the young lady being found wandering along the beach? Dr Wilmot informed me her ship went down in the Swale.'

'She's a conniving little thief who's trying to cheat Edward out of his inheritance. That's how *I* account for her,' Elizabeth replies.

'Ship?' asks Jane, her interest piqued higher than ever. 'The princess was involved in a shipwreck?'

'Yes.' Sir William nods. 'It's a miracle she survived. She was forced to swim all the way to shore.'

'No, she most certainly was not. She's making it up. Such a feat would have been impossible. Tell him, Edward.'

'Enough! This is hardly the time or place for idle talk,' says Neddy, tersely, causing Elizabeth to stiffen and shaming the pew into silence.

While the others might read her brother's piety as a symptom of his early upbringing as the son of a clergyman, Jane can tell by the tic at his jaw how agitated he is. It must be humiliating to have any threat to his position discussed before his wife's family and, owing to the confines of the church, within earshot of the entire congregation. But, to her dismay, Jane finds her sympathy lies with her sister-in-law. Neddy will not resolve this matter by refusing to discuss it. As the elderly priest shuffles down the aisle, she bows her head and prays that, for her brother's sake, they can work together to untangle this mess before his prospects suffer any lasting damage.

By Monday, Jane is increasingly fraught that she has not managed to consult her brother in private. If the situation was as innocuous as he claimed, he would allow himself to be drawn rather than remaining in a thunderous mood and hiding in his study. She is sanguine, however, that she will have the opportunity to quiz him that very afternoon: Neddy has arranged to escort her to Godmersham Park. The knowledge that Jane is to meet with Mrs Knight and, in all probability, her mysterious house guest imbues her with an uncharacteristic amount of patience for Elizabeth's disparaging remarks.

While Jane has failed to pin down Neddy, Elizabeth has pinned Jane in all manner of places in preparation for introducing her into society. Jane attempts to look grateful rather than pained as Mrs Green, Elizabeth's dressmaker, does her best to make the yellow silk of the latest cast-off gown meet the floor. Really, it is all a terrible waste of effort. Jane will not be using her time in Kent for husband-hunting. Apart from anything else, Cassandra will need her at home. It would be most cruel of Jane to abandon her sister in favour of her own marital bliss, at a time when Cassandra is still mourning the loss of her beloved fiancé.

'Up straight now.' Mrs Green turns Jane to face her sister-in-law's judgement.

'I sincerely hope it didn't look that ugly on me.' Elizabeth appraises Jane from a chaise-longue in her crowded dressing room. The small chamber, adjacent to Neddy and Elizabeth's bedroom, is overstuffed with hatboxes and chintz-covered furniture. 'I fear that shade makes you look sallow. Shall we try the gold stripes instead?'

'Mmmf . . .' replies Mrs Green, through a mouthful of pins. The harried dressmaker hardly has time to arrange each garment before Elizabeth finds a reason to object to it.

'Yes, terribly sallow. And stop slouching, Jane. Otherwise, the hem will be all wrong. Oh, this isn't going to work. You're too tall. We'll have to get you some new ones made up.'

As much as Jane might prefer to select her own attire, her father would not be pleased to be presented with the bill for a new wardrobe at the end of her stay. Her eye drifts to the carriage clock over the mantelpiece. Only another hour of this torture to go before Neddy has ordered her to be ready to leave. 'Honestly, Beth. It's fine. There's no need for you to go to all this bother for me.'

'Oh, but there is, dear.' Elizabeth beats a cushion against the head of the chaise-longue and squirms against it. With the weight of the baby pressing down against her midriff, it seems impossible for the expectant mother to be comfortable. She hasn't sat still for a moment since Jane arrived. Her condition must be partly to blame for her terrible mood.

Jane must not begrudge her being so fractious and she must really try to be more forgiving of Elizabeth's well-intended insults. After all, the season is far too hot to be lugging around another being inside oneself.

She sucks in her own trim waist for Mrs Green's measuring tape. 'But I can wear what I brought from Steventon.'

'No, Jane. Believe me, you can't.'

Then again, maybe her sister-in-law does possess a rather disagreeable nature. Thankfully, Jane is prevented from responding to this latest slight by Kitty, who hoists the rejected garment over her head before she can speak. Mrs Green holds out the striped gown for her to step into and together they wrestle her into the low-cut bodice.

'That's better. It almost fits, and we could add a flounce along the bottom.' Elizabeth pushes herself up to a sitting position. 'You could be quite elegant, if you put your mind to it.'

'Why, you are gracious.' Jane tries to curtsy, but Mrs Green grips her shoulders and pulls them back sharply.

'Not at all. As I said, it's no more than I would do for any of my sisters. And if we can get you well settled, you'll be less of a drain on our resources. When the time comes.'

Elizabeth's words dash the smile from Jane's face just as surely as if she had struck her. Presumably, 'the time' she refers to is when Mr Austen shuffles off his mortal coil. She closes her eyes, forcing down her ire at Elizabeth's willingness to consign her father to his grave. He may be elderly but, unlike Mrs Austen, he's always been of robust health. He certainly does not complain as much. It could be many years before Jane is forced to face the eventuality of his death, and anything could happen to improve her circumstances before then. She knows she will probably have to marry eventually: it would not be fair to expect to live off her father or her brothers for ever, especially now it seems even Neddy's future is far from secure. But while she is young, with her writing to occupy her, it is only prudent not to be hasty. If she waits long enough, Tom might even manoeuvre himself into a position where he can afford to marry her without requiring the approval of his family.

Or Jane might find some other means, apart from marriage, to support herself. Thomas Cadell is rumoured to have paid Frances Burney a thousand pounds to publish her latest work and she raised the same amount again from her subscribers, among whom Jane was proud to be listed. The enterprising authoress is said to have bought a cottage in Surrey with the proceeds and named it after her eponymous heroine, Camilla. If Jane applies herself, she is confident she can pen something worthy of publication. Despite Elizabeth and Mrs Austen's design that she secure a match among Kent's elite, Jane suspects she would be happier in a humble country cottage, with leisure to read and write all day, and in the company of one she truly loved. She is not foolhardy enough, though, to admit indulging in such outlandish fantasies to Elizabeth.

'Why don't you tell me what you can about the situation with Mrs Knight's house guest, if I'm to call on her this afternoon?' she asks, keen to divert her sister-in-law's attention as far from herself as she can. 'Everything I've heard has only left me more perplexed.'

'You're perplexed? All I get is garbled nonsense from Edward and placatory notes from the great lady herself,' replies Elizabeth. 'I want you to ingratiate yourself with her and determine exactly what's going on. You're my emissary, Jane.'

'I am?'

'You are.' Elizabeth casts a doubtful eye over Jane, as if she, too, is incredulous at entrusting her with such an important task. 'Remember how you got Georgy out of that pickle with the necklace.'

'I suppose I did ...' says Jane, as Mrs Green and Kitty undress her. 'But I had to. Georgy's life was on the line, and I had Henry to help me.' Eighteen months have passed since Jane's brother Georgy was accused of stealing the necklace of a murdered woman. It was a dreadful time for all of the Austens, and they rarely speak of it in hopes they will soon forget.

Elizabeth sighs. 'That will be all for today, thank you, Mrs Green. You have her measurements. We'll purchase some new cloth and have it sent on. Do what you can with the stripes in the meantime.'

As Kitty shows Mrs Green to the door, Jane cannot find

her original gown. She fears the dressmaker has carried it off by mistake as she pads around the room in her petticoat, searching for it.

'The truth is, Jane, I'm reliant on you. You must find some proof the girl is lying. She can't be a *princess*. The whole charade is ridiculous.'

'Have you raised your concerns with Mrs Knight?' Jane lays a hand on her exposed bosom, the skin on her arms turning to gooseflesh.

'I have written to her, yes, but it's too easy for her to fob me off by letter. Since Mr Knight passed away, she hardly ever leaves Godmersham, and I can't very well go around making enquiries like this.' Elizabeth nods to her distended belly. 'I'm hesitant to take any long carriage journeys in case the motion brings on the baby. I'll not be forced to labour by the side of the road, like some wretched beast.'

'You fear the baby may arrive early?' A worrisome pregnancy would explain why relations between Neddy and Elizabeth are quite so strained. If so, why has Providence entrusted Jane with Elizabeth's care? Elizabeth will have a midwife, of course, and possibly a doctor on hand for the actual birth – but, as the female relation designated to attend her, it is Jane's duty to make sure she is well cared for throughout this hazardous period. She should defer to Henrietta. Indeed, Jane was surprised to realize Elizabeth had chosen herself as her companion over her own sister, but she supposes Sir William can hardly be expected to manage with only his retinue of servants to assist him while Lady Bridges is away.

'No, I'm sure that won't happen.' Elizabeth creases her forehead. 'But I've been having these twinges – a tightening as if labour is about to commence, but then, thankfully, nothing further occurs.'

'You must consult your physician immediately.' Jane spies her chintz gown, strewn over a footstool and masquerading as a cushion. She throws it over her head and fiddles with the bodice. As inexperienced as she is, even she knows that the baby must be allowed the proper time to develop before it begins its descent into the world. Jane herself arrived a full month after the date on which her parents had anticipated her arrival. Mrs Austen often complains that she has continued to disappoint her expectations ever since.

'Not yet. It's probably the situation with Mrs Knight that's aggravating me. And this will be my fourth lying-in. As you'll discover, carrying a baby to term gets harder each time, not easier. I'm several years older than I was when I had Fanny, and believe me, Jane, I feel every day of those years.'

Childbirth is one of the very few experiences upon which Jane has no desire to satisfy her curiosity first-hand. She can tell just how wearisome it must be for Elizabeth by the shadows beneath her eyes and her permanently fraught expression. 'You really should tell Neddy. Ask him to call in the physician, just in case.'

'No, Jane. And don't you dare breathe a word either. Dr Wilmot would insist on complete rest, and I'd be powerless to object. I'd go out of my wits, cooped up in here all day, with nothing to do but torment myself with my concerns. Besides, I can't have Neddy fretting about me, not when he should be exerting his energy on driving that artful wench out from under his mother's notice. Now, before she does any further damage to his prospects.'

'Beth, calm yourself.' Jane sits beside Elizabeth, covering her hand with her own.

'You're the *only* other person I can trust to place Neddy's interest above all else. You must expose her, the lying, cheating little strumpet.'

'I'll do whatever I can, I promise. Anything for you and Neddy.'

'It's not just for us, Jane. Need I make myself any clearer? If Neddy's disinherited, your own prospects will be ruined too. Who do you think will marry you then?'

Jane rears back, but it is impossible to avoid being skewered by the truth of Elizabeth's words. Without Neddy's anticipated wealth to prop up the family, her parents would be considerably worse off. It is not only Georgy's future that would be in jeopardy. Jane would have to forgo dedicating any more years to her writing while she waited to see if Tom ever found his way back to her. She'd be obliged to accept the first man who asked for her hand. If there was one. And what about poor Cassandra? How could she bear to pledge herself to another so soon after losing Mr Fowle? It could take years before Jane's beloved sister is ready to contemplate marriage to anyone else.

'You're right, Beth. I'll do whatever it takes to oust her, I promise.'

'Good girl.' Elizabeth squeezes Jane's hand tight. 'I knew I could rely on you.'

1. ***Letter to Cassandra Austen***
Rowling Farm, Monday, 12 June 1797

My dearest Cassandra,

To the great disappointment of your niece and nephews, I am safely ensconced in Kent. So far, no amount of rolling around in the nursery playing Spillikins has proved sufficient to make up for being the 'wrong aunt'. Their mother is hardly more delighted to see me. One Susan says I must not take it personally, as her mistress lives in continual dissatisfaction with all members of her household, while the other fears Beth's condition is responsible for her sour temper. I will leave you to guess which Susan I am inclined to agree with. In even worse news, I am not the only interloper in the Garden of England. Mrs Knight has taken in a beleaguered foreign princess. I am yet to meet the young lady, but I suspect she will prove herself even less at ease than myself among such venerable society. Fear not, I am resolved we will both return to our natural stations forthwith.

Yours always,
J.A.

P.S. I regret to inform you that no letters of yours have arrived. I can only assume some calamity must have befallen them, for I know you would not leave it so long without writing to your faithful sister. Have you left your missives lying about somewhere that James's hounds might discover them? They are a hungry pack, but I do not think even they can be hungrier than I for some token of your affection. Please check and rectify this matter immediately.

Miss Austen
Rev. Mr Austen's
Deane
Hants

Chapter Four

Godmersham Park lies to the west of Rowling, on the far side of Canterbury. A buzzard disturbs the serene blue sky with its constant cry of 'keeyah!' as Jane and Neddy racket through the narrow lanes. For miles, the bird hangs above them, resting its weight on the grace of its enormous wings, and scanning the flat expanse of lush green fields and bushy hedgerows for its prey. Each time it swoops, Jane holds her breath, expecting to see it collide with a smaller bird, but instead the buzzard pulls up short and soars even higher – more interested in showing off its spectacular form than in finding its dinner. The sultry disquiet affords Jane the perfect opportunity to corner Neddy. He may be able to evade her when they're at home, but in the confines of the phaeton he's her captive and she's determined to interrogate him. 'Where did Mrs Knight make the acquaintance of her foreign princess? I presume they didn't meet at court.'

Neddy flicks his eyes away from the road for a fraction of a second. 'Must we discuss it?'

'Alas, we must. If we're to call on them both, it's best you prepare me. What can you tell me about this mysterious young woman?'

'Nothing. I've barely laid eyes on her.' Neddy exhales loudly, resting his elbows on his knees as he handles the reins. 'Dr Wilmot and his wife found her on the beach at Whitstable a week ago.'

Jane waits for him to elaborate, but he remains stubbornly silent. 'And she indicated to them that she'd swum ashore after being shipwrecked?'

'She must have. I'd have delivered her to the nearest bridewell, but they thought the incident warranted reporting to the Riding Officer.'

'The Riding Officer?' asks Jane, unfamiliar with the term.

'Since the navy has been called away to fight the French, the local Revenue Office has appointed a man to ride on horseback up and down the coast looking out for smugglers. He's their only hope of enforcing the King's dues.'

Jane ties the lace band of her straw hat tighter under her chin, to prevent it being carried away by the breeze. She doesn't fancy the Riding Officer's chances. One man and his horse are hardly sufficient to prevent a ship full of brigands creeping through the blockade. It is a wonder he has not been murdered already. 'Did he confirm whether any vessels had been lost?'

Neddy shrugs. 'One of the sailors recognized a few words

of Spanish and offered to translate for her. That's when this ridiculous story about her being a princess came out.'

'She doesn't speak English?'

'No. Apparently she's a native of the Canary Islands but she claims to have been kidnapped and held for ransom ever since she was a girl.'

'Kidnapped?' Jane stares at the grim set of her brother's profile. She knows she need not point out to him that a rich, lonely widow like Mrs Knight would make an easy mark for a trickster, and this young woman's story sounds too fantastical to be true.

'By pirates, arggh.' Neddy glances sideways, making a fist and swinging his elbow in his best impersonation of Blackbeard.

Jane's heart twists. The action calls to mind a rare memory of young Neddy, wearing a paper hat and organizing his siblings in a game of pirates. First, he'd force her and Cassandra to 'walk the plank', which involved teetering along a fallen branch in the garden while he brandished a stick in place of a cutlass and shouted, 'You're fish food, wench!' The sisters would jump off the log and pretend to flail in the sea, before Frank and Charles came to their rescue. Then the real fighting would begin, and she and Cassandra would have to get out of the way before their brothers were whacking each other mercilessly.

Jane shakes her head slowly. This is not sport and she cannot let Neddy's pretended levity at the situation distract her from getting to the truth. 'I fear you're not affording this matter the gravity it deserves.'

'I am. Honestly, I am. If this young woman is out to cheat Mother, then, believe me, I shall take it very seriously indeed. But indulging Beth's concerns will only make her more agitated. You can see how upset she is. She'll wear herself out with worry. I'm so glad you elected to join us. Hopefully, while you're here, Beth will be able to rest and restore her strength before the baby comes.'

'Hmm . . .' While the sentiment is admirable, Jane cannot help thinking the best way to preserve Elizabeth's health would be if she and Neddy were to employ the simple regimen of separate rooms. Not that Jane would ever dare suggest such a thing. She is not supposed to know what goes on in the marriage bed, much less have an opinion on it. Although, how it would be possible to maintain such ignorance coming from a family of eight children, and growing up in a boarding school for boys, is beyond her.

'You've got to admit it's a fantastic story. Like one of yours.'

'It's really not. If you'd let me read to you, you'd see my work has matured vastly since the last time you heard any.' Jane folds her arms and sits back in her seat, trying not to let Neddy see just how vexed she is that he and Elizabeth have thus far declined her offers to entertain. She left *First Impressions* on the sideboard, hoping a glimpse of the title page beneath the ribbon securing the sheaf of papers, would pique their curiosity. Reading her work aloud is the best way to gauge its effectiveness. Cassandra is always willing to listen and will respond to each draft of Jane's manuscript as if it's the first time she's heard the story. Simply by studying her sister's expressions, Jane can tell if her words are provoking the intended reactions. It is usually when she's performing to her sister that Jane is struck with the inspiration for how to improve her composition. 'Was Mrs Knight present in Whitstable while all this occurred?'

'No.' Neddy shakes his head. 'Mother rarely leaves home. The Wilmots invited the girl to stay with them in Canterbury, gullible fools that they are. The doctor even wrote to the King with a message to pass on to his Spanish counterpart.'

'And did His Majesty reply?' Jane arches an eyebrow.

'Don't be ridiculous.' Neddy snorts. 'It'll have been thrown on the fire by one of his courtiers, along with the rest of the begging letters.'

'If she was the doctor's responsibility, how did Mrs Knight come to accommodate her?'

'That's the thing . . .' Neddy sighs heavily, tossing the reins into one leather-gloved hand. 'Something untoward must have taken place as, overnight, the Wilmots washed their hands of her. Mother was visiting Mrs Wilmot at the time, which is peculiar in itself. As I said, she hardly ever pays calls. But rather than seeing the girl turned onto the street, she offered to take her.'

Jane swivels in her seat to face her brother. If Mrs Knight's friends have already turned against her protégée, it is odd that she should insist on maintaining her. 'Did you hear why the Wilmots rescinded their hospitality?'

'I'd hazard a guess they caught her making off with the family silver,' he says. 'I've little doubt she'll show herself to be a gold-digging tavern wench, but you know how tender-hearted Mother is.'

Jane's mother is many things but tender-hearted she is not. A beat too late, she realizes Neddy is referring to Mrs Knight, rather than Mrs Austen. The family have long since reconciled themselves to Neddy's adoption, but it will ever be strange to hear him defer to the Knights as his parents. She wonders when he began to think of Mrs Knight, rather than Mrs Austen, as his 'mother', and on what terms he now considers the original holder of that title. She knows her parents will never cease to describe him as *their* son. 'Did you not quiz the Wilmots yourself?'

'It's difficult. I cannot go against Mother's wishes, or I risk a total breach. She's always been such a champion of the ill-served. If I make any unfounded accusations about the girl, it could very well encourage her to cleave to her even tighter.'

'She sounds like a very singular lady, your mother.'

Neddy slows the carriage to a crawl as an attendant waves them through the gates of Godmersham Park. Lebanese cedars and evergreen oaks are enclosed by a high brick wall, and further encased in a belt of valuable woodland. Once inside, an air of artificial tranquillity settles over the landscape. 'She is. I'm so looking forward to reintroducing you. Mother has long expressed a desire to become better acquainted with my brothers and sisters. At the very least, our time here will give you some respite from Beth's match-making schemes.'

'Can you not call her off? I appreciate her good offices, but I'm in no humour at present to be courted.'

'In her defence, she's trying to be of service.'

'I know. It's just . . .' Jane bites her lip, unwilling to detail the many reasons she does not relish the prospect of marrying into Neddy's world. He and Elizabeth would think her pathetic for clinging to the hope of Tom's return, and they would no doubt laugh heartily if she dared to articulate her dream of seeing her work published. Or, worse, they might be scandalized that she could even consider such a vulgar notion as exchanging her words for money. Elizabeth would accuse her of planning to bring the entire family into disrepute and give her a long tiresome lecture on the various pastimes befitting a young lady – every one of them designed to conceal any spark of wit or ingenuity she may have.

'Just what? It'd be wonderful to have you settled nearby. Our children could grow up together, as we did.'

Jane simply smiles, fearful of offending him by pointing out that they didn't actually grow up together. During the first three years of Jane's life, Neddy lived at the rectory while she was cared for by her dry nurse in the village.

Shortly after Jane returned to the family home, Neddy began his prolonged visits to the Knights. Within two years he had decamped to Kent to learn all the habits that separate a fashionable young man of fortune from an ordinary gentleman. Shooting at things, mainly. She is not sure there has ever been a time when all eight of the Austen children resided at the rectory together. Georgy only ever came home on fleeting visits, James and Henry went up to Oxford at fourteen and seventeen, and Frank and Charles left for Portsmouth at eleven and twelve. Among her siblings, Cassandra is Jane's only constant companion, remaining at her side even during the two brief periods when they were sent away to school.

'Look, there's the house.' Neddy pats her arm.

Jane catches her breath as a Palladian mansion rolls into view from behind a cluster of weeping willows. It's enormous. A huge expanse of redbrick, slates and freshly painted window frames. Three oval-shaped portholes above the front door are its only concession to femininity or restraint. If Mrs Austen were here, she'd be counting the glass panes and the number of steps it took to cross the imposing façade in order to boast to the neighbours back in Hampshire. A matching pair of box-like structures flank an even larger central portion. Neddy has already explained these wings house a magnificent ballroom and an extensive library, but Jane must not expect entry to either. Since Mr Knight's death, his widow has closed off large parts of the house, claiming it is too big for her to manage alone. Which begs the question: why has she not invited her adoptive son and his young family to share it with her?

Neddy leans forward, resting his elbows on his spread thighs. 'Well, what do you think?'

Godmersham Park is so large it appears to span the entire valley. Either of its superfluous wings could swallow Steventon Rectory whole. A peacock saunters towards the carriage, baring its plumage and squawking as if it fancies itself a guard dog. Jane's chin has dropped towards her chest and she is having trouble getting it to move. 'It's very . . . grand.'

'Yes. Impressive, isn't it? That's the marvellous thing with these newer houses. It's all very well adding an extra bay or two to an old place like Rowling, but the proportions are always going to make it feel poky. If you knock it down and start again, as Grandfather Knight did, you're able to rebuild on a much grander scale. It's a temporary inconvenience, certainly, but I dare say it's worth it in the long run. Don't you agree?'

Jane blinks at him. How is it possible she shares the same blood as this man, who thinks nothing of demolishing a perfectly good home and raising a grandiose mansion from the ashes? She spares a thought for the 'poky' Elizabethan manor the first Thomas Knight demolished to make room for this monstrosity.

As Neddy helps her from the carriage, the butler and several footmen appear. Jane brushes herself down and pats her coiled hair while the servants bow and scrape before her brother. They are all adorned in matching black breeches, with brash gold-and-purple-striped jackets and old-fashioned powdered wigs. Beneath Jane's tawny pelisse, she is hiding her best morning dress in a strawberry flower print. Even compared to the household staff, she looks like a country bumpkin. Perhaps she should be more grateful for the sumptuous silks Elizabeth is so determined to throw her way.

'I take it Mother's in the north drawing room, Penling-ton.' Neddy walks swiftly through the open front door into the entrance hall. Jane trails behind, trying to orient herself in the new surroundings. A magnificent chimney piece dominates the centre of one wall while a carved frieze rests beneath the panelled ceiling. Several doorways promise sumptuous locations beyond, while a marble nymph dances in a scallop-shaped alcove. Merely admiring the grandeur causes Jane to feel light-headed.

Neddy strides towards the most ornate exit: an archway topped with a triangular pediment and framed by a pair of Corinthian columns. The family portraits are lined up on either side. Thomas Knight the Elder manages to look genial, even with the hilt of his sword poking out from behind his waistcoat, while his son and namesake appears more thoughtful. Mrs Knight is depicted exactly as Jane remembers her, with handsome features and penetrating eyes. The pale silk of her gown is so luminescent it might have been fashioned from the bark of a silver birch. There is even a painting of Neddy as a boy. He is all curls and pouting lips, trying to look dignified in a frilly collar.

Penlington jogs beside adult Neddy, his buckled shoes tap-tapping over the black-and-white tiles as he dives to reach the handle before the visitors. 'She is. Yes.'

Neddy halts, drawing himself up to his full height and puffing out his chest as he waits for the butler to open the door. 'What is it? You're in my way, man.'

Penlington's neck flushes scarlet, clashing horribly with his purple livery. 'Princess Eleanor is with her, sir.'

'P-Princess Eleanor?' Neddy spits the words, astounded that a stranger is hailed as royalty in a home he has long been taught to think of as his by right.

'And since Mr Blackall's visit, we're under strict orders not to let any male persons into the room while she's present.'

'But that's ridiculous.' Neddy's voice booms around the cathedral-like space.

Jane draws a sharp breath at his outburst. He is clearly riled by this latest relegation, and who can blame him? She cannot imagine the anguish of being refused notice by one's own mother. 'Perhaps we should return at a later date, Ned.'

'Mrs Knight did leave a message in anticipation of your arrival, sir.' The butler's spine curls into the shape of a snail. He takes no pleasure in delivering this humiliation. 'She'd be most pleased to receive your companion, but asked if you could possibly inspect the boundary to the east. We've received reports that one of the great oaks fell during the storm.'

Neddy splutters, a deep blush crawling up his cheek. 'Can't the steward do it?'

'She instructed me to inform you personally, as she fears there may be substantial damage and is anxious for the timber to be collected before any of the tenants discover it.'

Jane swallows, fearful of what her brother might say next. He may be reluctant to risk a breach with his mother, but she is not averse to demeaning him before her household. Has Mrs Knight forgot she named Neddy her son, not her servant?

'If you'd be so kind as to have Armand convey Miss Austen back to Rowling after her meeting with my mother?' Neddy's clipped tone betrays his fury.

'I will, sir.' Penlington peers at Jane as Neddy flicks up his collar and turns on his heel. She tries to smile, wanting to reassure the butler he has not mortally offended his prospective lord and master by following the orders of his current mistress, but her mouth is so dry that her lips stick to her teeth. As Neddy's footsteps retreat, followed by the sound of the front door slamming after him, the butler opens the entrance to the drawing room just wide enough for Jane to slip through.

Chapter Five

Jane finds herself in a large, square chamber. Red damask clothes the walls and velvet curtains the deep windows, obscuring the parkland. Two figures sit in the furthest corner – a distance of at least twenty feet away. Jane must squint to make them out clearly in the dim light. In the near two decades since Jane was last in her company, Mrs Knight has aged into the archetype of a grieving widow in her sombre black mantua and veil. Her companion, meanwhile, looks to have stepped straight out of an illustration from Cook's voyages. Neither woman rises to greet her. She hesitates, wishing she had found an excuse to accompany Neddy on his inspection of the estate, before forcing herself to take extra care as she crosses the slippery parquet flooring. By appearing before the latest in their line of benefactors, Jane is holding up not just herself but her entire family for inspection. It is not only incumbent upon her to restore Neddy to Mrs Knight's good graces: Jane's parents will be furious if she fails to make a favourable impression on her own account.

'Miss Austen, I presume?' Mrs Knight wafts a lace fan over her severe features. Her dark mane may be streaked with silver and her lively eyes grown cold, but she is still recognizable as the glamorous creature from Jane's youth. A mourning brooch of woven hair surrounded by pearls is pinned to her bosom.

'Yes, ma'am.' Jane bobs a curtsy, but she is too distracted by Mrs Knight's more flamboyant house guest to retain her gaze.

The girl, no older than herself, sits with her chin high, her back ramrod straight. With her coppery red hair, she reminds Jane of an oil painting she once saw of the shrewd, calculating Queen Elizabeth. Her hands rest, upturned, on the arms of her chair, as if waiting to be passed her orb and sceptre. She casts her russet-brown gaze over Jane, nostrils flickering with disdain, eyes unblinking in her freckled countenance. Her entire demeanour is one of aggressive haughtiness. But now that Jane is closer, she can see her cape is actually a quilt, and her headdress is fashioned from a linen pillowcase, some ribbon and three peacock feathers. No wonder the bird looked so disgruntled.

At a loss for how to greet the stranger, Jane places one foot at an angle to the other and bends low into a demure curtsy. 'Your Royal Highness.'

Mrs Knight makes slow claps, causing the heavy jewels

on her fingers to sparkle. 'Very droll. I was warned you considered yourself a wit. My house guest, Eleanor, does not require you to adhere to protocol while she resides with me.'

'She doesn't?' Still, Jane cannot tear her eyes from the girl. Eleanor certainly possesses the arrogance of a princess. Despite Jane's deferential greeting, she refuses to acknowledge her presence. What mischief is she up to?

'Was that my son, storming about the hall? I hoped he'd grown out of such infantile behaviour by now.'

'It was Neddy, yes, ma'am. He was most looking forward to seeing you.'

'If that's the case, instruct him to return on Thursday. He can accompany me to Canterbury. I have a great many errands to run, and shall be in need of someone to carry my purchases.' Mrs Knight's lips purse, as if she'd bitten into a rather sour quince when expecting a nice juicy apple. While Jane is relieved Neddy's mother has requested his presence, she cannot help noticing that, yet again, she has relegated him to the position of a servant. 'I can never remember, are you the Miss Austen who paints or the one who plays the pianoforte most indifferently?'

Jane looks about for a seat, wondering who's been defaming her musical abilities. It must have been her sister-in-law. While she may not have been fortunate enough to receive instruction from court musicians, as Elizabeth did, Jane is more than proficient, and she practises every day when she's at home. She perches on the edge of a chintz sofa. 'I'm afraid I'm the musician, and I also compose my own stories. My elder sister, Cassandra, is the artist. She was meant to come, but . . .' The memory of Cassandra clutching the tear-stained letter from Mr Fowle's devastated family stops the words in Jane's throat.

The sisters had been lying on the grassy slope at the back of the rectory, avoiding their mother and her never-ending list of domestic duties for them to complete. As soon as their father's horse came clip-clopping along the lane, Cassandra scrambled to greet him. Mr Austen had been to Basingstoke and had promised to call at the Wheatsheaf inn to collect the mail on his way home. Cassandra had been expecting news of her fiancé every day for weeks, but no letters had arrived. Jane went back to dozing in the spring sunshine, daydreaming her way through her next story, when the most appalling noise came from inside the rectory. Her first thought was that a fox had got itself trapped in the pantry. But when she rushed inside, there was Cassandra on her knees, bent double. The crumpled letter, with its horrid black seal, was still in her hand, while Mr Austen, his face ghostly, looked on.

Jane blinks away the threat of tears. 'Well, she's indisposed at the moment.'

'I know the true purpose of your visit, Miss Austen.' Mrs Knight glares at her.

The sofa is so low Jane is forced to crouch before the other women. 'Do you? If so, pray can you tell me? I thought I was coming to help with the children, but it seems my sister-in-law intends to arrange a bride auction on my behalf.'

Mrs Knight recoils. 'How old are you?'

'One-and-twenty.' Jane braces herself to be told she should be married already and therefore should show more gratitude for Elizabeth's efforts to find her a husband.

'You speak your mind very freely, for one so young.'

'I do apologize.' Jane twists her hands in her lap. She dearly wants to be agreeable, but it is most distracting trying to converse with Mrs Knight while they both ignore the strange woman sitting beside her, festooned in peacock feathers. 'Sincerely, I don't mean to offend. I have all these words, and they tend to come tumbling out. Especially when I'm ill at ease.'

'You're here because Neddy fears I'm entering my second childhood.'

'He would never dare make such a presumption . . .' Jane cannot let the gulf between her brother and his benefactress widen any further than it already has. She has promised to act as Elizabeth's emissary and she will do whatever it takes to find out the truth of the girl's story but, above all, she must act in a manner deferential to Mrs Knight. 'Neddy has the greatest respect and regard for you. Indeed, all our fam—'

Mrs Knight flicks her fan, silencing Jane as the door to the entrance hall opens. A vaguely familiar maid, holding a silver tray laden with what smells like coffee, crosses the room.

'Here, Grace.' Mrs Knight makes a pile of small, leather-bound books on the mahogany side table to clear a space. As Grace unloads the items, Mrs Knight eyes a folded leaf of paper beside the pot. Instantly, all colour drains from her pinched features. 'That's not another already?'

Grace's features turn wan. 'I'm afraid so, ma'am. Mr Penlington found it on the front step.'

'Is it . . .' Mrs Knight trails off, stroking her neck.

'Like the last? Yes, ma'am. I'm sorry to say it is.' The maid stands, clutching the now empty silver tray to her chest so tightly her knuckles are white. 'Shall I leave it here for you?'

'No! I don't want the dreaded thing anywhere near me. Take it away at once. I'll deal with it later.' Mrs Knight flicks her wrist, as if she could shoo the note from her table like a stray dog. She glances briefly at Eleanor, but the princess keeps her eyes trained on Jane. Whatever the mysterious note entails, Eleanor will not let it distract her from taunting Jane and her family. Indeed she shoots Jane the kind of filthy look, which, if they were really in high society, would signify she had been cut from the *bon ton* for ever.

'As you wish, mistress.' Grace curtsies before dropping the note onto the tray, equally unwilling to touch it. Jane is desperate to ask what kind of message could have upset Mrs Knight and her maid so, but Mrs Knight's demeanour tells her she would be expelled with a flea in her ear if she dared to ask outright. Perhaps Grace will reveal more if Jane can engage her in conversation.

Mrs Knight takes a moment to recover as the maid departs before fixing her attention back to Jane. 'As I was saying, Miss Austen, I know why Neddy's sent you here, but there's really no need –'

Without warning, Eleanor jumps to her feet, opens her small, round mouth and a stream of babble flies out. '*Si, si . . . Lieto di conoscerti. Fijar con listones la escotilla. Merci beaucoup.*' Jane stares up at the girl in astonishment. She does not speak much Spanish, but her father taught her French and a smattering of Italian, and she is pretty sure Eleanor just combined all three. Mrs Knight reaches out a hand and places it gently over the girl's wrist. Eleanor peers down at her, indignant. '*Soy la Infanta de Castilla.*'

'The Infanta of Castile?' asks Jane. 'I thought Neddy said the princess hailed from the Canary Islands?'

'Do take some refreshment.' Mrs Knight releases Eleanor to pour three cups. The girl sits heavily beside her, shaking out her cloak and huffing at the closed door.

Enquiring into Mrs Knight's private correspondence may overstep the bounds of propriety, but surely it is only polite to converse as to how she formed the acquaintance of her house guest. 'I'm most eager to hear more about how the princess came to be under your protection. If that's not too impertinent to ask? I've heard rumours of a terrible tragedy taking place at sea.' Jane reaches for the tongs and has almost selected the perfect-sized lump of sugar to sweeten her coffee, when Eleanor dumps her cup directly onto the table, splashing steaming liquid onto the polished surface, snatches the bowl and deposits the entire contents in her saucer.

Jane's hand is frozen, tongs poised over the empty bowl. She looks to Mrs Knight for a reaction, but instead the widow remains focused on Jane as she speaks. 'I believe these rituals are conducted quite differently where my guest hails from.'

'So I see,' says Jane, as Eleanor licks her finger and rolls it across her saucer of sugar, coating it in delicious crystals, then sticks it into her mouth. When she withdraws it, she flicks it against the inside of her cheek to make a popping sound. This is done with such a dignified air that Jane could almost believe it is how all ladies of quality take their afternoon refreshments, and she is simply not well bred enough to be familiar with the custom. 'Which is?'

Mrs Knight frowns. 'Why don't you read to us, Miss Austen?'

'Oh ... If you'd like me to, I can.' Jane reaches for the small leather-bound tomes on the coffee table. If she's not mistaken, among them is a copy of *Letters for Literary Ladies*.

'Not those. I can read my own books whenever I please.' Mrs Knight raps Jane's hand with her closed fan. 'One of your compositions.'

'Mine?' Jane clutches her hand to her breast. It was only a light tap, but it stung and made her start.

'Yes, yours. I remember your father boasting that your stories could be quite amusing.'

'Did he really?' Jane shouldn't be surprised. Mr Austen has always been her greatest admirer, but being so far from home and all those who appreciate her talent has eroded her confidence. 'I'm sorry, I didn't bring any of my work with me today. But I could next time. If you'd *really* like me to?'

'I wouldn't have asked if I wasn't in earnest.'

'Then I shall.' Jane sits back in her seat, cheered by the prospect of an audience and already wondering which of her compositions would be most favourable to Mrs Knight. *First Impressions* is by far the most complex work she's ever written; her father says he prefers it to everything in his library. But the Bennet family, with their constant lament at not having a son to continue the entail of their estate, might be a bit too near the mark. On the surface, *Catherine* is too silly, and Jane wouldn't want the widow to conflate herself with her most whimsical heroine. No, as unfinished as the manuscript is, it will have to be *The Sisters*.

This might even turn out for the best, as the Misses Dashwood are most in need of her attention. Without Cassandra there to reflect Jane's words back at her, the story remains a puzzle. She began with the intention of contrasting their characters: the elder Miss Dashwood is a woman of sense, while her younger sister succumbs too readily to the fluctuating tides of her emotions. Alas, in its current form, Jane fears the work veers towards a medieval morality play rather than a subtle exploration of human nature.

She forces down her unsweetened coffee while making her resolution. Jane's vanity is not so robust as to preclude her from suspecting Mrs Knight's motivation in asking her to read was to distract her from Eleanor's antics but, with so much on her mind, she almost forgets to observe the girl. That is, until Eleanor plucks the jug from the table, holds it aloft and pours a rivulet of cream directly into her mouth.

Mrs Knight rests her forehead in one hand. 'You may call again.'

'Thank you. That is most hospitable of you,' says Jane, without tearing her eyes from Eleanor. How is it possible she has not spilt a single drop? The jug must be twelve inches from her mouth. 'I shall very much look forward to it.'

'Good day to you, Miss Austen. My coachman will see you back to Rowling.'

'Oh, very well.' Jane jumps up, belatedly realizing she is being dismissed. 'Good day to you, Mrs Knight.' Still no wiser as to how to address Eleanor, Jane walks backwards to the door, bowing every few steps until her bottom collides with the knob. Mrs Knight has declared her guest does not require Jane to stand on ceremony, but 'Miss Eleanor' feels far too familiar. Perhaps the princess's self-styled title would feel less of an insult to both Jane and Eleanor's dignity. 'Infanta.'

All the cream finished, Eleanor smacks her lips together. '*Cambia tu rumbo a estribor. Buona notte.*'

'Quite,' replies Jane, as she reaches behind herself, fumbling for the handle to let herself out.

Once Jane is in the sanctity of the entrance hall, she takes a deep breath to regain her composure. She has witnessed enough to agree Elizabeth and Neddy's fears are well-founded. Mrs Knight's house guest is a spurious interloper. Eleanor's bizarre behaviour would be enough to arouse suspicion, but her costume is ridiculous and it is obvious she speaks no more Spanish than Jane. Her ruse is so preposterous as to offend the comprehension of any intelligent person.

The real question is why a woman as intelligent as Mrs Knight cannot see this for herself. What hold does the girl have over her that she would invite Eleanor to share her home and place her comfort above that of her son and daughter-in-law? Jane's only consolation is that she has been invited to return. Through a few well-placed hints, she might open Mrs Knight's eyes to Eleanor's mendacity.

There are no servants to be seen, and the marble floor keeps the hall wonderfully cool. Her nerves calmer, Jane moves to check her reflection in the surface of a silver tray left on a marble pedestal. A folded leaf of hot-pressed paper sits abandoned on it. Jane's throat catches as she realizes it is the same note that Mrs Knight refused to read. There is no seal and no postmark, indicating it was delivered by hand. How curious that Mrs Knight should be so disgusted by a message from a near acquaintance. Jane's fingers hover towards it. Before she can stop herself, she has flicked open the page. In contrast to the excellent-quality materials, the handwriting is crude and clumsy – not at all appropriate for the correspondent of a great lady. Large, spidery letters, blotted with black ink, spell out just a few words.

The whore's feet run to evil, whosoever harbours her shall know no peace. Turn her out or I will deliver her to judgement myself.

Capt. Fairbairn

Jane whips away her hand, as if she'd grasped the handle of a kettle straight from the stove. No wonder Mrs Knight didn't want to read it. How dare this Captain Fairbairn write such a profanity and have the gall to present it at the very entrance of Godmersham Park? *Another?* This is not the first disgusting note Mrs Knight has received. Jane closes her eyes, shaking her head to dispel the image of the obscene scrawl from her mind. Who is Captain Fairbairn and what does he know about Eleanor's history? Could he be party to the girl's true nature and whatever devious plans she has to defraud Mrs Knight? His method is despicable and his words are beyond coarse, but his missive is clearly intended as a warning. Has Mrs Knight told Neddy? Or the authorities? If Neddy's benefactress is embroiled in a nefarious affair, Jane must do what she can to extract her from it. Quickly, before she places herself – or, more crucially, Neddy's inheritance and the Austens' future happiness – in danger.

Chapter Six

Unlike Godmersham, Rowling Manor wears its long history with pride. The next evening, when Jane comes down for dinner, she enters the dining room through an archway carved with Tudor roses. Dust motes shimmy before the complex arrangement of lead lights, which make up the windows looking out onto the garden. The encaustic tiles are cool and smooth beneath her slippers. Oak panels cover the walls, and ivory roses stand upright in a crystal vase, perfuming the air with the scent of summer.

So far, Jane has spent her day cutting out paper dolls for the children while puzzling over the identity of the odious Captain Fairbairn. If she were in Steventon, she would start by searching for his name in *The Navy List*. But Neddy does not subscribe and, as he has already pointed out, the vast majority of naval officers on active service have been despatched to fight the French. Which means Fairbairn is more likely to be a captain in the army, unless he is retired altogether. In which case, he may be a neighbour, or perhaps a tenant, given he has access to the park. The contents of the note may have been upsetting, but Jane is hopeful that, once she and Neddy have located its sender, they can determine what he knows and use it to extract Mrs Knight from Eleanor's pernicious scheme.

However, Jane has not seen her brother since he escorted her to Godmersham Park. Neddy is either occupied with estate matters or avoiding Jane after the humiliation of being refused admittance. As requested, Mrs Knight's coachman, Armand, ferried Jane home. Not the genial fellow who retrieved Neddy from Steventon all those years ago, but a surly Swiss man who barely said two words and rode with a blunderbuss on the seat beside him. No doubt his pride was grievously wounded at being asked to retrieve the magnificent coach and his team of six horses for the sake of his mistress's poor relation. He was so abrupt, Jane feared he might bear her some malicious intent. All the way, she kept looking out for landmarks to reassure herself they were following the correct route. But, really, with the endless fields of hops it was impossible to know whether to bother panicking that she had been abducted until after he had deposited her safely at Rowling.

A door on the far side of the room opens and Elizabeth wafts through, her statuesque frame wrapped in a pale blue and white cloud. Jane's sister-in-law was so incensed by her account of Eleanor's freakish behaviour and Mrs Knight's coldness towards her son that Jane could not bring herself to alarm her further by telling her about the note. Jane should not have been snooping, and it seemed inappropriate to mention something so obscene to a woman in Elizabeth's condition. The shock of it might somehow harm the baby or bring on labour. Now, Elizabeth pauses to admire her reflection in the gilt-edged mirror above the fireplace before she notices Jane. 'Oh, you're here already. I've only just sent Susan to see to you.'

'There's no need for that. I'm perfectly capable of dressing myself.' It did take quite a lot of wriggling for Jane to lace herself inside Elizabeth's striped gown, now elongated by the addition of a clever flounce. Not to mention risk of personal injury, as she pinned the bodice in place. But Kitty and Alice are already overstretched, both girls complaining the other is negligent in her duties, leaving themselves to carry out the majority of Elizabeth's commands. Jane does not want to add to their workload or their list of grievances.

'Hmm . . .' Elizabeth frowns, as she adjusts Jane's neckline to reveal more of her bosom. Roger, Neddy's obliging manservant, enters clasping a green glass bottle and heads for the crystal decanter on the sideboard. 'I said two bottles. And of the Bordeaux, not the Rioja.'

Roger frowns at the Rioja, as if it has deliberately attempted to catch him out. 'But my master said –'

'Never mind what your master said. He'll thank me for making sure we're well provisioned later.'

Jane bites her lip. Despite his affluence, Neddy must have inherited their father's approach to husbandry. Two bottles of wine seems rather excessive for a quiet family dinner. Mr Austen would likely settle for half, diluted with plenty of water. But when Jane lowers her gaze to the table, she realizes it is set for four. 'Are we expecting company?'

'Only the Reverend Mr Blackall. Edward's giving him a tour of the garden.'

'Would this be the same Mr Blackall who calls at Godmersham Park?' Jane asks, remembering the visitor who had so upset Eleanor that she had persuaded Mrs Knight to banish her son.

'That's right. Mr Blackall has the living of Godmersham and the smaller parish of Crundale, which brings him an income of around two hundred and fifty pounds a year. He employs a curate, but that can't cost more than fifty, and his mother left him a good two thousand invested in the four per cents. Crundale is a very pretty village. The parsonage is fit only for a bachelor at present, but he intends to refurbish. He doesn't keep a carriage as he prefers to ride on horseback, but I see no reason why he couldn't in future.' Elizabeth smiles brightly. 'Say, for instance, if he were to take a wife.'

'Is that so?' Jane's skin prickles. The eligible Mr Blackall explains why Elizabeth was so eager to send her maid to dress her, and for Mrs Green to adjust her cast-off evening gown in readiness for tonight. While Jane is grateful for the unexpected opportunity to quiz Mr Blackall, she must disabuse Elizabeth of the notion she is prepared to entertain a suitor. 'Really, Beth, it's very kind of you to invite this young gentleman here on my behalf. But as I said previously –'

'Who said anything about young? I'm not a miracle worker, Jane. Do I need to remind you that entire legions of our young men have been called off to fight General Bonaparte, and you have not a penny to your name?' Elizabeth picks up one of the tall-stemmed wine glasses, inspecting it against the late-afternoon sunlight. Roger, having returned, tries so hard to pretend indifference to their conversation that his hand trembles as he pours Bordeaux into the decanter.

Determined not to betray her mortification, Jane focuses on inhaling the wine's comforting aroma. It is not true that she is completely without money of her own. The ever-generous Thomas Knight II bequeathed her a modest legacy of fifty pounds. It is all she can expect to take with her into her marriage and she will not provoke her sister-in-law's scorn by reminding her of this when Elizabeth brought two thousand and the leasehold of Rowling to her union with Neddy. 'Is Mrs Knight usually on good terms with the clergyman?'

'Of course. He's most respectable.' Elizabeth continues listing Mr Blackall's attractions on her fingertips. 'He enjoys fishing and professes to have an ear for music, but his voice is a little flat. He collects earthenware tankards in the shape of little men, and visits family in East Anglia every couple of years. Oh, and he detests women who wear too much rouge.' She takes out a pocket handkerchief to wipe Jane's cheeks, but Jane's offensive colouring is all her own.

'You seem to know rather a lot about him.' Jane squirms out of Elizabeth's reach, checking her appearance in the looking glass. Her complexion is a touch more flushed than usual. Her countenance has not yet recovered from riding about in the phaeton. Aside from that, the subtle gold stripes of Elizabeth's former gown suit her rather well.

Undeterred, Elizabeth licks a finger and twists one of the natural curls that Jane left loose around her face, encouraging it to form a smarter ringlet. 'With an unmarried sister advancing thirty, and two more penniless sisters-in-law, I make it my business to know every eligible bachelor in the county and beyond.'

Jane's spirit deflates at Elizabeth's inclusion of Cassandra in this threesome of desperate spinsters. Despite Jane despatching a letter to Hampshire every day, Cassandra is yet to reply. It is the longest the pair have ever gone without any direct correspondence. Each morning, when Roger retrieves the post, Jane's hopes of hearing from Cassandra ever again are diminished. With her parents still travelling, Jane is forced to rely on Mary for news. Never one to avoid harsh truths, Mary warns that Cassandra will not dress and barely eats. Instead, she lies in bed all day with the curtains drawn, white-faced and tearful as she nourishes her grief.

Elizabeth turns to fiddle with the arrangement of roses so that the fresh buds take centre stage; the open flowers, their petals already turning brown and falling loose, are hidden at the back. 'Mr Blackall has never been married, so there are no dependants to worry about and there will likely be no division of assets when he passes away.'

Jane mirrors Elizabeth's over-bright smile. 'Unless he keeps a brood of by-blows up in East Anglia.'

'Jane, that's not amusing.' Elizabeth scowls. 'Don't you dare say anything like that in company, or you'll destroy your chances completely.'

'I'm sorry.' Jane is quite sure Cassandra would have found it hilarious. The old Cassandra would, anyway. She's not sure the new broken version of her sister will ever laugh again. Everyone dishes out the platitudes, reassuring Cassandra that time will prove the best healer. In Jane's experience, distance may remove the sting of lost love, but the dull ache only grows heavier. Immediately, she suffers a twinge for comparing Cassandra's devastating loss with her sentiments for Tom Lefroy. Next to Cassandra's devotion to Mr Fowle, Jane's affair with Tom was nothing – a trifling flirtation, over almost as soon as it began.

'Ah, there they are …' Elizabeth peers through the window, where two figures are wandering up the brick path through the shrubbery. 'I saved his most attractive feature until last – he's a published author.'

'He is?' Perhaps Jane is being too hasty in dismissing any

potential suitors out of hand. There would be no harm in her considering other options, just in case Tom never reappears. She presses her nose to the glass to get a better look. Outside, Neddy throws his head back laughing. Beside him, a thickset man remains dour. He is dressed in a clerical black frock coat and breeches, with a Geneva band and a wide-brimmed hat, just like Jane's father.

'Yes. What a coincidence. I'm sure you'll have so much in common.'

As the two men draw closer, sunlight illuminates the grey threaded through Mr Blackall's side-whiskers, signifying he must be closer in age to Mrs Knight than to Jane – not quite the romantic young poet she might have hoped for. 'What exactly did he publish?'

'Oh, let me think.' Elizabeth returns to her roses, refusing to meet Jane's eye. 'Sermons, I believe.'

Jane straightens. 'That's not an author, that's a priest with access to the printing press.'

'But he's working on something new. A treatise of some kind. That's bound to be more exciting.'

Jane catches another glimpse of herself in the mirror. How Tom would laugh if he could see her now, all dressed up to impress a dour-faced man of the cloth. She represses the urge to snatch away Elizabeth's vase and hurl it at the silvered glass. It's not Jane's fault she hasn't managed to extinguish the hope Tom will one day rekindle their brief affair. If she could go out into the world, forge a path for herself, like her brothers, it might be different. Stuck at home, with only her writing to occupy her, she's forced to dwell on past feelings. Oh, God, if it's this painful for Jane to move on from her short dalliance, how can Cassandra be expected to bear her genuine heartbreak? It's enough to make Jane want to lie down and weep with grief for her beloved sister.

Over a dinner of succulent roast lamb (formerly a member of Neddy's flock), the gentlemen converse at great length about which members of the local gentry have it within their power to grant access to the best fishing. Jane learns more about the preferences of the aristocratic and aquatic inhabitants of Kent than she ever cared to. Whenever there is a lull, Elizabeth looks at her expectantly. While Jane is tempted to use these pauses to dive headlong into an interrogation of Mr Blackall's interaction with Eleanor, she suspects it would be politic to wait for Neddy to introduce the subject.

In the interim, she does her best to walk the fine line between being civil and restraining herself from giving Mr Blackall any false encouragement. It is a delicate dance and only possible if one's partner is willing to follow one's lead. 'Do you visit Canterbury often, Mr Blackall? Perhaps, for such entertainments as the theatre?' she asks, hoping to divert him from any further consideration of country pursuits, and that the mention of players might lead towards the strange creature masquerading as a princess at God-mersham Park.

'Not often, Miss Austen. It is my opinion that very few plays are fit to be staged in public. Even the most moral work can be degenerated when performed in front of a bawdy crowd.'

'Oh ...' Unfortunately, Jane's polite enquiries are no match for Mr Blackall's pomposity. Ever since her parents took her to watch a pantomime as a child, she has longed to see more of the theatre. Real theatre – not the amateur efforts her brothers put on in Mr Austen's barn in their youth. Although she must respect the earnestness with which James undertook his management of these family productions, rounding up his younger siblings to paint the scenery and forcing their cousins, Jane Cooper and Eliza, and even a young Mr Fowle, to audition for their parts. 'But I understood Canterbury was home to a very respectable establishment.'

'The Orange Street? I haven't attended a performance there since I had the misfortune of watching *Doctor Faustus* under a shower of missiles thrown by a troupe of redcoats. I will not return until Sir Edward Hale has completed his new facility and only the most high-ranking officers are granted leave to remain within the city's walls. I only wish Sir Edward had chosen a plot even further out of the way to house the cavalry.'

Jane straightens at the mention of army officers.

Canterbury is less than ten miles from Godmersham, close enough to make it a possible location for the mysterious Captain Fairbairn to reside. 'The militia is billeted there?'

'Far too many of them, yes. And up to two thousand more just outside, at the new barracks on Northgate Street. This particular regiment was the most undisciplined group of ruffians I ever saw. They all but ruined the play.'

Jane cannot blame Mr Blackall for his hostility towards the militia: they have hardly been careful to guard their reputation. When soldiers have been ordered to disperse crowds voicing their displeasure at the rising cost of bread, they have joined in to protest at their own meagre rations. Only last April four hundred men of Henry's regiment, seized by hunger and the devil, laid waste to the town of Newhaven on the Sussex coast. For two days, the gang ran riot, helping themselves to meat and liquor while attacking local farms and mills. By some merciful act of Providence, Henry was on leave at the time. He returned to watch the ringleaders kneel in their coffins and be shot by ten of their former comrades.

'I wonder, do you know if there is a Captain Fairbairn among their number?' Jane watches Neddy to see if the name means anything to him, but there is not the slightest flicker of recognition in his features.

Elizabeth, meanwhile, looks horrified. 'Let me assure you, Mr Blackall, Jane is not the type of young lady to associate with young men from the barracks.'

'Of course not.' Jane rushes to defend herself against her own imaginary impropriety. 'He served with our brother, Captain Henry Austen of the Oxfordshires. Henry mentioned Fairbairn was stationed nearby and asked me to enquire of anyone who might have news of his friend.' Neddy gives her a quizzical glance, knowing that, even if one of Henry's acquaintances was stationed in Canterbury, he would hardly task his unmarried sister with retrieving word of him.

'I do not, Miss Austen. I avoid fraternizing with the armed forces, and I would counsel you to do likewise. A soldier, or even a sailor, may be welcomed readily into society, but that doesn't make him a gentleman. As for the theatre, I am of the opinion that great works of literature are best enjoyed in private. Even then, I restrict myself to the histories and tragedies. I do not think the comedies suitable for a clergyman.'

'Jane will agree with you there. She's an avid reader, hardly ever without a book in her hand.' Elizabeth tops up Mr Blackall's glass of Bordeaux almost to the brim before Neddy gently wrestles away the decanter.

'Are you, Miss Austen?' Mr Blackall smiles, placing his knife and fork on his plate and looking ready to listen for the first time that evening. 'And what, in particular, do you care to read?'

Jane enjoys Marlowe and Shakespeare – Mr Blackall's comment about histories and tragedies perhaps referred to their works – but she doesn't want to risk elevating herself in his esteem. 'Novels, usually.'

'Novels?' he splutters, as if Jane has revealed she reads runes.

'Exclusively novels,' she replies, delighted he has taken the bait. 'Histories, romances, any kind of novel I can acquire through the circulating library. I devour them. All our family are great novel readers, aren't they, Neddy?'

'Um . . .' Neddy pauses, glass halfway to his mouth.

'Apart from our eldest brother, James, but he's always had far too great a sense of his own self-consequence.' Jane can tell Neddy and Elizabeth are on tenterhooks lest she embarrasses them further by revealing she not only reads novels but writes them. They need not be so alarmed. Jane is conscious enough of the precariousness of her reputation to know she must keep her literary ambitions within the family. Plus, she doesn't care to invite any disapprobation or, worse, pity from Mr Blackall by admitting she dreams of doing what he has so effortlessly achieved.

Mr Blackall wipes his mouth with a napkin and throws it onto his plate. 'I would be failing in my duty as a clergyman if I did not censure you in that regard. Novels are hardly suitable reading matter for young ladies.'

'Oh, really? What makes you say so?' Jane picks up her glass, swilling her drink and hoping its heavenly scent will quell her temper as she's forced to endure more of Mr Blackall's drivel. Beneath the initial taste of berries, the wine has an earthy undertone, like the smell of wet gravel, or a freshly licked pencil. Bordeaux must be very expensive, not to mention difficult to obtain, since all trade with France has been proscribed.

'They are effusions of fancy designed to provoke pleasure, which can only distract a woman from her religious and familial duties.' Mr Blackall frowns. 'Such compositions risk exposing the impressionable female mind to ungodly thoughts and leaving her ripe for seduction.'

If anything, the novels Jane has read have served to strengthen her resolve against temptation by a handsome rogue. It is a rare breed of heroine who can resist the traps laid out for her by her creator, and Jane has no desire to share the fate of Samuel Richardson's Clarissa. She will not exert her energies explaining this to Mr Blackall, however, lest he flatters himself as a rational creature. 'I suppose you would rather I read conduct books? Or sermons?'

'Sermons are much more suitable, I agree.' Elizabeth uses all her might to push the conversation towards the safer arena of her guest's literary accomplishments. 'Did I mention Mr Blackall has published his own collection? It has been very well received, so I believe.'

'Indeed. After such a favourable account by Mr Croker of the *Critical Review*, my publisher informs me we are obliged to print a second edition.'

'That is good news.' Neddy picks up his wine. 'Isn't it, Jane?'

'Capital.' Jane is forced to raise her glass as her spirits sink through the floorboards. How can Mr Blackall's sermons be selling so well? Who is buying them? Unless it is interfering relatives, foisting them upon unsuspecting young ladies who would much rather lose themselves within the pages of a well-drawn and thoughtfully written novel.

As dinner is cleared away, Jane ruminates on how best to raise the topic of Mrs Knight and her strange house guest. While she longs to be released from Mr Blackall's company, she is loath to let him depart without deepening her understanding of what passed between him and Eleanor. The incident must have been serious for Mrs Knight to take the precaution of barring all male persons, including Neddy, from Eleanor's presence.

Roger returns, with a heavy platter of cheese, nuts, gooseberry pudding and a jug of egg custard. It is a far cry from Steventon, where even on feast days the family fight over one dessert. Mr Austen maintains a rule that whoever slices is last to select their portion, ensuring all his children have an eagle eye and a head for fractions. 'Did Beth mention Mrs Knight requested you accompany her to Canterbury on Thursday, Ned?'

Neddy unwraps the cheese. It is kept in a round container with French writing on the top and would be excellent for storing ribbons. Jane plans to purloin it, but when Neddy lifts the lid, the acrid stench of ammonia pervades. The smell will have permeated the wood, rendering it useless. It must have been in the pantry since before the French declared war. 'This Thursday? That's unfortunate. I have a prior commitment on behalf of Sir William. I'm to meet his gamekeeper and assess the stock.'

Given their strained relations, Neddy should be taking every opportunity he can to spend time with his mother. 'Can't that wait?' asks Jane.

'Not really. Grouse season will be on us before we know it. And I must do everything I can to oblige the baronet, especially with Midsummer approaching.'

'What's so pressing about Midsummer?' Elizabeth serves Mr Blackall a dainty slice of pudding, which he promptly smothers in custard. 'We must oblige my brother at all times.'

'Indeed we must.' Neddy pulls at his cravat. 'Forget I mentioned it.'

Jane recalls their conversation on the way to Rowling. Tenant farmers pay their rent on quarter days. Neddy took his additional acreage on Lady Day, meaning the next instalment of his increased rent will be due at Midsummer. She doubts it would be conducive to her brother's domestic harmony if she were to explain this arrangement. If Neddy is concerned he will not be able to meet the repayments, it is up to him to inform his wife. 'Someone should certainly accompany Mrs Knight. We must do all we can to encourage her in her participation in society.'

Neddy turns to Elizabeth. 'Can you go, darling? I'm already committed to helping your brother.'

Elizabeth pauses with a sliver of pudding halfway between the platter and her bowl. 'Well, I could . . .'

'Don't be silly. Beth can't go.' Escorting Mrs Knight to Canterbury will involve hours of being bounced around the country lanes. Even if Elizabeth is hiding the full extent of her suffering, Neddy should know the exertion is too much to ask of a woman in her condition. 'She's weeks away from lying-in.' How can he be so inconsiderate? Mary has only recently announced she's expecting, yet James is treating her as delicately as one would handle a Dresden shepherdess.

At the reference to Elizabeth's pregnancy, Mr Blackall grimaces into his overflowing custard. Neddy, however, continues to stare at Jane, impassive. 'I'll put some cushions in the phaeton.'

'It's no matter. I'll go.' Elizabeth places her pudding back on the platter, rather than into her bowl.

'No, you absolutely must not.' The air turns thick with silence as Jane senses she's broken some unwritten rule in challenging Neddy's authority. But surely if he knew how much Elizabeth was already suffering he wouldn't want to cause her any more discomfort, or risk bringing on the baby before its time by forcing her out in the carriage. 'Really, Neddy. It would be most taxing for her.'

Elizabeth's cheeks flush. 'I said it's no matter.'

Jane glances between her brother and an increasingly

agitated Elizabeth. Mrs Knight's errands may involve calling on the Wilmots, in which case Jane would very much like to solicit the doctor's opinion of his former charge. The visit may even afford her the opportunity to make some discreet enquiries as to the whereabouts of Captain Fairbairn. 'Why don't I go? I may not be familiar with Canterbury, but I'm very willing to act as a companion, if it will save your mother from travelling alone.'

'Thank you, Jane. That's very kind of you.' Neddy smiles, but there is no real warmth in his features. 'Mother will hardly be alone. Whenever she is minded to leave the park, she takes Armand with her. And this time I'd hazard a guess her foreign princess will cleave to her too.'

Jane places her napkin on the table, relieved that Neddy has finally raised the thorny topic. 'Actually, Ned, I'm quite sure I have evidence she's not foreign, never mind a princess. She certainly doesn't speak Spanish. Did you converse with her when you visited, Mr Blackall?'

'I did, and I concur with you, Miss Austen.'

'You do?' Jane is gratified that Mr Blackall can appreciate her skill in detecting the inconsistencies in Eleanor's speech. Perhaps he will prove himself a useful ally in uncovering the girl's true history. 'Tell me, did you recognize any scraps of French or Italian amid her babble?'

Having just placed a spoonful of custard into his mouth, Mr Blackall presses his corpulent lips together and swallows slowly. He is either thinking very carefully about his answer or savouring the exquisite hint of vanilla. 'Neither. She speaks with the devil's tongue.'

Jane stares hard at Mr Blackall, trying to work out if he is joking. From the deadpan expression on his face, he is clearly not. 'What?'

'The devil's tongue?' Elizabeth repeats, as if this is a fashionable European language she should have been introduced to at school.

'Indeed.' Mr Blackall nods gravely. 'It is my learned opinion that the girl has made a compact with Satan. Mrs Knight would not permit me to examine her fully for a mark but, from her behaviour, it's evident to me she's been invaded by a demon and is in urgent need of exorcism.'

Elizabeth and Neddy continue to stare at Mr Blackall, faces frozen. Excitement bubbles up in Jane. This dinner has the potential to be far more entertaining than she had hitherto thought. 'Possessed by a demon? How frightful. Pray tell us, Mr Blackall, is this a condition you are familiar with? In all the time my father has been a clergyman, I've never heard him speak of any of his parishioners succumbing in this way. I implore you to share with us everything you know of the matter.'

Neddy splutters. He tears his napkin from his collar and balls it in his hand as he makes coughing sounds into it. Jane is satisfied by the knowledge that he too is trying to contain his horror. The Austens are a pragmatic breed. Their father would dismiss any supernatural leanings as preposterous.

'Not in person, but I have read numerous accounts. It is obvious that the girl has entered into an unholy conspiracy with Lucifer himself. That's what my collection of sermons is foremost concerned with – how to spot the devil in his many earthly guises.'

'Goodness me,' says Jane. 'I didn't realize I was in the presence of such an authority. But Mrs Knight refused to let you examine her house guest, you say?'

Mr Blackall sets his dumpy features in a frown. 'I'm afraid so. Otherwise I'm certain I would have found proof.'

Jane arches her brow. 'Proof?' During England's witch trials, hundreds of women were put to death for no greater evil than a blemish in some intimate part. Whatever Eleanor's intentions, Jane can hardly fault her for becoming distressed if Mr Blackall attempted to examine her naked.

'If I'd carried out a thorough interrogation of her person, I'm confident I would have found the spot where the demon entered her.' Mr Blackall turns to Neddy, placing his meaty hand on his host's shoulder. 'I'm sorry to alarm you, but the possession will only get worse. I've already witnessed lapses in the girl's ability to control the demon festering inside her. Very shortly, she'll descend into uninterrupted fits of raving. Then your mother will be forced to admit the necessity of driving it out.'

At the mentions of 'fits', Neddy's features grow stern. Several members of the Austen family, including Jane's brother Georgy, are prone to convulsions. The insinuation that such difficulties are anything other than unfortunate physical ailments is no laughing matter.

'Well, thank goodness you're here to preserve us.' Jane smiles sweetly. How dare Mr Blackall accuse novelists of peddling fantasies when he is no more than a purveyor of superstitious nonsense? 'Do you happen to have a copy of your collection of sermons with you? I'd be most eager to read –'

Elizabeth leaps up from her seat. 'Actually, Jane, I think it's high time we left the gentlemen to it.'

Jane looks down at her half-eaten pudding. 'Oh, but I've not finished yet.'

'Well, never mind, you don't want to get fat.' She places a hand under Jane's armpit and practically drags her from the table.

In the tapestry-lined drawing room, Jane tries her best not to snigger as Elizabeth makes her swear on pain of death not to encourage Mr Blackall to converse any further on his macabre interest in the occult. 'I agree it's rather quaint, but men with ample incomes who remain single until later life will develop strange habits. Once you're married, you'll be able to steer him towards a more palatable area of theology,' she says, then launches into a full-blown lecture on the fragility of a man's pride. 'And you must promise me never to disagree with your brother in company again. What were you thinking, so brazenly questioning his command I accompany Mrs Knight to Canterbury? Didn't your mother teach you anything? A woman must be seen to submit.'

'I was only trying to save you from the discomfort of making an unnecessary journey. You told me yourself of your reluctance to wander far from home,' Jane replies, as she takes a seat on the carved oak bench beside the hearth. Now the heat of the day is past, the antique house is chilly, and a log fire burns in the steel grate.

'Yes, but disputes between married couples should be handled with discretion. If you'd left it to me, I'd have dealt with it in a far more feminine manner. A wife must prevail upon her husband, until the very thing she wishes seems to him to be his own design,' Elizabeth continues, seemingly unaware she has done nothing but chide Neddy on his inability to deal with his mother since Jane's arrival. 'Only think of the anarchy that would ensue if every female in the country took it upon herself so violently to usurp her master? The system would collapse, and chaos would reign supreme. Look at what's happened in France, where the entire social order has been upturned by the will of the mob, and the blood of the Royal Family runs like a river through the streets of Paris!'

Fortunately for Elizabeth's equilibrium, Neddy and Mr Blackall soon join them in the snug chamber. With the one topic that can afford Jane amusement prohibited, she sits quietly while Mr Blackall eulogizes on the comfortable situation of Rowling Manor and how it puts him in mind of the repairs he intends to make to Crundale Parsonage. Jane's only contribution to the conversation is occasionally to bend forward and stroke Conker's elongated tummy. Like Jane, the dog is on his best behaviour, stretched out in front of the fire with his paws in the air.

'That beast should be kept in the coach house,' Elizabeth mutters, already disregarding her resolve that a husband's way of managing things ought never to be called into question.

'I know, darling, but he complains so much when he's out there it distresses the horses.'

'It distresses me when he remains in here.'

To Jane's surprise, Neddy turns to Mr Blackall. 'Shall we take a walk out to the coach house? I don't believe I've shown you my new team yet and I expect you'll want Roger to prepare your mount. It's a long ride back to Crundale.' Neddy is so practised at being genial, it can be difficult to read his true sentiments, but the cleric's offhand remarks must have annoyed him if he is so eager to see him gone. It is not yet eight o'clock. There are another couple of hours before darkness will descend over Kent, making travel on horseback undesirable.

When Neddy returns, having disposed of Mr Blackall but retaining his dog, Elizabeth stands to greet him. 'Well? Did he express any preference for Jane?'

'I didn't think there was much point in asking, not unless Jane was partial to him.' He slumps into an armchair before the fire. 'So, Jane, how would you like to be Mrs Blackall?'

'I'd rather be ducked in the River Medway with my thumb tied to my big toe.'

Neddy roars with laughter, causing Conker to raise his ears in consternation. 'I knew you were going to say something amusing.'

Elizabeth sighs, wilting into the bench beside Jane. 'Never mind. You didn't do too badly, Jane. And you'll have the chance to revise your opinion of Mr Blackall at the ball. I'm told he's a very elegant dancer.'

'We're to attend a ball?' Jane perks up. It is clear Mr Blackall and his irrational notions are going to be of little assistance in unmasking Eleanor. If Jane is to discover where she came from and her dastardly intentions towards Mrs Knight, she must speak to a wider pool of witnesses. That means finding the opportunity to converse with the Wilmots in Canterbury, and anyone else who might have visited Eleanor during her brief stay with them.

'Have I not mentioned it?' Elizabeth places a hand to her cheek. 'I've been so preoccupied helping William with the arrangements, I assumed you already knew. The Goodnestone Midsummer Ball, my family host it every year on the summer solstice. On this occasion we will use it to mark your entrance into society.'

'Really?' As a country girl, Jane had not been granted the pomp and ceremony of coming out. She had slipped from a child to a young lady unheeded in much the same way that Mrs Austen warns she's in danger of sliding into an old maid. It does not bother Jane. She's always preferred to be the observer rather than the observed. 'That's tremendously kind of Sir William, but there's no need to fuss over me.'

'We may as well. All of my sisters are out and we're committed to holding the event. It's only a week away, so remember to choose some silk when you go into Canterbury and have it sent straight to Mrs Green.'

Neddy pokes his head out from his chair. 'I thought you were going to have one of your old gowns adjusted?'

'That won't do.' Elizabeth frowns. 'Fashions have changed far too much since we married. Besides which, Jane is too tall.'

'Nonsense. She can't be more than an inch taller, and your gowns are not outmoded.'

'Has Sir William invited any of the cavalry?' asks Jane, wondering if this foray into Kent society might bring her into contact with Captain Fairbairn. Even if he is not present, one of his brothers in arms might recognize his name and be able to throw light on his whereabouts.

'Goodness, no,' replies Elizabeth. 'You heard Mr Blackall, they're a most uncivilized bunch.'

'Don't you think he should? It would maintain morale. I agree with Sir Edward Hale – it's our duty to accommodate the men who stand between us and the French.'

Elizabeth peers at her. 'What are you about? Imagining yourself flirting with a smart young colonel, I expect.'

'I am not!' Jane exclaims. How can she explain her interest

in the officers without revealing to Elizabeth Captain Fairbairn's unsavoury accusations?

'You cannot afford a soldier. Tell her, Edward.'

'She's right, Jane. You don't want to attract the attentions of a penniless rake with more charm than fortune to recommend him. You know how mercenary some of these army fellows can be. Just look at Henry.'

'Honestly, it's not that. And don't be so uncharitable towards our dear brother. Henry assures me he's very much in love with Miss Pearson.' While it's true that Henry once had the temerity to propose to Eliza, despite her superiority in fortune and station, not to mention that she is his first cousin and ten years his senior, he has since found a far more suitable match in the seventeen-year-old daughter of a naval captain. And as Jane sees it, all her brothers, including Neddy, are ambitious in their affections.

'Look, Jane, don't think me immune to the charms of a redcoat.' Elizabeth sighs, 'but you're bound to choose some gallant who'll go off and be killed on a foreign battlefield. And then where will you be? Back where you started, but with his children to support, and you having surrendered your bloom. Believe me, a clergyman is a much safer bet. And do promise not to do that thing with your wine.'

Jane stares into the empty glass in her hand. 'What thing?'

'Closing your eyes and sniffing it. You almost put your whole nose in it at one point.'

'Did I?' Jane hiccups. 'I do apologize, I couldn't help myself. It's very good. Was it terribly expensive?'

'Yes, it was.' Neddy huffs. 'I thought I told Roger to open the Rioja. And we hardly needed two bottles.'

'You told me you had a very reasonable supplier,' says Elizabeth.

'I did, but I haven't heard from him in a while and I'm growing quite anxious.'

'Anxious?' Jane echoes. It seems an excessive reaction to a lack of correspondence from one's wine merchant.

'Concerned as to where else I'd be able to source such excellent wine. As you said, it's very good – and my cellar is running low.'

Elizabeth stands, pressing into the arch of her back with both hands. 'Well, I'm going to bed. I know it's early, but I'm exhausted after all that entertaining.'

Neddy drains his glass. 'I'll join you, darling.'

'But there's still plenty of sunlight,' says Jane, considering how best to persuade Neddy to remain so she can tell him about Captain Fairbairn's note. She spots her manuscript, still tied up with ribbon and abandoned on the sideboard. 'I could read *First Impressions* to you. Even James couldn't help loitering outside the parlour door to listen to it.'

'Another night.' Neddy dismisses her with a flick of his hand, following his wife out of the room.

As the house creaks and footsteps sound from the landing above, Jane takes Elizabeth's glass and sips the remainder of her wine. Conker lifts his head in mild rebuke, but he is soon settled with a firm rub to his snout. Perhaps it is for the best Jane did not have the chance to tell Neddy about Fairbairn. Now that she has the opportunity of meeting the Wilmots and enquiring after the captain in Canterbury, it may prove more prudent to keep this knowledge to herself. Her brother is so protective, he may well forbid her to insert herself into any investigation. And while it may be a woman's duty to obey her master, Neddy cannot order Jane to desist in searching for Captain Fairbairn unless he is aware she is doing so.

2.   *Letter to Cassandra Austen*
                    Rowling Farm, Tuesday, 13 June 1797

My dearest Cassandra,

How am I to understand how things go on in Hampshire if you will not tell me? Kent continues to grow fresh and verdant, but for all I know you could be plagued with black frost and hailstorms. Can you give any credence to the elder Susan's claim that it is breeding which makes a woman ill-tempered? As difficult as it is to discern between each of Mary's dark moods, compared to Beth she is a continual procession of warm, sunny days. Fanny requires me to tell you that I am not as proficient with a cup and ball as she remembers you being. Do you have any message for me to pass on in return? Perhaps something that will help elevate me in her estimation and keep me there, since that is your forte. I am now acquainted with Mrs Knight's infanta but I do not consider myself familiar with her motives or her nature. I have a plan, however, to seek out one who professes to know her better.

Your affectionate sister,
J.A.

P.S. You may assume Mary is keeping me sufficiently abreast as it is certainly her custom to pass on everything she hears, regardless of its veracity. And while I am grateful for Mary's letters, I consider it most ungracious of you for making me so. Father always preaches against incurring a debt one has no intention of paying, and I have long since fixed on giving little pleasure to either of my sisters-in-law. Please compose yourself so that I may be released from this obligation.

Miss Austen
Rev. Mr Austen's
Deane
Hants

Chapter Seven

Thursday is another bright, cloudless morning. Jane wears her pelisse, but she is too hot and regretting her choice before she reaches Godmersham Park and finds Mrs Knight's coach and six stationed in the gravel drive. Roger conveyed her in the phaeton as Neddy, having an early appointment with Sir William's game, passed the previous evening at Goodnestone House. The two estates sit at the outer points of a squat triangle with Canterbury at the apex, meaning Jane must skirt the city and return on herself to escort Mrs Knight there. She remains hopeful the excursion will afford her the opportunity to investigate Eleanor's story. There must be someone in Canterbury who knows of Captain Fairbairn, and the Wilmots will have had good reason to turn against the girl. If Jane can seek out an introduction to either of these parties, she will be satisfied her visit has not been in vain. As for furthering her own composition, she has not explicitly been invited to read today – or invited at all, for that matter – but she has brought *The Sisters* in hope of exhibiting her accomplishments on their return. She instructs Roger to leave her writing box with Grace and proceeds towards the house, but Mrs Knight's coachman opens the door of his vehicle to reveal his mistress impatiently ensconced alone.

'Make haste, Miss Austen, if you will insist on accompanying me. The morning is already receding, and I have several important deeds to accomplish.'

'Is the *Infanta* not joining us?' Jane asks, as she clambers into the velvet-lined coach. After she volunteered to assist Mrs Knight with her errands, Jane wondered if Neddy was right in predicting Eleanor would come too. The resolution that Eleanor should remain secluded from all male company presented itself as a symptom of some wider scheme to isolate Mrs Knight from her friends. Now Jane is party to what may have prompted Eleanor's distress, she cannot help considering it a sensitive precaution.

'I'm afraid my house guest is … How did you put it? Indisposed.' Mrs Knight maintains her position in the centre of the forward-facing seat, forcing Jane to endure the journey backwards and risk carriage-sickness.

'I'm sorry to hear that.' Jane forces down a quip about how Eleanor must find it tiresome to be consumed with royal duties in such fair weather. She can already tell it is going to be a long day, and Mrs Knight is in no humour for ribbing. Jane will have to employ the utmost discretion if she is to elicit any information from her or her friends. As the coach wobbles into motion, she extracts a tidy square of folded paper from her reticule. Mrs Knight starts at the sight of it, recalling her reaction to the horrible missive from her mystery correspondent. 'It's a message from Neddy,' Jane reassures her, 'detailing the progress, or lack thereof, of repairs to your perimeter wall. I believe he's having trouble locating a bricklayer. They've all been lured away to London. And he gives his sincere apologies for not being able to oblige you today, but he had already pledged himself to Sir William.'

'He does have many demands on his time.' Mrs Knight slips the letter, unopened, into a pocket and returns her hooded eyes to the expansive façade of her home. In her widow's weeds, she is no more prepared than Jane for fine weather. Jane fears she will be forced to suffer the entire journey in stifling silence but, once they are out on the open road, Mrs Knight begins an interrogation of her own. 'Why is it you are not married yet, Miss Austen? You are certainly old enough.'

'I ... I haven't met anyone I find amiable enough to marry,' Jane lies, hating the insincerity of her own tongue. She would have liked to marry Tom, dearly. But she would not marry him without his family's approval and to the detriment of both their futures. They would have grown to resent each other, and the slow heartbreak of seeing him live to regret his choice would have been worse than giving him up altogether. At least, that is what Jane tells herself in her bleakest moments.

Mrs Knight narrows her eyes, considering Jane from across the carriage. 'I had no idea Hampshire was so devoid of eligible gentlemen. It's the war, I suppose.'

'I expect you're going to tell me that any gentleman of means will do, and I need not trouble myself with liking him much.' Catherine Knatchbull, as Mrs Knight was previously known, was the daughter of a humble rector and in her mid-twenties when she became the bride of Thomas Knight II, who himself had long surpassed forty. Despite the disparity in age, it was widely lauded as an excellent match: for she was handsome and, by then, he was rich. What two qualities could form a happier union?

Instead of responding immediately to Jane's barb, Mrs Knight turns towards the window. Her eyes mist as they fix on fields of gleaming buttercups speeding by. 'Thomas was my saviour. My protector,' she says, after a while, in a low voice. 'I thank God for sending him to me, and for every day He saw fit to grant us each other's company. I was extremely fortunate to be blessed with such a husband. I do not know how I could have endured if I had been forced to accept a lesser man.'

Jane catches her breath, thrown off guard by Mrs Knight's declaration. She is certainly a formidable woman, but she is just a woman. And in this moment, with her fingers resting on her mourning brooch and her mind clearly dwelling on her late husband, she is as vulnerable as any other. In the past, Jane had never known her to exhibit anything but the most tremendous kindness towards Neddy. Mr and Mrs Austen would not have released their son to the care of a couple who lacked affection, no matter how wealthy they promised to make him. It is most distressing that she should grow cold towards her adoptive son now. The only explanation Jane can fathom for her doing so is that Eleanor is manipulating Mrs Knight's grief to her own advantage. She will discover what the girl's game is, before they are all made losers.

No sooner do they arrive in Canterbury than Jane is assaulted with the hopeless naivety of her plan. The city must be thrice the size of Winchester, with its majestic cathedral, ruined Norman castle, and variety of irregular timber-framed buildings occupying any nook left over by Church or King. As Mr Blackall warned, the cobbled streets heave with soldiers standing on guard to defend Kent from Bonaparte's forces. The insignia of more regiments than Jane can count pass in a blur as the carriage makes its way through the confusing jumble of passageways. Even if she could escape Mrs Knight's notice, she could hardly go up to an unknown officer and ask if he knows the whereabouts of a 'Captain Fairbairn'. She risks making herself look like a jilted country girl, forced to search for her errant lover in desperate need of making him pay for the consequences of their illicit tryst.

Mrs Knight thumps on the door of the coach, and it draws to a halt as they emerge into a wide thoroughfare. A long crowd of people, from cheerful market girls shucking oysters to ragged pilgrims serene at having reached their holy destination, stretches endlessly in both directions. 'I'll conduct my business here on the high street first,' she says, as Armand hands her down from the carriage. 'After that, I have an appointment with my lawyer. It should not take much more than an hour, two at most, leaving us time to call at Briar Farm on our way home.'

Armand nods to the footman sitting on the rumble seat and then, instead of remaining with the vehicle, follows Jane and his mistress into the mixed multitude. His blunderbuss is tucked into his wide leather belt. Jane frets he will blow away his kneecap but Mrs Knight doesn't so much as bat an eyelid at the enormous gun reaching halfway down his leg. Instead, the widow warns Jane to remain in close step and beware of pickpockets. Jane's eyes latch onto the colourful displays in the procession of shops for some landmark to cling to in the eventuality she is lost. Alas, if the milliner sells her coquelicot confection, Jane will never find her way back to the coach. 'Are we not to call on your friends the Wilmots?'

'No,' replies Mrs Knight, without drawing a breath.

'You risk appearing impolite if they discover you have visited Canterbury without paying your respects. Especially as you so rarely come to town.'

'I do not require instruction on my social obligations from you, Miss Austen.'

But Jane is unwilling to abandon her ambition of questioning at least one person of interest while she is in the city. The street is so congested – surely everyone in the locality is employed in walking up and down it. 'Then I expect there's a high probability we'll meet either with Dr Wilmot or his wife while we're about our errands.'

'I sincerely hope not. The last people one wishes to happen across when one is in town are one's friends.' Mrs Knight scowls as she leads Jane towards a draper's shop. Once inside, the widow issues decisive orders on her own account, then sighs impatiently as Jane compares the most inexpensive bolts of muslin and records every detail of her expenditure in her pocketbook.

Jane had hoped, since this was her first independent foray into society, her father might despatch her with a long letter full of tender sentiments and paternal advice covering every practical or moral dilemma she might encounter, as he did for Frank and Charles when they went to sea. Instead, he sat her down and gave her a lesson in bookkeeping. During her time away, Jane must account for every penny incurred on her behalf, from her laundry to her postage, and before she returns, Mr Austen will send a draft for the exact amount. Should it exceed the five pounds he has awarded her quarterly since she came of age, he will simply subtract the surplus from her next instalment.

As she is tallying up, Jane attempts to calculate the cost of Mrs Knight's commissions. While a length of silk long enough to suggest a new pelisse is not enough to obliterate Neddy's inheritance, even if it is shot through with regal purple, it is evidence of the insidious control Eleanor has over Mrs Knight. Unfortunately, Jane's indecision over which of the many Indian cottons might prove of sufficient quality to satisfy her sister-in-law, while remaining cheap enough to appease her father, prevented her from being able to account for the full list of Mrs Knight's purchases.

The fear that Eleanor is controlling Mrs Knight from afar is further heightened when they arrive at a warren-like set of rooms in Burgate, and the widow instructs Jane to wait in the outer lobby while she converses with her lawyer, Mr Furley, in private. Still hot from their visits to various merchants, and hotter still from the agitation that she is sitting idly by while Mrs Knight reconsiders the terms of her will, Jane twists and turns in the collapsed seat of a leather armchair. The clerk, a young man of about her age, studiously ignores her in favour of scraping his nib too hard across the page of his ledger. Mrs Knight's business must be of a sensitive nature for her to exclude Jane from it so deliberately. She stares at the closed door to Mr Furley's office, willing her eyes to absorb what her ears cannot. At last, the violence of the clerk's inscriptions proves too much for his pen to sustain and, as he steps into an anteroom to retrieve another, Jane resorts to pressing her ear to the keyhole.

'My dear madam, I must protest. You cannot give up so much to enrich another,' says Mr Furley, causing Jane to lay her palm over her heart. Can Elizabeth's worst fears be justified? Is Mrs Knight really planning an act of unbridled generosity towards her beleaguered princess? She curses herself for volunteering to come in Neddy's stead. If he were here, he would be able to stop this madness.

'On the contrary, I will retain everything necessary for my ease and comfort.'

'But the scheme you propose would greatly reduce your circumstances.'

'I assure you, the circumstances attached to large, landed possessions are entirely lost on me at present.' This is even worse than Jane suspected. Neddy's mother is not rewriting her will to favour Eleanor, she is planning to surrender her wealth while she lives.

'Then you are certain?'

'I am.'

'And forgive me, ma'am, but no one is placing undue pressure on you to pursue this course of action? By the terms of Mr Knight's will –'

'I am familiar with my late husband's instructions, but this is how I am resolved to act and you cannot deny it is within my power to do so.'

'Even so, I see no reason for such haste. Return to me in a month's time, and we'll discuss it further.' Even Mrs Knight's lawyer is determined to save her from her imprudence.

'Mr Furley, if you cannot do as I describe, I will take my custom elsewhere.'

'There is nothing I can say to persuade you otherwise?'

'Indeed, it is the fondest wish of my heart.' Jane rears back at Mrs Knight's words. What cruel, unnatural mother could cut out her son and embrace a stranger before him? Neddy has spent the last two decades proving himself deserving of the Knights' affections. Eleanor appeared less than a fortnight ago and shows every symptom of being a manipulative liar. Is this punishment for an imagined slight towards her? Can Mrs Knight be so angry with Neddy for refusing to escort her to Canterbury when she had the ill-grace to turn him away from Godmersham Park?

'With an estate of such magnitude, it will take some time to execute the transfer ...'

'I will give you a month, and no longer.'

Jane springs upright as the door swings open, leaving her face to face with the room's occupants. The widow's cheeks suffuse with colour. 'Were you spying on me?'

'I ... I dropped a pin,' Jane stutters, still trying to slow her racing heart. She must have misheard, yet it was perfectly clear. Mr Furley is drawing up a contract to transfer Mrs Knight's possessions. In a month's time, the fortune Neddy has been raised to expect as his own will be released to another. The widow is so taken in by Eleanor's ruse, that she will reduce her own circumstances to elevate her.

'And I suppose it just happened to roll to the foot of

the door?' Mrs Knight does not wait to hear Jane's answer. Instead, she barges past the returning clerk, jostling a stack of papers out of his hands and sending them fanning out across the floorboards. From within his office, Jane catches the eye of Mr Furley. His slack features attest that he is as bewildered as she is by Mrs Knight's rash determination to impoverish herself and her son.

What delusions can be motivating her to act in a manner so detrimental to herself and her family? How will Jane tell Elizabeth, or Neddy, that his mother is indeed resolved to behave so treacherously towards them? Elizabeth's health is not strong enough to bear the confirmation of her greatest fears, and Neddy would be heartbroken by Mrs Knight's shock betrayal. Will Mr and Mrs Austen ever be able to assuage their consciences when they realize they parted with their son for naught? How will Cassandra cope when Jane explains they can no longer rely on their brother and must do whatever is necessary to decrease the burden on their ageing parents? Jane's only hope is to remain by Mrs Knight's side, preventing her from her own folly, until she can unmask Eleanor and break the malevolent hold she wields over the Austens' benefactress.

Chapter Eight

As Jane follows Mrs Knight out into the lane, Armand is already waiting with the coach, enabling them to make a hasty exit from the city. Despite Jane's protestations of innocence, the widow practically vibrates with fury. Jane cannot look at her without feeling the vehemence of her disapproval crashing off her in waves. Too afraid to meet her fierce gaze, she stares out of the window at the ruins of what, prior to the Dissolution, must have been a magnificent abbey. The stone arches stand devoid of stained glass, and its hallowed foundations are left open to the elements. Jane feels equally exposed as she prays for the strength to withstand this latest disaster.

The one benefit to come from her prying is that she can warn Neddy of his mother's intentions, and they can work together to bring her to her senses. Jane may have failed to locate Captain Fairbairn or question the Wilmots, but Neddy is a man with resources at his disposal. Given a month, he is sure to track down the captain, and elicit from him whatever it was that turned the Wilmots against Eleanor. Perhaps Jane should persuade him to place a description of the girl in the local newspaper and appeal for witnesses to her character. Someone must know who she really is, and Mrs Knight is bound to withdraw her generosity once she realizes she has been duped.

Armand takes the main road for a few miles before twisting along an overgrown country lane until they reach a farmstead. Spires of yellow and pink hollyhocks grow along the base of the lime-washed building, softening the scene. 'I won't be long,' Mrs Knight says, over her shoulder, as the coachman helps her descend. 'You may bide here.'

Jane sighs, disappointed with herself for being so indiscreet that Mrs Knight will not even allow her to accompany her on a visit to a tenant farmer and his family. She wonders if the residents of Briar Farm are also in distress and appealing for Mrs Knight's charity. Neddy and Elizabeth should have done more to protect his isolated and vulnerable mother from those who covet her wealth. A woman of fortune remains a target for the unscrupulous, whether she is a youthful heiress or an aged widow.

As the iron-braced front door opens, Jane expects to see a harried farmer's wife, surrounded by children. Instead, an elderly woman with a humped back and a face as finely lined as crackled porcelain, dressed in what can only be described as a religious habit, appears at the threshold. Her austere white veil is tucked tight around her features, but her mud-coloured robe is loose, gathered below the waist with a plain piece of rope attached to a wooden crucifix. Papists are no longer barred from practising their religion, but a Roman Catholic nun making her home in the English country-side is a most unusual sight. Jane has vowed to protect Mrs Knight. That makes it incumbent upon her to follow the widow inside this makeshift convent. 'It's no bother, really.' She leaps down from the carriage and scurries up the path.

Mrs Knight's shoulders rise and fall before she proceeds '*Bonjour, Madame l'Abbesse.*'

'*Bonjour, Madame Knight.*' The abbess smiles, one side of her face rising in animation while the other remains slack. '*Vous êtes venue pour la menthe poivrée?*'

'*Oui. La menthe poivrée et votre sagesse. Si vous seriez si gentille?*'

You have come for the peppermint?

Yes. The peppermint, and your wisdom. If you would be so kind?

How odd. If Mrs Knight speaks fluent French, she must know her *infanta* is a fraud. Jane could tell after just one afternoon with the girl, and Eliza decries her French as merely passable.

'*Bien sûr.*' The abbess hobbles towards them. She takes painfully slow steps around the side of the building, hefting her weight to one side and dragging her other leg behind. She must have suffered an apoplexy that has left part of her body paralysed.

Mrs Knight shoots Jane a venomous look, keeping her at a respectful distance. Jane uses the opportunity to examine her surroundings. The settlement is unlike any farmstead she has visited previously and there is certainly an air of the divine about it. They round the house and emerge into a neatly swept courtyard, bordered on all sides by brick and timber outbuildings. Half-barrels are filled with soil and planted with cheerful points of mignonette flowers. Heavenly music drifts from somewhere unseen. At first it sounds like strings, but soon Jane recognizes a choir of female voices singing the liturgy in Latin.

The abbess creaks open a door to a wooden hut. Mrs Knight turns to Jane. 'This time, do as you are bade, and wait *here*.'

Chastened, Jane lowers her gaze to her walking boots. She is genuinely trying to preserve Mrs Knight's best interests, as well as being wildly curious. Through the leaded window of the main building, another nun is bent over a slanted desk. Every few moments, she dips a quill into an inkpot before resuming her work. A smile plays at her lips. She is so completely absorbed that she does not notice Jane gawping at her through the window. How many hours a day is she left alone to complete her scholarly tasks? Jane wonders. Could Jane turn her back on society in exchange for such blissful solitude? Giving herself wholly to the Lord would remove any obligation to marry. No, she could not do it. It's not that Jane lacks the faith to give her life to God, but, rather, she is too frivolous to maintain such a sombre existence. She would miss Cassandra too much, unless her sister could be persuaded to join her. But any mother superior would insist Jane reproduce lines of Latin as proof of her devotion, rather than allowing her licence to form her own compositions. Jane fears her restless mind would revolt at any such attempts to constrain it.

Laughter erupts behind her. Another woman, in the same cumbersome attire, leads a trio of small children across the courtyard. The boys and girls hold hands as they stumble over the cobbles. Their chin-length hair is cut into pudding-bowl shapes and they wear plain linen smocks. '*Allez, allez,*' the nun calls, as she hastens them inside a back door to the cottage. She is carrying a wicker basket, half filled with strawberries. The children's mouths and hands are stained red. They must have been 'helping' her to gather them.

The door of the hut swings open and Mrs Knight emerges with several packages. Jane rushes to her side. 'Let me carry those for you.'

'Be careful. That one is candles, and this is essence of peppermint.' Mrs Knight hands over her purchases one by one. Even through the cardboard, the herbals fizz, tingling Jane's nostrils. 'The sisters make the very best lozenges. They're essential for my digestion.'

'I will. You can trust me.' Jane juggles the packages, trying not to drop any while being afraid of damaging the fragile contents by holding them too tightly.

'Hmm ...' Mrs Knight's dour expression suggests she doubts Jane's assertion. She turns to the lady abbess, reaches into her reticule and presses a handful of gleaming gold coins into the nun's gnarled fingers.

The abbess whispers a blessing, placing both hands over Mrs Knight's as she does so.

Jane holds her tongue until they are inside the coach. 'Did you really just pay several guineas for some peppermint pastilles?' Poor Mrs Knight is liable to exploitation from every quarter. If Neddy and Elizabeth had taken more pains to assist in her reintroduction to society, she would not be at the mercy of so many swindlers. 'You could have sent word to my mother that you were in need of such a remedy. If I'd known, I would have brought something up from Hampshire. My friend, James's wife's sister Martha Lloyd, makes the most wonderful –'

Mrs Knight lifts her palm, encased in its black glove. 'Desist from your racket, Miss Austen. I am not duty-bound to account for my giving of alms to you. Or anyone else, for that matter.'

'Oh, I didn't consider it in that way.' The Knights have never been overly pious, and they are not Roman Catholic. 'Do they run a school?'

Mrs Knight faces the window. 'No.'

'Only, I saw children crossing the yard?'

Beneath the rim of her bonnet, Mrs Knight rubs her temples between thumb and forefinger. 'Upon my word, you ask a lot of questions.'

'Forgive me, I warned you I have an enquiring mind.' Jane's father has always encouraged her inquisitiveness, and even her mother indulges it. Outside the tightly knit family, she is aware her manner may be perceived as precocious, but she is too curious about the world to let other people's dim-wittedness prevent her from getting at the truth.

Mrs Knight takes a deep breath, and finally relents, providing an explanation. 'The order was originally from nearby. After she retired from court, my ancestor, Dame Lucy, resided there as a lay sister. Before that, she was a great favourite with both Queen Mary and Queen Elizabeth.'

'How diplomatic of her.' Jane smiles, as the carriage sets off.

'Indeed.' Mrs Knight narrows her eyes, seemingly deliberating as to whether Jane is being impertinent or not. 'She used her personal wealth to found a religious house in Picardy. My late husband and I were fortunate to make a pilgrimage there while we were in France for my health, many years ago. But now, what with the troubles, the sisters have returned to Kent, and I have granted them refuge on a portion of my estate.'

'Briar Farm is part of Godmersham? That's very gracious of you ...' Jane stalls, wanting to ask if the farm will be included in the list of assets Mrs Knight intends to transfer to Eleanor. As much as Mrs Knight might already suspect her of eavesdropping, Jane cannot admit it without incurring the full force of her wrath. 'It's a shame the sisters can't take back their original abbey. I expect that's some great lord's home now. Unless it fell into ruin, like the one we saw as we departed Canterbury. How did they come by the children? Were they orphaned by the fighting?'

Mrs Knight's features tighten. 'You are a young lady. It is not for me to disabuse you of your notions of the world.'

'What notions? I know all about massacres.' Jane assures her. 'How can I not when our mutual cousin, Eliza, was widowed by the guillotine?' The Comte and Comtesse de Feuillide had initially escaped the insurrection in France, along with their son Hastings. Unfortunately, the Comte was later executed when he made the mistake of returning. Eliza and Hastings have since been staying with friends in England, including the Austens, but after refusing Henry's secret proposal eighteen months ago, Eliza had fled to Brighton on the excuse of promoting Hastings's health. Poor Hastings has never been stout and Eliza is determined to spend what remains of her fortune on ensuring his happiness. Sometimes Jane feels her irrepressible cousin approaches widowhood and caring for her sickly child with more vivacity than other women can muster for a country dance.

Mrs Knight frowns. 'Then you'll know that one of the

requirements the new regime imposed on its people was to swear an oath of fealty to the state above all others. An oath that any devout member of a religious order would understand as blasphemous. Those who resisted were either executed or thrown into gaol, nuns as well as priests and monks.'

'Yes.' Jane nods blithely, recalling her visit to Winchester County Gaol. Thanks to Neddy's generosity, Georgy was spared the deprivation of the cells. Instead, the family was able to pay for him to board with the governor while he awaited trial.

Mrs Knight peers at Jane closely. 'A small number of the sisters were fortunate to be released, and to find passage to England. But during their time of incarceration, their status as holy women was not recognized. They were not protected, either from the male inmates or the guards.'

Bile rises in Jane's throat. This is not a story she wants to hear. It's too gruesome, even for her. What these gentle, quiet women must have been forced to endure is unthinkable. She cranes her neck to stare back at the farmhouse. 'Oh . . . dear Lord. No.'

'Yes.' Mrs Knight exhales. 'They have suffered a great deal. And so, if I choose to give alms in the form of over-generous payments for their produce, I consider it my prerogative. Mine, and nobody else's. Do you comprehend me, child?'

'I do.' Jane swallows. 'I promise. I won't say a word.'

'Good.' Mrs Knight reclines in her seat, eyeing Jane

carefully. 'It's the same with Eleanor. I'm well aware that my son, along with the rest of the county, thinks me a dupe. But whom I choose to give shelter to, in my own home, is my private business.'

Jane draws breath, readying herself to argue that giving a roof to Eleanor does not necessarily have to entail Mrs Knight sacrificing her own or Neddy's future security. 'Yes, but –'

'Enough!' Mrs Knight cries, so loudly that Jane startles. 'Your familiarity encroaches on insolence. I do not need to justify myself to *you*, of all people. Who are you, Miss Austen, but a young lady of little experience and no consequence.'

Jane's cheek tingles as if she's been slapped. Against her better judgement, she has unleashed Mrs Knight's ire with her tactless inquisition. Neddy's mother is as stubborn as an ox and has the same tendency to lash out violently when crossed. If Jane is not more cautious, she risks losing what little influence over, or at least access to, Mrs Knight she has, and failing in her role as Elizabeth's emissary. Throughout the remainder of the journey, Jane is silent – digging her fingernails into her palms lest she betray how shaken she is. She vowed to use discretion to break the spell Eleanor has cast over Mrs Knight, but she has proved herself as prone to blunder as Mr Blackall. Really, for Jane to have any hope of resolving this mystery, she must first become mistress of herself.

Chapter Nine

In the heavenly cool entrance hall of Godmersham Park, Jane appraises the version of Mrs Knight immortalized in oils while the living, breathing subject of the portrait issues instructions to her servants. Is Jane imagining it, or is there a guarded aspect to the lady in the picture she had not noticed before? The young bride sits with her hands clasped awkwardly in her lap, gazing directly out of the frame. At the time of sitting, Mrs Knight was only a few years older than Jane, yet her dark eyes and stern features betray a command beyond her youth and station. It's as if she challenges the viewer to hold her gaze while scolding them for their impertinence in doing so. Like Jane, Mrs Knight does not take kindly to being made the object of intense scrutiny. The beauty of her painted form may encourage admirers to linger, but her unflinching gaze soon hastens them away.

On entering the north drawing room, Jane is met with no such elegance or refinement: Eleanor stands in the centre, moving her body as if she is a sapling caught in a violent gale. Her arms flail, and the appropriated peacock feathers in her headdress flap, as she bends into a series of impossible postures.

'Ma'am.' Grace tucks her knitting behind her back, and stands to greet her mistress. The maid looks a sensible woman. How can she go about her work while Eleanor is intent on causing such mischief?

'Grace, will you send for some refreshment? I've had a very tiresome day.' Mrs Knight steps briskly across the room and takes her usual seat while Jane remains stupefied on the threshold. 'What is it, Miss Austen? Have you never seen a young lady practise her dancing before? My house guest is engaging in the traditions of her people.'

Jane does not reply that even the remotest tribe would exert more grace and poise than Eleanor, who races across the room before continuing her wild gestures. Once again, she is reminded of the illustrations of Cook's voyages. Is it possible Eleanor has seen these reproduced in the *Lady's Magazine* and is attempting to imitate them? It would be a cunning trick to exploit high society's craze for the exotic in order to extort their riches.

'Come, Eleanor, my dear. You must be fatigued by now.' Mrs Knight gestures to the chair next to her. Eleanor obeys immediately, pressing countless kisses to the widow's hand as she takes her place.

'How do you do, Infanta?' Jane sits on the low sofa

opposite. Eleanor merely sniffs in reply and continues to fawn over Mrs Knight. She really is a saucy minx. While Jane cannot support Elizabeth's design to banish her immediately to a house of correction, she is tempted to grab the girl by the shoulders and shake the truth out of her. However, Jane has already provoked Mrs Knight several times today and must not even think of doing so again. Her investigation will be better served by remaining at the widow's side, rather than being expelled from Godmersham Park for manhandling her guest.

After Grace returns with coffee and a selection of sweetmeats, Eleanor proceeds to jabber away in her made-up tongue. Mrs Knight smiles and pats her hand, showing no sign of suspecting her of manufacturing gibberish, despite what Jane now knows of her own proficiency in the French language. When Eleanor finally runs out of ill-remembered Continental phrases, Mrs Knight turns to Jane. 'Well, Miss Austen, I believe you promised to read to us. Or have you lugged that thing all the way from Rowling simply for me to admire it?' She nods to Grace, who drags the small mahogany table with Jane's writing box resting on it before the sofa.

'As you wish, ma'am.' Unfamiliar nerves dance inside Jane's frame as she unpacks her manuscript and reads hesitantly from *The Sisters*. Technically, as Jane's distant cousin by marriage, Mrs Knight is family, but Jane has never before read her work aloud to someone so remotely related or so ill-tempered. She is relieved rather than offended when, fifteen minutes into her performance, light snores drift from the direction of Mrs Knight's chair. Jane is hardly at her most riveting and it has been an exhausting day. She would be ready for a nap, too, if it wasn't for the assistance of Godmersham's exquisite coffee. Thankfully, Eleanor is so fascinated by the sweetmeats, she refrains from hogging the sugar bowl or putting on a spectacle with the cream jug.

Determined to make the most of this rare opportunity to work undisturbed, Jane continues to read aloud, alternating from each of the Misses Dashwood's letters to one another. Mrs Knight continues to slumber peacefully, Grace soon withdraws and, as Eleanor is utterly unaffected by anything Jane does, her inhibitions soon fade away. She reads each of the sisters' voices as clearly as she hears them in her mind. The elder Miss Dashwood is low and measured, while the younger speaks in a faster, high-pitched tongue. Without an audience, Jane does not hesitate to pause and mark corrections, or repeat the same passage. She gets through several of the letters, striking out and writing over her earlier work, but she cannot help thinking that something is lacking from the story. Both Misses Dashwood are shallow creatures, caricatures rather than portraits.

It is late afternoon by the time Grace pops her head around the door. 'The Rowling coachman is here for you, miss.'

'Thank you. Please tell him I'll be there in just a moment.'

Jane is relieved that Roger will be escorting her home, rather than Armand – who, after their morning's excursion, must be as worn out as herself and Mrs Knight, and therefore likely to be even surlier than usual. She continues to write until no more ink pours from the nib of her quill before scattering setting powder over the pages. When she finally looks up, Eleanor is bent forward, elbows resting on her knees, face cupped in her palms as waves of burnished copper hair cascade around her shoulders. Her quilt cape is discarded, along with her usual haughty posture, revealing a reed-thin figure in a plain morning gown, with sharp clavicles at the base of her throat.

'Goodness me! I didn't know I had your attention.' Jane shudders at the realization that Eleanor has been watching her. Her task was to study the girl, but instead she has become the focus of Eleanor's observations. What a sly creature – she must have been waiting for Mrs Knight to fall asleep before relaxing her pretence.

'You are Jane?' The lilt of Eleanor's voice betrays an Irish accent.

'That's right. I'm Jane.' So, this is the girl behind the mask. Will Mrs Knight rouse in time to see her true colours? The grand lady is reclined in her seat, eyes closed and the faintest hint of drool running from one corner of her mouth. Jane is sorely tempted to kick her awake. 'And you are . . . ?'

Eleanor stares at her, seeming not to comprehend that Jane has posed her a question. The door creaks as Grace enters, but Jane does not tear her eyes from the girl. She waits for her to flinch upright. Surely she will not want the servant to witness her slip in composure. If they reported her antics to Mrs Knight, her ruse would be over. But Eleanor remains hunched. Without her regal bearing and silly costume, she looks younger, more sorrowful. Almost a different being altogether.

Jane determines to engage her in conversation. If her tone is brusque enough, Mrs Knight might wake. 'I hope you enjoyed my ramblings?'

'Your ramblings?' Eleanor's forehead creases.

'Yes. If I'd realized you were listening, I would have made more of an effort to stick to the thread, instead of jumping about. It must have been quite bewildering for you.'

'No, it wasn't bewildering at all.' Eleanor leans forward, a light shining in her russet brown eyes. Her accent distinguishes her as belonging to the lower orders. If she is not native to Kent, or even England, it would explain why no one has recognized her. She holds out a hand, as if to lay it over Jane's, then withdraws it and stares down into her lap. 'I fear . . . I fear I understand you perfectly.'

'Oh.' It seems Jane has at last found someone in Kent to appreciate her talent. What a shame it is the artful wench who is out to steal her brother's inheritance.

Grace waits at Jane's elbow. 'Shall I help you with your box, miss?'

'There's no need.' Jane looks from Grace to Eleanor,

examining each for a reaction to the other, but Grace seems no more disconcerted by Eleanor's switch in demeanour than Eleanor is to have her witness it. Even more frustrating, Mrs Knight slumbers on. If only she would open her eyes or ears now. She would realize her *infanta* is no more than a doleful young Irish woman. Jane slams the lid of the box, hoping the sound might rouse her. 'Well, I'm afraid I must leave you,' she says, as loudly as she can, but Mrs Knight shows no sign of letting Jane disturb her peace. 'Adieu.'

Grace, ignoring Jane's instructions, lifts her writing box from the table. 'It's no bother.'

'You will come again.' Eleanor stares up at Jane as if she has only just made her acquaintance. 'The others will let you, when it's your turn.'

'You may depend upon it.' Jane attempts to make her farewell sound like a warning. What does she mean by 'the others'? Now that Elizabeth is indisposed to travel, and both Neddy and Mr Blackall are refused admittance, Godmersham Park is hardly inundated with callers.

'If you please, miss,' says Grace, labouring under the weight of Jane's writing box.

'Did you mark that?' Jane whispers, as she follows the maid towards the exit.

Grace heaves the box onto her chest, trying to manoeuvre one hand free to turn the handle. 'Mark what?'

'That?' Jane tips her head towards Eleanor as she opens

the door for them. Across the drawing room, Eleanor returns her gaze, mournful eyes cutting right through Jane. 'Mrs Knight's house guest – she completely disregarded her pretence of being a Spanish princess. She was even speaking to me in English, and she has an *Irish* accent. You must have noticed?'

Grace sighs heavily as she hands Jane's box to a waiting footman in the entrance hall. 'A good servant sees and hears only what her mistress wishes her to.'

'But you watch Eleanor all day – you were supervising her when we came in. Has this happened before? If so, why have you not informed Mrs Knight?'

'I'm afraid I cannot help you, Miss Austen.' Grace bobs the briefest of curtsies before darting towards a servant's staircase. How infuriating that she refuses to be drawn on the matter. Is Mrs Knight's maid colluding with the girl? Has Eleanor promised her a share of her spoils if she assists in her wicked scheme? Or is Grace afraid of disclosing Eleanor's duplicity in fear of being executed as the messenger? If only Mrs Knight had awoken in time to witness Eleanor's revelation. But Jane refuses to be despondent. If Eleanor's mask has slipped once, she is confident she can find a way to wrench it free again.

Chapter Ten

'Is Neddy returned?' Back at Rowling, Jane is impatient to confide in her brother. However distressing it will prove, she must tell him about the conversation she overheard in Mr Furley's office. They have a month to prevail on Mrs Knight not to disregard her late husband's wishes by bestowing all her wealth on an imposter. Eleanor is not an exotic princess and, like her father, Jane gives no credence to the belief that people can be possessed by demons – unless wickedness and a will to deceive count as evil sprites.

The most likely story is that she is a runaway servant determined to avoid being denounced as a vagrant. She may even have fallen into prostitution, if the horrible note from Captain Fairbairn is anything to go by. Perhaps Eleanor's (if that *is* her real name) former employers were in trade, and that was where she picked up the bizarre foreign phrases. Her manufactured tongue, combined with her approximations of native costumes, may have been enough to convince the Wilmots and even Mrs Knight of her provenance initially, but such naive attempts at deception cannot be sustained. Mrs Knight is a well-travelled woman who is fluent in French. A few discreet enquiries by Neddy should cause Eleanor's story to collapse as easily as a house of cards.

'I believe he's here somewhere. Or, at the least, not far off.' Elizabeth reclines on the nursery sofa, reading to the children from a book of fables as Kitty rubs her swollen feet. Fanny crouches over her mother's shoulder to see the illustrations, while Georgy sucks his thumb and rests with his eyes closed against her distended stomach.

'I must talk to him immediately. I'm afraid you're correct in your suspicions about the motives of Mrs Knight's house guest.' Jane stops short of revealing the full extent of Eleanor's schemes. 'But fear not, I'm confident Ned and I can return his mother to her senses.'

'Obviously I'm correct. Did you think for a moment I wouldn't be?' Elizabeth yawns. 'I heard Edward tell Roger he was taking Conker for a drill. I tried to get him to take Ted, but he didn't hear me call . . .'

On cue, Ted romps through the nursery on his hobbyhorse. Alice thunders after him, shaking the house as she admonishes her charge.

'Is that so?' Jane glances out of the window. Conker's spotted body lopes past the pond, disappearing behind the drooping branches of a weeping willow. If Conker is in the garden, Neddy cannot have gone far. She will catch him when he returns for his dog. 'Tell me, how long has Grace been in service at Godmersham Park?'

'Who?'

'Mrs Knight's maidservant, Grace. How long has she been in her employ?'

'I don't know. It's difficult keeping track of one's own household. I can't be expected to manage my mother-in-law's as well.'

Jane looks to Kitty, who is staring rather intently at the ball of Elizabeth's foot. 'Might you know, Kitty?'

'Over ten years, miss.' Kitty blushes. 'She's my second cousin. If you remember, ma'am, I came to Rowling on Mrs Knight's recommendation. Grace asked for her assistance in finding me a place.'

'We can assume Grace is loyal to Mrs Knight, then?'

Elizabeth straightens, 'Why? Do you believe the servants are in league with the girl?'

'Not at all.' Jane shakes her head vehemently. She doesn't want to be responsible for any false accusations. She has no proof Grace is conspiring with Eleanor, only that she does not appear to be working against her. 'But she might prove a useful ally. Grace was left in charge of the girl while Mrs Knight and I travelled to Canterbury.'

'Then you were granted a private interview with Mrs Knight. Please tell me you took the opportunity to remind her of her obligations towards her son.'

'I ...' Jane hesitates, she will not destroy Elizabeth's

equilibrium by telling her about Mrs Knight's instructions to her lawyer. Especially as she truly believes, if they work together, she and Neddy can easily expose Eleanor's true identity and foil her plot to steal Mrs Knight's estates. 'I certainly endeavoured to.'

'And do you think your words made any impression?'

Mrs Knight's rebuke echoes in Jane's aching head. *Who are you, Miss Austen, but a young lady of little experience and no consequence?* 'She was certainly struck by what I had to say.'

'Excellent. I admit I had my doubts about entrusting you with such a delicate commission, Jane, but it sounds as though you met with some success. Did you find something suitable for your new gown to be made up in while you were in town?'

'I did, yes. I bought some Indian muslin for only five shillings a yard.'

'Muslin? I said silk. Are you sure it's fine enough?'

'Mrs Knight said it was, and it meant I could afford to spend the rest of my allowance on a new pocketbook from the stationer on the high street.' Jane is already regretting this purchase. At eight shillings, it was quite expensive, and it was by no means a necessity as she has plenty of pages left to record her daily habits in her current book. She really should have bought some plain paper instead. If she continues to work on *The Sisters* at the pace she progressed this afternoon, she will exhaust her supply.

Elizabeth sniffs. 'Don't take her advice. Not unless you

wish to attend the ball as one of Queen Charlotte's ladies-in-waiting. When can Mrs Green expect the muslin to arrive?'

'Actually, Mrs Knight insisted I leave it with her dress-maker, since we were calling on her anyway.'

'Her dressmaker? I didn't know she still had one. Tell me, Jane, how many identical black silk mantuas does one woman need?' Elizabeth laughs at her own joke while Jane experiences a pang on behalf of the widow. Mrs Knight's outmoded clothing is a symptom of her broken heart. She has not dispensed with her mourning attire or re-entered society as she continues to grieve the loss of her late hus-band. Unfortunately, her miserable isolation has left her vulnerable to manipulation. By taking Eleanor to her breast, she must be trying to fill the void left by the death of her great love. Jane must help her to see that Neddy and his young family should be her rightful solace.

'She seemed a very capable seamstress, and I saw several smart-looking young ladies leaving her premises.'

'I certainly hope you're right.' Elizabeth rubs at her breast, grimacing.

'Are you well?'

'Perfectly so. My dinner is repeating on me, that's all.'

'I should have brought you some of the nuns' peppermint lozenges.'

'Nuns?' Elizabeth quirks an eyebrow.

Too late, Jane sees she has strayed into another thorny topic. She has no desire to break Mrs Knight's confidence – she is still smarting from her last rebuke. However, it was her overly generous payment for the convent's produce that Jane swore to keep secret, not the existence of the makeshift nunnery. After all, everyone in the vicinity of Godmersham Park must know who Mrs Knight's tenants are. 'The Benedictine sisters who are lodging at Briar Farm.'

Elizabeth shrieks, sitting bolt upright. Fanny wobbles, threatening to tip off the sofa, while Georgy lands face first in the newly vacant space behind his mother. 'Are you telling me Mrs Knight has let valuable farmland to the Roman Catholic Church?'

Jane rushes to comfort Georgy, whose face is as red as his mother's. 'Um, yes.'

'I bet that scheming wretch is one of *them*. They'll have sent her to convert her to Rome. The next thing we know, she'll have ripped up Mr Knight's will and transferred the whole estate to the Pope.'

'Whatever else she is, the girl is not a nun.' Jane recalls Captain Fairbairn's horrid turn of phrase. Eleanor cannot be one of the sisters in disguise. She is Irish, not French, and of humble birth. 'Mrs Knight is simply being charitable in letting the sisters dwell in one of her vacant premises. They lost their home in the insurrection in France, and they've suffered tremendously.'

Elizabeth presses the heel of her hand against her breastbone. 'They're French? That's even worse. They'll be spies, out to incite sedition ahead of Bonaparte's landing.'

Despite her best intentions, Jane appears to have added to rather than taken away from Elizabeth's concerns. 'They're trying to escape the Terror of the new regime, not import it.'

'There won't be a penny left by the time she thinks of us. We have to stop this madness!'

'Beth, endeavour to remain calm.'

Elizabeth stands, rubbing her lower back frantically. 'I knew I should have gone myself. One cannot entrust a child with a woman's job.'

Jane turns to Kitty, who stares open-mouthed at the sudden commotion. 'Could you possibly bring your mistress some tea?'

'Not tea. It prevents me from sleeping if taken this late in the day. Bring me port.' Elizabeth dismisses her maid before grasping Jane's hands between her own. 'Go and find Edward immediately. Make him swear he'll speak to his mother. He must remind her of her late husband's promise. Now, before it's too late, and we're all impoverished for the sake of that hussy.'

'I will. Please, try not to upset yourself.'

'Upset *myself*? It's not me, Jane. It's all these vultures, closing in before she's even dead. There'll be nothing left by the time they've picked over her bones.'

'That will never happen. I give you my word.' Jane leads Elizabeth back to the sofa, pressing her to take a seat. She was right not to reveal Mrs Knight's intentions to her sister-in-law. If a harmless community of nuns taking refuge at

Briar Farm is enough to provoke such a fit, how much further would the knowledge of Mrs Knight's conversation
with her lawyer distress her? Elizabeth is already unwell,
and Jane is meant to be ensuring she is protected at this
precarious time for mother and baby.

'Here, miss.' Kitty returns, handing a glass of port to Jane,
who passes it straight to Elizabeth. They both watch as she
swallows it, then pauses to take a breath.

'Why do you remain? I said go, Jane. Quickly!'

Outside, Jane chases her brother's shadow along the brick
path. All around her, the roses are in full bloom, their heads
too heavy for their sap-filled stems to hold upright. Instead,
they loll about, like drunkards at the end of a supper party,
enjoying themselves far too much to admit they have had
their fill and must retire to bed. A chestnut arbour, covered
with tangled vines of old man's beard, marks the end of the
garden. As Jane approaches, a latch clicks and Conker's
brown-and-white rear dashes through the open gate. Neddy
is taking the dog out, albeit far later than he pretended to. She
almost calls for him to wait when an unfamiliar voice silences
her: 'That's what I keep telling you, sir. She's lost to us now.'

'But you must at least attempt to recover her,' replies
Neddy.

Jane side-steps into the arbour, peeking around the vines,
like a curtain, to see her brother standing toe-to-toe with
a man in the lane. The stranger's face is half obscured by a

knitted hat, pulled low over his brow. Conker sits, begging, at the feet of his wide-legged trousers. It's easy to tell why. Even from a distance of ten feet, the man reeks of fish. 'I can't, sir, it's impossible.'

Neddy removes his tall-crowned hat, raking his fingers through his golden curls. 'No, Spooner. Tell me it's not too late, that you can get her back.'

'It's no good pleading with me, sir. *She*'s claimed her now, and that's it.' Spooner spits on the dusty ground. Ever since Jane arrived, she's watched the inhabitants of Kent defer to Neddy as a grand gentleman, but this man treats him with ill-disguised contempt.

'You cannot allow the *Infanta* to remain where she is. You'll ruin me.'

They are speaking of Eleanor. Does this ruffian know where she came from? Is that why Neddy has arranged to meet him? There can be no other reason. He is a coarse, low fellow, dirty and gross. Just looking at him makes the hairs on Jane's arms rise. And what does Neddy mean she will ruin him if she remains at Godmersham Park? Does he already suspect Mrs Knight's plans to cut him out? Jane's feet compel her to flee, dash back to the house and pretend she has not overheard such a troubling conversation, but her body is a dead weight and her ears strain for the truth. She pulls back the foliage to continue to observe her brother unseen.

The man leers. 'I'll procure you another. That will satisfy you, I'm sure. If you'll advance me a portion of the fee –'

'Another? What good would that do?' Neddy smacks his palm against his head. 'Damnation, this is my punishment for straying. I knew something terrible was bound to happen if I gave in to temptation and used her.'

Neddy *used* her? Jane recoils, dropping the vines. After growing up in a house of schoolboys, she is familiar with the various ways in which men refer to relations with the female sex when they believe no polite ears are listening. Surely no brother of hers would degrade himself by breaking his marriage vows or sink so low as to *pay* for another's favours. And yet Neddy certainly takes every opportunity to escape his wife's close observation, and Jane cannot deny the disharmony between him and Elizabeth. Such licentious habits would account for the extra night away from home when he retrieved Jane from Dartford. It could also explain the breach between Neddy and Mrs Knight. If his mother suspects he has fallen prey to vice, she may well be angry enough to disavow her late husband's intentions of making Neddy heir.

Spooner wipes his dirty palms on his trousers. 'I'll find you a perfect beauty, just like her. As soon as you grant me the funds.'

'No. I will not accept it. You *must* retrieve the *Infanta*.'

'I can't,' Spooner replies, twisting his weathered face. Black bristles cover his jaw.

'You must. You're not listening to me.' Neddy takes a step even closer to him, so they are almost nose to nose.

'No, sir. You're not listening to *me*. Advance me the money, or I'll . . .' He puffs his chest, until their bodies are touching. Spooner is a head shorter than Jane's brother, but his wiry frame looks powerful all the same.

'Or you'll what?'

'Or I shall keep your secrets no longer. I'm sure you wouldn't want your wife to know –'

A scuffle breaks out. Neddy's hat falls to the ground as both men push and shove against each other at once. 'How dare you threaten me?' Neddy grabs Spooner by the throat. 'You will not breathe a word about my association with the *Infanta* to anyone. Do you hear?'

Should Jane do something to help rid Neddy of this odious man? No: as Neddy lifts Spooner by the collar of his pea-coat, it is clear her brother is equal to his brutishness. And, after her discovery, Jane is in no mood to assist him. Conker barks, startling Jane by appearing at her side. The dog tugs at her dress with his teeth, willing her to break up the fight. She pushes his nose away, but his barking grows more insistent. When she looks up, Neddy has released Spooner and is retrieving his hat. His face is white: he is as stunned as Jane by the ferocity of his own violence.

Spooner staggers backwards, rubbing his neck. 'Aye, sir. And I think you're finally beginning to hear me.'

Jane darts into the garden with Conker yapping at her heels. She must away, before the dog reveals her presence. It is bad enough to be burdened with the knowledge of her brother's transgressions, but she cannot face him knowing she has found him out. Her skirts swish with her quick steps, brushing the lavender and disturbing the bees. Their angry buzz fills her ears as she scurries along.

'Jane.' Neddy's footsteps beat up the brick path behind her. 'Were you looking for me?'

She glances backwards, without meeting his eye. 'I . . . I was just taking some air.'

He jogs along until he is at her side, spots of colour rising in his cheeks. 'That was one of the shepherds. Come to grumble, as usual.'

Inside, Jane's head is screaming that Neddy is a liar. Spooner is not a shepherd. He is a purveyor of debauchery who intended to extort money from her brother in return for his silence over his guilty connection to Eleanor. Instead of confronting Neddy on his many lies, Jane dips her chin and lets him pass. She came into Kent believing she could strengthen the bond between herself and her most distant brother, but she has been as sorely duped by Neddy's charm as the Wilmots and Mrs Knight were by Eleanor's ridiculous antics. Jane was a fool to think she and Neddy could work together to save his inheritance when all this time he has been hiding the truth from her. If the exchange with Spooner was innocent, there would be no reason for him to lie. He stoops to pet Conker, lifting his handsome Austen features to smile at her benevolently. His shape is so familiar, yet his character is a complete mystery. It has been more than a decade since the siblings lived under the same roof. Neddy was raised in a different world, to an alternative moral compass. Jane's flesh crawls as she realizes she does not know this man at all.

3. *Letter to Cassandra Austen*
Rowling Farm, Tuesday, 20 June 1797

My dearest Cassandra,

It is almost a fortnight since I left Steventon and still you have not written. I would never have volunteered to travel to Rowling in your stead if I'd known you intended to be such an indolent correspondent. If you cannot bring yourself to pick up a pen, ask James to scribe for you. I would cheerfully wade through ten thousand of his dreary couplets for one line of your sweet voice. I cannot bear to lose your confidences at a time when I am losing confidence in all around me. I have never been so utterly adrift – sister to a brother who is little more than a stranger, forced to observe Mrs Knight paying court to a destitute wretch out to steal her fortune, and trying my utmost to have the girl expelled as a trickster while my sister-in-law seeks just as eagerly to unburden herself of me. Tomorrow evening we are to attend the Goodnestone Midsummer Ball. Under the scrutiny of Kent's most distinguished society, I shall be looking for proof as to where Mrs Knight's infanta truly came from and fathoming how I may prevent her from ruining our family, and all our future hopes. Help me, Cassy. I am in dire need of your guidance if I am to navigate these perilous waters and arrive safely at the truth.

Yours ever faithfully,

J.A.

P.S. If the reason for your hesitation in writing is a fear of inciting disillusionment within my breast at my own compositions, you needn't be so abashed. As favourable as my trifles may ever be regarded, I have long since reconciled myself to the knowledge that you are the finest comic writer of the present age.

Miss Austen

Rev. Mr Austen's

Deane

Hants

Chapter Eleven

There is an acrid taste in Jane's mouth as Neddy's phaeton draws up beside Goodnestone House. Early-evening sunlight casts a shadow over its crisp stucco façade while illuminating the red bricks of the adjacent coach house. The Queen Anne-style mansion is tall and elegant, and looks over the Kent countryside as any being of such lofty refinement must be forgiven for peering down its nose at its more bucolic surroundings. As Jane dressed for the ball, she scrubbed her teeth thoroughly, working the bristles of her little wooden brush furiously into the furthest reaches of her mouth. But try as she might, she has not been able to dislodge the bitterness resting at the back of her throat ever since her disturbing discovery. She wishes she was wrong, but Elizabeth's fourth pregnancy in five years is proof enough of Neddy's unquenchable appetite. By his own admission Neddy, the Austens' most blessed child, is 'straying' from his pregnant wife and fornicating with harlots. Jane draws her shawl tight and attempts to swallow her disgust.

In the days since the revelation, Jane has fought to reconcile what she heard from the man she knows as her brother. As tempting as it is to confront him outright, she has seen how easily the lies drip from his mouth. Neddy made his way in the world by charming people. He would, no doubt, have a ready answer for all of Jane's accusations, and leave her questioning her own rational mind. She believed him wholeheartedly when he claimed he had 'barely laid eyes' on Eleanor. Yet her senses had not deceived her. She had heard him confess to having 'used' the girl with her own ears while the disgusting Spooner offered to 'procure' him another. Jane's only option is to gather as much irrefutable evidence of Eleanor's true history as she can before broaching the topic with Neddy, so that it would be impossible for her brother to deny any part he may have played in her downfall.

If Mrs Knight has an inkling of Neddy's despicable behaviour, it would certainly explain why she has decided to disinherit him. She would hardly wish to bequeath her very great fortune to one likely to disgrace the name of Knight. But as she is planning to part with her wealth while she lives, impoverishing herself in favour of Eleanor, Jane's suspicion is that the girl has exploited her association with Neddy to gain the information necessary to manipulate his mother. Mrs Knight is an isolated, grieving widow with a sympathetic heart – a ready target for a trickster practised in the art of manufacturing attachments. Has Jane's brother invited this disaster on himself by consorting with a woman capable of such mischief? Either way, if Neddy were to fall from grace, then every one of the Austens would suffer.

How would Jane's family manage without the security the anticipation of his wealth affords? Her father would be obliged to continue his priestly duties well into his dotage. James is expected to be presented with Mr Austen's livings after him, but this choice remains at the discretion of who-ever owns the Steventon estate. Frank and Charles will win their fortunes at sea or perish in the pursuit of a prize, but Georgy will always need to be provided for. As will Mrs Austen, should she outlive her husband. Without Neddy's anticipated wealth to prop up the family, Jane would be forced to forgo her dream of remaining at liberty until she has written something worthy of being published, and find a man, any man with the means to support her, to marry instead. Worse, so would Cassandra.

Disgusted with his selfishness, Jane has thus far avoided Neddy's company by dining with the children or feigning a headache to retire early. But tonight, as guest of honour at the Goodnestone Midsummer Ball, she can hardly turn her face from him. She will have to rely on the splendour of the occasion to cover the rottenness of her heart. Poor Elizabeth. Does she suspect her husband of philandering? If so, why ask Jane to carry out her espionage, rather than her sister, Henrietta? Does Elizabeth want Neddy to know that *she* knows, or does she want Jane to know, as a way of shaming her husband into some semblance of decency? Relations between Neddy and his wife have become even more fraught, with Elizabeth increasingly vexed at his failure to persuade his mother to evict Eleanor and the Benedictine sisters lodging at Briar Farm.

Out of guilt by association with her brother's actions and pity for Elizabeth's predicament, Jane is complying with all her sister-in-law's tiresome attempts to civilize her. In preparation for the ball, she has suffered through insults to her wardrobe and lectures on deportment without a whisper of complaint. She even let Kitty singe her natural curls into uniform ringlets and lace her, too tightly, into her column-like gown. The effect is rather elegant, but Jane cannot help feeling like a game bird trussed for market.

As Neddy hands Elizabeth down from the carriage, her face betrays no hint of animosity towards her husband. She is clearly uncomfortable, at less than a month away from the baby's expected arrival, her swollen belly wrapped in a sail of white silk. Jane tried to persuade her to stay at home and rest, but Elizabeth insisted on being present to see Jane open the ball by dancing with Sir William. There is no possibility Jane can reveal what she knows to her sister-in-law. The blow of Neddy's betrayal added to Mrs Knight's disaffection really could bring on the baby early, placing Elizabeth and her offspring in even greater peril.

In Kent, there is no one Jane can confide in. Cassandra, always her most trusty correspondent, remains choked with grief and refuses to answer her letters. If Jane must be an island, she is resolved to turn herself into a fortified one. With Elizabeth's assistance, she has contrived to visit Mrs Knight and her foreign princess almost every day. Neddy's mother makes polite enquiries as to the welfare of her son and his family, without expressing any desire to see them. Jane reads the Misses Dashwood's letters aloud while studying Eleanor closely for any hint of her true character. Grace refuses to be drawn on her charge and Jane's inexperienced eye cannot tell if Eleanor is an artful strumpet with a highly sophisticated plan to deceive her superiors, or a pitiful wench who has concocted an elaborate ruse in a desperate attempt to escape her bully. Either way, it does not excuse the vulgar manner in which Neddy, Spooner or the vile Captain Fairbairn refer to her. She has been 'used', passed from man to man, like a bottle of port or an amusing anecdote.

'Are you ready, Jane?' says Neddy, reaching up a hand to help her descend.

'Yes. I'm ready.' Jane shuffles along the bench and pinches his hand with the lightest of touches, grateful for her kid leather evening gloves. Without them, it would be impossible not to recoil from his touch.

Damn Neddy. Let him think she is his placid little sister – the doting child he left behind, rather than the woman of astute observation she has grown into during his long absence. Jane will seek out the truth. She may be completely alone and inexperienced in the ways of the world, but she is not afraid of diving into this murky pool and testing the depths of his depravity. Tonight, Jane will speak to some of those involved in the discovery of Mrs Knight's strange house guest. If she can arm herself with the truth, she can use it to confront Neddy and force her brother to forgo his licentious ways before he sinks any further into his own ignominy, dragging down all of the Austens with him.

'Where are the family? William should be here to greet his guests.' Elizabeth strides past the footmen gathered in the circular entrance hall, pausing briefly to correct one on his posture. The right-hand side of the round room opens to a long gallery, cleared for dancing, while the left leads to an identical space filled with tea-tables. 'He'd better not have let any dances commence. I warned him several times he's to wait for you, Jane.'

'I'm sure he wouldn't dare.' Neddy hurries to keep pace with her.

Jane's spirit is already calmer, having escaped the confines of Rowling. Perhaps the evening will not be such a trial, and she will feel lighter for being forced into company. Unknown to herself, Elizabeth has made Jane's mission to quiz all those involved in Eleanor's discovery significantly easier by tasking her with seeking an introduction to everyone in their fashionable set. The original list of eligible bachelors Elizabeth composed – ranked by their position in the hierarchy of East Kent, and annotated with their annual income, estimated investment in government bonds, and helpful hints as to which topics might seduce them into conversation *(Adores blancmange! Keeps an African grey parrot! Suffers terribly with chilblains)* – was consigned to the fire shortly after it was handed over. But inside Jane's reticule sits her own list of persons of interest, chiefly Dr Wilmot and his wife. The Wilmots were the first to circulate the report of a shipwrecked foreign princess, and therefore Jane will begin her attempt to discredit it by interviewing them.

Unfortunately, the Wilmots, with the rest of the guests, are yet to arrive. In the echoey ballroom Henrietta, in a gown twice as sheer and cut even closer to the body than Jane's own, plays a maudlin tune on a grand pianoforte. She may be older than Elizabeth, but Henrietta is more willing to embrace the daring new fashions. A huddle of professional musicians stands idle beside her, eyeing each other disdainfully while twiddling the strings of their instruments.

'Thank goodness you're here,' Sir William calls, from a semi-reclined position in front of a grand fireplace. 'Can you remember what time we put on the invitations? It was eight o'clock rather than half past, was it not?'

Elizabeth glides to him across the polished parquet, decorated with a giant chalk rose to prevent the dancers slipping. 'Yes, yes. Don't fret. You know the guests are always late. Why aren't you in the round room to greet them? What will Sir Edward and Lady Hale say if they arrive to find you lounging about like this? It's most disrespectful.'

Sir William dabs his flushed forehead with a handkerchief. 'I can't help it, it's my gouty big toe. The damn thing's playing up again. It must've been all that traipsing about looking for game.' His foot rests on a stool, level with his chest. It is the shape of a bowling ball, and the laces of his dancing pump will not meet. Jane's own foot throbs in sympathy. So much for her glittering entrance into society on the arm of a baronet. She berates herself for her disappointed vanity. However much Jane rebels at Elizabeth's attempts to refine her, she is horrified to realize that a small part of her was looking forward to playing the bashful debutante. No matter her troubles, dancing never fails to distract her.

'Surely you can manage one set.' Elizabeth bobs down beside him, switching her gaze from the swollen foot to its less remarkable partner.

'I'm afraid not. The footmen had to haul me in here. I've no idea how I'm going to get out again.'

Neddy claps Sir William on the shoulder. 'Bad luck, old fellow. I told you to leave the grouse to me.'

'This is infuriating.' Elizabeth stands, surveying the small party. 'Who will open the ball with Jane now? She can hardly stand up with her brother.'

'Honestly, Beth, it's no matter.' Jane tries to placate her sister-in-law. It's a far cry from arriving at a raucous public ball in the Basingstoke assembly rooms, where half the county squash themselves inside, and the air is thick with perspiration and possibility. She tries to muster a shadow of the enthusiasm she knows she should feel on such an occasion, hopeful that a little excitement will spur her on in her mission. It's no use: the butterflies have long since fled her breast, leaving only the dried-out husks of their chrysalises. 'The most important thing is making sure Sir William is comfortable.'

'Thank you, Miss Austen.' The baronet smiles up at her. 'Would you be so kind as to fetch me a glass of wine?'

'Wine?' Elizabeth scowls. 'When your gout is already inflamed? You know it will only unbalance your constitution further.'

'Spare me your raillery, sister. It is enough that I am at the mercy of Dr Wilmot's constant sallies. Do you know he's added roast beef, red wine and butter sauce to the list of pernicious substances I'm to forgo to stave off these attacks?'

'I don't see how that would help,' says Neddy. 'You need to keep your strength up.'

'Hush …' Elizabeth nods towards the long windows opening onto the drive. 'That's the doctor arriving now.'

Jane turns to note a trio of guests edging tentatively towards the entrance. She guesses Dr Wilmot is the senior figure, while the lady clutching nervously at his side must be his wife. The other man, wearing a similar pair of spectacles and expression of bewilderment as the lady, must be a relation of hers.

'What could have persuaded you to invite him?' Sir William huffs. 'Don't let him anywhere near me, I entreat you. If he sees my foot, he'll spend the whole evening proscribing the pleasures I'm to abstain from. And can you speak to the kitchen? Have them serve the white soup at ten o'clock sharp. Last year they left it too late and the company were ravenous.'

'Can't Hen do it?' asks Elizabeth.

Sir William gestures towards the pianoforte where Henrietta continues her morose performance. 'She's exhibiting.'

'Yes, and it would be a good excuse for her not to,' Elizabeth sighs. Jane senses Elizabeth is just as frustrated with her unmarried sister as she is with her sisters-in-law. 'Jane, will you attend to the baronet? Red wine, if he must, diluted with plenty of water. And, Edward, will you take up station in the round room to welcome the guests on the family's behalf?'

'Actually, Ned, would you mind calling for Sir William's wine so that Beth can introduce me to the Wilmots?' Jane is reluctant to risk the room becoming noisy and crowded, thereby forfeiting her opportunity to quiz the Wilmots in relative comfort.

'Well remembered. Mrs Wilmot's cousin, Dr Storer, is on your list.' Elizabeth beams at Jane's apparent studiousness. 'Rather close to the bottom, but I suppose we have to start somewhere. Did you bring the list with you?'

Jane holds up her reticule, dangling it by its drawstring

loop. By happy coincidence, one of the names on Elizabeth's original list overlaps with the objects of Jane's own curiosity. 'How could I forget, after you went to such efforts?'

Elizabeth shepherds Jane towards the entrance hall by her elbow. 'As you know, Dr Wilmot runs his practice from Canterbury but Dr Storer's clinic is in Harley Street.'

'I expect London is *the* most convenient place to gather invalids.'

'Dr Storer is intending to reside with his cousin for the duration of the summer months. He says it's to get away from the worst of the air, but I suspect it's because he's about to come into a great deal of money and is fishing for a well-connected wife. Which you could be taken for, Jane. Here in Kent, anyway.'

Jane raises an eyebrow. 'Pray how can you foretell such a lucky event for Dr Storer? Does he have a rich relation on their deathbed?'

'Unfortunately not, but he *has* invented an ingenious medical device.' Elizabeth's eyes sparkle with the news. 'It acts as an artificial leech.'

'An artificial leech?'

'So as not to frighten children. A glass cup is attached to the body, while a mechanical foot pump encourages the flow of blood. It's so much more effective than the old-fashioned way. Apparently, Mrs Wilmot claimed he withdrew twenty ounces before she'd even noticed.'

Jane resists the urge to vomit into her reticule.

'Don't look so disgusted. It's not as if you can afford to be squeamish. He's registered the design with the Patent Office and, when it comes through, he'll be a very wealthy man.'

'Capital, his patients will be haemorrhaging cash!'

Elizabeth shoots her a warning glance.

Jane forces her features into a grave expression. 'Just a quip. I won't repeat it in his presence, I promise.'

'You'd better not. I only condescended to invite the doctor and his party for you.'

'Me?' After Elizabeth's previous outburst, Jane has attempted to keep the detailed machinations of her investigation to herself. She didn't think Elizabeth knew how keenly she wished to speak to the Wilmots.

'Yes. I thought you must be partial to clever men. After the lawyer?' Elizabeth says, as if looking for a spark of intelligence in one's life partner is as quaint as having a preference for red hair or a dimpled chin. 'I can't see the attraction myself. No, for lasting happiness, I believe it's much better to select someone more malleable.'

Jane is sorely tempted to ask Elizabeth if this was why she chose to marry Neddy, but it is no jest. Neddy has proven himself neither dull nor governable.

'Dr Wilmot, Mrs Wilmot, Dr Storer,' says Elizabeth, the moment the trio enter, causing all three to stand to attention. 'Please allow me to introduce my sister-in-law, *Miss* Austen.' She emphasizes the single syllable of Jane's title, clearly finding it the most objectionable part of her name.

Jane curtsies politely. 'How do you do?'

'I'm afraid you'll have to excuse me if we're to have any hope of being fed this evening.' Elizabeth departs to orchestrate the refreshments. She pauses briefly at the pianoforte to bark at Henrietta, whose fingers strike up Bach's Toccata and Fugue in D Minor in reply. The Wilmots and Dr Storer greet Jane over the disjointed, angry music, their stiff manners signifying they are as ill at ease as she is.

As stalwarts of the middling classes, Jane doubts they are accustomed to socializing with the scrupulously discerning Bridges family. Yet, up close, Dr Storer is not such a terrible prospect. He can only recently have turned thirty, if at all, and there is nothing outright offensive about his countenance. If he shows the slightest evidence of being a rational creature, Jane might be persuaded to stand up with him. That is, if Henrietta ever surrenders her place at the pianoforte. Her musical accompaniment is more likely to drive the guests away to weep over life's cruel disappointments than entice them to dance.

By silent agreement, the party drifts towards the round room to make their small-talk audible. Jane answers a handful of banal questions about the climate and topography of Hampshire compared to Kent, its neighbour of only one county removed, before losing patience and diving headlong into her investigation. 'And we have an esteemed acquaintance in common, I believe?'

Dr Wilmot peers down at her. 'We do?'

'Yes. I have the pleasure of assuring you that your foreign princess was quite well when I left her yesterday.'

Given how expeditiously Dr Wilmot took up and discarded Eleanor's cause, Jane expects him to blush at this description of her. He must have revised his opinion of the authenticity of her account to expel her so unceremoniously. Instead, the doctor's expression grows animated at the mention of his former charge. 'You've met the princess?'

'I have. If one is to believe that is what she is.' Jane resorts to provoking his confidence.

'Why should one doubt it?' He blinks.

'No particular reason ... But I did wonder if you would be willing to relay the circumstances of her discovery. I'm having difficulty in understanding exactly what persuaded you to place her under your care and, as you know, the princess is rather unintelligible. What condition was she in when you found her?'

Mrs Wilmot takes a step closer to her husband, placing her hand in the crook of his arm. She opens her mouth to speak, but Dr Wilmot gets there first. Which is most frustrating as, in Jane's experience, women are generally better at recounting events. It is the little details they like to include, which a man may not think important enough to impart.

'I'd be only too pleased to relay the terrible nature of the princess's arrival in this country.' He puffs his chest, reminding Jane of James's performance when delivering one of his self-penned prologues to the many plays he directed in Mr

Austen's barn. 'I'm afraid she was in a remarkably forlorn state when we found her. It took all my skill as a physician to revive her. It was apparent to me that she had very nearly drowned.'

'She was unconscious?' asks Jane.

'Not unconscious, but confused. If it hadn't been for my intervention, I fear she would have succumbed from exposure to the elements. Despite her injuries, she was tumbling about in a state of undress.'

Jane nods, but Dr Wilmot's description could apply as readily to a harlot suffering the consequences of imbibing an excessive amount of gin as it could to the survivor of a shipwreck. 'And how exactly did you revive her?'

'My wife offered the princess her cloak and some smelling salts.'

'I see.' Jane tries to catch Mrs Wilmot's eye, but the lady glances down at her slippers. Dr Wilmot's success as a physician owes as much to his wife's compassion as to any medical knowledge on his part. 'And where exactly did you find her?'

'On the beach towards the promenade. We regularly spend our mornings there, for the promotion of Mrs Wilmot's health.'

'Not *in* the water, then?'

'No.'

'And were there any other signs of a shipwreck?' Jane asks, wondering how a sunken vessel could escape the notice of the various authorities. 'Debris washed up along the shore, perhaps, or any other survivors?'

'None that I met with.'

'Then, if I may, sir, what prompted you to take Eleanor to the Riding Officer, rather than treating her as any other unfortunate soul in need of charity?'

'Ah, but one can always tell a woman of quality,' the doctor scoffs. 'There is something in her air that marks her as distinct. From the moment I discovered the princess, it was obvious by her disdain for all around her that she herself was of far nobler rank.'

Dr Wilmot may have revealed himself as a pompous fool, but Jane has some sympathy with his reverence for Eleanor. While the girl's manners are beyond bizarre, she is so determined in them that even Jane has doubted herself in her presence. 'It was her air that led you to take her to the Riding Officer?'

'Yes, and once there, he corroborated her story.'

'He confirmed there had been a shipwreck?'

'No. He called forth a sailor fluent in her native tongue. The man listened for a great while before relaying the details of her birth and the terrible events that have since befallen her. Princess Eleanor is a daughter of the most noble house of Spain.'

'She doesn't look like a Habsburg to me,' says Jane. Two centuries of marrying only their close relations had made the features of Spanish royalty rather distinctive.

'A minor branch of the family, I concede,' Dr Wilmot continues, impervious to Jane's scepticism. 'It was on a return voyage from the Canary Islands that the convoy carrying her entourage was attacked. When the brigands found they had stolen a most precious jewel, and could likely demand a great deal of gold for her return, they were persuaded to spare her life with the intention of claiming the bounty.'

'There's a reward on offer?' Jane wonders if the lure of an imaginary prize is part of Eleanor's scheme to extort money. Is she promising to reimburse her benefactors for their generosity?

'I'm certain there will be, yes. But when her kidnappers' vessel encountered difficulties while passing through the Swale, the princess seized her chance of liberty and risked death by swimming ashore to escape their clutches.'

Jane frowns. She is quite sure one would have to be conversant in a variety of European languages to interpret for Eleanor. And, even then, she's not convinced it would be possible to determine any sense from her strange babble. 'A Spanish sailor told you all this?'

'The man was a lascar.'

This news does not inspire any more faith in the tale. When Aunt Phila and Eliza returned from India, their ayah, Clarinda, came too. Clarinda constantly switched between English and Bengali but, to Jane's knowledge, she never uttered a word of Spanish. 'But lascars are from the Indian subcontinent. Are they not?'

Only Mrs Wilmot colours at this observation. Her husband merely smiles in a most irritating manner. 'My dear Miss Austen, I did not realize you are a scholar. As you must be, for you certainly profess to owning an exceptional knowledge of geography for one of your sex.'

More than you, Jane resists replying. Perhaps this sailor was an accomplice of Eleanor's, and the pair conspired together to deceive the Wilmots. 'So it was the lascar's testimony, more than anything else, that persuaded you to offer Eleanor your hospitality. And you're certain neither he nor any of the other sailors or townspeople recognized her?'

'How could they when she had so recently arrived on our shores?' The doctor ignores the implication he may have been duped – but Jane knows that Eleanor must have arrived in England prior to the morning when she was discovered by the Wilmots; as Spooner, Neddy and Captain Fairbairn had already had the opportunity to know her. 'As the young lady was quite bereft, I thought it incumbent upon myself to take her under my protection.'

'How generous of you.' Jane is certain Dr Wilmot's benevolence towards Eleanor was motivated foremost by the promise of pecuniary emolument. 'But you did not accommodate her for long because she soon came to reside with my kinswoman, Mrs Knight.'

'Indeed, I was making preparations to exhibit her at court –'

'Exhibit?'

'To *present* her at court,' he corrects himself, but Jane has already grasped the doctor's designs. Eleanor is a curiosity and, even without a reward, such a spectacle could be made profitable. 'Foreign dignitaries are sure to receive a warm welcome at the Court of St James, and through the good offices of the courtiers there I hoped to inform King Charles of Spain of her deliverance. I had gone so far as to write to His Royal Highness and the Spanish ambassador and am certain both were in fond anticipation of her arrival, when the princess revealed herself to be somewhat unpredictable. And while I would have preferred to maintain her myself, I do not have the resources necessary to restrain her as your cousin does.'

Jane presses a hand to her throat. If Eleanor represents a risk to those around her, she must be expelled immediately. 'Are you saying she's a danger?'

'Not if handled appropriately. It's simply a case of the vapours.' Dr Storer steps forward to dash Jane's hopes of finding any semblance of rationality in her prospective dancing partner. 'It is a common complaint. I've observed it among several of my female patients. You must not alarm yourself.'

'I assure you, I'm not in the least alarmed.'

'It can be treated but, it requires the delicate art of rebalancing the body's optimum state. Unfortunately, the princess ...' Dr Storer continues, but Jane's attention is diverted elsewhere. Tom Lefroy, in his distinctive ivory swallowtail coat, has swaggered into the ballroom. With his back to Jane, he bows to greet Sir William. Her mouth dries, as she searches for the words to say to him after all this time. Does he know she is here? Has he come to find her? He turns, brushing his straw-coloured hair out of his eyes to reveal his irresistibly handsome features. Except, somehow, in only eighteen months, his nose has grown beak-like and his chin has receded beyond all recognition.

It is not Tom.

It is never Tom.

It is just some young fop who wears an outmoded coat and, from a certain angle, bears a fleeting resemblance to him. Good God, will Cassandra's mind play this cruel trick on her in constantly seeking Mr Fowle? At least Jane's pathetic hope that Tom will resurface is plausible if not rational. He could very well reappear one day. Their circles cross all the time. He may make a fortune of his own and seek her out. If he's as brilliant as he promised to be, he may even have been called to the Bar by now. He may win a case that could see him established for life. Or he may inherit a fortune he never expected from a long-lost cousin. Someone too distant to grieve and rich enough to rejoice.

Jane forces her attention back to Dr Storer's incessant droning: 'It is the inherent weakness of the female sex, you see. It makes women so susceptible to these fits of hysteria . . .'

Mrs Wilmot sags against her husband. He catches her by the elbow, just as she is about to fall. 'Are you well, wife?'

This time, the lady is allowed to answer through short, puffy breaths. 'Merely a trifle light-headed. It must be all the excitement. I don't socialize much, I'm afraid, Miss Austen.'

'I said it would be too much, but you would insist on accompanying us,' Dr Wilmot says tersely. 'Allow me to send for our carriage.'

'Oh, no, I cannot permit you to retire so early . . .' If Jane can get Mrs Wilmot alone, she might be able to retrieve more sense from her. It was clearly her kindness that had led to the couple's initial interaction with Eleanor. Dr Wilmot became interested in her case only *after* he suspected it might prove a return for himself. 'Sir William is most eager to consult you on his constitution.'

Dr Wilmot stands taller. 'He is?'

A tiny flicker of guilt pulses through Jane's veins, but it may be no bad thing to act in her own *and* Sir William's best interests. 'He was adamant he was going to seek out your opinion. He's at the far end of the ballroom, laid up with another attack of the dreaded gout. Poor fellow, he's in agony. I believe he'd especially like to hear more about how restricting his intake of certain foodstuffs may help. Why don't you go and talk to him? Both of you, at once. I'll take care of your good lady.'

Mrs Wilmot releases her husband to lean on Jane's arm.

'Do go on, dear. Don't worry about me. This may be your opportunity to make an impression, at last.'

'If you're certain?' asks Dr Wilmot. But his younger colleague's heels are already clacking across the parquet towards his target. Not one to be defeated, Dr Wilmot speeds after him without waiting for his wife's reply.

Chapter Twelve

Jane steers Mrs Wilmot towards a sofa in the tea-room, shielded from view by an arrangement of parlour ferns in Japanese vases. She pauses for a few moments, checking her companion is not going to pass out, then sends for a cup of tea, sweetened with plenty of sugar. 'There,' she plants the saucer between Mrs Wilmot's trembling hands, 'that should restore you.' The two women sit quietly, watching the guests arrive through the long windows. Outside, the glowing sun recedes over the flat Kent horizon, leaving a grey chill in its path. Jane senses Mrs Wilmot is content in her company and may need little prompting to share her doubts about Eleanor's origins. The doctor may see only what he wishes to, but his wife is more attuned to the thoughts and feelings of others. When the lady's breath has finally steadied, Jane asks, 'Was it your idea, to take Eleanor in?'

'Me? Goodness, no! The doctor never listens to me.' Mrs Wilmot titters mirthlessly. 'He was confident Spain would reward him with his own weight in silver for her recovery.'

'But it was you who paused to help her initially, as you were walking along the promenade?'

Mrs Wilmot takes slow, thoughtful sips of her tea. Her gloves slip down her arms to reveal bandages on both, indicating she has been recently bled. 'I did. It was clear she'd been mistreated, and if one forsaken woman cannot turn to another for aid, from whom can she expect such protection and regard?'

'That was very charitable of you. Whatever the girl may reveal herself to be, you made the only Christian choice in offering her your assistance. For I believe you suspect, as I do, that her tale is false?'

Mrs Wilmot smiles knowingly. 'It would seem rather ... far-fetched.'

'Her Spanish, for one thing, is a little ...'

'Inconsistent?' Despite her physical frailty, Mrs Wilmot's wits are as sharp as pins.

Jane softens, relieved to have found a confidante. 'Exactly.'

'Don't think too poorly of my husband. He's not ignorant, only bewitched by the opportunity he believed the girl represented. I'm afraid he's grown to dislike the practice of physic, especially now his apprentice, my cousin Dr Storer, looks set to eclipse him with his various contraptions. A foreign princess, with all her strange habits, would have made a lucrative specimen for him to exhibit.'

Could Eleanor have recognized the desire to escape his profession in Dr Wilmot and concocted her ruse on the spot to exploit it? 'She deliberately set out to captivate the doctor, then?'

Mrs Wilmot presses her lips together and shakes her head. 'Not exactly. She was barely capable of uttering a word when we first discovered her. There she was, poor child, stumbling along in her wet things. Her lips and fingers were blue, and she was shivering so violently that I feared her teeth would crack.'

Jane is circumspect. She assumed the entirety of Eleanor's account would prove false. 'She was definitely *in* the water, then? That part of her story is true?'

'I believe she was.' Mrs Wilmot tips her head to the side, appraising Jane. 'You seem to be a sympathetic young lady so I will tell you, in confidence, I cannot attest to *how* she came to be there. Whether it was an accident, or she entered the waves of her own volition, I do not know.'

'Oh ...' Jane catches Mrs Wilmot's meaning. Could Eleanor, prior to being taken up by the Wilmots and then Mrs Knight, have been so destitute that she submerged herself with the intention of ending her suffering? If Jane is right, and Eleanor is a runaway servant sunk into prostitution, her existence may have become intolerable. Self-murder is a crime against the King and, worse, a sin against the Almighty, but that does not make its siren call any less appealing. The threat of having one's property confiscated after one's death, as well as being damned for all eternity, has done nothing to curb the craze for taking one's life in a fit of romantic passion after the style of Young Werther – a most unfortunate literary hero who made the mistake of believing the best cure for disappointed love was to discharge a pistol at one's brain.

'When my husband assumed she'd fallen overboard, I didn't want to suggest otherwise . . . It wouldn't have ended well for the poor girl if I had. She'd likely have been thrown into gaol, and I do not see how that would have encouraged her to act with more regard to her life. By the time we reached the Riding Officer, she'd drawn quite a crowd. I suspect most merely wanted a glimpse of a woman in her shift. That was when she started up with her babbling. I wondered if she'd hit her head, and it had affected her speech. Or perhaps she had suffered an apoplexy. That happens sometimes, you know.'

'I do.' Jane nods, thinking of how Georgy is bewildered for days after his fits. Eleanor's behaviour may be confounding but, unlike Georgy after one of his seizures, she does not *seem* confused. And Jane already knows there are times when she can present a different, more rational countenance.

'But after the lascar gave his account, my husband grew so animated I could hardly contradict him in front of so many people.'

'That's the part of Eleanor's story I find the most

inexplicable. I don't believe a lascar would be any more likely to understand her than you or I. But what reason would he have to lie? Unless they planned the entire feint between them to take advantage of your good nature.'

Mrs Wilmot frowns, a small crease appearing in her forehead. 'Sincerely, I do not think so. We've heard nothing from him since. And Eleanor was initially reluctant to come away with us. It took some persuading on my husband's part. He can be quite forceful,' she lowers her voice, 'when he believes he is justified in being so.'

If Eleanor set out to hoodwink the Wilmots, it makes no sense that she would resist their hospitality. 'So it was the lascar, rather than Eleanor, who explained she'd been kidnapped and had escaped a shipwreck.'

'Yes, it was.'

Perhaps Mrs Wilmot is correct and Eleanor was confused after her trial in the water – at least temporarily. It could have been the lascar, motivated by pity rather than anything more sinister, who claimed she was of notable birth as a way of entreating the respectable couple to take care of her. 'And was it also he who first suggested she was a princess?'

'Oh, no. That was the one phrase we all recognized.' Mrs Wilmot turns to face Jane, eyes widening behind her spectacles. 'It's why my husband refused to let her go. If she'd been an ordinary girl, I've no doubt he would have taken her straight to the poorhouse. "*Soy la Infanta de Castilla.*"

She kept repeating it and pointing to herself, then out to sea, over and over again.'

The *Infanta*. Jane grows weary. This is not a terrible misunderstanding. Neddy really is involved with whatever ordeal Eleanor has been through.

'But when we got her home, she became even more uncooperative. I tried to impress upon her that it would be better for her if she kept quiet and went along with the doctor's treatments, but she would not listen. Then my cousin arrived, and the way he proposed to deal with her unruly behaviour was barbaric. That is why I sent for Mrs Knight.'

'*You* sent for Mrs Knight? I thought she just happened to be visiting.'

'Oh, my dear, you should have noticed that lady never goes anywhere unless she absolutely must. And now I rather fear what I have begun . . .' Mrs Wilmot exhales, her slight frame sagging into her chair.

'Why Mrs Knight?' Jane asks, wondering if Eleanor could have known about the Wilmots' connection to the widow before she appealed to them for help. If so, perhaps she thwarted the couple's attempts to accommodate her in favour of a greater prize. 'Please think very carefully. Was there any way Eleanor could have put into your head the idea of calling for her specifically?'

'Eleanor? No.' Mrs Wilmot stares directly at Jane. 'It was simply that before she was widowed, and my health deserted me, Mrs Knight was forever calling for my assistance in organizing the poor relief. I hoped she might know of somewhere more compassionate that might take Eleanor in. I never intended for her to be deceived. And I certainly never meant to cause any difficulties between her and her son, if that's what is driving your concern?'

Jane rests a hand on Mrs Wilmot's arm. She has stopped trembling, but her frame is birdlike and Jane is overcome with sympathy for the trials she must face in living with her brutish husband. 'It was very kind of you to offer succour to Eleanor, whatever her motives may turn out to be. As for Mrs Knight, I promise I'll do everything I can to help her arrive at the truth.'

'Jane!' Elizabeth's furious face pokes through the leafy palms. 'What are you doing hiding behind here? You're supposed to be opening the ball. It's getting late.'

Jane startles, returning her hand to her own lap. 'But I haven't a partner. Can someone else do it?'

'No.' Elizabeth pulls her to standing. Jane lets herself be drawn along, reasoning she has learnt all she can from the Wilmots. The interview has thrown up as many questions as it has answers. If Eleanor is engaged in a deliberate ploy to extort money from Mrs Knight by posing as a beleaguered princess, why was she initially so reluctant to accept the Wilmots' invitation and how did she contrive to be transferred to the widow? 'I've spent weeks managing the arrangements for this ball,' Elizabeth continues. 'I'll not let some young lady I have no association with steal the advantage. Come along, I've found you a replacement. We didn't think he was going to make it, but the darling boy decided to surprise us.'

As they reach the ballroom, an extremely fashionable young man with mischievous dark brown eyes attracts Jane's notice. The points on his starched collar reach his sharp cheekbones, and his buff breeches are so tight across his lean thighs, Jane presumes he must have been sewn into them. He is the perfect dandy, swept straight from the cobbles of Bond Street. He should be running with the Prince of Wales, not dallying with the spinsters of Kent.

'Which one is *he* on my list?' Jane murmurs.

'He's not. Strictly off limits, I'm afraid. Excellent family, but he's a younger son. The third living, far too low in the pecking order for you. And there's an unmarried sister yet to be dispensed with. No, he'll need to marry his fortune. But I don't think that will be a problem. Do you?'

Jane is inclined to agree. It is always the way. The more attractive they are, the poorer they turn out to be. The young gentleman tucks a hand inside his blue-black frock coat to retrieve a silver snuff box. In a practised motion, he tips a tiny portion of tobacco onto the back of his hand before inhaling it. She is pleased to see that, apart from being an obvious profligate, he has at least one other unforgivable flaw: the odour of tobacco combined with his foppery *should* be enough to keep her heart safely buried in its shallow grave.

Elizabeth leans closer, her rosewater perfume filling

Jane's nostrils. 'He's far too young and flighty to know his own mind. Only eighteen, would you believe, despite the size of him. He's still up at Oxford and yet to settle on a profession. Don't take a word he says seriously, but you have my permission to monopolize him for the first two dances.'

'Are you sure it's wise for him to dance in those breeches?' Jane eyes the seam along his inner thigh, wondering if his tailor thought to reinforce it against splitting.

'Two dances. And absolutely no flirting.'

'All right. But it's only fair to warn you that I didn't pack a needle and thread in my reticule.'

'I'm in earnest, Jane. After that, you must promise to relinquish him, and seek out the gentlemen who *are* on your list. I'll be off home to bed once you get started, so you'll have to rely on Edward for assistance. Don't squander this opportunity. A young lady only comes out into society once. From this point onwards, your desirability can only depreciate.'

Jane nods, feeling like a fast-wilting lettuce but sensing Elizabeth will not release her hand to make the introduction until she does so. They cross the final few steps, to where the young gentleman is standing beside Sir William. The unfortunate baronet is still being harangued on both sides by medical advice.

'Miss Austen, I'm delighted to make your acquaintance.' The dandy sweeps into an elegant bow, then proffers his arm to Jane. 'It would, indeed, be the highest honour if you would condescend to grant me the first two dances.' With his dark colouring and lithe limbs, he's like a long stick of liquorice. Unfortunately, Jane has long held a partiality for liquorice.

'With pleasure, sir.' She curtsies, making a mental note to be on her guard. Now is the time to employ her island defences – let her cliffs soar and her battlements tower. Never again will she make the mistake of looking upon an attractive young man as a harmless creature.

Elizabeth smiles proudly. 'May I present Mr Brook-Edward Bridges.'

'He's *your* younger brother?' Jane replies, but Mr Bridges is already leading her insistently towards the area marked for dancing. He raises his free hand towards Henrietta, still stationed at the pianoforte, and clicks his thumb and forefinger together. 'Enough of that funeral dirge, Hen. Play us a quadrille or let the professionals take over.'

Henrietta flushes, and Jane knows she should be mortified on her behalf, rather than thrilled when the musicians take advantage of her stunned silence to strike up with their bows. Mr Bridges propels Jane into the centre of the chalk rose. Her skirts fan out around her, as he twists her into an allemande. She searches for some witty remark, to seize back some semblance of control. 'I didn't realize you were expected at home, Mr Bridges.'

'It was a last-minute decision. And I insist you call me Brook.'

'I most certainly will not.'

'Why? We're practically family.' He raises one highly flirtatious eyebrow. 'Are we not?'

Jane forces her mouth into a straight line, determined not to betray her amusement at his impertinence. 'I was told you were spending the summer with friends in the Scottish Highlands.' Three other couples join them in making a square. Even Henrietta has recovered from her smart and is standing up with Mr Blackall.

Mr Bridges greets his sister and her partner, then turns back to Jane. 'I am. But I couldn't cross Hadrian's Wall without saying goodbye to my nearest and dearest. What if I get lost in the wilderness and never make it back? And I could hardly miss the opportunity to admire the Austens' brightest star.'

'Well, you're out of luck there. My brother, Captain Henry Austen, isn't due in Kent until mid-August.'

Mr Bridges lowers his voice to a rich baritone. 'You know very well I'm alluding to yourself. Your lively mind – not to mention your charming countenance – is legendary around these parts.'

Despite herself, Jane grows warm. 'Is it? I rather thought Elizabeth found me infuriating.'

He leans close, tickling her ear with his tobacco-spiced breath. 'She does. Which means *I'm* all the more inclined to find you delightful.'

Jane lets out a peal of laughter. Mr Bridges is a fully

seasoned flirt. Under his corrupting influence, she suffers a temporary amnesia. When he suggests a third, and then a fourth dance, she forsakes her promise to Elizabeth and concedes readily – with no thought to propriety, lists of potential husbands or even witnesses to Eleanor's discovery. It is not until her limbs grow heavy and her feet throb from pounding the parquet flooring in her silk slippers that she realizes, for a few blissful hours, she has completely forgotten all her cares. Her concentrated attempts to master the Baker's Wife and other cotillions popular in Kent had left no room for thoughts of the Austens' benefactress surrendering her wealth to an imposter. Jane had even forgot about her sister languishing on the precipice of despair in Hampshire. But when the sun emerges across the hop fields of Kent, and the unflinching daylight forces her to look at Neddy, she soon remembers his infidelities and her vow to prove his illicit association with Mrs Knight's foreign princess.

Chapter Thirteen

Jane and Neddy walk home in the early hours, as Roger had driven Elizabeth in the phaeton and Neddy insisted he stable the carriage and horses for the night rather than return. Rowling is a mere stone's throw from Goodnestone. Jane imagines taking a pebble and skimming it across the fields, which are as flat as the surface of a lake. She is sure her brother Frank could do it, allowing the stone to bounce only three or four times before it reached its destination. Neddy had retrieved a pair of top boots he keeps at the great house for whenever he joins Sir William in an impromptu bout of field sport. Further proof, if any was needed, of her brother's tendency to wander from his own fireside whenever he pleases. A thoughtful maid had found a pair of ladies' boots for Jane. Presumably they once belonged to Elizabeth or Henrietta, but the girl assured her they had long been discarded and would not be missed before she returned them. The buttery soft leather is of the best quality and they are in greater repair than the ones Jane brought with her from Steventon.

As Neddy walks ahead, his outline silhouetted by the rising sun, Jane fixes her eyes on his back and contemplates how best to interrogate her brother on his connection to Eleanor. Is there anything in Mrs Wilmot's testimony that could help draw the truth from him? She is mindful that, on several ill-fated occasions in the past, she has been guilty of leaping to conclusions and accusing others without just cause. Such injudicious behaviour laid her open to criticism and resulted in nothing but her own disgrace. On this occasion, she would rather not reveal her suspicions until she has enough evidence to make Neddy's culpability for Eleanor's appearance at Godmersham Park irrefutable. If Jane can gain this one advantage over him, she may be able to use it to force him to act in a manner that would protect the fortunes of his wider family.

Neddy half turns, flashing his strong profile against the pale morning light. 'What did you make of Dr Storer? You were talking to him for quite a while.'

Jane kicks small stones from the dusty footpath as she trudges after him. 'If I wanted to listen to a quack for the rest of my life, I'd ask Mother's advice on hatching a duck.'

He lets out a booming guffaw, sending the chaffinches nesting in the hedgerow into frenzied song. 'I told Beth you'd be ill-suited. You seemed to have more in common with young Mr Bridges.'

'We only danced together.' She bristles, preparing herself for a lecture on how she cannot afford to dally with Elizabeth's younger brother when there are older, richer and altogether far less appealing prospects waiting to be snatched up.

They reach a stile, leading to a field of ripening wheat. Neddy offers his arm. 'I know that. He's a pleasant fellow. Not much of a sportsman, but I wouldn't hold that against him.'

'Aren't you going to warn me off? I don't think Beth would approve.' As she climbs over, reluctantly holding onto Neddy as lightly as she possibly can without risking injury, Jane's skirt catches on a splinter of wood. She tugs it lightly to release it, cautious not to rip the delicate fabric on the post-and-rail fence.

'I wouldn't dream of it. As you said, you were only dancing. And he won't be here long enough for you to form a serious attachment. It was a relief to see you enjoying yourself. I was afraid your spirits had become rather oppressed since you arrived.'

'I'm merely tired, that's all, what with helping Beth with the children and travelling to Godmersham every day. I'm not accustomed to so much gaiety.' Can Neddy sense Jane has grown wary of him? She does not wait for him to climb over the fence before she treads the narrow strip of hard-baked earth at the edge of the field. All around her, ears of wheat point to the sky, their stems still strong enough to support the tightly packed kernels of their burgeoning heads.

'I know you're worried about Cassy. We all are. Her loss is still so fresh. Given time, she'll rally.'

Neddy's sudden mention of Cassandra causes Jane to falter. He is not worthy to utter her beloved sister's name. He is hardly worthy to be an Austen at all. How dare he pretend to be so amiable, encouraging a friendship with the only interesting young man Jane has met in months, and expressing concern for her sister? He must be the real thespian in the family. James would be most incommoded to discover what a superior actor his younger brother is. As much as Jane wishes Neddy is right in his assertion about Cassandra, she scrutinizes every line of Mary's letters for the truth of her sister's condition and can see no evidence that she will ever recover. In her latest missive, Mary writes that Cassandra will not even leave her room. James has taken to sitting at her bedside, patting her hand as he composes verses to their dead companion. Poor Cassandra. As if she wasn't suffering enough without the jarring accompaniment of James's half-rhymes.

'I didn't see you dance much. Were you in the card room?' Jane asks, unwilling to share her anxiety with such a brute.

'I was, more fool me. I lost two hands to Sir William. Pray don't mention it to Beth. I fear she'll have my guts to tie as garters if you do.'

Perhaps the rift between Neddy and his wife will prove an opening large enough for Jane to exploit. By examining Elizabeth's concerns, she may be able to ascertain the extent of his own. 'Oh dear. Is there often disagreement between the two of you?'

'I was speaking in jest,' he huffs, from several steps behind her.

'Everything is well, then, in your marriage?'

'Why wouldn't things be well? We have everything we could ever wish for.'

'Do you, really?'

'Maybe not quite everything. You must understand, Beth expects a certain style of living. It can be difficult to keep up. She's not used to rough it, like one of us.' He laughs softly, leaving Jane wondering who 'us' can be. Has Neddy failed to notice he keeps a manservant and a fashionable carriage, and was groomed to inherit a fortune, while the rest of his family eke out every penny? 'And all marriages need work. Even if you begin with a fond fit, you invariably need to make accommodations for each other at some point.'

'Hmm ...' Jane is in no mood for a lecture on fidelity, from Neddy of all people. 'Only I can't help but notice how nervous Beth appears to be.'

'Well, it's getting very close to her time, and you know she's very concerned about the situation with Mother.'

'Aren't you?'

'I've said I'll handle the matter and I will.'

'Yes, but are you sure you haven't done something to arouse Mrs Knight's displeasure?' Jane watches Neddy for any hint he is aware of his mother's intentions.

His countenance remains unperturbed. 'Has she said something to you to indicate she's displeased with me?'

'Not to me, no,' she replies, thinking of the conversation she overheard between Mrs Knight and Mr Furley. Unfortunately, she caught only the tail-end, but Neddy's mother must have expressed a great deal of disappointment with her son in the course of instructing her lawyer to transfer her fortune elsewhere. 'But you don't wait on her very often.'

'I admit I may be guilty of neglecting her of late. I am rather straitened for time. Alongside my own concerns at Rowling, Mother has me overseeing the management of the plantations, preparations for the harvest, repairs to the perimeter wall. If I have eschewed her company, it's because I have been busy carrying out her commissions.'

The path is not wide enough for brother and sister to walk side by side. Neddy is forced to let Jane lead, while he follows. She wonders if Mrs Knight, having some notion of his licentious ways, is deliberately keeping her son occupied. After all, the devil makes work for idle hands. 'Shouldn't that be her steward's responsibility?'

'Yes, but Mother's keen for me to oversee it. She's always impressed upon me my duty to be useful to the neighbourhood. Besides, I can't call on her at present because her house guest remains with her.'

Jane pauses, eyeing Neddy over her shoulder. 'You're keen to avoid Eleanor?' Perhaps he had not accompanied Mrs Knight to Canterbury because he assumed Eleanor would be with her.

Neddy blusters, flapping his arms at his sides. 'She, or rather Mother, will not admit me to her presence.'

'You were mistaken. I was attending to the Wilmots rather than Dr Storer.' Jane takes a breath, readying herself to confront Neddy with the little she has learnt. 'Dr Wilmot is still under the impression he plucked Eleanor fresh from the waves, but his wife is not so convinced. She believes, as do I, that the girl was present in Whitstable before that morning. If so, someone must recognize her. Don't you think?'

'I dare say you're right.'

Jane refuses to move, blocking his path as she continues to level her gaze at him. 'Do you recognize her, Ned?'

'Me? Where on earth would I recognize her from?'

'You certainly go abroad.'

'On estate business.'

'And sport.'

'You mean assisting Sir William in taking stock of the game rather than escorting Mother to Canterbury, I suppose. I had to, Jane. You can see he's not in the best of health. And he may be my brother-in-law but he's also my landlord. It's important I remain on good terms with the baronet, as I am in his debt.'

Jane bites her cheek, resisting the urge to release her temper. Her brother is being deliberately obtuse. 'Why did it take you an extra night to retrieve me from Dartford? Your wife certainly did not expect you to be away for so long.'

'I departed a day early to ensure I was there waiting when you arrived. Beth is not always sympathetic to my feelings towards my Steventon family, but I wanted to spend every second I could with Mother and Father before they were obliged to return. I so rarely see them, Jane. I so rarely see any of you. Why? Are you accusing me of something?'

'I wouldn't dare.' Jane wraps her shawl tighter around her shoulders and gives an exaggerated shiver as she walks on, hastening her step to put as much distance between herself and her brother as she can. She is tired of baiting Neddy to no effect, and desperate to kick off her borrowed boots and sink into bed. If their conversation has proved anything, it is that Neddy is adept at bending the truth to his advantage. He is too practised in the art of deception to disclose himself to Jane, and she does not yet have the information necessary to accuse him outright. The field emerges onto a narrow lane, snaking up to what must be the main road to Canterbury. Rowling is visible through a small copse, the tiled roof gleaming above the treetops. She heads straight towards it.

'Wait! We can't go that way.'

'But I can see the house.' Jane climbs the steep bank and

enters the modest woodland, sheltered by a cover of spindly alder and willow. The ground is soft underfoot, carpeted with graceful ferns. An old path, not quite grown over, runs straight through it.

'Come back, will you?' Neddy calls from the lane. 'That's one of Sir William's favourite shooting spots.'

She ignores him, padding onwards through the dense foliage. 'He's hardly likely to be out at this hour, and I'm not walking all the way round to avoid disturbing his grouse. My feet are throbbing.'

Neddy comes crashing through the undergrowth, grabbing her wrist. 'I mean it, Jane. You can't cut through here.'

'Let go!' Jane tries to shake him off, but Neddy is holding her so tightly she fears her skin will bruise. There is an edge to his voice. It is the same sharp tone she overheard him use when arguing with Spooner in the lane. 'You're hurting me.'

He releases his grip, just enough to prevent it from smarting but not loose enough for her to walk on. 'It's too dangerous. There are traps.'

Jane casts her eye around the woodland floor, well shaded by the trees' canopy. The ferns are up to her knees in places, but the path is clearly visible. 'So? They'll be in the undergrowth, not near the path. If Sir William's gamekeeper is snaring hares, he'll be careful to keep the traps away from where anyone might accidentally step on them.'

'No, you don't understand.' Neddy's eyes widen, features pained. 'They're *man*traps.'

'Mantraps!' Ever since she was a little girl, such instruments of devastation have been the subject of Jane's imagination – and her nightmares. Yet she has never seen one in real life. Plenty of rabbit and other game traps, but never anything designed to wound, trap or even kill a fully grown man. According to the advertisements in her father's agricultural magazines, the giant spring-loaded steel jaws can weigh more than six stone and have teeth an inch and a half long. She is both repulsed and strangely thrilled at the notion of stumbling across one. 'But why?'

'He's grown intolerant of poachers. We'd probably be safe walking single file on the footpath, but I don't want to risk it. Or get into the habit of cutting through this way. I'm always warning the staff to stick to the lane. If they see me taking the shorter route, they're bound to follow. And God forbid the children get the impression it's safe to play in these woods.'

Jane claps a hand over her mouth, sickened at the prospect of Fanny or Ted being clamped in half. 'You must tell Sir William to remove them. Now, before the little ones are old enough to wander off on their own.' She tries to remember when she was considered mature enough to play unsupervised. Come to think of it, she cannot remember a time when she was not free to roam out of doors.

'I have. I will. And I'm sure he'll relax his efforts once the Enclosure Bill goes through.'

'He's enclosing the estate?' An increasing number of landowners are applying to Parliament for permission to fence off great swathes of what was previously thought to be 'common land', thus ending the freedom to graze animals and gather kindling that the lowliest members of society have enjoyed since time immemorial. Jane is forced to listen to her father rant against the practice for hours every time a new Act is reported in the newspaper. 'That's abominable.'

'It's his right, as squire. Otherwise it's too tempting for his tenants to help themselves. He lost so many birds last year that the hunting party was rather an anticlimax.'

'And we can't have families providing for themselves when there's sport to be had.' Despite herself, Jane's voice rises with her ire.

'It's more complicated than that, Jane. He's only enclosing a few choice shooting spots. Hopefully, it'll give him the peace of mind to remove these ghastly devices. I don't agree with them either. But it's his land, not mine.'

'Would you enclose Godmersham in the same manner?' Jane may not be able to pass judgement on the way Neddy manages his marriage, but she can at least take him to task over the way in which he intends to govern his land. If he ever inherits it.

'I won't have to. There's already an eight-foot wall running all the way around it.'

'The park is walled off, yes. But what about the commons and the meadows that make up the wider estate? There are bound to be families who've relied on access to them for generations.'

Neddy shrugs. 'I'll see. I'd rather not.'

'Good.' Jane is glad some part of her parents' pragmatism has been communicated to their most affluent son.

'It's an awful lot of trouble and expense to go to, if I don't have to.'

Jane recoils, drawing her arm away from her brother's grasp. It's an Act of Parliament Neddy is keen to avoid, not starving and freezing his tenants. His principles are risible. She turns her face towards the wilderness, lest he see her contempt for his character writ across her features. Through the greenery, at the base of an ancient alder, something glints. Is it a deadly contraption, or are her eyes deceiving her? 'Show me a trap, before we go.'

'There's one.' Neddy puts a hand to her waist and guides her, as if they are dancing, two steps further along the footpath. 'See, at the base of the alder with the bleeding canker?'

As Jane gets closer, the livid bruises scarring the tree move into sight. The ugly marks blotch the pale green trunk, oozing reddish-brown sticky liquid down to the woodland floor. The gamekeeper will have set the trap at the base of the distinctive tree so that he could keep track of it. The ferns, rising in a perfect circle, signal the earth has been disturbed. Most of the mechanism is covered with greenery, leaving only a few jagged iron teeth exposed. A strange, nefarious desire pulls Jane towards it, tempting her to walk right into the deadly device. Is this the same thrill that Neddy experiences when stepping outside the bounds of loving husband and doting father – the triumph of staring one's own destruction in the face, and cheating it?

'That's enough. Promise me you won't come back and try exploring on your own.'

'Very well, I promise,' Jane says meekly, letting him tug her back towards the lane. All the way, she fights the urge to twist her neck and look back into the jaws of death. Who would have thought such an ugly device could be hidden among such a pretty wilderness? The Garden of England is fraught with more danger than she imagined. Beneath the bucolic scenery, barbaric devices are laid out by men who feel the need to hoard their wealth and stake ownership of that which ought not to be owned. For now, Jane is content to let Neddy lead her to safety, but if she wants to know the truth, she'll have to find her own way.

Chapter Fourteen

Despite Neddy's protestations, Jane's warning that he has been neglecting his mother must have found its mark: the next time she visits Mrs Knight he will not be dissuaded from accompanying her. That is, until they arrive in the entrance hall of Godmersham Park and Penlington turns him aside to deal with estate matters that must be attended to urgently. Repairs to the perimeter wall have stalled again, due to a disagreement with the neighbouring squire over gaining access from the aforementioned's land. Furthermore, in Kent as in Hampshire, the balance between drought and deluge is elusive. With the lack of rain, two of Mrs Knight's tenants have accused each other of diverting streams to the severe detriment of themselves. Neddy is tasked with resolving these disputes in a manner satisfactory to all parties but, most of all, to the benefit of Mrs Knight.

As he stalks off, grumbling about the impossibility of meeting his mother's demands without so much as being

granted an audience, Grace shows Jane to the north drawing room. There she is given a warm welcome by the great
lady's excellent coffee, while Mrs Knight curls her top lip
and Eleanor turns her face to the wall, as if Jane is so far
beneath her notice it would be a grievous insult to her pride
if she were to acknowledge her presence. Ever since that
one early slip in composure, Jane has watched the girl like a
hawk and has even tried to coax her into conversation while
Mrs Knight dozes. But Eleanor either meets her enquiries
with a haughty string of babble or ignores her as she acts
out her bizarre tea rituals with all the dignity of the King's
Guard on parade. Perhaps Jane is being unfair in assuming
it is entirely a malicious act. As Mrs Wilmot said, a person's
speech *can* be affected by a blow to the head. Maybe, after
trying to end her life and being tumbled in the waves, Eleanor really did sustain such an injury, which left her unable to
remember who she was. But finding her way into the heart
and home of the wealthiest woman in Kent, and persuading
her to part with her riches in reparation for having lost her
own imaginary fortune, certainly implies masterful cunning
and Jane is as determined as ever to uncover it.

When all avenues of conversation between Jane and Mrs
Knight are exhausted (and there aren't many – the weather,
the roads, the imminence of Elizabeth's lying-in), Grace
drags out the small mahogany table and hoists Jane's writing box onto it. The maid's exaggerated huffs and puffs
suggest that, rather than being in league with Eleanor,

she, too, is growing frustrated with Mrs Knight's decree that neither the footmen, nor the butler, nor even a stable boy attend her house guest. It must be galling to serve in a house where an imposter is raised so far above her station. The maid's obvious displeasure gives Jane hope that her alarm will eventually outweigh her subservience, and that Grace will eventually respond to her persistent pleas that she shares her opinion on the credibility of Mrs Knight's foreign princess.

Heedless of the season, the enormous house is draughty. Jane sits on the low sofa, beside the stone fireplace, stifled by the enthusiastic flame flickering in the grate. Her spine aches as she pulls herself upright and throws her voice across the cavernous room, attempting a rousing performance of the Misses Dashwood's early letters to each other. Between lines, she flicks her eyes to the two women, in their comfortable buttoned chairs, to check if they are listening. The slightest nod, from her hostess, would be enough to sustain the hope that she has not lost her gift to entertain. But very soon Mrs Knight's hooded eyes flicker closed as she rests her dainty feet on an embroidered footstool and begins to make light breathy snores. Beside her, Eleanor sits ramrod straight and fixes all her attention on the dust motes dancing in the middle distance.

Jane hunches over her writing box to read and reread the letters she has composed since she arrived at Rowling. They are terrible. The most conceited drivel she's ever written.

The elder Miss Dashwood is a haughty prig, while the younger, Marianne, is a brazen hussy. In her latest despatch, Marianne confides she wanders around the Devonshire countryside with no servant and no degree of caution. Why Marianne would confess this to her elder sister when she is bound to scold her, Jane does not know. Only that as Jane tells Cassandra everything, delighting in provoking her into ever more violent admonishments, Marianne must tell Miss Dashwood her secrets too. It starts to rain. Of course it does: anyone who has visited Devon will testify to the reason the hills are a renowned patchwork of green. Marianne falls, twisting her ankle. She is stranded a good way from home and without assistance. Too late, she realizes the folly of her actions.

Through the misty drizzle a tall, dark figure appears. A hunting rifle is slung over his shoulder, and two enormous black hounds sniff at his heels. Marianne's limbs are seized with panic. He is coming towards her. He bends, scooping her into his arms. Marianne makes a futile attempt at resistance, flailing and kicking, but she is weak with cold and fear, and he is a hundred times stronger than she is –

'Argh!' Eleanor bolts from her chair. Her makeshift headdress and her gold quilt lie abandoned as she scuttles backwards across the floor.

Startled, Jane's hand raps against her ink jar, toppling it. Black liquid pools across her pages. Without thinking, she throws onto it a handkerchief Cassandra embroidered, desperate to save at least some of her work. Instead, she spreads an even greater smear across the page and ruins the precious handkerchief. When Eleanor reaches the furthest corner, her retreat blocked by a sideboard, her placid features twist into a snarl and she hisses like a feral cat. Jane is frozen in disbelief. Is this outburst one of the hysterical fits the doctors referred to? Should she call the footmen to restrain Eleanor?

Mrs Knight's head snaps upright. 'What? What did you do?'

'Me? Nothing ...' Jane continues to dab at the mess, hoping at least to preserve the surface of Mrs Knight's polished mahogany table.

Across the room, Eleanor squeezes herself under a marble-topped sideboard hosting a collection of porcelain creatures. Jane jumps to her feet, racing to remove the ornaments before she upsets them. As she approaches, Eleanor rears back, hissing even louder. What is the girl playing at? This is not a mere slip in composure, more of a wild departure from it. Such behaviour is hardly conducive to persuading Mrs Knight she can be entrusted with her estate.

'Was it Penlington?' Mrs Knight levers herself up from her chair with both arms. 'I've warned him, time and again, not to come in here under any circumstance.'

'No. No one came in. I was just sitting there, quietly reading ...'

'Eleanor, dear. Come out from under there. You'll hurt

yourself.' Mrs Knight's knees crack as she crouches. At the sight of her, Eleanor contorts herself into a ball. Her arched spine bumps the underside of the sideboard, wobbling the surface as she rests her face in her hands and whimpers. She is frightened – a danger only to herself. Or, very possibly, Mrs Knight's porcelain menagerie. Jane gathers the ornaments into a doily, transferring them to a card table.

A firm knock sounds at the door from the entrance hall.

Eleanor screams, forcing Jane and Mrs Knight to start in unison.

'Stop! Don't come in!' Mrs Knight cries.

But it's too late: Grace has already entered. Panicked by her mistress's distress, she sends a silver tray clanging onto the floor. A folded piece of paper skids along the polished parquet. 'Oh, no – is she at it again?' Grace stoops to pick up the note before hastening to join the women. 'What was it this time? I told the gardener's boy not to pass by the window, but he will not do as he's bade.'

Mrs Knight places a hand across her forehead. 'Don't blame him. It was Miss Austen.'

Jane gasps. It's hardly fair to accuse her of causing the girl's outburst. 'I was simply reading aloud, as you asked me to.'

Grace gets down on all fours, shushing softly as she crawls towards the sideboard. Beneath it, Eleanor is making keening noises as she wraps her arms around herself and rocks back and forth. Her red hair falls over her face, like a curtain, hiding her features.

Mrs Knight's eyes dart to the white paper tucked into Grace's bib. 'That can't be another, so soon after the last.'

'I'm afraid so, ma'am. Mr Penlington found it on the front step.' Grace fishes out the letter, handing it to her mistress.

Once again, it is unsealed and there are no postmarks or stamps. Unlike one of Jane's neat letters, which she arranges into a perfect envelope to protect her message from prying eyes, the paper is not even folded properly. She makes out a few spidery lines written within. Unwilling to confide in Elizabeth or Neddy, Jane has kept her ire on Mrs Knight's behalf close to her breast. Now, though, it is bursting forth. 'That's one of those dreadful missives from Captain Fairbairn. Isn't it? How dare he? The wretched beast.'

Mrs Knight fixes Jane with her steely glare, jaw tightening. 'And how would *you* know anything about my correspondence with Captain Fairbairn, Miss Austen?'

'I . . . well . . .' Jane stammers, her skin prickling. She has revealed herself to be a dreadful sneak. 'I was here when you received a note from him previously. It was sitting, half open, in the hall as I departed . . .'

'And your curious mind led you to pry into my private business, did it?'

'I'm so sorry. I know I shouldn't have. It was very shabby of me. But the note wasn't sealed, and the page was half open. I couldn't prevent my eye from alighting on the obscene language. It was so shockingly vulgar. Who is he, this Captain Fairbairn? And how dare he send you such vile messages?'

'He's nothing but a nasty coward who would rather hide behind his pen than reveal himself.' A flash of anger ignites Mrs Knight's countenance. 'My steward has made some discreet enquiries as to his identity, but we are yet to ascertain the scoundrel's whereabouts. He began harassing me as soon as I took in the poor girl.' She gestures towards the trembling Eleanor, limbs folded like a contortionist's and trapped beneath the sideboard as Grace tries patiently to coax her out. 'I suspect he did it to the Wilmots, too, and that was why the doctor let me take her. But I don't like being told what to do. And at my time of life, in my station, I will not stand for it.'

Jane swallows. Is this the real reason Mrs Knight has offered Eleanor her protection? Not because she believes her story about being kidnapped by pirates, but because she fears she is at threat from a vicious bully. If so, her intentions are laudable but handing over her fortune would seem rather a disproportionate act of charity. 'You never believed for a moment that she was a Spanish princess, did you?'

'I've told you before Miss Austen,' Mrs Knight draws herself up to her full height, 'I am not obliged to explain myself to you. Or anyone else, for that matter.'

On this occasion, Jane is determined not to be cowed. Mrs Knight has invited a complete stranger, whose behaviour has proven entirely unpredictable, into her home and Jane has promised Elizabeth and Mrs Wilmot that she will steer her towards sense. 'But she's not your responsibility.

You don't even know who, or what, she is. Not unless she's told you anything more about where she came from.' Jane holds her breath, waiting to hear if guilt on behalf of her son's behaviour is motivating Mrs Knight's benevolence.

'She's a young woman in obvious distress without a friend in the world. And I can't, in all good conscience, abandon her.' Mrs Knight's fingers brush the brooch pinned to the black silk of her bosom. 'I know what it's like to be utterly alone. It can drive a person to despair.'

Jane tries to sympathize, but the sentiment sticks in her craw. Mrs Knight is not alone: she has Neddy. She and her husband *took* Neddy and introduced him to the habits of wealth. If he is dissolute and expensive, it is because they made him so. None of Jane's other brothers has wandered so far from her mother and father's good principles. And now Mrs Knight has a daughter-in-law in Elizabeth, and three cherubic grandchildren but a short carriage ride away at Rowling. If she is lonely, it is because she has chosen to absent herself from the company of her friends and family. At five-and-forty, Mrs Knight is hardly a decrepit old woman. She is in no way infirm, and her official year of mourning has long since expired. There is no expectation on her to continue to avoid society.

Grace turns her face towards the ladies, breaking the tension. 'Shall I fetch her some warm milk, ma'am? That seemed to settle her well enough last time.'

'That would be very helpful. Thank you, Grace.' Mrs

Knight walks towards the fireplace, resting her hand against the mantel, 'And perhaps sherry for myself and Miss Austen.'

'Please.' Jane nods vigorously. She is in desperate need of something to steady her nerves.

Grace rises, dipping into a curtsy before withdrawing. From beneath the sideboard, Eleanor makes a whimpering sound. She may not pose a physical threat, but her behaviour is erratic and her mere presence at Godmersham Park is attracting undesirable attention that could place its inhabitants in danger. The realization that the captain has drawn so close makes her shiver. But Mrs Knight merely screws the offending note into a ball, eyeing the fire as if she intends to feed it to the flames.

'Wait.' Jane rests a hand on her forearm. 'Aren't you going to read it?'

'Whatever for? It'll be the same as the others. Full of vile accusations about Eleanor's character, and threats about what the captain will do if I don't give her up. But I shan't let some villain browbeat me.'

While Jane admires the widow's refusal to be intimidated, she fears her bullishness will leave her vulnerable. 'There's no postmark on the letters. The culprit must be delivering them by hand. Have you asked your servants if they have witnessed any strangers coming or going?'

'Of course I have,' Mrs Knight snaps, irritation audible in her clipped tone. Whether it is directed at herself or the elusive Captain Fairbairn, Jane can no longer tell. 'We have a constant watch on the gatehouse, and the gardener and his men patrol the park all day, but still the scoundrel manages to elude us.'

'That's not enough. If he's making threats against you, you must ensure you are protected at all times.'

'Believe me, I take the security of myself and my household very seriously indeed. Since the incident in the kitchen, Penlington ensures all the doors and windows are kept locked.'

'What incident?'

Mrs Knight purses her lips, clearly vexed at betraying her own secrets. 'It was nothing. My cook was adamant she'd bolted the kitchen door, but Armand was alerted by the sound of it crashing open in the night. He and several of the grooms came over from the coach house to investigate, but she had already discovered it and was in the process of securing it again. Armand insisted, quite rightly, on reporting it to me and carrying out a thorough search of the house. I'm afraid it caused some bad blood among the servants.'

Jane gasps. 'The captain tried to break into the house?'

'I'm confident it wasn't him. There was no obvious sign of an intruder – nothing was taken, and no note was left. It was probably a forgetful kitchen girl but, after all the furore, whoever was responsible is too afraid to come forward. Don't you dare tell my son about this.'

'Why ever not?' Jane asks, her mouth suddenly dry. What does Mrs Knight suspect about Neddy's involvement in

Eleanor's past? And is it too late for her brother to restore his mother's good opinion of him?

'Because he'll fret. And, just now, he has enough on his mind. I've already burdened him with the running of the estate while I'm distracted. If Neddy knew someone was threatening me, he'd be here all day, every day, pacing the perimeter and determined not to sleep until he caught the blackguard. And I *can't* allow him to do that. Not now, while Elizabeth needs him at her side. It wouldn't be fair of me to deprive her of her husband. She's so close to giving birth that the slightest shock could place her and the baby in danger.'

It is the same reason Jane will not confide to her sister-in-law the more disturbing details of what she has learnt through the course of her investigation. However much Elizabeth refuses to admit it, she grows more uncomfortable by the day. Childbirth is a perilous business. As soon as Mary knew she was breeding, she began collecting stories of dead mothers and their doomed offspring. Since Jane left Hampshire, Mary has written to inform her of two more such cases: a village woman, brought to bed of a baby boy far too early for him to survive longer than an hour outside his mother's womb; and a lawyer's wife from Basingstoke, who laboured for a week before she passed away without delivering the child. After she died, a surgeon cut her open and found the babe in a macerated state. Apparently, it had been dead for so long they could not even tell the sex.

'What about the authorities?' Jane asks. 'You must set the local magistrate on this Captain Fairbairn immediately. He'll know how to find him, and if a gentleman of rank was to warn him off, I'm sure he'd desist in this ghastly behaviour.'

Mrs Knight exhales through her nostrils. 'I cannot do that either, because Neddy *is* the magistrate.'

'I'm sorry. I did know that.' Jane gnaws her lip, berating herself for giving Mrs Knight yet another reason to think her a fool. Even before Mr Knight died, Neddy had taken over his duties as justice of the peace. 'But what if Captain Fairbairn is telling the truth about Eleanor's character? We don't know who she is, or where she came from.'

'Do you think I'm susceptible to a corrupting influence, at my age? Besides, Eleanor needs my help, not my scorn.' Mrs Knight gestures towards the sideboard, beneath which the girl remains sobbing into the crook of her arm.

Grace creeps back into the room balancing two brimming glasses, and a delftware dish full of milk, on a silver tray. Eleanor peeps over her elbow and wipes her nose along the sleeve of her gown. As Jane and Mrs Knight reach for their sherry, Grace places the dish of milk on the floor. 'There, there. Drink up, miss. It'll make you feel better.'

Eleanor crawls slowly towards it, until she has extracted herself from beneath the furniture, and laps the milk straight from the dish. She is either genuinely bewildered, or the most accomplished actress Jane has ever had the privilege to see perform. Gone is all her haughty dignity, replaced by a snivelling wreck.

Jane motions towards the note, still balled tight in Mrs Knight's hand. 'May I read it?'

'Why? I've already told you, it'll be nothing but black-hearted vitriol.'

'Because it might hold some clue as to the identity of the writer. Please.'

'I suppose it can't hurt, not if you've already seen the other. But only if you swear you won't breathe a word to my son. I mean it. I don't want to burden Neddy, or Elizabeth, with this nasty business. At least, not until after the new baby has arrived safely.'

'I give you my word.' Jane nods. She has no intention of disturbing Elizabeth's peace, and she has already tried confronting Neddy to no avail. Mrs Knight relaxes her fist, allowing Jane to pluck the paper from her hand. She takes it to her writing box and spreads the damp page over the slope, smoothing the edges. Three lines of large, blotted handwriting are scrawled across the page.

Heed my warning or ye shall face the sword of righteousness. Cast the whore out, for I will not stop to spill the blood of the innocent who stand between us.

Capt. Fairbairn

Jane's chest tightens, but she fights to keep her features impassive. While the contents of the message are highly disturbing, it is the means of its delivery that has caught her attention. There is something alarmingly familiar about the paper it is written on. Captain Fairbairn's small white hot-pressed sheet bears a startling resemblance to her brother's. Jane recalls Mrs Knight's reaction in the coach when she handed over Neddy's message about the perimeter wall. Did she flinch because she noticed the similarity, too? Jane holds it to the light to get a better look at the watermark – it is an elaborate shield surrounding a post-horn with the initials B B underneath.

'Well?' Mrs Knight stands over Jane, her shadow blocking the light.

Jane shakes her head, 'Nothing but vitriol, as you warned. May I keep it?'

'Why?'

How can Jane explain she wants to retain the note to compare it to one of Neddy's? Is sending threatening missives to frighten his mother and discredit the girl Neddy's way of 'handling the matter'? The captain's untidy scrawl does not bring to mind her brother's hand. All of the Austen boys use the same bold, cursive script, drilled into them by their father as children, but if Neddy is writing to his mother under an assumed identity, he is bound to disguise his pen. Jane cannot bear to think he would stoop so low, yet it is a strange coincidence that both notes should appear on the days he escorted her to Godmersham Park. 'Because sometimes, if I keep turning over a piece of writing, it helps me to see something I missed before.'

'No, it's too much of a risk. I can't have Neddy stumbling across it.'

'I assure you, my writing box is private.' Jane motions towards the tiny brass key resting beside the Misses Dashwood's letters. The box is the one area of her life over which she has complete dominion. When she is not working, the key is either in her pocket or hanging from the mirror on her dresser, meaning her papers are protected. Except for when she nearly lost the entire thing to the West Indies. Her body makes an involuntary shudder at the memory.

'I said no.' Mrs Knight snatches the note. Jane opens her mouth to object, but before she can Mrs Knight has tossed it onto the fire. The paper curls, blackening at the edges. Jane moves to the hearth as it dissolves to ash. There is no need for her to rush to copy out the words: she'll remember them for ever – she always does. It is the paper, with its distinctive watermark, she is keen to memorize as the clue that might help solve this mystery. Mrs Knight may not be fooled by Eleanor's claims to nobility, but she is clearly attached to the girl – which means she really does have the potential to divide Neddy from his mother and his inheritance. It is more imperative than ever for Jane to find out what is driving Eleanor's strange antics. Quickly, before Mrs Knight discovers Neddy's dastardly behaviour and an irrecoverable breach occurs between them, casting all of the Austens into financial precariousness.

4. Letter to Cassandra Austen

Rowling Farm, Friday, 23 June 1797

My dearest Cassandra,

Why do you not write? Is Mary neglecting to feed and water you, so that you are too weak to wield a pen? She can be ruthless in her pursuit of economy. If so, could you flag down a passing stagecoach and appeal to the driver's compassion? Breathe on your bedroom window and trace a message asking for help? Hang your pink Persian petticoats out of the front door – I'll send Father round to check. Which reminds me, can you ask him how much he receives per ounce for his wool? Neddy is worried he's being fleeced. I have a hankering to travel to Whitstable, to interrogate the Riding Officer as to the provenance of Mrs Knight's house guest. Fortunately, owing to the subtle art of my own suggestiveness, my sister-in-law finds herself plagued by a relentless craving for fresh oysters and is in desperate need of more muslin for the new baby. She will resolve this dire state of affairs by sending me to the seaside in her stead. For reasons I shall not burden you with, I do not want Neddy to escort me. Therefore Beth proposes to place me under the watchful eye of the eligible Mr Blackall, local clergyman and Kent's foremost exorcist. I have a great deal of everybody's love to give you, but am most anxious you should accept mine above all others.

Yours truly,
J.A.

P.S. I refuse to travel with the witchfinder general. Since you will not stir yourself to provide your wayward younger sister with guidance as to the bounds of respectable behaviour, I shall purloin a pair of the stable boy's breeches, lop off my curls, and beg a ride with a band of passing brigands.

Miss Austen
Rev. Mr Austen's
Deane
Hants

Chapter Fifteen

While Jane bitterly laments her inability to dissuade Mrs Knight from incinerating the captain's latest missive, she remains determined to obtain a specimen of Neddy's paper to compare with it. She very much hopes to be mistaken, and that the paper will not match, but a piece of physical evidence linking Neddy to Mrs Knight's nefarious correspondent would lend weight to her suspicion that his diabolical behaviour is in part to blame for his predicament and allow her to confront him outright.

When he disappears, the next evening, on some flimsy excuse pertaining to a few unruly members of his flock straying on his neighbour's land, she finds his study locked as usual. But through her own masterful act of cunning, Jane has already obtained the key. She began by asking Alice for access to the mysterious room. When the maid replied, as expected, that it was always kept locked owing to her master storing his firearms in there, Jane mused aloud if she should ask Kitty for it: as the upper servant, surely Kitty would be given greater dominion over the house than Alice. Shortly afterwards, to Jane's great satisfaction, Alice found she was able to produce the key.

As soon as Elizabeth can be persuaded to rest, Jane takes the opportunity to enter. Unlike Mr Austen's library, which is the beating heart of Steventon Rectory, Neddy's study seems to belong to a separate house. It even smells different – of stale tobacco and neglect. His guns, two enormous, long-barrelled rifles, take pride of place over the mantel. Hunting scenes line the walls; excited beagles and slain stags are depicted in watercolours. Surprisingly few volumes occupy the glass-fronted mahogany bookcase. She heads for the leather-topped desk, spotting a small pile of letter-writing paper already cut to size. Her hand moves instinctively towards it, gently caressing the smooth texture. It is certainly the same style, but the watermark will render it distinctive beyond all doubt.

'What are you doing in here?' Elizabeth, who clearly lied about intending to rest, throws the door wide open. 'It should be locked. Who gave you the key?'

'Susan.' Jane would rather not inform on Alice for having provided her with the means of entry, especially as it was Jane's own deviousness that had put her up to it.

'Which one?'

'I'm afraid I couldn't say.'

'Then I shall have words with both. A gentleman's study is his private domain. Women and children are not permitted.'

'My father never barred me from his.'

Elizabeth flushes. 'Well, he should have. Perhaps then you wouldn't be so ... so ...'

'Articulate?' supplies Jane.

'Come out at once. There's nothing to concern you in here.'

Jane's fingers hover over the stack. If she can purloin just one sheet, she'll be able to hold it to the light and see the mark. 'I was seeking paper. I've almost depleted my own supply, and I didn't think Neddy would begrudge me some of his.' As Jane is already sorely aware of how Elizabeth resents her, indeed resents all the Austens, for sponging off Neddy, it pains her greatly to use this excuse. But it is unthinkable to admit she is searching for evidence that Neddy is guilty of harassing his mother under a false identity.

'Can't you use the pocketbook you bought in Canterbury?'

'Not for my composition.' Jane is genuinely horrified at this suggestion. She needs a blank sheet to draft her manuscripts as she delights in filling every part of the space herself, crossing out mistakes and squeezing new lines between existing ones. A page torn from a pocketbook, decorated with scrolls and illustrations along the margins, would not do at all. She picks up a clean sheet in protest. 'The pocketbook is too pretty. I can't bring myself to despoil it.'

'Then I shall give you some of mine. Edward does not

like to have his belongings disturbed.' Elizabeth forcibly removes the ill-gotten paper from Jane's hand, returning it to the stack before guiding her towards the door.

Jane wants to resist, but she can hardly continue to trespass in Neddy's study now that his wife has discovered her. 'Oh, no, Beth, that's too kind. Just a leaf of Neddy's would do . . .'

'Come and sit down with me for a moment.' Elizabeth turns into the hall. 'I'm afraid I have some bad news for you.'

'Is it Cassy?' Jane's heart lurches as she hurries after Elizabeth, all thoughts of paper discarded. Every day that Jane's beloved sister does not write, she lives in fear of receiving the news that Cassandra has managed to starve herself to death, or found some other, more violent means to end her agony.

Elizabeth locks the door behind them, pocketing the key, which Jane had foolishly left in the lock. 'No. You read your brother's letter. Cassandra is adjusting to her loss. She shows every sign of rallying soon.'

Jane had read James's letter, or most of it, aloud to the family over breakfast – in which he assured them Cassandra was responding to her grief with 'all due propriety'. Therefore, Jane knows her brother is lying and Cassandra must be worse than ever. At least she can rely on Mary to tell her the truth. She writes that Jane mustn't worry as she has hidden the kitchen knives, and removed the sashes from

Cassandra's wardrobe. That Mary felt the need to take these precautions only sends Jane into a paroxysm of concern for her beloved sister. Oh, God, she must remind Mary to lock away the laudanum too.

In an uncharacteristic act of tenderness, Elizabeth wraps an arm around Jane's shoulders. 'I do hope your sister will be recovered in time for next year's ball. She's such a favourite here, you know.'

'So you've told me, several times.' Jane does not need reminding that Elizabeth would far rather Cassandra was her companion, while Jane remained in Hampshire. If Cassandra's life had not been so devastated, Jane would much prefer that arrangement too.

'I don't mean to imply you're not. It's just that Cassy is so beautiful, and so sweet-tempered. It will be much easier getting her a husband.'

'Beth! She's only just lost her fiancé.'

'I know. But, as I said, she'll rally. And with my help, I can foresee she'll go on to win a much greater prize.'

'How can you say that?' Jane is run through with grief on her sister's behalf. 'You know how devoted to each other she and Mr Fowle were.'

'I do, but with no money on her side and only a curacy to support them on his, you cannot deny the match was ill-fated from the start.'

'They would have been happy.'

'They would have been poor. Even with the Shropshire

living Lord Craven promised, every passing year would have seen the arrival of another child, which would have stretched them beyond their means. Cassandra would have had to be a very clever mistress of economy to survive.' Elizabeth's face is grave. 'Both of you must take this unhappy event as a sign to consider your futures carefully. I know you don't like to discuss it, but your father won't live for ever.'

It takes an enormous effort for Jane to swallow her rebuke. She cannot argue with Elizabeth's reasoning as to poor Mr Fowle's prospects or her father's mortality, but it demonstrates Elizabeth's lack of empathy. 'You need not worry about Cassandra. Mr Fowle bequeathed her a legacy.'

'He did? What a noble young man he was. Do you know if it's a fixed sum or an annuity that must be surrendered upon marriage?'

Jane relies on her vexed features to inform Elizabeth that she will not supply the answer. It was the only part of James's letter that Jane could not bear to read aloud for fear of losing all composure. Without telling anyone, Mr Fowle had seen a lawyer before he set sail for the West Indies and made out a will leaving everything he had, a legacy of one thousand pounds, to Cassandra. Invested wisely in government bonds, the inheritance will yield an income of up to forty pounds per annum. Not enough to live on, but it will give Cassandra some independence and means she need not worry quite so much about becoming a burden to Mr and Mrs Austen in their old age. Jane's sister is effectively a widow, without enjoying one precious moment of marriage to the man she loved.

'I'm afraid the bad news pertains to Mr Blackall,' Elizabeth eventually concedes. 'He will not be able to escort you to the coast tomorrow, after all.'

'Why not? Is *he* dead?'

'No, Jane. He's been called away on parish business.'

'That's a shame.'

'Isn't it?' Elizabeth scowls, as if wanting to chastise Jane on her flippancy but not being quite fast enough to pin it down. 'Especially as I had managed to persuade Edward to allow Mr Blackall to convey you there in his phaeton. The one benefit of him insisting on retaining that ghastly open carriage was that I could wave you both off without a chaperone. But not to worry, you'll see Mr Blackall on Sunday at evensong in Crundale.'

'Evensong? But we'll have attended the morning service at Holy Cross. Is that not devotion enough for you?'

'Under normal circumstances, yes, but as no other gentleman took your fancy at the ball, I insist you give Mr Blackall another examination.' Elizabeth brushes a crumb from her fichu. 'Better still, give Crundale Parsonage an examination. It really is very handsome. With the addition of a portico, it might even be made elegant.'

'But I don't like Mr Blackall. Twenty porticoes could not make his character any more compatible with mine.'

'Ah, but that doesn't matter as the gentleman in question has professed to a liking for *you*.'

'How can he say he likes me? The fool! He doesn't know the first thing about me.'

'Perhaps that's part of the attraction.'

Jane refuses to be defeated. She needs to get to the coast and speak to the Riding Officer. Now that she has witnessed Eleanor's bouts of instability, she is even more certain that someone from Whitstable will know who she is. Such behaviour cannot be hidden and, whether working as servant or harlot, she is bound to have developed a reputation as ungovernable. 'Can Roger take me instead? I wouldn't want the new baby to run short of clouts due to my suitor's lack in dedication.'

'There's no need. My brother has volunteered to escort you.'

'Sir William?' Jane can hardly imagine the baronet putting himself out for her. He's already expressed his disapproval of any unnecessary travel. An afternoon in his company is the last thing she needs. How could she make it all the way to the coast and back without admonishing him on his selfishness in enclosing the estate? Never mind the sheer idiocy of leaving mantraps lying around for innocent passers-by to walk into.

'No, my younger brother.'

Despite herself, Jane's spirits rise. Why is her dancing

partner still in Kent? He was meant to begin his journey to the Scottish Highlands on the morning after the ball. Could his delayed departure have anything to do with seeking to further his acquaintance with her? They had spent a most agreeable evening together. The knowledge that he would be gone as soon as the sun rose had allowed Jane to let down her inhibitions in a manner she could not have done with any serious prospect. 'Mr Bridges is still here? I thought he was planning to remain only the night.'

'So did I. But he called while you were at Godmersham, not long after I'd received Mr Blackall's note, and insisted on offering himself as a replacement.' From Elizabeth's sour expression, Jane can tell she had tried her best to convince her brother his services were not required.

'That's very obliging of him.'

'He'll be here, in his gig, bright and early tomorrow morning.'

Jane sets off up the staircase, lest Elizabeth senses her pleasure at the prospect of Mr Bridges arguing for her company. 'Then I'd better rest.'

'But, Jane . . .'

'Yes?'

'About my brother. Do remember he's out of bounds, won't you?'

'Naturally.' Jane sways her hips in victory as she ascends. It is extremely flattering to think Mr Bridges might have altered his plans for her, and even more satisfying to watch Elizabeth's attempts at matchmaking ricochet. But she must not, in all good conscience, allow herself to develop an appetite for forbidden fruit. As Mrs Austen warns, the sweeter the temptation, the more acrid the regret.

Chapter Sixteen

The following morning, the air is crisp but heavy with the promise of heat yet to come. The pink roses stretching across the façade of Rowling House tentatively loosen their petals, as if all too aware they are about to be scorched by the blazing sun. Mr Bridges sits on the bench of his two-wheeled gig in his too-tight breeches, looking immensely pleased with himself. Really, his attire is most impractical. The slightest sudden movement and the seam between groin and buttocks would give way entirely. 'Good morning, Jane.' He smiles, revealing sharp canine teeth.

'Mr Bridges.' Jane ignores his outstretched hand in favour of the handle to hoist herself into the gig.

'I've told you to call me Brook.'

'And I expressly have *not* given you permission to address me by my Christian name.' She wraps her pelisse around herself, and shuffles into the corner of the seat, as far away from him as possible. It is no good: her knee remains in danger of scraping his thigh.

'You're prickly this morning.'

Jane ignores him. She *is* prickly. She has a conundrum to solve. Somehow, she must obtain one of Captain Fairbairn's letters *and* a slip of paper from Neddy's study, without aggravating Mrs Knight or causing either of the Susans strife with her mistress. If the paper matches, Neddy can hardly deny sending them, and can Jane use this knowledge to persuade him to reform his licentious ways. Even if Mrs Knight knows about his involvement in Eleanor's downfall, it may not be too late to save his prospects. Eleanor has revealed herself to be far too unstable to manage a grand estate and, if Neddy is duly contrite, Jane is hopeful Mrs Knight could be persuaded to forgive him. In the meantime, she will return to her earlier plan of interrogating the Riding Officer. There must be something about the circumstances in which Eleanor was found that will reveal who she is and where she came from. And, after dwelling on it all night, Jane concedes Elizabeth is right. She must school herself to remember that no good can possibly come of her developing a preference for Mr Bridges. Thankfully, he is doing his utmost to prevent her from finding him agreeable, as he tips a small quantity of snuff onto the back of his hand and snorts it noisily up his left nostril.

'That's a disgusting habit.' She tuts to underscore her disapproval.

'I know, but what's a gentleman of fashion to do? One

must comply with the times.' He tucks the snuff box inside his frock coat before replacing his gloves and gathering the reins with both hands. 'Shall we?'

Jane nods, and he works his chestnut cob into an easy canter. It has not rained since Jane arrived in Kent and the countryside is showing signs of being parched. Sprays of creamy elderflowers weigh down the tired shrubs lining the hedgerow, and wilting umbels of cow parsley spill lazily into their path. As they advance towards Canterbury, Mr Bridges explains he will take the new turnpike road to the coast so that he can give the horse licence to gallop. This news does not thrill Jane in the way he intended. The gig is so light, she fears the slightest bump will overturn it, sending them both somersaulting through the air to meet their maker in spectacular style.

'So,' he glances at her, from beneath the brim of his tall-crowned hat, 'what are we *really* about in Whitstable?'

Jane flinches. 'As your sister instructed. We're to run her errands.'

'Come now, it must be more than that.'

'Why?'

'Your eyes. They're sparkling. Even more so than usual. It's as clear as daylight you're up to something. And whatever it is, *I* want in on it. Remaining in the country for too long can leave a gentleman vulnerable to the most terrible *ennui*. I need you, Jane. You're the only one who can rescue me from myself.'

Jane diverts her gaze. All around, the gently sloping fields are planted with neat rows of apple trees, speckled with pink and white blossom. As she pretends to admire the view, she is acutely aware of Mr Bridges watching her, waiting for an answer. Heat rises in her cheeks at the prospect of his scrutiny. She cannot reveal all and risk this would-be Lothario blundering into her investigation. Or, worse, alerting Neddy that she is on to him.

She opts to distract him: 'Why do you remain at your family seat if you find it so objectionable? I thought your appearance at the Midsummer Ball was a mere break on your journey towards the Highlands.'

'Indeed, I'm determined to see Scotland before the summer is behind us. A very dear friend from Oxford is expecting me.' Mr Bridges passes both reins into one hand so that he can scratch the back of his long neck. 'But I've . . . er . . . rather overspent my allowance. And I can hardly arrive empty-handed at McBride's castle. So, I'm waiting for my brother to throw me some coin. Alas, he's doggedly determined not to part with any.'

'Oh . . .' Jane folds her arms across her chest. Mr Bridges remaining in Kent has nothing to do with her. He is simply a profligate, who is used to being indulged by his rich relations. When will she learn to be properly wary of a gentleman's intentions?

'I expect William will keep me here for at least a fortnight, while he gives me a set-to about applying myself to my studies, not to mention deciding on a profession. Then, before he knows it, he'll relent and send me on my way with a more generous handout than I asked for. I merely have to wait for him to grow tired of admonishing me. Or of me making a nuisance of myself. Whichever comes first. It's very trying, not having one's independence.'

'Hmm ...' Jane glances sidelong at him. She should have known he'd be just like his brother. Sir William is so accustomed to the privilege of his circumstances that, rather than exercising the moral responsibility that should rightfully accompany it, he guards his riches jealously. Through his adoption and marriage, Neddy has become as entitled as the rest of his set.

'What? Spare me your judgement. I've already sat through more lectures since I got home than I attended during the entire Michaelmas term.'

'Really, Mr Bridges.' They are only a few miles into their journey, and Jane is already sick of his complaining. She may be obliged to defer to the baronet and suffer her sister-in-law's self-absorption, and she is certainly resolved to win at the long game with Neddy, but there is nothing to bar her from speaking her mind to this impudent coxcomb. 'You're a young, able-bodied gentleman, well-educated and from an excellent family. Can you not see that you have every advantage in making your way in the world? Are you so impotent that, with such an array of intellectually stimulating and lucrative opportunities open to a man of your good breeding and connections, you cannot decide which one to grasp first?'

Mr Bridges' jaw settles on his cravat. Evidently a Bridges lecture isn't enough to prepare one for an Austen-style castigation. 'I . . . I will. I just need a little more time, that's all. There are so many factors to consider.'

Jane runs her eyes over his frame. A small part of her cannot resist comparing his person to Tom Lefroy's. She is shocked to realize his lithe limbs do not come off too unfavourably. 'Have you considered the law, for example?'

'Too dull.' Mr Bridges sniffs. 'I haven't the patience for it.'

In Jane's experience, the law is sadly anything but dull. But she supposes he is right in that it takes a studious mind to comprehend the myriad ways in which it can be applied to one's advantage. 'The navy, then? I have two brothers at sea. Frank has recently been appointed lieutenant on board a new frigate. Charles is only a midshipman, but he's so bold we have high hopes he'll be made an officer, too. And then they'll both have a chance of winning their fortune.' Either that or be killed in action Jane does not think it will be helpful to add.

Mr Bridges fixes her with his honeyed brown eyes, one dark brow quirking in provocation. 'I may appear to you to be in the prime of my life, Jane, but I believe I would already be considered too old to join the navy. Besides, although I was raised by the sea, I am no seaman. I suffer from acute *mal de mer.*'

'The army?' she continues, ignoring his outrageous coquetry.

He tilts his head to one side, pretending to consider her advice in earnest. 'Well, the regalia certainly appeals. I do think I'd look rather dashing in scarlet. But . . .' He trails off.

'But?'

'In case you haven't noticed, there's a war on. And *I* am a terrible coward. I faint at the sight of blood.'

Jane pokes her tongue into her cheek to still her laughter. It is impossible not to warm to a man who can own his inadequacies. 'What about trying for a seat in Parliament?'

'Do you mind? I do have some principles.' He shakes the reins as if casting off her insult. 'No, if I had the power of forcing people to listen to me, I'd be a poet and proclaim in verse my objections to sacrificing any more of our countrymen at the feet of the French.'

This causes Jane to check herself. She had not known Mr Bridges had philosophical tendencies – but perhaps she might have guessed. While the government is determined to quash any dissent to the war on British soil by means of military might, there remain a few who dare to express their dissatisfaction by means of the quill. What would Elizabeth say if she knew her brother was prone to seditious fancies? 'That won't do. There's no money to be had in writing. Not in my experience, anyway.'

He flashes her a conspiratorial grin. 'Neddy boasts you compose your own stories. May I read one?'

'No.' She surprises herself by snapping. While she is delighted to hear that Neddy has shared his esteem for her compositions with his wife's family, even if he will not indulge her by listening to them, she cannot allow Mr Bridges to read her work. It would create an intimacy between them she is not prepared to permit. 'I cannot trust you not to steal my ideas and pass them off as your own.'

'You're probably right. Plagiarism is my one academic strength. No, all things considered, it'll probably end up being the Ch—'

'Oh, for the love of God. Please, don't say it.'

'The Church? What's wrong with being a clergyman? My brother will soon have it in his power to provide me with a decent living. The present incumbent of Holy Cross is almost as Gothic as the building itself.'

'It's not that there's anything wrong with the Church, per se. I just feel it lacks imagination, when there are so many other avenues open for you to explore. It must be the oldest profession known to man.'

'Not quite the oldest. Now that really would be a bold choice.' He cocks his brow at her, and Jane's cheeks flush: she has just compared priesthood to prostitution.

'Are you sure you won't consider the militia? That way, you wouldn't have to do any actual fighting until the French invade. And everyone will have to take up arms then.'

'Will you choose a sabre or a pike, do you think?'

'Stop with your jests.' Jane laughs at the image of herself

armed to enter the fray. She does not tell him that her friend and Tom's aunt, Mrs Lefroy, is so concerned about the imminent French invasion that she sleeps with a spiked club under her bed. A moment later, she catches her breath: Mr Bridges' prevarication over his intended profession could be her ticket to enter the garrison. She would dearly love to be proved wrong about Neddy and find Captain Fairbairn does exist. Even if Jane is disappointed in her search, and there is no such person entered on the roster, this information is bound to prove helpful when she eventually confronts her brother. 'Why don't you speak to a recruiting officer? There must be one at Sir Edward Hale's new facility in Canterbury. I'll come with you.'

'Absolutely not. I shan't go near that dreadful place. Why are you so passionate about turning me into a soldier? Are you working on commission? I'd better not come in for refreshment when we get back to Rowling, lest I find the King's shilling nestled among my tea leaves.'

'I'm speaking in earnest. My brother Henry was all set to enter the Church, but he volunteered for the militia instead. Now he's a captain and acting paymaster for the Oxfordshires. By all accounts, he's doing very well for himself.'

'Ah, but I'll wager he's not doing quite as well as the brother who is set to inherit his wealth.'

Jane tries to keep her features placid. It is more than a week since Mrs Knight visited her lawyer. The widow must have her doubts about transferring her estate to Eleanor now that she has witnessed her strange outbursts, but that does not mean she has reinstated Neddy in her affections or her will. As Elizabeth pointed out, Godmersham Park is Mrs Knight's to dispose of as she sees fit. 'No, not quite as well as that.'

Mr Bridges lets out a defeated sigh. 'Unfortunately, a legacy is the most expedient route to one's independence.'

They drive on in silence until Jane realizes that, in reconciling himself to take holy orders, Mr Bridges is showing far more diligence than his sister expects. She cannot resist testing him on it. 'I didn't think you'd need to lower yourself to enter a profession. Beth says you're to marry your fortune.'

'Ugh . . .' He slumps forward, elbows resting on his knees as he steers the horse. 'Look, Jane. Far be it for me to speak ill of my own sister, but you must have noticed Beth's a bossy old trout. After my mother died, she took it upon herself to act as matriarch. Nobody asked her to, and her interventions are far from welcome. She's forever placing her oar where it's not needed, telling the rest of us how to go on.'

'Well, I . . .' Jane reaches for a tactful answer, but it seems she's prodded a particularly sensitive spot and there is no need for her to say anything at all, even if she agrees.

'Don't believe everything she tells you. When I'm ready, I'll make my own decision. She's even worse with my sister. Hen had begun to despair of ever receiving an offer. Now she's finally secured the attentions of a respectable country parson, but Beth keeps raising objections. She doesn't think he's smart enough to be one of the family, but it shouldn't be her opinion that matters. Hen is the one who will be obliged to live with her choice.'

'That's appalling.' No wonder Henrietta's taste in music is so melancholy: she must be pining for her forbidden love.

'You might have met the gentleman. He has the living of a place on the Godmersham estate. What's it called? Crudner? Crummy-vale?'

'Are you referring to Crundale?'

'That's the one. Do you know it?'

Stunned, Jane sinks back into the seat. It seems Elizabeth is far more of a strategist than Jane had previously given her credit for. Perhaps it is *she* who should be introduced to the King's recruiting officer if the British forces are to outwit Bonaparte. 'No, but Beth is certainly very keen to send me there. Ideally for good.'

'She's not trying to lure away the good cleric by dangling you in front of him, is she? Poor Hen won't stand a chance. What a shame. She's never warmed to any of the fools Beth has thrown her way previously, but I do believe she has a genuine preference for Mr Blackall.'

'On the contrary, I have no intention in becoming mistress of Crundale Parsonage. Please inform Henrietta her sweetheart is quite safe with me.' Jane cannot understand why Henrietta would want to be Mrs Blackall either but, as her brothers' choices of mate have consistently taught her, there is no disputing taste. She wonders if the clergyman's loyalty to Henrietta is the real reason he failed to escort her to Whitstable.

'You see?' Mr Bridges laughs. 'If Beth is trying to govern your marital prospects, too, we have more in common than we do apart. We should form an alliance, while I'm here. You can start by telling me the true purpose of our visit to Whitstable.'

Jane dips her chin, fearing her flushed cheeks will con-firm her duplicity. She retrieves her tired old pocketbook from her reticule and pretends to check her list. 'First, I must visit the haberdasher and barter a good deal on muslin. Then it's on to the fishmonger, where I shall place an order for a hefty quantity of shellfish. And then . . .'

One corner of Mr Bridges' mouth turns up. 'And then?'

Jane eyes him carefully. He has been charged with escort-ing her to the coastal town and back safely. There is no way she will be able to complete her mission without confiding at least some of the details in him. 'And then I'd like a brief interview with the Riding Officer.'

'Ha, I knew it!' He drops the reins from one hand to slap his lean thigh. 'You're out to discredit that flimflammer Mrs Knight has taken in, aren't you?'

Jane presses the pocketbook to her chest, opening her eyes wide and batting her lashes. 'What on earth would give you that impression?'

'Beth told me about her. She's a threat to your brother's

inheritance. And we both know how critical an inheritance is. Even, or should I say especially, when it's not your own.'

'I simply want to get to the bottom of her story. That's all.'

'You should have come straight out with it. I'd be more than happy to do your bidding. It will provide an excellent distraction from my own concerns.'

Jane peers at him, trying to decipher if he is sincere. How is a lady to know, before it is too late? One thing she cannot deny is that she is in need of an accomplice and this pliable young man is eager to fill the vacancy. 'And you won't tell Beth? Or Neddy? Or anyone else for that matter?'

Mr Bridges shakes his head vigorously. 'Absolutely not. You have my word as a gentleman. How thrilling, to be taken into your confidence.'

Jane stuffs the pocketbook back inside her reticule. 'Don't make this out to be anything more than it is. You're a convenience to me, that's all.'

'Oh, I understand completely. Now, let's hurry up and fetch your bobbins and whelks and whatnot so we can get to the exciting part of our little adventure together.' He gathers the reins, prompting the horse forward.

Jane digs her teeth so hard into her bottom lip to prevent herself from smiling that she fears she'll draw blood. Despite her best efforts, she is genuinely enjoying the young man's company. It is an attraction that could prove most inconvenient. She is not prepared to expose her heart again and she reminds herself that, even if she was, it would be reckless to form an attachment to such an unsuitable choice. As a younger son, Mr Bridges can no more afford to marry Jane against his family's wishes than can Tom Lefroy. Elizabeth has already stated her objections to such a match and she expects Sir William will be inclined to agree with her. What a shame so many brothers lie, or rather stand, between Mr Bridges and the magnificent Goodnestone House.

Chapter Seventeen

After the sky fills with squawking gulls and the flat road sinks between the dunes, the small town of Whitstable draws into sight. Mr Bridges stables the horse at an inn at the start of the crooked high street, then he and Jane proceed towards the front on foot. The air is thick with salt, and the fierce breeze blows Jane's curls into her eyes and flaps her skirts around her legs as she jogs to keep up with his long strides. She is eager for her first glimpse of the sea, and even more anxious to conceal her childish delight in it from Mr Bridges. The thoroughfare is crowded with shoppers, and she is surprised to note so many well-dressed and well-fed but seemingly idle men loitering on corners with their mounts. They cannot all be as indolent or as fortunate as Mr Bridges. At last, the undressed masts of a handful of cutters rise over the tiled rooftops and a narrow lane reveals a tantalizing flash of calm grey water stretching beyond the misty horizon. Jane's pulse quickens at the limitless possibilities it represents. If

Providence had made her a man, she would not have been able to resist its allure.

Determined to succeed in her commissions as well as her investigation, Jane compares muslins and drives a hard bargain on fresh oysters while Mr Bridges questions the shopkeepers on the most likely whereabouts of the Riding Officer. As Neddy explained, the Royal Navy are preoccupied with the war effort so the Revenue Office has employed a local man, a Mr Skeete, to keep watch along the shore. It is Mr Skeete's job to ride continuously up and down the Kent coast, looking for vessels entering the Thames estuary with the intention of smuggling licensed goods to or from the Continent. However, the merchants cheerfully report that he can usually be found at the harbour, playing dice with any unoccupied sailors, or along the promenade offering guided tours to visitors.

Armed with this knowledge, Mr Bridges carries Jane's basket and leads her along the Island Wall: a low stone structure that purportedly protects the cluster of clapboard cottages from dissolving into salt marsh. On the other side of the partition, a shingle beach leads to the sea, lapping lazily at the muddy shoreline. Today, the waves are as level as the surrounding countryside and the Isle of Sheppey sits squat and leafy in the distance. Whitstable is situated at the point where the Swale river meets the sea, and the shallow water makes a perfect breeding ground for various species of shellfish. At least two dozen small boats bob on the surface, dredging for oysters. Mr Bridges explains these are called yawls and are distinct to the area. Although he has professed himself not to be a seaman, Jane is amused to note he is as animated as any of her brothers as he explains the different configurations of bows and sterns employed by the fishermen of Kent.

'I'll wager there's our Riding Officer.' Mr Bridges breaks off his instruction to signal towards a weaselly young man perched on top of the wall. The youth holds a telescope to one eye, and squints at the curved bay below. 'Ahoy there, sirrah.'

Mr Skeete removes his telescope. 'Sir.'

'Mr Bridges, of the Goodnestone Bridges.'

'Mr Skeete, at your service.' He bows in deference to the Bridges family name. How much easier these interactions are, Jane notes, when one is male and a member of the local gentry.

'We'd like to talk to you about the strange woman found wandering along the beach by Dr Wilmot and his wife. I believe they brought her to you in the first instance.' Mr Bridges climbs up to Mr Skeete's level. Jane remains at the foot of the steps, next to a group of fishwives gutting flounder on a trestle table in front of a ramshackle collection of huts. The women chatter while they work, grazing their paring knives over the fish's scales as their eyes dart to small children playing at their feet. They remind Jane of the way she and Cassandra converse as they sew, their minds paying little heed to what their fingers are doing. She smiles at the party in greeting, but only the lopsided faces of the spotted fish return her gaze.

Mr Skeete scratches the fluff along his top lip. 'The Spanish princess?'

'If you believe she is a princess, or even a Spaniard,' replies Mr Bridges.

Throughout the rest of their journey, Jane primed him most thoroughly for this conversation. So far, she is delighted he is sticking to her script word for word.

'She's a Spaniard, all right. Kidnapped and held at the mercy of pirates since she was a girl. One of the lascars translated for her,' says Mr Skeete, although his eyes stray from Mr Bridges' face down to the curve of the bay.

Jane stands apart, trying not to make it obvious how keenly she is listening. She knows from bitter experience that Mr Skeete is far more likely to confide in Mr Bridges than herself. Especially if he suspects anything unsavoury about Eleanor's past. She gazes down towards the bay to see what has attracted his interest. Around twenty yards out to sea, a draught horse is submerged up to its flanks, tethered to what looks like a privy on wheels. It must be one of those newfangled bathing machines. Jane read an intriguing account of the facility in one of Elizabeth's copies of the *Lady's Magazine*, but she's never seen one in person before.

'And you're sure she wasn't already known to this lascar? Or anyone else hereabouts?' asks Mr Bridges.

'Known, sir?'

'You didn't recognize her? And the lascar did not seem familiar with her?'

'He couldn't have been. His ship only docked that morning.'

'And where might I find this lascar?'

'You won't. His ship's gone out again.' Mr Skeete shakes his head. 'But she was definitely a Spanish princess, I'd stake my life on it.'

Mr Bridges hesitates. 'She also claimed she was involved in a shipwreck, yet no vessels have been reported lost along this stretch of coastline recently. If any had, the wreckage would have washed up by now. Wouldn't it?'

Mr Skeete furrows his brow, as if he is just as confused by this discrepancy in Eleanor's story as Mr Bridges is. 'There've been no wrecks along my stretch, sir. Not since the winter.'

Jane releases a breath, turning back to the beach. Eleanor is a slight thing. It would be impossible for her to swim ashore in a storm. Mrs Wilmot's suspicion, that she entered the water of her own accord, is far more likely. Was she so ground down by her circumstances that death seemed a preferable alternative? Jane wonders if Mr Bridges would agree to circulate the girl's description in the less salubrious taverns they passed on Whitstable's high street. He could pretend he was a philanderer with a penchant for redheads – masquerading as a rascal could prove an interesting cure for his *ennui*. Perhaps Mr Bridges has even frequented such places in the past. Jane would never have suspected any of her brothers capable of entering a bawdy house, yet she knows Neddy must have. But what would she do if a tavern reported that a girl answering to Eleanor's description was missing? The next logical thing would be to enquire if her brother had ever patronized the establishment. Could she involve Mr Bridges in such a sordid investigation, and does she really want to know the answer?

Out in the bay, two burly female dippers pull down the ladder on the back of the bathing machine, and wrench open the door. A lady steps out, dressed in a loose red gown and cap. The dippers jump into the lapping waves, calling to and motioning for the lady to join them. Understandably, she clutches tight to the rail, her posture rigid with fear. It is very rare for ladies to learn to swim. Jane has never so much as paddled her bare feet along the shoreline. If the dippers were to let go of their charge, even for a moment, she could be swept away by the elements.

Mr Bridges shrugs his shoulders at Jane, having exhausted all her predefined prompts. She glares at him, willing him to continue until he discovers something useful. With a sigh, he turns back to Mr Skeete. 'What about inland? Are you in communication with the watch towards Uplees?'

Mr Skeete sucks in a sharp breath. 'If there was a wreck, and I'm not saying there was, I reckon it must have gone down further out. Around Margate, say. Terribly dangerous around there.'

The lady is in the sea now, submerged up to her shoulders. Her shrieks of delight carry all the way to shore. The dippers laugh as she splashes around. Jane tries to imagine how the briny water would feel on her skin: delightfully cool on this stifling day. Perhaps she should convince her parents to take Cassandra to the coast. She could visit Eliza and Hastings at Brighton. A spot of sea bathing could be just the thing to revive Cassandra's spirits. Or not, given how poor Mr Fowle was buried at sea. Would it have helped to ease Cassandra's grief if she had a grave to visit? As it is, Jane's sister will have to mourn Mr Fowle every time she is confronted with the endless waves.

Mr Bridges scratches his temple. 'What? Are you suggesting she could have swum upriver to make it to shore?'

'Yes ... Or perhaps the vessel didn't go down, and she jumped ship to escape her captors. Those blackguards will be long gone, by now. Across the Channel, on to the Continent. Or maybe even across to the New World. The West Indies, most likely. I hear the waters around Jamaica are particularly infested with pirates.' Mr Skeete warms to his theme. 'There'll be no hope of catching –'

A blood-curdling scream cuts him off mid-sentence.

Jane's heart constricts as she trains her eyes out across the water. She searches for the lady in her red cap, fearing she has eluded her dippers and gone under.

But it is the lady who is screaming as she scrabbles up the stairs of the bathing machine. The two dippers wave frantically to the shore. Beside Jane, one of the younger fishwives stands. She tosses aside her paring knife. It lands with a thud as she lifts her skirts and runs, barefoot, up the steps and down onto the beach. For a few awful moments, she is the only one to react. Jane and everyone else stare on in stunned silence, trying to decipher why she is so panicked when the lady and both her dippers are accounted for.

But then Jane spots something floating in the water *beside* the bathers.

Mr Skeete lifts his telescope and presses it to one eye. 'God's teeth, not another.' He sets off after her. Some of the other women follow. All along the beach, people halt in their promenade and fishermen pause in their work. Everyone is staring anxiously towards the horizon. Jane turns to Mr Bridges, who is frowning in confusion. The object bobs in the water, long and pale. Could it be a piece of driftwood? If so, why are the women alarmed?

The young fishwife has reached the shoreline. The waves drag at her skirts, but she advances undeterred through the foaming water. The dippers have caught the object between them and are towing it through the waves. The scene pulls Jane towards it. Her feet climb the steps of their own accord, despite the leaden weight of her legs.

'Jane, wait.' Mr Bridges reaches for her wrist as she passes, but she shakes herself free. The women have hauled the wreckage onto the beach. They huddle around it, obscuring Jane's view. But she can tell, by their reverent silence and the way the object bends to their will, that it is not a piece of driftwood.

It is a corpse.

A man. Now, laid out in the shallows – his arms spread wide as if nailed to a cross. His lips dark blue, his features all but destroyed, but wearing the distinctive striped jersey of a sailor. The fishwife who led the charge falls to her knees beside him. The other women stare at each other, white-faced and mute with shock. Jane stumbles over the shingle, nearly twisting her ankle, to reach them. One of the oystermen has rowed to the shore and passes a rough felt blanket to the Riding Officer. Deftly, Mr Skeete shakes it over the body and barks directions. The women roll the remains into a tight bundle. Four of them haul it up and trudge towards the huts.

Mr Skeete follows, leaving the first fishwife and an older woman on their knees in the mud. He swore there had been no wrecks along this part of the coast. Yet Eleanor was found in just her shift, blue and shivering as if she'd spent some time in the water. And now here is a dead sailor, washed up before Jane's very eyes. And he is not the first. *God's teeth, not another*, Mr Skeete had exclaimed, when he saw the man's deceased form drifting in the waves. Is it possible Eleanor really did survive a shipwreck?

Jane breaks into a run, desperate to reach the last two women before they depart. She must uncover details of this tragedy. The knowledge could help her sort through Eleanor's jumbled account to find out who she is and why she is cleaving to Mrs Knight. 'Excuse me,' she cries.

The older woman stares up at her, open-mouthed. There is a yellow bruise at her temple and both of her front teeth are missing.

'Do forgive me for asking but was that . . .' Jane braces herself '. . . was that a lost sailor washed up onto the beach?'

The older woman staggers to her feet. 'What's it to you? That ain't a revenue man, is it? I ain't one to peach.' She motions behind Jane, where Mr Bridges is stumbling along the shingle.

'Oh, goodness, no. Pay no mind to him. He's a very fine gentleman, never worked a day in his life.' Jane places a hand to her throat. 'It's just . . . if it was a lost sailor, and if a vessel did go down hereabouts recently, I think I may know someone who was on it.'

The woman makes a curt nod, confirming Jane's suspicions.

'But how strange. We were just this very moment talking to the Riding Officer and he claimed to have no knowledge of any ships getting into difficulty along this stretch of coast.'

'He knows all right. Useless beggar!' The woman shouts over Jane's shoulder: 'When are you going to tow in the wreck and retrieve the rest of the bodies? Or are you leaving it out there, so you can cut the tubs free and take the loot for yourself?'

Mr Skeete turns to sneer at her. 'Watch your tongue, Molly. Unless you want it cut out.'

Jane flinches at the violence of their exchange. Could Mr Skeete be lying, while Eleanor is telling the truth? 'You're expecting *more* bodies?'

Molly narrows her eyes, clearly assessing Jane – trying to decide why she should tell her anything at all. 'Only three have washed up, so far. But there's another dozen or so sailors from the town missing. My old man included. All gone, since the night of the terrible storm, three weeks back.'

'I'm so sorry.' Jane steps closer, reaching for Molly's hand. 'Do you know which ship he was aboard?'

Molly rears backwards, tearing her calloused fingers from Jane's grasp. 'No. And I *won't* be sorry if he washes up dead. He was an idle brute. Only went out when he was short on coin for rum and whoring. And he never told me when he did. God forbid I look to him to feed his own children.'

'Oh . . .' It is not often Jane is speechless, but this is one of those rare occasions.

'Whatever vessel our menfolk were aboard must have got caught in a swell and flipped over, somewhere upriver. I expect it happened so quick most of them were trapped below deck or caught in the rigging. That's why it's taking so long for the tide to bring them back to us. But the sea will rattle them free, eventually. Please, God, my old man'll turn up. So I'll have the peace of knowing I'm rid of him, at last.' Molly turns to the first fishwife, still sobbing in the muddy shingle. She grabs her by the elbows and hoists her to her feet. Evidently the younger woman cannot reconcile her loss so easily.

'Three men, you say?' Jane swallows, afraid of the answer to her next question before she has even asked it. 'I wonder, have any women washed up at all?'

'What makes you ask that?'

The hairs on the backs of Jane's arms rise. She and Molly are caught in a moment of silence, both wondering how much they dare reveal to each other. 'No reason . . .'

'Not a woman, more of a girl.' The older woman looks out to sea.

'Oh . . .' Jane's heart sinks.

'Must have been the captain's daughter. No women on board a boat. Not honest ones, anyway.' Molly wraps her arms around her companion and half carries her towards the jetty.

The muscles in Jane's forehead stretch tight as she watches them go. She already knows that Eleanor is not an 'honest woman'. If she was on that ship, it is likely she and any other women, or girls, were there to entertain the sailors. But, despite the slurs against her character and Mr Skeete's protestations about there being no wrecks nearby, it is just possible Eleanor is telling the truth about swimming to shore.

'Is that proof enough of a wreck for you?' Mr Bridges edges gingerly over the pebbles, echoing Jane's thoughts.

'I dare say it is. Why do you think the Riding Officer lied to us?'

He spreads his arms wide. 'It's obvious, isn't it?'

Jane stares back at him. 'Is it?'

'He'll have been paid to keep quiet. Any boats sailing up and down the Swale in secret are likely to be involved in smuggling.'

The whisper of a memory lurks at the edge of Jane's consciousness. *No one sails this way in a storm. Not unless they're trying to escape paying their dues.* The smell of dried hops, a rising panic in her chest. An old man sitting before a fireplace with a pipe clenched between his teeth, the night her writing box almost made its way to the West Indies while she waited anxiously at the inn for her father and Neddy to retrieve it. *A cutter went down off the coast of Harty not five nights since.* 'Mr Bridges, is there a place called Harty along this stretch of coast?'

'Yes. It's on the Isle of Sheppey, just over the water. Look, you can see it from here.' He points across the estuary. On the other side, Jane can just make out a square tower rising above the trees. She has the answer. She has had the answer all along. The old man from the Bull and George inn at Dartford gave an eyewitness account of the disaster. But

Jane was not paying him any attention, and she did not think to connect it afterwards, because, as usual, she was too preoccupied with her own affairs. *Every one of those poor souls perished that night. All the crew drowned. Must have been twenty men at least, on board a ship like that. If the skipper had lived, he'd be up in front of a justice by now – with a noose around his neck.*

What if the old man was wrong and not everyone perished? Could Eleanor have been on board that ship, and somehow made it to shore, followed by its skipper, the vile Captain Fairbairn? It would be a blessed relief for the captain to prove a real villain and for Jane to abandon her suspicion that Neddy is behind the malicious notes. If so, Eleanor would know enough about the man's crimes to see him hanged – not only smuggling, but also the loss of every other soul on board due to his negligence. The knowledge would put Eleanor, and anyone harbouring her, in a hazardous position. Perhaps she constructed her alternative identity and is hiding at Godmersham Park because she does not want the captain to know she survived.

Except Fairbairn has found her anyway, and is calling for Mrs Knight to turn her out, so that he can silence her for good. He may even have tried to enter the mansion to reach her but was frightened away by Armand and his blunderbuss on the night the kitchen door was found swinging open. That the captain and Neddy use the same paper, and are both involved in Eleanor's past, seems too suspicious to ignore – but it *could* be an unfortunate coincidence. Fairbairn may be an independent mariner with ties to the area. Perhaps he commanded a vessel in the merchant fleet and bought the paper at the stationer's in Canterbury, which Neddy may also frequent. 'Mr Bridges, do you think, if a boat went down between here and Harty, it would be possible for someone to swim all the way to where we are standing?'

'It would take a superhuman amount of strength. But it's been known to happen.' Mr Bridges sways, catching himself before he stumbles.

Jane rushes to his aid. 'Are you quite well?'

'Give me a moment. I warned you my constitution could not withstand the sight of blood. Or putrefied corpses, as it turns out.' He retrieves a flask from his frock coat and takes a nip. 'Actually, I don't think that helped. Do you happen to have any smelling salts?'

'No, because I'm not an eighty-year-old dowager duchess and neither are you.' Jane peers at him. His face is ashen. 'Shall I fetch a physician?'

'No!' He launches himself bolt upright.

'Then take command of yourself. This is most unmanly.'

'Unmanly? I'm beginning to think my sister's right about you, Jane. You *are* trouble.'

'Then give me your arm and I shall return you to your nursemaid forthwith.'

'Don't you dare,' he says, latching onto Jane's elbow. 'A

man likes to encounter a little danger every once in a while. It makes one feel alive. Unlike that poor fellow, God rest his soul.'

'Hmm . . .' Jane struggles to maintain her own balance, as she leads Mr Bridges back to the Island Wall. Despite its unpleasantness, the expedition to Whitstable has proved most fruitful. She now knows why Eleanor lied: she was mortally afraid of Fairbairn discovering that she survived the shipwreck and is witness to his crimes. If Jane wants to move Eleanor on, all she has to do is persuade her it is safe to come forward with the truth of the disaster she witnessed at sea. Eleanor is not the only person able to testify against the captain. If Jane can trace the old man from the inn, he will corroborate her story. Now that she has evidence to suggest someone other than Neddy is sending the notes, her faith in her brother's ability to redeem himself is revived. And, with Mrs Knight's and Neddy's help, Jane is sure she can remove Eleanor to safety and see the captain served justice.

Chapter Eighteen

On the journey home, Jane mulls over her revised plan. Her first priority must be to find a way of contacting the old man from the Bull and George. Unfortunately, she did not speak to him directly or even catch his name. Their paths crossed only fleetingly as they shared a roof for one evening while travelling in opposite directions. However, Jane has reason to be sanguine as she has never known her mother let a piece of news, no matter how seemingly unrelated to the Austens' fortunes, pass her by. At her first opportunity, Jane will write to Mrs Austen, on the premise of wanting to relay all the details of their strange encounter with the old man to her Kent relations, and ask her to respond with a full report.

Once Jane has a way of tracing this second witness, she will tell Neddy he must use his authority as a magistrate to find the captain and press charges of unlawful killing against him, or she will reveal to the world what she knows of his liaison with Eleanor. Blackmail did not work for

Spooner, but Neddy can hardly shake Jane by the scruff, and it is ultimately in his interests to make it safe for Eleanor to move on. In the meantime, Jane must impress upon Mrs Knight the importance of improving the security of Godmersham Park and persuade Eleanor that Jane can be trusted with her secrets.

Jane does not share her deliberations with Mr Bridges, as this would entail betraying Mrs Knight's confidence and surrendering what little power she might wield over her brother. She senses that Mr Bridges is as reluctant to converse with her, owing to his concentrated efforts to regain command of his constitution, which makes for a gratifyingly peaceful ride home. Really, Jane has done Mr Bridges a huge favour by exposing him to his first corpse. He may have been right in his assertion that he was never intended for a career in the armed forces, but his disposition must be fortified if he is in earnest about entering a profession in which one of his core duties will be to shepherd his flock, body and soul, from one realm to the next. He slows the horse as they approach Rowling to find an unfamiliar chaise stationed in the drive. At the sight of it, Mr Bridges loses what little colour he has recovered. 'What the devil is he doing here?'

'Who?' Jane asks, but he alights and races for the house without pausing to help her down. He must have grown tired of all his gallantry and be eager to dispose of her. Once Roger has restored Jane to her feet, she follows Mr Bridges inside. Neddy stands at the entrance to his study with a deep crease in his forehead.

'What's happened? Why did you call for the doctor?' asks Mr Bridges. He must have recognized the conveyance. No wonder he made a dash for the door. Mr Bridges may have had some terribly sharp words to say about Elizabeth, but she is his sister and, after the way his mother died, he's bound to be fraught until both she and her baby are out of danger.

'It's Beth. She fainted.'

'Fainted?' repeats Mr Bridges.

'How so?' asks Jane.

'I don't know. One moment we were having a lively discussion –'

'You were arguing.' Jane recalls Elizabeth's fit of discomfort on the day she arrived. Was Elizabeth berating Neddy over Eleanor's continued presence at Godmersham Park, or has she discovered her husband's infidelities for herself? He is hardly discreet. For all Jane knows, Eleanor may not be the only harlot he is using behind his wife's back.

Neddy holds his hands aloft '– the next she was lying on the floor and I couldn't rouse her. I knew Dr Wilmot was expected at Goodnestone for Sir William, so I sent Roger to retrieve him immediately.'

Mr Bridges places a foot on the first stair. 'May I see her?'

'Not yet. Let the doctor work. Come and wait with me until he's gone. Jane, you go up.' Neddy claps Mr Bridges on the back, before drawing him into his study and closing the door.

Alone, Jane stares up at the elaborate staircase. It has never looked so imposing. Not for her a glass of port and a stilted conversation about the scarcity of game as she waits to hear Elizabeth's fate second-hand. Oh, no. This is the reason Jane came to Kent. If there are any unpleasant consequences from Elizabeth's fainting fit, it is Jane who must bear witness. With a heavy tread, she ascends the stairs to Neddy and Elizabeth's chamber on the first floor. The door is slightly ajar. She pauses as she reaches the landing – not deliberately eavesdropping, just too much of a coward to enter.

'Really, Mrs Austen. You *must* rest.' Dr Wilmot's voice is audible from within.

'But I have been resting, haven't I, Susan?' replies Elizabeth. She most certainly has not been resting, but neither of her maids would dare disagree with their mistress. Poor Kitty or Alice, to be placed in such a position.

'You will remember,' the doctor continues, 'I advised you very strongly, after your previous lying-in, that it would be prudent to recover your health before conceiving another child.'

'You try telling my husband.' Elizabeth laughs. An uncomfortable silence ensues as Dr Wilmot refrains from joining her. Damn Neddy, is there no end to his selfishness? Jane calculates there must have been just a few months between

Fanny's birth and Ted's conception, even less between Ted and Georgy. Her mother and father did a much better job of spacing their children, granting Mrs Austen leave to recover between each subsequent pregnancy. 'It's too late to regret that now. Are you certain my labour has not commenced?'

'I am. The distress you are experiencing is brought about by dropsy. But you must desist from exerting yourself or you really will bring on the baby before its time.'

'But the tightening, the pains. I feel just as I did in the hours before I birthed Georgy. Is it because there's some deficiency with the child?'

Jane's throat catches at the obvious distress in Elizabeth's tone. Is her sister-in-law's suffering the direct result of Neddy's infractions? If he has contracted some dreadful disease through his philandering, and passed it to Elizabeth and the baby, Jane will never forgive him.

Dr Wilmot sighs. 'As far as I can judge, the child is perfectly well developed, and I detect a very strong heartbeat.'

'With *me*, then?' Elizabeth's voice is on the point of cracking. Jane has never heard her so desperate.

'As I've already told you, you carry an excess of water around the baby. Perhaps it would be best if I were to drain some of it? I can insert an instrument to rupture the caul.'

'No! There's no need,' Elizabeth cries.

'But if you're uncomfortable?'

'No. I'll rest. I promise.'

Jane swings the door open, eager to save Elizabeth from

whatever instrument of torture Dr Wilmot keeps in his bag. 'I'm so sorry I wasn't here.'

'Ah, Jane.' Elizabeth is lying in bed, wearing a cap and nightgown. She reaches her arms out, grasping Jane's hands and using them to lever herself upright. 'You see, Doctor? I did follow your advice. My sister-in-law is here to assist me. I expect it's because she abandoned me today that I came over faint. I did ask her not to go.'

'But . . .' Jane opens her mouth to rebut this accusation by pointing out that, despite her best efforts, Elizabeth has not once left the children under her sole care while she rested. It was Elizabeth who originally sent Jane to Godmersham Park to watch Eleanor, and Elizabeth who expressly desired Jane to do her bidding in Whitstable (albeit, as a result of Jane's subtle manipulations, but she is not to know that). However, Elizabeth squeezes Jane's hands so tightly that she is reminded of the urgency of dispensing with the doctor's services.

'Miss Austen, I'd appeal to you to be more diligent in exercising your duties in future.' Dr Wilmot wipes a bloody scalpel with a rag and places it in his valise. Kitty stands next to him, holding a bowl of what Jane assumes is Elizabeth's blood. He must have bled her to ease the dropsy.

'Certainly, sir,' Jane replies, pressing Elizabeth's fingers in return as Kitty shows the doctor out. 'Why didn't you tell me you were unwell?' she asks, as soon as she and Elizabeth are alone. 'You know I'd be all too happy to take charge of the children. It's why I'm here.'

'I wasn't unwell.' Elizabeth withdraws her hands.

'Neddy said you fainted?'

'A trifling swoon, that's all. It would never have happened if he hadn't angered me so.'

'Why were you arguing?' Jane asks, fearing the answer.

'Because he refuses to demand his mother evicts that conniving little wretch. Why else? Honestly, Jane, you swore you'd help oust her, but all I see you doing is flirting with my brother. If Edward allows Mrs Knight to go on like this, my poor children will be swept aside for that hussy.'

'Beth, calm yourself. With a mother like you to defend their interests, your children will always be remembered.'

'And what if I'm not here to defend them?' Elizabeth's eyes are bright with terror at the prospect of being torn from her children.

Jane draws breath. She cannot argue away her sister-in-law's fears. There is good reason that it is customary for an expectant mother to prepare her last will and testament. 'Mrs Knight has already begun to suspect Eleanor is lying and I am confident she will be keen to move her on very soon.'

'Has she? Truly?'

Confident might be an exaggeration, but Jane is optimistic her plan will work. The old man was so furious about the negligence he had witnessed, she is sure he will be all too glad to testify against Captain Fairbairn. The only difficulty is locating them both. 'Yes. You mustn't make yourself ill over it.'

'I was probably just hungry. Did you get my oysters?'

'I did. Shall I fetch you a couple?' Jane plumps up the goose-down pillows behind Elizabeth. She may not be able to solve all of her sister-in-law's problems, but she must do whatever she can to make her comfortable.

'Make it half a dozen. And some of Neddy's French cheese on a slice of bread, if there's any left.'

'The stinking kind?'

'It usually turns my stomach – but I have the most peculiar craving for it at present.'

Jane nods. She's known pregnant women to have stranger fancies. She caught James's first wife, Anne, chewing a stick of chalk when she was weeks away from lying-in with their daughter, Anna.

Kitty sticks her nose around the door. 'If you please, ma'am, if it is the dropsy, you'll remember the midwife prescribed foxglove tea. Shall I brew some?'

Elizabeth slumps against her pillows. 'If you must but bring me a large glass of port to wash it down, will you? It tastes vile.'

Jane pats her hand. 'We'll set you right. Just rest and let me take care of everything.'

As soon as Elizabeth is easy, Jane will write to Steventon. She muses on how long it will take to receive a response from her mother. From her father's letters to Neddy, she knows that Mr and Mrs Austen have left Town and begun their journey back to Hampshire. Alas, they have not seen

Frank, who, in the true sailor way, was expected at Deptford but turned up in Madeira. It wasn't an entirely wasted journey as her parents met his friend, Captain Gore, and had the pleasure of seeing the *Triton* launched on her maiden voyage. She prays her mother is party to the old man's intended destination. Her initial relief that Neddy is not behind Fairbairn's notes is giving way to the disquiet of remembering a dangerous scoundrel is at large: a man so villainous he has disregarded bringing about the deaths of all under his care and is so determined to maintain his freedom that he has sworn to spill the blood of anyone found harbouring the witness to his crime. It is no wonder Eleanor is afeard for her life. Jane must find a way to warn Mrs Knight and gain Eleanor's trust before the captain makes another attempt to penetrate Godmersham Park.

Chapter Nineteen

etermined to give her sister-in-law some respite, Jane presses Elizabeth to spend the next day in bed while she constructs paper boats with her niece and nephews and sails them across the garden pond. Fanny, Ted and Georgy have a splendid time, and only Conker needs the occasional reprimand for his tendency to dive in and make off with the fleet. Afterwards, Kitty serves the children dinner in the nursery and Alice promises to give them a good scrub before their mother sees quite how much sport they have had.

Jane withdraws to her bedroom, finally composing her letter to her mother and afterwards labouring over *The Sisters*. Her composition is not progressing well and, with her last few sheets of precious paper, she produces nothing more valuable than kindling. No matter her intentions, the Misses Dashwood's correspondence bears the same dull woodcut of a pattern over and over again. Marianne, driven by her reckless sensibility, does something foolish.

The elder Miss Dashwood admonishes her, while keeping her own frustrated desires corked up inside. And still neither can admit what she is really feeling, or empathize with the other. Unless they can bear to expose their wounds, and give way to compassion, there will be no satisfactory finale.

Jane is even more irritated than usual, therefore, when a newly revived Elizabeth invades her private chamber to insist she change in and out of several gowns, curl her hair and borrow a pair of her best stockings. All of this finery to attend evensong at St Mary the Blessed Virgin, parish church of the listless hamlet of Crundale, near Godmersham.

'That's better. I'm positive he'll prefer you in that one.' Elizabeth rests one hand on her bump, appraising her work.

Jane stands rigid as Kitty pins her into the modest white frock. It takes all her self-control not to object to making herself attractive for Mr Blackall, especially now she knows the prime reason Elizabeth wants her to marry him is so that Henrietta cannot. 'Why are you so confident he has any preference for me, at all?'

'Must you be so tiresome? You're a tolerably smart young lady from a good family. Added to that, you asked pertinent questions about Mr Blackall's pursuits, and had the good breeding to sit quietly while he expounded upon them. You know that's all the encouragement a gentleman needs.'

Jane gawps at her, mortified that her wicked curiosity could be mistaken for romantic inclinations. This is the problem with never being allowed to speak her mind.

Anyone outside her inner circle would assume her interest is genuine, rather than a malicious attempt to encourage the many fools with whom she is forced to converse to hang themselves by their own rope. 'That can't be the case. If it was, I'd be betrothed to half of Hampshire by now.'

Elizabeth ushers her down the stairs to the entrance hall. 'As well you might be, if I was there to guide you.'

'But he was so disapproving of my taste in literature. Are you not afraid I repulsed him with my penchant for novels?'

'On the contrary, he'll be itching to correct you. If there's one thing a man enjoys even more than perfection, it's the opportunity to offer instruction.'

'But there must be so many young ladies whose tastes are more in sympathy with his.' Jane reaches for her pelisse, which is hanging on the row of hooks.

'None. You are very fortunate.' Elizabeth bats away Jane's arm and hands her one of her own Canterbury wool shawls. 'I truly believe he's perfect for you, in every way.'

'But I wouldn't want to tread on another's heels. Not if there's one who already has her heart set on claiming the honour of being Mrs Blackall.' Jane cannot resist making a final, veiled reference to Henrietta.

'Don't be ridiculous.' Elizabeth shoos her out of the front door and towards the waiting carriage as pique colours her cheeks. 'Make haste or you'll miss your chance altogether.'

In the drive, Neddy steps into the phaeton, grabbing the reins from Roger. 'Are you sure you won't come too, darling?'

'No, Ned.' Jane answers for Elizabeth, risking another lecture on the danger of intervening in her brother's marriage. She is too vexed at his lack of regard for his wife to heed Elizabeth's earlier reprimand. 'Dr Wilmot warned she must not exert herself.'

'I'm sorry, dear. But Jane's right. I must rest. And I've the children to supervise. You know how Ted misbehaves when I'm not here.' In the last couple of days, the bulk of the baby has migrated downwards, settling in Elizabeth's pelvis and forcing her to waddle. There are another three weeks before her confinement is expected, but Jane cannot imagine Elizabeth will be able to delay for so long. 'And without me present, Jane is likely to be the only lady in attendance – which will certainly show her off to her best advantage.'

Neddy grimaces, looking as enthusiastic to peddle his sister to Mr Blackall as Jane is to be peddled. 'As you wish, my dear.'

Roger hands Jane up into the phaeton, and Elizabeth waves cheerfully as they set off at a clip through the crisp summer evening. The sun recedes beyond streaks of pink clouds, taking its warmth with it, so that Jane is grateful for Elizabeth's shawl gathered around her shoulders as they speed through leafy lanes. Overhead, the trees are so full that the branches meet and form a tunnel of dappled light for the carriage to pass through. She eyes Neddy as he handles the reins. It is excruciating to be alone with him at such close quarters. Jane may have quashed her suspicion that he is the author of Fairbairn's malicious notes, but she cannot pardon him for his use of Eleanor. In the silence, she recalls his initial assertion, on their very first journey to Godmersham Park, that Eleanor would 'show herself to be a gold-digging tavern wench'. In retrospect, it is obvious his argument was founded on his prior knowledge of her.

Molly claimed the sailors aboard the captain's ill-fated ship were from the town of Whitstable. Jane is still convinced that Eleanor must also have ties to the town, and she has read enough lurid novels to hazard a guess as to how she came to be there. Eleanor would have arrived in England, young and fresh, looking for work in service. Her downfall will have been heralded by an innocuous-seeming fat woman, offering her small beer and an easier way to make a living. Once in the clutches of the procuress, Eleanor's innocence will have been eroded as she was passed from man to man. Eventually, she'll have contracted some terrible disease and been ejected from her bawdy house. At that point, she'll have been forced to walk the streets – until she found less salubrious employment in one of Whitstable's many taverns.

There she would have fallen in with Fairbairn's gang of devious smugglers and joined their expedition hoping for a rich reward across the Channel. France is a dangerous place but, as Jane's brothers have proved, with war comes opportunity. Even, or perhaps especially, for a woman adept at selling herself. When the ship capsized, Eleanor will have used all her might to swim ashore. Exhausted and frightened, she will have concocted her ruse to evade the captain. She was probably as astounded as anyone when the lascar confirmed her story, and first the Wilmots, then Mrs Knight took her in. Now she has worked her way into the widow's affections, she will be determined to remain within the walls of Godmersham Park. Far safer than falling back into the villainous Captain Fairbairn's clutches, or returning to a life of vice and dying alone of the pox in a sponging house. Jane knows she is giving way to 'effusions of fancy', as Mr Blackall would describe them, but she doubts her surmises will prove far removed from the truth.

One thing she knows for certain is that Neddy is party to Eleanor's real history, and she is determined to prise it out of him. 'Whitstable was very refreshing. Do you visit often?'

'Never.'

Is she imagining it, or is he purposely refusing to meet her eye? 'Not at all?'

'I have neither the time nor the inclination to do so. Why would I?'

'One or two of the taverns looked inviting.'

He snaps upright. 'Did Mr Bridges take you into one?'

'No!' Jane is outraged that Neddy should accuse Mr Bridges of behaving improperly when his own behaviour is in question.

'Good. I'm a liberal man, but you should know better

than to dine alone with a gentleman to whom you have no formal attachment.'

'I wondered if that's where you might recognize Eleanor from, if you sometimes go there to meet with your associates.'

'I've already told you, Jane. I do not recognize the girl and I do not associate with the kind of low company who frequent "taverns" in Whitstable.' He enunciates the word harshly, indignant at her insinuation, when Jane is sure Mr Spooner is exactly the type of low fellow to be found enjoying his liquor at an establishment along the high street.

If Neddy will not admit to knowing Eleanor, Jane will try panicking him with the prospect of the girl revealing their connection instead. 'I believe Mrs Knight is beginning to suspect her of lying. It will not be long before she reveals who she really is.'

He nods, already resigned to this outcome. Since the moment Mrs Knight took Eleanor in, he must have been preparing himself for their sordid connection to become known to her. But perhaps it is not too late to salvage their relationship. If Eleanor is cleaving to Mrs Knight because she is afraid, Neddy may redeem himself in part by helping to prosecute Captain Fairbairn. To save his fortune, he may even be amenable to helping Eleanor find a new place. 'Once it is safe for her to move on, you could offer her some money. So that she might start again somewhere where her past is not known and she might have the benefit of character.'

'I will do no such thing. If she has blackened her reputation, she has only herself to blame.' He leans back, spreading his legs wide. Jane swivels away to make sure they do not touch. She is so full of loathing for her brother's hypocrisy that she cannot bear to have any part of herself in communication with him.

'Just a couple of hundred pounds. You owe her that much at least.'

'I owe her nothing of the sort,' he says, voice terse. 'Even if I had the money to hand, I would not give it to her.'

Jane remembers his concern over meeting his repayments to Sir William. The money Elizabeth brought into their marriage is likely to be tied up in trusts, but, even so, his affairs cannot be so dire. 'Surely you can spare her something.'

'I really can't, Jane. And why should I reward her for her offences?'

'Because I imagine there was a time when her soul was as spotless as any other's. If she is a sinner, it is because others have embroiled her in their own misdeeds. Father always says, let him that is without sin cast the first stone. Wouldn't you agree?'

At this, Neddy has the good grace to colour. He raises his whip above the horses' hinds. The leather cracks as he vents his frustration on his team. 'She is not a heroine from one of your stories. I know you're fond of conjecture, but in the real world there are circumstances beyond your grasp.'

Jane turns her face to the dense hedgerow racing by, too full of contempt to gaze upon her brother. If he knew how close Mrs Knight was to signing away his anticipated riches, she doubts he would remain so uncharitable. That he will not spare the girl the means to begin her life afresh, even to remove a burden of his making from his mother, speaks to his indomitable selfishness.

By the time Jane and Neddy turn off the main road, and into a narrow lane leading to Crundale, the bells are ringing for evensong. It has not rained for more than a fortnight and the surrounding pasture is turning to straw, while brambles, dotted with dusty-white flowers and threaded with hemlock and red campion, crowd the path. As the carriage ambles towards the square tower of the Anglo-Saxon church, a haze of gnats plagues the horses. Desperate for relief, the mares swish their plaited tails and rear their blinkered heads. 'Is that Mrs Knight's coachman?' Jane asks, spotting the Swiss man, in his distinctive purple livery. He stands in the middle of the lane, lifting one hand above his head in greeting, exposing the blunderbuss tucked into his belt.

'Whoa now.' Neddy slows the horses. 'Yes, it is.'

'Why does he always carry his weapon? It's most disconcerting.' While Jane is pleased Mrs Knight is so well defended, she hopes the widow has chosen her protector wisely. It strikes Jane that if her brother is not behind the malicious notes, then one of Mrs Knight's household must be enabling Captain Fairbairn's access to the park. How else could a messenger sneak in and out of Godmersham undetected? And every one of the staff has good reason to resent Eleanor. Could the cook have left the kitchen door unbolted for the captain? What if Armand, instead of chasing away an intruder, was discovered in the act of escorting him inside?

'I'm afraid Armand has witnessed more than his fair share of troubles. He was a captain in the Swiss Guard and fought at the Tuileries.' The Swiss Guard were the last forces to remain loyal to King Louis XVI and Queen Marie Antoinette. The vast majority were eradicated in the vicious attack on the palace where the Royal Family were held captive. Mrs Knight's surly coachman is either an excellent soldier or a deserter. 'Is there a problem, Armand?' Neddy asks.

'I am here to prevent anyone taking the bend at speed and colliding with the carriage.' He gestures to the corner of the churchyard, where the rear of Mrs Knight's black coach extends from behind an ancient yew.

'Can you not drive on?' Neddy asks. 'You're blocking the lane.'

'*Non.* Madame is within.' Armand takes the reins from Neddy, offering no further explanation as to why his mother has driven all the way to evensong at St Mary's, only to remain outside in her coach. Jane and Neddy exchange a glance of equal bemusement before alighting. Another two footmen stand idle in the lane, their glossy shoes and white stockings incongruous against the dusty path. Both touch their hats. Without pausing to acknowledge them, Jane heads directly for the coach. The door is ajar and the low murmur of female voices drifts from inside.

'Please, dear,' says Mrs Knight. 'You must come inside the church with me. There's nothing to be afraid of.'

'I'm sorry, mistress, but I can't enter the Lord's house. Not yet,' Eleanor replies, in the same distinctive Irish brogue Jane heard her use while Mrs Knight was asleep.

Neddy places a hand on Jane's arm, preventing her from getting any closer. 'It sounds as if Mother has company.'

Jane cranes her ear to the vehicle. 'That's Eleanor. It's as I warned. Mrs Knight has discovered her ruse.'

Neddy takes a step backwards, removing his hat and wiping the sweat along his hairline with the back of his hand. 'Then I will not interfere.' Even Neddy does not have the audacity to greet his mother and his harlot at the same time. Jane has no such compunction. If the axe has fallen, she must know where the blow landed. 'Wait!' Neddy reaches for her elbow, but she has already hoisted herself onto the steps of the coach.

Inside, Mrs Knight faces away from the door. Her black silk skirts flood the carriage. 'You must accompany me inside. I will not abandon you, but it would be terribly rude of me to leave without acknowledging Mr Blackall and his congregation. The villagers will have recognized the coach and be anticipating my attendance. I expect we're holding up the service.'

On the opposite bench, Eleanor sits with her feet drawn up and her reed-thin arms wrapped around her shins. Today, she is unrecognizable as the jabbering princess or the wild creature hiding under sideboards. With her wavy hair pulled into a loose plait and pinned to the back of her head, she could be a farmer's daughter or a respectable young maid on her afternoon off. 'The next time, I promise.'

Jane pokes her head into the coach, 'Is all well?'

'Miss Austen?' Mrs Knight startles. 'What do you mean by sneaking up on us like that?'

'I do apologize for the intrusion, but the coach is blocking the lane. I came to see if I could be of any assistance.'

Mrs Knight presses a hand over Eleanor's. 'Don't upset yourself. I'll instruct Armand to restore us to Godmersham forthwith.' Eleanor sniffs into her skirts as Mrs Knight returns her attention to Jane. 'It's my fault entirely. I persuaded her to accompany me to evensong. I thought it would benefit her to say her prayers, but now we're here, I concede it's far too much. I shouldn't have pressed her before she was ready.'

Eleanor backs further into her seat. 'I can't confess. He'll smite me for what I've done.'

Mrs Knight squeezes Eleanor's hand. 'Oh, you poor child. Whatever it is you think you've done, I promise you the Lord *is* forgiveness.'

Jane senses an opportunity to gain Eleanor's confidence.

She may have surrendered her ridiculous claim to be a princess, but she appears too afraid to disclose the truth of her past in case of any repercussions from Captain Fairbairn. Jane glances at Neddy pacing the lane in distress. 'There's no need for you to have made a wasted journey. I can remain here with Eleanor, while you attend the service with Neddy.'

Mrs Knight brightens. 'Neddy's here?'

'Yes.' Jane bites her lip. If she can gain a private interview with Eleanor, she can reveal what she knows about the shipwreck and reassure her it is safe for her to come forward. Once Eleanor understands that she is not the only witness, her courage will be bolstered. And if he is wise, Neddy will use the time alone with his mother to make a confession of his own. 'I'm confident he'd be only too happy to escort you inside. He's been most forlorn at the lack of your company.'

'What do you think of that, dear? Would that be tolerable? You know Miss Austen. You're safe with her.'

Eleanor peers over her knees, pressing her lips together as she nods. Jane jumps off the steps, clearing the way for Mrs Knight to descend.

'What's occurring?' asks Neddy, voice clipped with impatience.

'It's all resolved.' Jane glares back at him. 'You're to escort your mother inside to evensong and redeem yourself in the eyes of the Lord, while I wait here with Eleanor.'

'Make haste, Ned. I've inconvenienced Mr Blackall long

enough.' Mrs Knight tucks her hand into the crook of her son's arm, pulling him towards the arched doorway.

'Perfect,' Jane calls after them. 'With a bit of luck, we'll be able to hear the music from here, and the singing, if not Mr Blackall's sermon.'

Jane waits until Neddy and Mrs Knight are through the studded oak door of the church before climbing inside the coach. She shuts the window, acutely aware of Armand lingering nearby. The two footmen followed their mistress to evensong, but the coachman remains in the lane – ostensibly to guard the carriage. If there is even the slightest chance that he could be acting on behalf of Captain Fairbairn, Jane cannot risk him overhearing her conversation. Once sealed inside, the smell of freshly buffed leather is overpowering. She squeezes onto the bench beside Eleanor, rather than taking the seat opposite, before passing her a handkerchief from her reticule. The girl takes it eagerly, blowing her nose and wiping the tracks from her cheeks. She wears no gloves, and the cuticle around each of her fingernails is bitten to the quick.

The bells cease clanging, and an organ strikes up. A pathetic choir attempts to make its musical offering heard above the pipes. Overhead, a murmuration of starlings hovers, a cloud of black, twisting and turning across the dusky pink sky. Jane takes a deep breath to steady herself. She must get this right. She cannot have Eleanor thinking she is rounding on her, sending her clamouring to hide behind her lies or bringing on another hysterical fit. 'Thank you for letting me bide with you, Eleanor,' she begins, voice low and shaky. 'I was hoping to speak to you alone as, although we haven't been acquainted for long, I want you to know that you can trust me.'

Eleanor drops her feet into the footwell. 'It's Agnes,' she whispers.

Jane falters. Will it really prove so easy to be taken into the girl's confidence? 'Agnes? That is your real name, not Eleanor?'

Agnes fixes Jane with her mournful stare. Her eyes are red-rimmed, causing the glassy irises to border on the colour of dried blood. 'Please don't think I was lying to you, miss. I was Eleanor then.'

Jane's shoulders drop. She thought the girl was about to make a full confession, yet here is more sport. 'Are you saying you changed your name?'

'No. I *was* Eleanor. She's untouchable, the princess. Nobody would dare harm her. But today I find I'm Agnes again.' A look of abject misery crosses her features, as if she is as confounded as everyone else to discover she is not a kidnapped princess, but rather a penniless, destitute and friendless young woman.

'I don't understand,' says Jane.

'Do you really not?'

'No. How could I?'

'Oh.' Agnes slumps forward, burying her face in her lap. 'I so hoped you might.'

Jane raises her hand to pat Agnes's shoulder, but her fingers recoil. Peeking from the scooped back of the girl's dress is a mass of angry red and silver scars. The raised lines all follow the same direction, overlaying each other like a wheatsheaf of wounds. Agnes has been flogged to within an inch of her life. Some of the injuries are recent, for in parts her skin has only just begun to heal. This must have been the obvious sign of mistreatment that stirred Mrs Wilmot to take pity on her.

After the ringleaders of the Oxfordshire militia mutiny were shot, Henry told Jane that any soldiers found guilty of participating in the uprising were handed down sentences ranging from three hundred to fifteen hundred lashes. She thought he was exaggerating, that it would be impossible to survive such a punishment. Now she fears she has seen living proof of the body's ability to withstand such barbarity. What kind of monster could inflict such savagery on another being? Was it the villainous Captain Fairbairn? Is this how a young woman is made compliant in her own debauchery? Does Mrs Knight know? She must: such an injury would be impossible to hide. And Neddy? No. Jane's brother may be as susceptible as any other man to vice, but she cannot believe him capable of violence. There is no way Neddy could inflict, or even condone, such brutality.

Her fingers hover an inch from the tangle of welts. 'Oh, Agnes. How could *I* possibly begin to understand?'

Agnes takes a shuddering breath, turning to face her. 'Because you are Jane . . . But sometimes you are Marianne. And at other times, you are Miss Dashwood.'

'Yes,' Jane murmurs, her hand still poised over Agnes's wounds. She wants, so desperately, to comfort her. Agnes's life must have been wretched indeed. Who could blame her for concocting such an outrageous story to escape her suffering?

'And they're all different . . .' Agnes's eyes shine directly into Jane's. She reminds Jane of her father in the school-room, when he is waiting for her to comprehend something so very obvious, yet Jane's mind cannot grasp it.

'Yes. Yes, they are . . .' Jane places her hand in her lap. Touch will not comfort a woman who has been so violently assaulted. 'But I'm not really Marianne or Miss Dashwood. Am I?'

'You're not?' The light fades from Agnes's eyes.

'No, I'm just playing a part. Reading their letters aloud, pretending to be them. They're characters of my own inven-tion. It helps, you see. When I'm feeling oppressed and I need an escape, I compose stories and fill them with all sorts of people. But they're not real.'

'Are you certain? None of them?'

'No. How could they be?' Jane asks, but even as she says it an unsettling feeling washes over her. During Jane's periods

of extreme dejection, her characters are more vital than any
of the friends and family who populate her daily life.

'Oh.' Agnes lowers her eyes to the floor of the carriage,
lips trembling.

She looks so crestfallen that Jane almost wishes she had
lied – pretended the letters were a set of correspondence
between actual sisters that she had stumbled across. If thinking the letters were real gave Agnes comfort, what would be
the harm? Tentatively, she reaches for Agnes's hand. 'Isn't that
what you were doing? Pretending to be someone else, so that
you could escape those who might hurt you?'

'No.' Agnes withdraws her fingers, pivoting her frame
towards the window. 'Never mind, forget what I said. It
doesn't matter.'

Jane leans against the padded seat, squeezing her eyes
closed. For the briefest of moments, Agnes was an open
book, ready and willing to have her pages riffled through.
Now she is shut tight again – an enigma locked inside a
leather-bound case. Through the glass, the starlings continue to swarm. An amorphous shadow, pushing and pulling
against each other, switching the direction of their forma-
tion before they are gathered.

In desperation, Jane resorts to directness. 'Look, Eleanor.
Agnes. I know exactly what occurred the night of the storm,
and why you're so determined to hide who you really are.'

'You do?' Agnes's eyes stretch wide.

'Yes. I know you're telling the truth about swimming to

shore after the ship sank. And I'm not the only one. There
was a witness. An old man was watching from the coast of
Harty and he will testify to what happened.'

'Oh . . . that.'

'And I really think, given how charitable Mrs Knight is,
if you are honest about why you lied, she'll help you find a
way out. We all will.'

Agnes stares mutely at Jane, as if met with a stream of her
own senseless babble. 'But how could there ever be a way
out from what I did? From what I am?'

'Well, our first priority would be to ensure it is safe for
you to move on. And believe me, Agnes, Mrs Knight would
never dream of parting with you until she is assured of your
safety. But once justice has been served to anyone who might
threaten you, we could give you some money. You could
leave your past behind and start a new life.' Jane calculates
how much a woman like Agnes might need to begin afresh.
Neddy scoffed at her request for two hundred pounds, but
he does not yet know how much more he stands to lose.

'But where would I go?'

This is more like it: they are entering negotiations. Jane
knows there are places where penitent prostitutes are tolerated, if not welcomed. She could ask James for the details.
A Magdalene House is just the type of joyless enterprise he
would subscribe to. On second thoughts, perhaps returning to her people might be best. 'Have you any family who
might take you in? In Ireland, say?'

Agnes's bottom lip trembles. 'I can't. My mammy said I had to go with him. He gave her money to take me away.'

'Your *mother* sold you into this life?' Jane has read of women betrayed by the very people meant to protect them, but she had hoped such unnatural behaviour was confined to the most salacious novels.

'She had to. We were half starved, with nowhere to go.' Agnes leans her forehead against the window. Her breath steams the glass, and she traces her fingertip lightly over the mist. 'We could barely make the rent for the farm when my father was alive. After he died, our debts were the only things that grew. The landlord sent his middleman to turn us out. In his temper, he broke everything Mammy had not sold so we gave up the cottage and walked to the harbour. At times, we had to carry all three of my younger sisters between us, and it rained so hard my brother took a chill to his chest. But Mammy said if we could find the strength to keep going, she would get work or a place for my brother on one of the tall ships going to America. Only, when we finally made it, there wasn't work for all the men waiting. No one would give a place to a sickly, scrawny boy. Then, the man on the smaller ship, he offered her money to take me.'

'Oh, good Lord . . .' Jane chokes on the words.

'It was enough for food and shelter, and medicine for my brother so I told Mammy not to cry, that I would be brave and bear it for the sake of the other childer. But I couldn't, not any more.'

A FORTUNE MOST FATAL

Jane presses herself into the seat, involuntarily sliding along the bench towards the opposite door – away from Agnes and her pain. 'I'm so sorry, Agnes. I had no idea. How old were you?'

'Nine,' Agnes whispers, in her sing-song voice.

'Nine? But that's unconscionable.' Jane recalls Molly's words about the only female victim of the shipwreck found washed up along the shore: *Not a woman, more of a girl.* By law, the age of consent is set at twelve, but no decent man would consider a twelve-year-old to be a woman. Is it possible she was forced onto that boat to be used by the sailors, just like Agnes? And now the poor child is dead, slain by the captain's negligence. Jane's throat closes, smothering her words. All her life, she has believed – no, she has been told – that a fallen woman has brought about her own condition by some weakness in her moral fibre. But at no point in her story was Agnes or her companion on that ship given the opportunity to be the author of her own fate. Agnes no more chose to be a prostitute than Jane chose to be a clergyman's daughter. 'But you mustn't despair. There are places you can go, where Mrs Knight can help locate you, out of Captain Fairbairn's clu—'

Agnes whips round, grabbing Jane by her upper arms. 'How do you know about the captain? Has he made himself known to you?'

'He's been sending Mrs Knight nasty letters. You know this. You were there when the last one arrived.' Jane squirms to free herself, but the girl's vice-like fingers dig deep into her flesh. 'Ouch. Agnes, you're hurting me.'

'But have you seen him? You must not get in his way if you do. He will smother anyone who stands between us.' Beneath her freckles, all blood has drained from Agnes's countenance. 'What letter do you speak of?'

'The note that arrived the first time we met, while you were pretending to be a princess?' There is not the tiniest spark of recognition in the girl's panic-stricken face with regard to the letters, but she is clearly terrified of the captain.

'I told you, that wasn't me. It was Eleanor.'

The hair on the back of Jane's neck rises. Agnes's mind must be as damaged as her body if she cannot remember the events of only a few days ago. 'Then another came, while you were hiding under the sideboard, crawling around on all fours like a trapped animal?'

'That sounds like Nessa.' Agnes closes her eyes, shaking her head. 'You mustn't mind her, she's only playing. She'll have known you didn't mean any harm. She wouldn't dare be so bold if you were a real threat.'

'Nessa? Agnes, this is ridiculous.'

'I know it must sound that way, but the others ... they don't always talk to me. I try to remember, and I try to keep them out. But they force their way in ...' Agnes withdraws her hands, rubbing at her temples. 'There are so many of us, and all the time we're fighting for possession. Sometimes I wake, and hours, days have gone by without me. I don't know where I am, or how I got there. And I cannot stop them. Try as I might, I cannot stop them.'

'Please, Agnes, slow down and try to explain.'

'You won't understand. I hoped you would, but you don't.'

Although Jane cannot yet articulate her thoughts, deep within her breast a kinship stirs. When faced with a reality she cannot bear, Agnes finds solace in becoming someone other than herself. But, unlike Jane, she is able to will herself into such a state that she leaves behind the person she was before. 'I may not comprehend you fully, but I can try. I want to help you, Agnes. Sincerely, I do.'

'Just promise you won't let the captain take me.' Agnes grabs Jane's hands, squeezing her fingers. Jane can taste her fear as the peppery scent of fresh perspiration fills the carriage. Agnes's story might be fraught with lies and make-believe, but her terror is genuine. 'He'll make me go back there, and I can't. I can't let them stab me any more.'

'Stab you?' Jane asks, thinking of the welts on Agnes's back. Has Captain Fairbairn tortured her with a blade, too?

'With their swords. The ones they keep hidden, beneath their breeches.'

Jane is assaulted by the urge to fling the door wide, leap out of the coach and run as fast as her feet can take her from this wretched tale. Failing that, she will tear her fingers from Agnes's grip and clamp them over her own ears to block out the girl's words. But having encouraged Agnes to share her suffering, the least Jane can do is bear witness to it.

'Who?' she asks, terrified that Agnes will name Neddy. He has already admitted to using her, but hearing from Agnes that her brother has taken her against her will would be even worse. Surely he cannot be so depraved. Jane will not believe him so wicked. 'Who is doing this to you, Agnes? You can trust me, I swear.'

'I don't know who they are.'

'The men on the ship?'

'Men on the ship, men on land. I try not to look at their faces or hear their names. I try not to be there at all.'

'And money is exchanged?'

'Sometimes.' Agnes nods miserably. 'At others, I am given to earn favours, or to distract the revenue officers. But I'd rather die than go on like that. I tried to die. I never meant anyone else to be hurt. All I wanted was for it to end. Promise you won't let the captain take me back there. Anything but that.'

'I promise,' Jane hears herself say. It is as if she were outside the carriage, a spectator to the scene. Agnes breaks down in sobs, her body heaving. Jane wraps an arm around her, tentatively pulling the girl into her lap and smoothing a hand over Agnes's hair as she wonders what she has committed herself to.

Jane was meant to find a way to move the girl on – but Agnes, with her fractured mind, is far too vulnerable for Mrs Knight to turn out of doors, even with money of her own. What if protecting Agnes from Fairbairn means

denouncing Neddy as a scoundrel? If Jane reveals everything she knows about Agnes's past to Mrs Knight, she
risks exposing her brother in the process. For the captain to
be prosecuted for the full extent of his crimes, Agnes must
be interrogated and give up her abusers – if she can identify
them. Could Jane really destroy the Austens' good name,
and their best chance of financial security? Elizabeth would
be devastated and Jane's parents horrified. No one likes a
tattle-tale – Jane would likely be ostracized for ever, with no
way of supporting herself. But how else can she, one lone
young woman, conceive of keeping another safe from the
leader of a gang of villainous smugglers? As impossible as
it seems, Jane knows she will find a way to save Agnes from
the vile captain. A promise, once extracted, *must* be kept. If
nothing else, Jane is a woman of her word.

5. *Letter to Cassandra Austen*
> *Rowling Farm, Sunday, 25 June 1797*

My dearest Cassandra,

*Our formidable cousin, the Comtesse de Feuillide, once
told me there is only so far a woman can bend before
she breaks. But what if, when pushed past the breaking
point of any ordinary female, some women shatter? And
these separate shards, splintered and slivered as they are,
find a way to persevere? Might the good Lord, in His
infinite kindness, grant peace through a cauterization of*

the mind? Enough of your silence – I cannot do without you. Gather your wounded parts, my beloved sister. Mrs Knight's house guest is more troubled than she is trouble. I have pledged to assist her, but what can I, one poor and powerless young lady against the world, do?

Yours ever,

J.A.

P.S. Purloin some of James's paper, if you must. Just think, with every sheet, you'll be saving his friends and family from the expense of his self-indulgent scribble. If you have no compassion for your own correspondents, will you not think of your brother's?

Miss Austen
Rev. Mr Austen's
Deane
Hants

Chapter Twenty

'I cannot comprehend what you are telling me.' Elizabeth places her cup in its saucer. 'If the girl, Eleanor, Agnes or whatever we are supposed to call her, has admitted she lied to elicit sympathy and accepted your mother's hospitality under false pretences, why have you not charged her with deception?'

As Elizabeth was asleep by the time Jane and Neddy returned from Crundale, Neddy has been relaying the events of the previous evening to his wife over breakfast. At some point during the service, probably amid Mr Blackall's lengthy sermon, Mrs Knight had confided to Neddy that Agnes had confessed to being nothing more exotic than a destitute Irishwoman. Elizabeth is responding to the news with all her usual sweetness of temper. 'You're the magistrate. It's your duty to ensure justice is served. She's owned to being a vagrant. She should be locked in a pillory and flogged in front of the entire parish.'

Neddy pours himself more coffee. The dark circles beneath

his eyes indicate his night was as devoid of sleep as Jane's. Judging by how cordial he and Mrs Knight were when they left the service, Jane does not believe he confessed to any involvement with Agnes's past. 'It's also my duty to comply with Mother's wishes, and she has no wish to see the girl punished.'

'She's a vagrant. Why is your mother condoning her crimes?'

'Mrs Knight simply wishes to be charitable,' says Jane. Although she does not yet know how charitable, she is confident Mrs Knight will have revised her plan to transfer her fortune to Agnes. While she may wish to continue supporting the girl, it is clear Agnes is not capable of bearing the responsibility of being a wealthy landowner. Her affliction would leave her vulnerable to exactly the kind of trickster Jane once thought her to be. 'Providing Agnes with a refuge is her way of paying alms.'

'But for how long does she intend to keep her?' asks Elizabeth.

Jane has no answer for this. It is tempting to reveal the reason Mrs Knight cannot release Agnes is that she is being threatened by a vicious scoundrel, and that if Neddy would only use his powers as justice of the peace to locate and prosecute Captain Fairbairn, he would clear the way for her to depart. But even if Neddy agreed to help, Agnes is in no fit state to testify. Jane may take her word for the abuse she suffered at the captain's command, but she doubts Agnes's performance would be enough to satisfy a judge and a jury. Rape is a capital crime and men have been known to hang for it. When Frank was serving as a midshipman on the *Perseverance*, one of the men was found guilty of raping another's child aboard the ship and sentenced to death. But in Agnes's case, so much time has passed since her initial abduction, it would be impossible to prove. Her fragile state would make her testimony all too easy for the defence to pick apart. And, with no guarantee of victory, a trial would be a terrible ordeal that would most likely exacerbate her confusion.

The captain would stand a far better chance of being served justice if Jane could bring forth another to corroborate her story about the shipwreck. Unfortunately, Mrs Austen is yet to reply to her letter and Jane is growing so anxious she has even contemplated writing to the innkeeper. Alas, she fears her witness will prove to be one of many grey-bearded, pipe-smoking old men who like to sit by the fire and spout what sounds suspiciously like nonsense.

'For as long as that girl is tolerated at Godmersham Park, she remains a threat,' Elizabeth continues, fixing her husband with an icy glare. 'I will not be able to rest until your mother dismisses her entirely.'

Jane's sister-in-law speaks more truth than she realizes. Agnes attracts danger. The captain is a ruthless, violent man and, by his own admission, he will stop at nothing to silence her. He has already tried to enter Godmersham Park, and

Jane fears he has an accomplice, possibly in the shape of the cook or even Armand, who will allow him entry whenever he is ready to strike again. She can only hope Mrs Knight's increased security measures are enough to prevent him from gaining admittance. She remembers Agnes's warning: *He will smother anyone who stands between us.* By continuing to harbour the girl, Mrs Knight is placing herself and her household in peril. Jane must find a way to warn her that Fairbairn's threats should be taken in earnest.

Without saying a word, Neddy scrapes his chair from the table. He tears his napkin from his collar and throws it onto his unfinished breakfast, sending egg yolk splattering across the white linen.

'Where are you going?' asks Elizabeth.

'Out.'

'Don't think of disappearing, not today. You're to escort Jane on a picnic.'

'A picnic?' Neddy's neck flushes red.

'Yes. Remember how taken she was with the remains of St Augustine's Abbey on Sir Edward Hale's estate? I've persuaded Lady Hale to grant her permission to enjoy a closer viewing.'

'You have?' Jane pictures the tumbledown ruin she spotted on the way from Canterbury. She had described it to Elizabeth in order to provoke some compassion for the sisters lodging at Briar Farm, doing her utmost to make their destitution sound like a romantic tragedy. It was kind of

Elizabeth to follow up on her throwaway remark. Almost suspiciously so.

'Can't that wait?' asks Neddy. 'I've important matters to attend to.'

'This is an important matter. Jane's time with us is coming to an end, and she's made no progress at all in securing her future.' In all the commotion, Elizabeth did not appear to have noticed that her plan to thrust Jane and Mr Blackall together was thwarted. But now Jane's indomitable sister-in-law pulls an ace from her sleeve. 'Lady Hale's former housekeeper, Mrs Roche, has volunteered to give you a guided tour of the site at noon. More to the point, Mr Blackall and Dr Storer have both confirmed their attendance.'

'Have they, indeed?' Jane crosses her arms tight over her chest, but she does not object. While she has no desire to see Mr Blackall again, she is willing to give Dr Storer a chance to redeem himself as a physician if not a suitor. Given the doctor claimed to have encountered Agnes's condition before, he may know of a medical precedent for treating it. If anything can be done to ease Agnes's torment and make her a more credible witness, it would be remiss of Jane not to solicit his advice. Can the girl really be so frightened that she constructed Princess Eleanor, and then, for a time, convinced herself she was really her? Jane is incredulous. And, yet, who better than Jane to understand? She, who longs to wear another's cloak so that she can say and do the things in her stories that she could never allow herself to do in real life.

But even Jane does not give herself to her characters entirely. She holds them at the sharpest point of her pen. Maybe that is why *The Sisters* remain a pair of card cut-outs, rather than lifelike portraits. What would happen if Jane were to allow herself to delve inside the mind and heart of Miss Dashwood, evoking all her innermost thoughts and feelings? Could she, *should* she, do such a thing? She may very well risk her equilibrium in recording the torment of her own grim fortitude in Miss Dashwood; even worse, by confronting the extent of her fears for Cassandra's sanity through Marianne's determined path to self-destruction. But, then, giving herself fully to her work might just be the saving of her wits. She dismisses the terrifying thought, returning her attention to her sister-in-law. 'Would you like me to flirt with both gentlemen at once or by turns?'

Elizabeth chews her toast thoughtfully, one hand holding the bread, while the other flicks crumbs from her swollen belly. 'I do believe you're finally catching on. There's nothing like a little competition to strengthen a man's desire.'

Neddy sighs, still lingering on the threshold. 'Then you'll have to accompany her, since it was you who made the arrangements.'

'Don't be a blockhead, Ned.' Jane's patience with her oafish brother is stretched so thin it's becoming brittle.

'She's about to be brought to bed. Whatever business you have can wait.'

'I'm afraid Jane's right.' Elizabeth takes a sip of tea, dabbing her lips with a napkin. 'It would be inadvisable for me to wander so far from home at this late stage. And when we were filling the hamper, Cook and I noticed the larder is in a terrible state. If we don't clear it out soon, it'll be infested with mice come winter. We're going to take everything off the shelves and give it a good scrub.'

Neddy glowers at the pair of them, 'Surely that's the kitchen girl's job.'

'Indeed, but it's imperative I'm there to supervise. You know the servants can never be trusted if left to their own devices. I want everything spick and span before the new baby arrives.'

A cold drip of dread runs down Jane's spine. She's witnessed this urgent need to put the world to rights before. James's late wife, Anne, insisted he replace all the curtain rails and re-thatch the poultry house immediately before her pains began. Elizabeth is nesting. Which means, very soon, she'll be lying-in. There may be another three weeks before the baby was anticipated but, at any moment now, Elizabeth's labour will commence and Jane will be called upon to assist. If only Cassandra would respond to her letters asking what she should do. But Mary writes that, although Cassandra now allows herself to be laced into a house gown each morning and joins the family in the parlour for their meals, she barely touches her food and remains entirely mute. All this despite Mary's best efforts to tempt her appetite with such irresistible delicacies as ox cheek and cold souse. Jane even wishes her mother was there to bark instructions in her impatient tone. Assistant midwife is not a role Jane was ever intended for. How is she to bear it?

'There was a light shower earlier, but now it looks to remain fine.' Elizabeth stares pointedly out of the window. 'I've instructed Susan to wrap the children up for the carriage ride and to pack a change of clothes in case of any accidents.'

Neddy's ire looks set to explode. 'We're taking the children?'

'It's a picnic. Of course you're taking the children.' Elizabeth's forbearance sounds just as fragile. 'They wouldn't want to miss it.'

'I'll manage them, Ned,' Jane volunteers. She can cling to her niece and nephews as a shield against Mr Blackall's instruction, but she fears she may need to find a more compelling distraction for the clergyman if she's to consult Dr Storer on the delicate matter of Agnes's condition.

'Thank you, Jane. And Conker. Don't forget to take the dog, will you?'

'Why should we take the dog? We're not going shooting,' Neddy replies.

'Well, neither am I!' Elizabeth retorts.

Neddy harrumphs as he resigns himself to his fate. 'I'll go and ready the carriage.'

Elizabeth rubs her belly, and gives a satisfied sigh, and Jane realizes that, rather than being solely for the purpose of marrying her off, the picnic is an elaborate ploy to get everyone out from under her feet. The poor woman is subject to the demands of her rowdy family day and night. Since Jane arrived, Elizabeth has not enjoyed so much as five minutes of peace. With her very real concern over her children's fortunes, added to her apprehension of her own impending trial, it is understandable she should wish to banish the lot of them. In her current state, Elizabeth is clearly not a woman to be trifled with. But, happily, neither is Jane. Before she finishes her breakfast, she tears a page from her pocketbook and scrawls a note to Mr Bridges instructing him to convey Henrietta to the ruined abbey for a serendipitous encounter with her sweetheart, bribing a groom to deliver it to Goodnestone forthwith. Hopefully, Henrietta is as artful as her sister and will command all of Mr Blackall's attention. A terrible picture of herself imprisoned in Crundale Parsonage, surrounded by earthenware tankards in the shape of little men as well as her and Mr Blackall's big-boned children, flashes through Jane's mind. She gives a shudder and washes away the horrifying image with a gulp of sweetened tea. Now, *that* really would be enough to drive her insane.

Chapter Twenty-one

'And this is Ethelbert's Tower, where the heretics who refused to swear allegiance to King Henry the Eighth were burned alive!' Mrs Roche, a silver-haired crone with a knowing glint in her eye, grins as she waits for her audience to react. Neddy, Henrietta, Mr Blackall and even Dr Storer all contort their features into suitable expressions of horror, while little Fanny and Ted shriek and dissolve into giggles. When Jane had formulated her plan to consult Dr Storer discreetly on Agnes's condition, under the guise of acquiescing to Elizabeth's demand she spend time in his and Mr Blackall's company, she had not reckoned on receiving such lively instruction from Lady Hale's former housekeeper. Mrs Roche's tour of St Augustine's Abbey is protracted and Jane is dubious of its veracity. For one thing, there is not a single scorch mark on the yellow stone of the ruined tower. She is beginning to realize Mr Bridges' decision to sit out the faux-history lesson, in favour of sketching the ruins from afar, was a judicious one.

Henrietta runs a gloved hand over the crumbling stone. 'I expect it's haunted.' All that is left of the once magnificent Norman church is a rugged square tower tufted in red valerian, and a portion of its nave. Through the empty arched window, the finer and far better-preserved tower of Canterbury Cathedral stares mockingly.

'Must you encourage her?' replies Jane. It has finally rained and her feet sink into the damp grass as she carries the weight of not-so-little Georgy on her hip. The child must have doubled in size since she arrived.

'Oh, yes,' Mrs Roche replies. 'Even the dragoons are too afraid to walk this way after dark.' Far from lying in romantic seclusion, the abbey perches beside a busy route linking Canterbury and Sir Edward Hale's new barracks to the east, and a constant stream of vehicles rattles past. 'For no sooner than darkness has crept over the fields, the monks return. In the quiet, their disembodied voices can be heard, still chanting vespers centuries after their slaughter. But, just lately, a new and even more terrifying apparition has begun to haunt the abbey. We call her "the bloody nun", for she wanders the ruins at dusk, dressed in a white habit with a mass of blood and gore oozing from a terrible gash on her forehead.'

Georgy bursts into desperate wails. Jane shifts him onto her opposite hip, holding him tight and attempting to hush him into quiet sobs. 'Why would a nun haunt this place? I thought it was a monastery, not a convent.'

'It was,' says Mrs Roche. 'Every one of the brothers went up in flames. There wasn't a soul spared among their ancient order to tell the tale. Now, if you'll let me take you to the cursed well ...'

While the rest of the party rushes to follow, Neddy lingers with Jane and the children. She senses he is not nearly as engrossed in Mrs Roche's far-fetched stories as the others. Something is troubling him. She wonders if it is simply the business he intended to manage today, or his wider conscience. 'You don't believe this codswallop either, do you? She lifted that part about the "bloody nun" straight from *The Monk*.'

'Which monk?' replies Neddy, brow furrowed. 'She just said there weren't any left.'

'*The Monk*. It's a novel. Haven't you read it?'

'No.'

'Well, you must. Everyone else has.' Once again Jane is reminded of how disparate Neddy's pleasures are from those of the rest of their family. Even James had read *The Monk*, if only to discover what had so scandalized Mary. Perhaps if Neddy had remained in Steventon, with only books to amuse him, he would not have wandered so far from the path of virtue.

'Why? Is it good?' Neddy pauses at the edge of the party, waiting for Jane to catch up.

'No, it's atrocious – but that's not the point.'

'Then what is the point?'

'You can't enjoy scorning something so thoroughly unless you've read it yourself.' Jane moves into the small patch of shade cast by the ruin's remaining wall. Georgy squirms and reaches for his errant siblings, but Jane is too wary of the sharp flint foundations that Fanny and Teddy are clambering over to let the toddler join them.

'It's far from codswallop, miss.' Mrs Roche turns, her hearing evidently much sharper than Jane had anticipated. 'The bloody nun has been witnessed by several travellers late at night. The innkeeper, across the way, is compiling a record. You can enquire of him if you don't believe me.'

Jane halts. 'I meant no offence.'

'This I can verify.' Mr Blackall nods solemnly. 'I interviewed the man myself – for my treatise on supernatural occurrences at sites of historical import.'

'How chilling.' Henrietta slips her arm into Mr Blackall's, eyes shining. Far from being chilled, Henrietta's giddy expression suggests she is thoroughly titillated by the housekeeper's histrionic performance. Away from Elizabeth, Henrietta is much more animated and she really does seem partial to Mr Blackall. With such a wealthy family, there cannot be any imperative for Henrietta to marry. Unless, like Jane, she is at risk of suffocating under the notice of her rich relations.

Mr Blackall places his hand over Henrietta's. 'Yes, but I have faith the Lord will protect those who do His work.'

'God bless you, sir.' Mrs Roche crosses herself. 'Your very presence will keep the evil spirits in check.'

'Why do you presume the spirits guilty of any malicious intent?' asks Jane. 'It was their abbey. Surely, they have every right to haunt it. If they were Benedictine monks, they'd be more likely to offer you a jug of ale and a bed for the night than do you any harm.' All of the party groans. Really, Jane cannot understand why everyone, apart from herself, is accepting Mrs Roche's assertions unquestioningly. Even Dr Storer, who is meant to be a man of science, is lapping them up. And now they are all frowning at Jane, as if her constant interruptions are akin to throwing rotten vegetables at the players on stage at the Theatre Royal. 'Forgive me, I'm sure you know more than I,' she mutters, through gritted teeth.

Mollified, the housekeeper walks on, leading Dr Storer, Mr Blackall and Henrietta to the open well – where, no doubt, the skulls of several brothers can be spotted whenever the water dries up. Jane remains with Neddy and the children. 'You know she's fabricating all this to inflate her tip. The innkeeper will be colluding with her. An apparition will be good for business.'

'Don't be such a killjoy, Jane,' Neddy replies. 'What does it matter if her stories are true or not, as long as everyone is enjoying them? Even the children are entertained.'

Jane bristles. Trust Neddy to employ such a casual attitude to the truth. Fanny and Ted are not even listening. Instead, they are climbing the lumpen remains of the stone pillars, then shoving each other off the top as Conker barks his enthusiasm. Georgy fusses, kicking to get down and join in, but he is too little for such hazardous play. Jane dare not return him to his mother with grazed knees and bloodied elbows, and does not trust anybody else, least of all Neddy, to supervise him properly.

But the real reason Neddy's comment nettles her is because he's right. She *is* being a killjoy, and her bitterness arises from no nobler sentiment than petty jealousy. The housekeeper will receive a generous reward for her spurious tales and will be invited to repeat them for tourists through-out the summer. Whereas Jane, who labours in private night and day over her thoughtful compositions, has little hope of receiving a penny for hers. Ever since she was a child, she has dreamt of being lauded as a professional authoress. Now she has reached her majority, and her dream feels as unattainable as ever. Unlike Frances Burney and the other authoresses she idolizes, Jane does not mix with men and women of letters, or even booksellers. Sometimes she fears she is foolish for daring to believe she will one day find a way to break into such a world. 'Keep an eye on Fanny and Ted. I don't like the look of that well. I shall distract Georgy with a slice of pork pie.'

Happily for everyone's comfort, Henrietta readily dis-pensed with her pride in her pursuit of her beau. Rather than maintain the illusion that she and Mr Bridges had met the St Augustine party by chance, she rode ahead in Sir William's coach with several of the Goodnestone foot-men, an enormous gazebo, a large picnic table, several comfortable chairs and what looks to be a very tasty spread. Jane is well satisfied with Henrietta's willingness to cast aside the veneer of serendipity. It's a very hot day, and she doesn't want to wilt under a scarcity of refreshments. On her way to enjoy the much-needed food and shelter, she finds Mr Bridges bent over his easel. 'What are you about?'

He reaches out to tickle Georgy under the chin. 'Insulting the scenery by attempting to capture it in a line drawing. That's what one is meant to do on these romantic excursions, isn't it?'

From where Mr Bridges is sitting, the view is most picturesque. Seagulls rise over the apex of the open church, as the sun warms the ancient brick and stone that make up the ruined tower. Jane could almost believe it was not surrounded by farmers grazing their cattle and a constant onslaught of thunderous traffic. If only Cassandra were here, she would be enthusing about the light and eagerly unpacking her watercolours. No, that is not right. Cassandra refuses to wield a quill, let alone a brush. When Jane returns to Steventon, she must encourage her sister to seek the same solace in her painting and drawing as she herself has found in her writing. Jane forces her attention back to the present. 'You weren't tempted to partake in the tour, then?'

Mr Bridges shrugs, affecting an air of nonchalance. 'I've heard it a thousand times.' He must be growing impatient, waiting for the baronet to grant him an extension to his allowance. He'll be gone soon, and Jane may never see him again. She must not let herself grow accustomed to his company. 'Did she tell you about the singing monks?'

'Yes, and the bloody nun. That was what upset Georgy here.'

'The bloody nun?' A flicker of interest crosses his refined features. 'That's a new one. Her stories get better every time, unlike my sketches.'

Jane leans over the easel, squinting at his feeble attempt to capture the scene. 'Your perspective is off.'

'Is that what's wrong with it?' He tucks his pencil behind his ear, leaning back to review his drawing.

'Yes – there, see.' Jane jostles the toddler, now happily gnawing his chubby fist, and releases one hand to point to Mr Bridges' interpretation of the ruin. 'The near corner of your tower is too short. I know it's seen better days, but in your version the foundations have sunk. It's teetering at a far too precarious angle. The slightest breeze and it would be reduced to a pile of rubble.'

'You're right. I'll start again.' He snatches the sheet, readying himself to tear the paper in two.

Jane places a hand on his forearm to stop him. 'What are you doing?'

'You said the perspective was off.'

'I know, but you can't discard it completely. No wonder your brother won't advance you any money when you behave like such a profligate. That's a perfectly good sheet of paper.'

'But it's spoilt.'

'No, it's not.' Jane takes the page from him, shaking it out to inspect it further. 'Look, you've only drawn on one side. How can you be such a wastrel?'

'You're the one who pronounced it a failure.' Mr Bridges glowers at her from beneath his dark brows. He grabs the sheet and smoothes his rescued drawing over his board with his fist.

'Yes, but if you want to be an artist, you cannot renounce your work at the slightest imperfection. As tedious as it may be, you must labour over it until it's right,' she says, with the heavy awareness that if she is in earnest about achieving her ambition of seeing her efforts in print, she must follow her own advice. Jane may lack the connections to make publication easy but, if she can write something entertaining that people want to read, no prudent bookseller will refuse her.

Mr Bridges huffs but he takes the pencil from behind his ear and draws over his lines, consciously elongating the nearest corner of the tower. Jane watches, with immense satisfaction. He really is most suggestible. She wonders if she could confide in him her fears for Agnes's fragile state of mind, without revealing Neddy's involvement in the horror that caused it. Cassandra's continued silence has left Jane desperate to unburden herself to someone. But it is an enormous secret to share, and she has not yet known Mr Bridges for a full week. Besides, Jane has learnt that handsome young gentlemen, with open countenances and easy manners, nearly always turn out to be the least reliable creatures.

Across the way, Mrs Roche finally releases Henrietta, Mr Blackall and Dr Storer. Jane tries not to scowl too fiercely as both gentlemen hand the housekeeper a fistful of coins. As the old lady departs, with an added bounce to her step as she crosses the fields, Jane bites back the urge to chase after her and decry her as a charlatan. The secret lovers loiter at the well, and Neddy remains at the broken pillars with Fanny and Ted, while Dr Storer, pink from the morning's exertions, heads towards the gazebo. Sensing her opportunity to consult him alone, Jane hastens to join him. 'I hope you're enjoying your visit to Kent, Dr Storer,' she says, as she seats Georgy at the table. Before Jane can prevent him, the toddler lunges for the food, grabbing handfuls of grapes from the opulent spread of cold meats, fresh bread and ripe fruit.

'Indeed I am.' Dr Storer takes a seat opposite. 'I find the county rich in beauty and history, but if Mrs Roche's stories upset you, you did well to remove yourself.'

Jane ignores his comment. She was horrified by the lies in Mrs Roche's account, not the facts. 'When we met at the ball you described my cousin's house guest as suffering from "a common complaint". I wondered if you could possibly expand upon the condition and its treatment, if there is one.'

He frowns. 'Your cousin's house guest?'

'The young woman Dr Wilmot and his wife found wandering along the beach.' Jane hands Georgy a slice of pie, which he proceeds to crumble between his fists rather than eat.

'Ah ... the princess.' Dr Storer nods. News of Agnes's confession cannot have made its way to her former protectors as the doctor seems unaware she may present herself as anyone other than Eleanor. 'I maintain it is curable, yes. I implemented a strict regimen of restraint and blistering to rebalance her constitution.'

'And did it help?' Jane asks, remembering the terrible ordeal Dr Wilmot threatened to cure Elizabeth's dropsy. This course of treatment sounds almost as unpleasant.

'Not immediately, but shortly after she removed to Godmersham Park, your cousin informed mine that the princess was much calmer. I am gratified, therefore, that my ministrations set her on her path to recovery.' He smiles, but Jane fears he is mistaken in his supposition. If Agnes was calmer once released from Dr Storer's care, it was because, unlike the physicians, Mrs Knight treated her with kindness.

'Pah!' Mr Blackall enters the gazebo in time to latch on to their conversation. 'Your remedies have no jurisdiction over her malady.'

'Let me assure you, Mr Blackall, it is only a matter of time before every ailment will be remedied with medicine. Only look at the King. It is thanks to the pioneering court physicians that our sovereign has regained his wits, not his clergy.'

'And let me assure you, Dr Storer,' Mr Blackall pulls out a chair for Henrietta – who seems rather aglow after being left alone in his company for so long, 'it was *my* spiritual guidance that returned the girl to her senses. If she is calmer, it is because I have been praying for her deliverance.'

'Such outmoded superstition.' Dr Storer removes his spectacles and rubs frantically at the lenses with his cravat. 'As a rational man, you cannot truly believe prayers alone restored her.'

'*I* instructed Mrs Knight to bring her to evensong,' Mr Blackall continues, 'and even though she did not dare cross the threshold while in the demon's thrall, her close proximity to holy ground drove it into hiding.'

'It was not a devil that took hold of the girl but an imbalance of her humours.'

'Admit it, Doctor, you were so taken in by the devilish imp, you would have presented her at the Court of St James, if only you'd been granted permission.'

'That is not true.' Dr Storer replaces his glasses, twitching his nose until they are comfortable.

Jane remembers their conversation at the ball. 'Dr Wilmot told me he was making plans to exhibit her.'

'But *I* did not. Indeed, Dr Wilmot and I disagreed greatly on how best to proceed with her treatment.'

'You did?' Perhaps Jane has maligned Dr Storer. Her theories chime far more with his than they do with Mr Blackall's. It is much more likely that Agnes's behaviour is due to an imbalance brought about by the terrible suffering she has endured, rather than an infestation by the devil. Dr

Storer's prescriptions may sound severe, but if King George's lunacy has been cured in this way, who is Jane to protest?

'We did,' the doctor continues. 'While Dr Wilmot thought it appropriate to present her at Court, I remain adamant she should be committed to an asylum.'

'An *asylum*?' Jane repeats the dreaded word, as if it might diminish its ability to terrify her. Unfortunately, she has had some prior exposure to the criminally insane. The mother of one of her dear friends is resident inside Bedlam Hospital. As a murderess, the lady is responsible for her own fate, but Jane cannot help feeling a pang of sympathy when she hears of the inhumane manner with which she is treated – secured in chains day and night, her head shaved to release the vapours, while spectators pay a penny to leer at her from the public gallery. As far as Jane can see, Agnes is more sinned against than sinner. She does not deserve to be treated with such savagery. 'But there's no need to lock the girl away. She's no danger to anyone.'

'She's a danger to society. Hysteria is contagious. You must take great care not to expose yourself to her company,' Dr Storer says, as a fly lands on the sliced ham. Instead of shooing it away, Jane watches it crawl over the pink flesh as he drones on. 'She must be kept in isolation from other women, even female patients. Mrs Knight's pandering will not end well.'

Jane rubs her throbbing temples. Pity the poor girl, at the mercy of the Church and modern medicine. 'How could frightening her possibly help? As Christians, we have a moral duty to treat the sick with compassion.'

Undeterred by the fly's progress, Dr Storer serves himself a slice of ham. 'Really, you mustn't concern yourself. I've seen such delusional behaviour before in a lawyer's wife I treated in London. That lady was obsessed with the idea her husband was about to murder her and steal her fortune. She left notes appealing for assistance wherever she went. Together, we decided the best course of action was to declare her a lunatic.'

'You did what?' Jane cannot believe the depths of this blundering quack's inadequacy. Dr Storer is meant to be an educated man, but he is starting to sound even more unhinged than Mr Blackall. Indeed, Jane is beginning to wonder if her ever-calculating sister-in-law invited him explicitly to make Mr Blackall appear more attractive by comparison. 'Can't you see? You played directly into her devious husband's thieving hands.'

Blotches of red suffuse Dr Storer's cheeks. 'It's perfectly legal for a husband to place his wife in an asylum.'

'I'm sure it is, and therein lies the problem.' Jane stands, unable to quiet her restless limbs any longer. If Elizabeth was successful in prevailing on her to marry Dr Storer, she would live in constant fear of being committed. One lacklustre supper or sharp word and he could see her locked away for life. There is no use asking for the physician's help in healing Agnes. She would likely die under any cure he prescribed. His barbaric methods were the reason Mrs Wilmot asked Mrs Knight to intervene in the first place. 'Miss Bridges, would you mind supervising Georgy? I must check where the other children have got to.'

As Jane turns to flee, Henrietta sidles closer to Dr Storer. 'You must forgive Miss Austen. I'm afraid she has been brought up in the most complete ignorance of the world. Her family are not rich and the people with whom they chiefly mix are not at all high-bred. If it wasn't for her brother's adoption, she would be very much below par.'

Desperate to be as far away from the suffocating conversation as possible, Jane takes quick strides to cool her temper. No doubt Dr Storer will attribute any signs of vehemence to her own hysteria, and Henrietta will revel in informing Elizabeth of any unseemly behaviour on Jane's part. But how can she be expected to keep her opinions to herself when the views of those around her are so ludicrous? She stalks across the grass, towards Fanny and Ted. The children are inside the remains of a small chapel, taking turns to jump off the stone altar – the little heretics. Nearby, Mr Bridges slouches against a jagged ivy-clad wall.

'Where's Neddy? I expressly told him to keep an eye on the children.' Her voice comes out much shriller than she had intended. She must refrain from inflicting her ire on Mr Bridges when he's the only one willing to offer any assistance.

'He went tearing after Conker. The dog must have seen a rabbit. He made an ill-advised dash for the road.'

'Typical. Trust my brother to be more concerned with his hound than his own offspring.'

'I don't mind watching them. They're far more rational company than the rest of our party.' Mr Bridges tips his head back to the gazebo, forcing Jane to give a tight smile. Was he close enough to hear her upbraid Dr Storer? Or Henrietta's comments about her own failings? 'And they're terribly sweet.'

'Aren't they just? Sometimes they make my teeth ache.' The children are atop the altar, kicking each other's shins while squabbling over whose turn it is to jump next. Ted protests, red-faced and stamping his feet; Fanny shoves him out of the way and leaps feet first onto the grass below. At what age is a girl's determination not to give way for her brother knocked out of her? Jane wonders.

Mr Bridges laughs softly at Fanny's lack of decorum. 'Staying at Rowling must put you in mind of having your own family.'

'No, it must not.' She frowns. 'Why go to the trouble of breeding, when I can borrow my brother's brood anytime I like?'

'But you must hanker after your own establishment? Poor Hen is desperate for her independence.'

'I expect she is.' Jane doesn't point out that marriage will not grant Henrietta independence. She will simply transfer her subjugation from her brother to her future husband. 'Believe me, just now, matrimony is the last thing on my mind.'

'Do you mean that?' Mr Bridges reaches out, catching Jane's wrist and shepherding her into an alcove.

'Most earnestly.'

'What do you think this was?' He offers her a rueful smile, surveying their semi-private surroundings. While Jane can still monitor the children, she and Mr Bridges are shielded from view.

'From the stench of it, I'd say the latrina.'

'You are droll, Jane.'

'Is that a compliment? I never can tell when a gentleman praises a woman's wit if he's celebrating her gift or pointing out a flaw.'

'The highest accolade, I assure you.' His eyes soften as his gaze rests on Jane's lips. 'Your lively company is the only thing making it bearable for me to remain here so long.'

How can he claim to be supervising the children when his eyes are fixed solely on Jane? In fact, he's watching her so closely, she is starting to worry she has some of Georgy's pork pie smeared across her cheek.

A movement catches in the corner of her eye. Down by the road, Neddy places his hands on his hips and leans back to address a man in a stalled dog-cart. Conker sits obediently at his master's heel. The man turns, revealing his face – half covered by a knitted hat. Jane shoves Mr Bridges' forearm away and steps out of the alcove. 'Who's Neddy talking to?' Her heart hammers in her chest as she squints at the driver. Could it be Spooner, the man she overheard

Neddy arguing with in the lane a few days after she arrived in Kent? Is he the important matter her brother was so desperate to attend to?

'It's a bit far to say for certain.' Mr Bridges holds his hand flat above his eyes, 'but he looks like one of our most infamous purveyors of goods originating from across the Channel.'

'He's a merchant?' Jane asks, desperate to believe Neddy's business is legitimate.

'Not quite. He's a free-trader. An associate of the Sea Salter Company, if I'm not mistaken.'

'Does Neddy have an interest in such a company? I thought all his money was safely squirrelled away in government four per cents.'

'Not that sort of company. He's an owler,' Mr Bridges says, as if this explains everything. Jane stares at him, not comprehending. 'A smuggler. Honestly, for someone so intelligent, you really can be incredibly green. I expect you pay the duty on tea in Hampshire.'

'Don't be ridiculous. Only a spendthrift like you would do that,' she quips, but this is not a joke. Why is Neddy consorting with a known villain in broad daylight in full view of the entire county? Does he have no care for his reputation? Here Jane is, working tirelessly to find a way to restore his fortunes, while Neddy is determined to condemn himself.

'They call him Spooner,' Mr Bridges continues. 'The blackguard will have earned it through some devilish deed.

Gouging some poor fellow's eyes out with a piece of dessert cutlery, most likely.'

'It's an alias?' Jane steps closer to the road. The man looks up, revealing his face. As she suspected, it is the same scoundrel with whom she witnessed Neddy brawling.

'Yes, all the best villains have them: Nasty Face, Towzer, Stick-in-the-Mud . . . I daresay they believe it helps them evade capture, but it only makes them more notorious among the schoolboys of Kent.'

A sickening realization stops Jane dead in her tracks. She should have thought of it earlier – but all the captains she has known previously have been debonair young men in uniform, gentlemen of self-import and ambition, like Captain Gore or her brother Henry. She assumed Captain Fairbairn would be obvious by his attire. It never occurred to her that this coarse-looking ruffian could hold any rank. But it would follow that the captain, or the 'skipper', of a smuggling ship would wear a different type of regalia. She turns to face Mr Bridges. 'Then what's his real name?'

'No idea. I've never spoken to him. I only know him by reputation. He's not the sort I'd ever accost, no matter how cheap his tobacco. Heaven only knows why your brother is conversing with him. Perhaps Conker ran out in front of his cart.'

'He must have . . .' Jane pushes down the rising fury in her chest. She has a horrible suspicion she knows what Neddy is discussing with the villain. The last time they met, Spooner threatened to inform Elizabeth of Neddy's treachery unless he handed over money. At the time, Neddy seemed determined not to comply and Jane believed her brother had bested him. But perhaps Spooner remained as persistent in threats to Neddy as he has been in his hounding of Agnes and Mrs Knight. Is Spooner the source of Neddy's financial woes? If Neddy has been paying for his silence, it would explain his concern about meeting his repayments to Sir William. Worse, if Neddy is susceptible to blackmail, he could be coerced into helping Spooner evade justice by silencing Agnes. Is this what he meant when he referred to circumstances beyond her grasp? Jane's stomach turns with revulsion. 'Could his real name be Fairbairn?'

'Fairbairn? It doesn't sound familiar, but it's just as likely as any other,' replies Mr Bridges.

Spooner releases the reins and his nag walks on along the road to Canterbury. Neddy heads back towards the ruin. His face is thunderous. Jane swallows. She has found him. Spooner *is* Captain Fairbairn, the skipper of the ship Agnes was travelling on. He is the man who brutalized Agnes as a child. He forced her and God knows how many other young girls into selling themselves to fill his own pockets. He is responsible for killing his entire crew, along with the unfortunate wretches forced onto his ship. And Neddy, the magistrate, is allowing him to evade justice in order to protect his own interests. Jane's worst fears are confirmed: her brother is in league with the Devil.

'Come, Fanny, Ted. You must be in want of refreshment by now.' She reaches for the children's hands, tugging them towards the gazebo without daring to look at Mr Bridges, lest he senses her distress. All this time, Neddy has been letting his adoptive mother nurse a broken girl, present-ing himself as the victim in Agnes's scheme to steal his fortune – when Neddy and his associates are responsible for her fractured state. With a lurch of her heart, Jane realizes it is not her brother and his inheritance that her conscience demands she protect but Agnes: she must save her from Neddy.

Chapter Twenty-two

By the time Neddy's phaeton, loaded with tired, fractious children, draws up at Rowling, Jane is determined to confront her brother. Neddy is a liar and a licentious brute. The Knights elevated him in society and made him their heir, and he repays their generosity by squandering his allowance on debauchery while his wife is carrying his child. The reason he is short on funds is because he is reduced to paying Captain Fairbairn to maintain his silence over his dissolute habits. Jane must apply the same pressure to force her brother to do the right thing. Her hints about his previous involvement with Agnes have been too subtle and easy for him to refute. As soon as she has handed over the children, she will reveal to him that she overheard his argument with Spooner in the lane and that she knows he is being blackmailed over his infidelity. Moreover, she will threaten that, unless he uses his authority to arrest Fairbairn and charge him with unlawful killing, she will repeat what she knows to Elizabeth and confirm Mrs Knight's suspicions that her son has fallen prey to dissipation.

In her heart, Jane cannot believe Neddy is so depraved as knowingly to harbour a murderer, even to protect his own good name. He may be unaware of the tragedy at sea, and the lengths the captain goes to in order to subjugate Agnes and the other girls, but he should know better than to associate with a man so deep in hardened villainy. Once she has informed him of Fairbairn's abhorrent crimes, she is confident Neddy will be eager to perform his duty as justice of the peace, even if it means forsaking his own reputation. If her trust is misplaced, and Neddy continues to deny what she has witnessed with her own eyes, Jane will confide in Mrs Knight and accept the consequences to herself and her wider family. Her father did not raise her in moral ambiguity. She cannot sit idly by while girls as young as nine are being enslaved to vice and a killer walks free.

A freshly revived Elizabeth tackles Jane as soon as she steps into the hall. 'Did you have a pleasant time?'

'Perfectly so.' With the tempest of opposing notions raging through Jane's mind, she cannot meet her sister-in-law's eye as she passes her a sleeping Georgy.

'It was exhausting. Look at these two.' Neddy staggers behind her, with Fanny and Ted tucked under each armpit. The children slide further down his legs with each step he takes. Kitty and Alice dash to retrieve one each before they hit the floor. Even Conker, with his snout pressed to his master's heel, looks ready to drop.

'A rousing success, then? Before you wander off, darling, some papers came from your mother. She wants you to look at them immediately. I put them in your study.' Elizabeth gestures towards the closed door. 'You'd better hop to it. The lease for Briar Farm is in there, along with some correspondence from her lawyer.'

Neddy's shoulders sag. 'As you wish.'

'Do check she's letting it to a respectable farmer, won't you? Not those dreadful nuns who've been trespassing.'

'They're not trespassing. They have Mrs Knight's permission,' says Jane, slighted on the sisters' behalf. As for the correspondence from Mr Furley, if Neddy's mother was still intent on disinheriting him, surely she would do him the courtesy of notifying him herself rather than asking him to oversee the paperwork.

'Then what do you call living somewhere without paying rent? Whoever takes on Briar Farm will be our neighbours.' Elizabeth turns to her husband. 'If you cannot prevent your mother from handing over the tenancy to a coven of papists, please ensure the arrangement can be dissolved at our convenience.'

'I'll see to it.' Neddy gives a half-hearted wave over his shoulder as he unlocks the door.

'Wait.' Jane steps towards the threshold. Once Neddy has barricaded himself into his study, he will be unreachable for hours. She must confront him while she remains fortified with righteous fury or risk losing her resolve. 'I would speak with you.'

Neddy halts. 'About what?'

'I ...' Jane glances at Elizabeth, a cherubic Georgy still wrapped around his mother's neck. She cannot even bring herself to hint at the topic before her. The shock of Neddy's betrayal could send Elizabeth into labour. As much as Elizabeth irritates Jane, she could not live with the death of her sister-in-law and her unborn baby on her conscience, never mind depriving her niece and nephews of their mother.

Neddy gives an exasperated sigh. 'Say what you require of me now, Jane. You heard Beth. Mother wants this paperwork seen to forthwith.'

'It's a private matter. It will take only five minutes of your time.'

'Then I'm afraid it will have to wait. I don't have five minutes.' He slams the door, causing a smattering of dust to emanate from the plaster.

'A private matter, Jane?' Elizabeth's eyes are lit with curiosity. 'Let me guess. Mr Blackall declared himself. I know he's not your first choice, but I really do think he's the best you can hope for, under the circumstances. Refuse him and you risk never receiving another offer for as long as you live.' She hands Georgy to Alice who, having already taken Ted, kicking and complaining to his bed, has returned for his younger brother.

Jane's nerves are too frayed for her even to pretend to submit to Elizabeth's designs. 'Mr Blackall most certainly did not declare himself to me. In fact, his attentions were entirely diverted towards another young lady.'

'*Another* young lady was present at the picnic?'

'Yes, a Miss Bridges of Goodnestone. I believe you're acquainted?'

All of Elizabeth's hard-won serenity dissipates from her features. 'Hen? What was she doing there?'

'We met her and Mr Bridges at the abbey. Quite by chance, they were out for a leisurely drive and insisted on joining us for the tour. A most fortuitous encounter, wouldn't you agree?' Jane knows she is shooting barbs at her sister-in-law because she has missed her real mark. It is hardly fair: Neddy's reprehensible behaviour is no fault of his wife. 'She and Mr Blackall were inseparable. If I were to guess, I'd say Crundale Parsonage won't lack a mistress for long.'

'I will talk to William. Hen must not be allowed to demean herself by making such a lowly connection.'

'But I should be encouraged to?' Jane cannot help but notice Alice, with a sleeping Georgy in her arms, ascend the stairs with exaggerated care. No doubt she is lingering to listen to the argument.

'It's different for you.'

'Why?' Jane's voice rises in pitch. She must be careful, or she will alert Neddy to their petty squabbling. If her brother was to scold her for her impropriety, she does not think she would be capable of holding her tongue about his.

'Because you're – you're –'

'A future burden on your purse, rather than Sir William's?' By now Alice has receded beyond view, and Elizabeth and Jane are the only two remaining in the entrance hall. They stand at the foot of the staircase, glaring at each other.

'How can you say that? Haven't I welcomed you here with open arms? I would never resent accommodating any of Neddy's family. It's just that you will insist on being so very . . . very . . . yourself.'

Jane grips the newel post, her knuckles turning white. 'Who else can you expect me to be?'

'An elegant, genteel, well-bred young lady. The sort who doesn't go around scheming to evade her suitors. If Hen waits just one more season, she could catch a far better sort of husband. I could persuade William to take her to Bath. It would help with his gout, and she's bound to find someone of nobler birth there. Oh, why must my brother be so resistant to travel?' Elizabeth continues, seeming to forget Jane is even there. 'Perhaps Edward could be convinced of the necessity of taking the waters.'

'Don't be ridiculous. Neddy doesn't even have gout.'

'He will do, eventually. All gentlemen of consequence have gout. And Edward will be of great consequence, one day.' Jane tries to leave, but Elizabeth reaches for her wrist. 'What about Dr Storer? Did you manage to further your acquaintance with him or were my efforts all in vain?'

'I made considerable progress with the doctor. I'd say I got to know his character much better.'

'And?'

'He's a leech. And not even an artificial one.' Jane wrenches her arm away and hurries up the stairs, desperate to retire before she says something she really will regret.

'Stop! A letter came for you too,' Elizabeth cries after her.

'It did?' Jane freezes. Please, God, let it be a note from Cassandra at last. Or her mother, with news of the old man's whereabouts. If Jane could present Neddy with an impartial witness to Fairbairn's crimes, he would have no choice but to act. Elizabeth jerks her head to the mantel, where a small square of paper is propped up against the mirror. Jane thunders down the stairs, scrutinizing it for Cassandra's or her mother's handwriting. But there is no mark and no seal, and only 'Miss Jane' written across the front in block capitals with a pencil, as if a child has been practising their letters. Even stranger, when Jane reaches for the yellowed sheet, she recognizes it as one of her own.

'It was tucked in with Neddy's post. I had to give the packet a good shake to get it free.' Elizabeth gives the note a fretful glance before Jane opens it to find only three lines written inside.

Dear Miss Jane,

I am seven years old and I live inside of Agnes. Please help, I am so frightened. He says he is going to kill me. If you do not stop him, he says he will kill us all.

Biddy

Jane reaches for the banister, swaying as if she's been doused with a bucket of water. Agnes must have taken the paper while Jane was working and now Biddy, another of Agnes's personae, has used it to call Jane back to her. The poor child is terrified. Jane must do whatever she can to reassure her that she has a plan to set Agnes free.

'Rather sinister, isn't it?' Elizabeth inclines her head. 'Tell me, who's Biddy? And how can she live inside Agnes?'

'You read it?' Jane affects an indignation she has no right to. In Elizabeth's place she would, and has, done the same.

'It wasn't sealed.'

Jane frowns at the note in her shaky grip. 'I can't say for certain, but I think Biddy is Agnes.'

'Agnes? Then who does she believe is going to murder her?'

Jane takes a deep breath. Elizabeth is so close to her time – only another three weeks at most. At the very least, Jane could collude with Mrs Knight to protect her from the awful truth until after she and her child are out of danger.

'Someone from her past who wishes her harm. But try not to be alarmed. The park is well guarded.'

'She's lying. This will be another of her tricks to encroach upon Mrs Knight's hospitality. First Eleanor, then Agnes, now Biddy. It's all a ruse.'

Jane fears the girl's affliction is beyond the limits of Elizabeth's compassion, especially as she is not party to the depravities Agnes has been forced to endure, but she must at least try to explain. 'Agnes has been subject to the most appalling abuse and it has left her mind fragile. The circumstances of her life are too cruel for her to withstand and, therefore, she imagines she's another and wills herself into inhabiting that character entirely. It's not a masquerade. She really did believe herself a princess and, when she wrote this, I expect earnestly thought herself a seven-year-old child.'

'But this is all Neddy needs to arrest her for deception.' Elizabeth jabs a finger at the page.

'No, Beth, he mustn't do that. Did you not hear me? None of this is Agnes's fault. We have to help her.'

'This is madness. You've all run mad. You'll be giving her the coin from your own pocket next.'

'She's not after money or Godmersham Park, just somewhere she can take refuge until her tormentors are captured. Which they will be soon, I am sure of it. Then, I pray, she will remember herself.' More than anything else, Jane wants this to be the case. She is resolved to do whatever it takes to bring the captain to justice, and she can foresee no other way of granting Agnes peace. 'I must go to her. It's the only way to resolve the matter. Please will you ask Neddy to convey me first thing tomorrow?'

Elizabeth nods mutely, and Jane pats her hand before retreating up the stairs to her bedroom. All the while, Jane's sister-in-law stares after her with as much misgiving as if she had danced the Carmagnole while sporting the colours of the French Revolutionary Army. But Jane knows, as treasonous as she may appear, her loyalty must lie with the true injured party.

Chapter Twenty-three

In the flower-garden at Godmersham Park, Penlington holds a parasol to shield Mrs Knight from the late-morning glare. Beside the butler and his mistress, Jane snips small clusters of Burgundian roses. Mrs Knight examines each posy in turn, before giving a small nod to signify Jane may place it in the wooden bucket resting at her feet or a shake of the head to indicate she should toss it into the gardener's wheelbarrow. Jane should be wearing her bonnet to protect her countenance, already chafed by the long ride to Godmersham with Roger – Neddy having fled Rowling on the tired excuse of urgent business before she had even risen.

Instead, she has pushed the bonnet to the back of her head in an effort to keep Agnes in her sights. The ribbons threaten to strangle her, but Jane must find an opportunity to explain to Agnes her plan to have Captain Fairbairn arrested for the slaughter of all those on board his ship. Unfortunately, maintaining a view of Agnes is as tricky as placing a lead on Conker. Today, the girl is ebullient as she skips along the York stone path, playing hopscotch. When she reaches the pebble, she cries out in jubilation before twisting back on herself and repeating the game. She is in such high spirits, she pays no mind to Penlington or the gardener's boy, on his way to retrieve the wheelbarrow with a handkerchief tied around his glistening forehead.

'Where is your hat, sirrah?' Mrs Knight asks the youth, in a tone of severe reprimand.

'I – I seem to have lost it, mistress.'

'How could you be so careless? What will I tell your mother when you expire due to this dreadful hot weather?'

Jane tucks the scissors into her pocket and drifts towards Agnes, hoping for a few moments of private conversation while Mrs Knight is distracted. She does not yet know how much of her deadly predicament Agnes has shared with her benefactress, and Jane anticipates keeping her secrets will be the key to maintaining her trust. At the very least, she suspects Mrs Knight is aware of the girl's fluctuating character, as she ignores her spirited play in the same way she paid no heed to her haughty impudence as Princess Eleanor.

'Agnes?' Jane whispers, trying to attract her attention. Agnes persists in her game, red hair flying out behind as she hops onto one foot and lands on two. Jane reaches for her arm. 'Agnes?'

The girl starts, as if only now becoming aware of Jane's

presence. 'Will you play with me?' She presses the stone into Jane's gloved hand.

Jane rears back. The girl's features are familiar but her eager expression is entirely foreign. 'I must speak with Agnes.'

'No Agnes today, only Biddy.' Biddy shakes her head, irritated. She snatches the stone, throwing it to the next slab along and hopping after it.

'Biddy? You wrote to me. I know you're frightened, but I can help you. Halt for a moment and let me explain.' But Biddy will not stop. There is a manic quality to her movements, which disturbs Jane. It recalls an account she once read of a group of Bavarian peasants who were possessed with a mysterious compulsion to dance night and day until at last they dropped dead. 'Please, I need to speak to Agnes about Captain F–'

'Sssh ...' Biddy rounds, cupping her hand over Jane's mouth. 'You mustn't speak of him. You mustn't even think of him, or he'll find a way in.'

Despite the extreme heat, Jane shivers. Biddy's words may resemble superstition but she is right to be afraid. Fairbairn is a wily enemy, loitering in shadows and waiting to pounce. His interactions with Neddy and his letters prove he is growing increasingly desperate to silence Agnes. The longer she is at large, the greater the threat she represents to his liberty. Jane must persuade Mrs Knight to increase her fortifications and place even her most trusted attendants, including Armand, under suspicion. Gently, Jane removes Biddy's hand from her lips and returns it to her side. 'You asked for my assistance, and I dearly want to help you. But how can I, if you will not allow me to broach the topic?'

'Play with me.' Biddy's eyes are pleading.

Jane glances along the path, but this is not the game she and Cassandra played on the flagstones leading to St Nicholas's Church. There is far more at stake here than whether Biddy can retain her balance as she skips back and forth. In her terror, the girl has reverted to a childlike state. 'I will, but first I must speak to Agnes. I need to tell her that she's not alone, that there is another witness who will attest to what the capt—'

'No!' Biddy stamps her foot. 'It's your turn. You must throw.'

Mrs Knight ceases upbraiding the boy to find Jane missing from her station. 'Miss Austen, are you disturbing my house guest?'

'She invited me to join in her game.' Jane lets loose the stone. It rolls over the uneven path, threatening to fall between the cracks before settling on the second slab along. Biddy bounces after it. Jane will get no sense from her while she is like this: she must wait until she has reverted to Agnes. But what if Agnes is too afraid to re-surface, and Jane is unable ever again to converse with the girl in a rational manner? She cannot save Agnes unless Agnes is willing to preserve herself.

'Then I suppose I shall have to tend the memorial garden.' The older woman kneels on a cushion and begins brushing wilted petals from one of the large pieces of quartz placed between each rose bush.

Jane hastens to her side, determined to spare Mrs Knight from such arduous duties. 'Oh, no, let me.'

'Thank you.' The widow rests on her heels.

'Are these dogs' graves?'

'No, Miss Austen, *not* dogs.' From Mrs Knight's stricken features and the way she places a protective hand to her stomach, Jane fears she's made the worst faux pas of her life.

The stones will signify the burial plots of the Knights' own offspring: those unfortunate beings who were expelled from their mother's womb far too early to draw breath, and who could not therefore be buried in consecrated ground. The unbaptized ought to be buried to the north of the church's boundary with the suicides. But in Steventon, Jane's father has given strict instructions to his sexton not to interrupt any persons found digging on the borders of the graveyard. Jane has even found Mr Austen praying over the patches of newly disturbed earth that appear at the base of the hedge- row after news of some unfortunate family's loss. 'I'm sorry. That was unforgivably heartless of me. My mother did tell me you'd suffered several . . .' Jane searches for a word that would be adequate to describe Mrs Knight's losses. There does not seem to be one. '. . . accidents.'

'It was a long time ago, before Neddy came to us.' The

widow takes Penlington's arm and rises to her feet, regaining her usual mask of composure.

Chastened, Jane returns to clipping the roses. She pictures Mrs Knight as the cheerful young bride in the ostrich-feather hat who visited the rectory all those years ago. She would have had no notion of the losses she would endure. If she is taking longer to adjust to her husband's death than society deems proper, who is Jane or anyone else to deny her that time? Grief will not be curbed by the expectations, or the impatience, of others. 'I'm sure that doesn't make it any easier.'

'Don't snip the bud like that.' Unwilling to listen to Jane's platitudes, Mrs Knight snatches the scissors from her hand, cutting the stem at a lower point directly above a leaf. She passes Jane the flower, before turning her attention towards the next shrub in the border. As Jane places it in the bucket, she pricks her finger. Wincing, she peels off her glove and squeezes her fingertip until she ejects a tiny piece of thorn from her flesh. A small red bubble rises on her finger. She puts it to her mouth. The metallic taste of blood settles on her tongue as she gazes across the lawn. Biddy has removed her stockings and slippers. Both lie discarded while she sits cross-legged on the lawn, threading daisies into a chain.

Perhaps the afternoon would be equally well spent in interrogating Mrs Knight. Even if Agnes was ready to accuse Fairbairn publicly of murder, there is little Jane can do to forward the case at present. She must give Neddy the opportunity to redeem himself by arresting the blackguard, and she has not yet received a reply from her mother with any clue as to the location of her second witness. And, as selfish as it may be, Jane must determine whether the knowledge of Agnes's condition has caused Mrs Knight to revise her intentions as to the disposal of her estate. 'Biddy is very animated.'

'She is indeed.' Mrs Knight's stern features refuse to betray the slightest reaction to the alternative name. As Jane suspected, she is not shocked by the revelation of Agnes's alternative identity.

'I had hoped that, after we exchanged confidences at Crundale, Agnes might remain.' Despite Jane's prompting, Mrs Knight is taciturn as she fiddles with a particularly large maroon rose. The wilted petals around the egg-yolk centre scatter to the ground. Agnes may have surrendered her secrets, but the widow is as unwilling to confide in Jane as ever. 'I suppose we should take it as a blessing that she has ceased to appear as Eleanor.'

'Ceased?'

'Yes, now she's returned to herself. Or someone more like herself.'

'On the contrary, she was Princess Eleanor this morning, directly before you arrived.'

'She was?'

'She was.' Mrs Knight's dark eyes soften as she gazes across the parterre. Biddy pokes her tongue between her lips as she focuses on her work.

'I wonder what brought about the change in her.' It was listening to Marianne's first encounter with Willoughby, exploring the peril Jane's heroine faced while knowing she was safe, that had prompted Eleanor to switch to Nessa. Could there be a specific set of circumstances that would prevail on Agnes to return? If Jane can identify it, she may be able to steady her.

'Our bucket is full, Penlington.' Mrs Knight nods to the butler. 'Would you be so kind as to fetch a new one? Ask Cook to add some ice to the water. It will prevent the flowers from wilting.'

'As you wish, ma'am.' A crease appears between Penlington's brows. He is either vexed at being sent away just as the conversation has become interesting, or there continues to be bad blood among the servants after the incident with the kitchen door.

Mrs Knight waits until he is out of earshot before she meets Jane with a grave expression. 'I cannot say exactly what prompted Agnes to return, but it is apparent to me that she has suffered a tremendous ordeal. It must be a blessed relief for her to have found a way to escape her torment, however briefly.' She glances down at her widow's weeds. 'I only wish I could find respite from past hurts.'

Jane's eyes slide involuntarily towards the memorial stones. There are six, no, seven lined up beneath rose bushes. With a pang, she remembers how mistaken she was in her original estimation of Mrs Knight. Beneath her brusque exterior, she is a deeply compassionate woman. While Jane no longer believes Agnes is a malicious imposter, out to manipulate the widow's grief to her own advantage, Mrs Knight's own suffering must have been what initially prompted her to act as Agnes's protector. The question remains of how far she is willing to go in this role, and to what extent it will affect the Austens' fortunes. 'Agnes is so very fortunate to have found such a generous benefactress as yourself. I know you sought to make her independent but, with her affliction, I fear she would not cope.'

'Still, I must see what can be done for her.'

'You are determined to do something for her, then?' Jane calculates what figure this might signify while Mrs Knight scowls back at her, stupefied by the question. 'Because I think the most pressing matter is to ensure her safety, and your own. I know you told me the house is kept locked and guarded, but there is still the risk he could evade your attendants' watch. He's a ruthless brute.'

'The captain?'

'Who else?' Jane asks, alarmed by the intonation of Mrs Knight's reply. Does she know Neddy is complicit in Agnes's distress? Surely not – if she did, she'd have broken with him completely.

'You ask too many questions.' Mrs Knight turns to where Biddy had been sitting. A cold terror seizes Jane's heart as she follows her gaze. The square patch of lawn is empty and the daisy chain lies abandoned, strewn over the girl's stockings and slippers. Has Fairbairn snatched her from beneath Jane's very nose?

'Penlington!' Mrs Knight cries, as the butler emerges from the side of the house. 'Have you seen my guest?'

'Don't fret, ma'am. She's playing with the kitchen cat.' Penlington sets a bucket of fresh water, filled with clanking blocks of ice, on the path.

Mrs Knight lets out a tinny laugh. 'Oh, that's a relief. I feared we'd lost her again.'

'You've lost her before?' The panic in Jane's chest refuses to subside. Neither Eleanor nor Agnes stirred far from Mrs Knight, but now the girl is exploring as Biddy she is so much more exposed.

'Only for a few hours.'

'But you mustn't lose her, not for any length of time. You should ensure someone is with her, always. Ask one of the footmen to watch her. Better still, ask two.'

'She's my guest, not my prisoner.'

'For her own safety.'

'You can take that back to the house, Penlington. We've finished now.' Mrs Knight flaps a hand towards the bucket before fixing her attention on Jane. 'I appreciate your concern, but it's impossible to monitor where everyone is in a house of this magnitude.'

Jane glances at the enormous façade of Godmersham Park. This mansion is not the refuge it purports to be. 'What of the captain? He's already tried to break in once. Have you discovered how he's managing to deliver those dreadful notes?'

Mrs Knight swallows. 'Not yet.'

'Have any more arrived?'

'Several. I'm afraid they're becoming ever more frequent. He's managing to leave one, sometimes two or three, a day. I've charged all my household with keeping a lookout, but the messages are always left in a different place, and nobody has seen any strangers come or go.'

This development quashes any lingering suspicions Jane may have that Neddy is delivering the captain's missives. He could not spare the time to travel to Godmersham and back several times in one day. Fairbairn must have another accomplice. If the servants have not spotted any intruders, perhaps one among their own number is leaving the notes. Armand, for example. Jane takes a fearful breath. 'Tell me, has the perimeter wall been mended?'

'Not completely. But, as I told you, I have men on constant watch.'

There is no time for discretion. Jane must act before Fairbairn, or his accomplice, harms Agnes. 'May I see another of the letters?'

'What on earth for?'

'I could compare the captain's handwriting to that of anyone else who has access to the park. He may have bribed an emissary to help carry out his campaign of intimidation, but I expect you have an account book that would contain samples of each of your servants' signatures.'

'Absolutely not. My staff are above suspicion. Besides, I have my steward making enquiries.'

Jane lays a hand on Mrs Knight's forearm. 'You must let me help you, help Agnes.'

'It's no concern of yours. You should never have pried into my affairs.'

'Please, I really think –'

'Your insistence borders on insolence.' The widow shakes her arm free of Jane's grasp. 'Besides, I couldn't, even if I wished to. It's my policy to burn all the notes immediately. They're all of a piece – full of nasty accusations about Agnes's character and vile threats about what will happen to me if I refuse to turn her out. He is a bully, but I have some experience with bullies and I will not be cowed.'

'They are evidence. You cannot simply destroy them or you risk letting the captain go unchecked on his reprehensible behaviour. You must set the law on him.'

'Will you stop this?' Mrs Knight's cheeks suffuse with red. 'I am perfectly capable of managing my own affairs. As I told you previously, I will not involve the authorities as I do not want Neddy to know about the captain and his insidious messages. I have a duty to protect my son and his family. My grandchild is due imminently, and nothing must be allowed to destroy Neddy or Elizabeth's peace at this delicate time.' Mrs Knight walks away, signalling an end to their conversation.

'Forgive me.' Jane has let her tongue get the better of her once again. She must speak calmly if she is ever to rise in Mrs Knight's estimation. 'But I won't rest, not until you let me help you snare this villain.'

'Miss Austen,' Mrs Knight turns to face her, 'if you really want to offer your assistance, then what I need is for you to show yourself as a friend to Agnes. For some reason, she trusts you. You said yourself she confided in you in the carriage at Crundale. Your friendship could prove the calming influence she requires.'

Chastised, Jane nods mutely. Poor Agnes does need a friend. It must be terrifying for her to be aware of her affliction, and yet have no way of controlling it. How frightening it must be for her to wake and have no recollection of what has passed. The uncertainty leaves her utterly defenceless. Feeling more pathetic than ever, Jane resolves to fall back on the one thing she knows she can always do. Before she leaves Godmersham Park, she will take the last remaining sheet of paper out of her writing box and pen a reply to the girl's note.

Chapter Twenty-four

By the next day, Jane is so thoroughly dejected at her failure to persuade either Agnes or Mrs Knight to collude with her in reducing the threat from Captain Fairbairn that the aroma of bacon pervading Rowling Manor turns her stomach. She glares at Neddy across the breakfast table, blissfully untroubled as he loads his plate with rashers. As soon as Elizabeth and the children retire, she will tackle him. She has nothing more than the overheard confession and his encounter with Fairbairn to reproach him with but, she fears, by deferring the confrontation, she is placing Agnes and Mrs Knight in danger. A deadly criminal is stalking Godmersham Park and Jane is powerless to prevent him from striking.

Without evidence to support her claims, Neddy may repel her accusation of his involvement with Agnes's past and refuse to comply with her wish that he arrest Fairbairn. Indeed, if it comes down to her word against his, she knows all their acquaintances are likely to believe her brother over herself. But, Jane prays, once Neddy realizes he has made a pact with the devil he will act swiftly to restore himself to virtue. He cannot know the extent of the captain's villainy. As pitiful as it sounds, Jane will not extinguish the tiny flicker of hope that some goodness remains in him. Whatever else he may have become, he is and will always be her brother.

'Were those more papers from your mother's lawyer?' Elizabeth asks, as she butters a roll for Ted. 'I saw Roger hand you a bundle when Jane arrived home yesterday.'

'They were, yes.' Neddy yawns, leaning down to pet Conker. The dog sits with his ears raised and one foot turned out like a dancer – confident that some scrap of breakfast will be thrown his way, if he can only maintain his good-boy posture for long enough.

'What portion of your fortune is she giving away this time?'

'We've talked about this. Mother isn't giving away any-thing that isn't hers to dispose of.'

'She *is* giving away something, then?' Elizabeth bristles.

'Honestly, it's nothing to concern us.' Neddy shifts his weight in his seat. Really, he is too big for Elizabeth's fash-ionable furniture. 'She wanted my advice on a small legal matter. That's all.'

'Which legal matter, exactly?' Elizabeth continues to hold her knife poised. Sunlight glints from the rounded blade as Ted stands on his chair, leaning across the table to claim his half-buttered roll.

'It's . . .' Neddy's smile recedes into a strained grimace. 'Well, it's a rather delicate situation involving her house guest.'

'I knew it! She's signing Godmersham Park over to that harlot, isn't she? That conniving little –'

'Don't be ridiculous.'

'Chawton, then? Or Steventon?' Elizabeth runs through the various properties that make up Mrs Knight's estate. Given the extent of her wealth, it could take some time – but even Jane holds her breath to hear what exactly the 'something' that Mrs Knight intends to do for Eleanor amounts to.

'Nothing of the sort. Mother might be tender-hearted, but she's nobody's fool.'

'Then what is it?' Elizabeth slams the heel of the knife onto the table, rattling the bone-china crockery.

'Yes, Neddy. What is it?' Jane catches Ted as he is about to climb over the table and swipe Georgy's breakfast in his impatience. Of all the people Mrs Knight could turn to for advice on dispensing with her assets, why has she chosen Neddy? Unless it is to punish him by making him bear witness to the consequences of his reprehensible behaviour. She may not know for certain about his involvement with Agnes, but something must have occurred for her to contemplate defying her late husband's instruction that she make Neddy heir to their entire fortune.

'I cannot say.'

'Why not?' asks Elizabeth.

Fanny hammers the shell of a boiled egg with her teaspoon, providing a military beat to the domestic dispute.

'It's a private matter. Mother asked me to handle it with the utmost discretion.'

'Private,' Elizabeth narrows her eyes, 'from your wife?'

'A man can never be expected to withhold anything from his wife.' Or his sister, Jane refrains from adding. She will find out how much Neddy's transgressions have cost, even if she has to break into his study and retrieve the papers herself. 'The ambiguity is upsetting Beth, and you know Dr Wilmot said we mustn't allow that.'

'It's, well . . .' Neddy's Adam's apple bobs against his cravat as his glance shifts between Elizabeth and Jane. His discretion is no match for their combined scrutiny. 'She received a message from a man claiming that Agnes is his ward. The girl's father is dead, but her mother appointed a friend of the family as her daughter's guardian shortly after she was widowed.'

Jane is aghast. This cannot be true. If there was anyone Agnes could trust, she would have told Mrs Knight or Jane when they were alone in the carriage. This mysterious claimant must be the reason Mrs Knight questioned who Agnes must be kept safe from. Jane watches Neddy carefully for signs of complicity. Is this desperate attempt to remove Agnes his idea? Who better than Neddy to understand how to manipulate the law to his own advantage?

'His ward? And he's willing to take her in? Then she must

go to him.' Elizabeth's dark eyes are as bright as those of a hunting hound waiting for the sound of the horn. Jane can almost see her tail wagging.

'He's more than willing. In fact, he's demanding she be turned over to him immediately. But Mother doesn't want to release her unless she knows for certain he has the girl's best interests at heart.'

Jane's limbs are seized with panic. Agnes is female and in her minority; she would be subject to the rule of any man who could persuade the authorities she belonged to him. 'We mustn't let her go.'

'Of course we must,' says Elizabeth, batting away Ted's greasy hands as he grows tired of waiting and makes a grab for the butter dish. 'She's his responsibility, not Mrs Knight's.'

'Who is he, this man? Did Mrs Knight give you his details?' Fairbairn cannot have claimed legal responsibility for Agnes in his own name after harassing Mrs Knight, but Jane already knows he goes by at least one alias. Mr Spooner, then? If only Mrs Knight had trusted Jane enough to confide in her, she could have warned her they are one and the same.

'Why should that matter?' Elizabeth spreads the butter over Ted's roll with such ferocity that she tears a hole in it. 'Whoever he is, the girl's place is beside him.'

'Could you two please slow down? You're giving me a headache.' Neddy presses the heel of his hand into his forehead. 'Mother didn't give a name. She didn't want to burden me with the details. Rather, she simply asked me to share my opinion on whether she's obliged to relinquish the girl to him. In the eyes of the law, that is.'

'But why consult you?' Jane asks.

'I am the magistrate, Jane.'

'Yes. He is the magistrate, Jane,' Elizabeth parrots. 'I expect you told her to hand her over immediately.'

'I know he's the magistrate.' Beneath the table, Jane balls her hands into fists. She is all too aware that Neddy, a man who is meant to be upholding the law, is blatantly flouting it. 'But still, why ask you and not her lawyer?'

Neddy lifts his palms. 'Ladies, please. One at a time with the questions. Mother *did* consult Mr Furley. But she didn't like his answer so she approached me for a second opinion.'

'Which is?' Jane grips the seat of her chair as she waits for Neddy to pronounce judgement on Agnes.

'It's perfectly reasonable for a man to lay claim to his ward. As Agnes is a minor, her guardian has every right to demand she is restored to him.'

'No!' Jane cannot prevent herself from shrieking.

'Take command of yourself, Jane.' Elizabeth turns to her husband. 'That's wonderful news, darling. Agnes will be restored to her guardian, and all will be right with the world.'

Neddy shifts, causing the mahogany chair to creak. 'Erm . . . not exactly.'

'But you just said –'

'I know what I said. But I also told Mother that if she

has real concerns over what would become of Agnes if she handed her over, then the best thing to do would be to keep her at the park.'

'You did what?' Elizabeth screams, so loudly that Georgy bursts into tears and Conker darts from the room.

'I know we'd prefer to see her gone, but I couldn't lie to Mother. The fact is, as long as Agnes remains at Godmersham, her guardian can't reach her without trespassing. He'd have to lodge a formal request to have her returned to him, and I doubt he's the kind of man with the resources or the wherewithal to do that.'

Jane is too stunned to speak. Her faith in Neddy was not without foundation. He does have some shred of decency left, after all. She reaches out to comfort Georgy, rubbing her hand up and down his chubby arm.

'Are you out of your wits?' Elizabeth fists the tablecloth, knuckles turning white. 'That girl is a threat to the financial stability of your family. Would you see that artful strumpet raised above your own children? Not to mention your wife!'

'Please, my love, don't upset –' Neddy falls silent mid-sentence.

Roger has entered with the post. The footman's flushed cheeks reveal he has overheard the family arguing. He lays two letters in front of his master, departing as abruptly as Conker. The frosty silence remains after he leaves. Neddy shoots Jane a sharp look, as he tosses one of the letters across the table. She grabs it, desperately hoping for a message from her mother, Cassandra or even Biddy. Instead, she's taken aback by her cousin Eliza's elaborate penmanship.

'Oh, look.' Neddy cracks open the seal on the remaining missive. 'Here's something that will restore our good humour. Henry is on his way. His leave must have been granted early.'

'Henry?' Jane is incredulous. 'But he's not meant to be arriving until mid-August so that he can escort me back to Hampshire *after* the baby is born.'

'Well, judging by the postmark, he's most certainly on his way. It's likely he'll be with us before the end of the week. And, look, here's the best bit, he's bringing his new bride.'

Elizabeth's eyes flicker towards the letter. 'He's married already?'

Jane's stomach plummets. 'Oh, good Lord, he can't possibly do that.'

'Of course he can,' says Elizabeth. 'Henry is always welcome at Rowling. He's a Godsend with the children. Even William is cheered by his visits. Will he remain long enough to join the hunt, do you think?'

Jane stares at the letter in her hand, rereading it in hopes she has misunderstood. 'No, he mustn't, because our cousin Eliza is making her way here too. She's headed to Margate to stay with friends, and asks if you'd mind accommodating her and Hastings for a night?'

'Splendid.' Neddy grins. 'The more Austens, the merrier. It'll be a family reunion.'

Jane cannot allow this to happen. 'You don't understand. We can't subject the former Miss Pearson to Eliza's company. It was only the Christmas before last that Henry wanted to marry Eliza instead. He went so far as to propose while she was residing with us at Steventon.' At this, Elizabeth lets out a spluttering laugh. Jane is so taken aback by her sudden change in demeanour, she fears she's having a fit. 'What is it? What have I said that's so amusing?'

Neddy leans in close to his wife, nudging her elbow with his own. 'Do you hear that, darling? *Henry* proposed to Eliza, the Christmas before last.'

Elizabeth pretends to wipe crumbs from her lips with a napkin to hide her merriment. 'What a terrible coquette your cousin is. I blame your aunt for bringing her out in Paris. It may have been cheap, but she'll never shed her Continental affectations. Only the most unscrupulous flirt could string the two of them along at once.'

'String which two along?' asks Jane. But Neddy's eyes are so full of mischief, she fears she already knows the answer.

'Our brother James also asked for Eliza's hand the Christmas before last.'

Jane falls limp with second-hand embarrassment. She had been so busy watching Henry and Eliza, she must have taken her eye off James. 'He never did.'

Elizabeth bites her lip. 'He wrote to Edward, asking for the funds to make Deane Rectory habitable for a family. Then, later, he told us he'd made his offer as he escorted her

345

partway to Brighton, but the foolish chit refused him. Still, I hear Mary's enjoying the refurbishments.'

Jane lets her face drop into her hands. No wonder the latest Mrs James Austen grows inflamed at the mere mention of the Austens' gregarious cousin. Mary has invited all her new family to visit her and James in their newly refurbished home. Everyone to whom Jane has even the slightest claim of kinship, except Eliza. Mary must know she was James's second, or rather third, choice. 'This will be a disaster.'

'I wonder who will try courting the Comtesse next?' Neddy nuzzles Elizabeth's cheek, causing her to titter like a schoolgirl. 'Charles or Frank? She'll have all the Austen boys trying for her.'

'This is not a jest.' Jane rises from her chair with as much gravity as she can muster. 'You simply cannot let their visits coincide.'

But now that Neddy has found a way to divert his wife, he will not be stopped. 'Not me, darling. You know I've only ever had eyes for one woman.'

Jane tucks Eliza's note into her pocket before she stalks out of the room, forcing down the urge to upend the entire table on Neddy's head. If Tom Lefroy ever did stir himself to write to Jane again, one of the many questions she would ask him is where the law stands on fratricide in cases of the utmost provocation. Jane is afraid she will soon be facing a double count. Allowing the newly married Captain Austen and his bride to reside at Rowling beside Eliza and her son is sheer lunacy. Yet Jane's temper is cooled when she recalls that, if her cousin and her brother are en route to East Kent, she will soon be blessed with the company of two friends she can rely on for assistance. By advising his mother on how best to protect Agnes from the man claiming to be her guardian, Neddy has proved himself capable of acting with honour towards her. If Mrs Knight's defences can hold for just a few more days, until Eliza or Henry arrives, Jane can elicit their help in prevailing on Neddy to arrest Fairbairn and deliver Agnes to safety.

6. *Letter to Cassandra Austen*
Rowling Farm, Wednesday, 28 June 1797

My dearest Cassandra,

If you will not murder yourself, and all who love you, you must resist being consumed by your grief. I remain in desperate need of your counsel. A calamity is hurtling towards me at the breakneck speed of two post-chaises. None of our Christian brothers are to be trusted. I don't mean to alarm you, but I'm beginning to suspect there is not a man on this earth whose principles can withstand the onslaught of his baser urges.

Yours affectionately,
J.A.

P.S. We must desist from teasing Mary about her petty rivalry with Eliza. If you don't write to me, I shall never, ever tell you why. And, believe me, you will want to know. It's a story of such thwarted romance and tortured desire that even I couldn't have made it up.

Miss Austen
Rev. Mr Austen's
Deane
Hants

Chapter Twenty-five

On Friday afternoon, Alice interrupts story-time in the nursery to alert Jane that a post-chaise has been spotted across the fields. Jane obediently troops downstairs and waits, with a roiling stomach, along with the rest of the household to greet either Henry and his new bride, or Eliza and Hastings. Whoever wins the race to Rowling will have the advantage of being able to fortify themselves against the others' arrival. As well as fretting over how her brother and her cousin will react to the other's company, Jane is appalled that they are imposing on Elizabeth at such a time. They know there is little more than a fortnight before she is due to lie in. Henry was not supposed to arrive until Elizabeth was out of danger and, since his marriage to Elizabeth, Eliza has rarely visited Neddy.

In an attempt to spare Elizabeth the inconvenience, Jane volunteered to ready the extra bedrooms. But Jane's sister-in-law is a most diligent mistress and insisted on supervising the preparations herself – between ever more frequent bouts of discomfort when she places one hand on her belly, the other on her lower back and fights hard for every breath. In this manner, Jane and Elizabeth transformed the second grandest chamber in the house into a fine suite for the newly-weds, and a draughty garret at the top, overlooking the stables, for Eliza and her son. Jane was mildly surprised to discover that she had not been allotted the lowliest accommodation Rowling had to offer and tried to exchange her room for Eliza's, but Elizabeth would not hear of it.

A draught horse, with a coachman riding postilion, neighs in the distance. Henry, the great oaf, sticks his beaming face out of the carriage window. So, it is Eliza who will be ambushed. As she had refused Henry's proposal, it seems only fair that he will have the advantage of being forewarned of their unintended reunion. And if either of them can withstand the shock of coming face to face unexpectedly in such close quarters, it had best be Eliza. Jane's cousin thrives on adversity, growing younger and more convivial with each setback life throws at her. Please God, Henry will be able to maintain his rictus grin when forced to compare his new bride with his former sweetheart. While there is nothing disagreeable in the former Miss Pearson's person, her beauty is bound to be overshadowed by the bewitching Eliza, and the young lady's wits are no match for a devil like Henry. Who knows what wiles he used to induce her to marry him?

'Whoa there, sirrah!' Neddy steps out into the gravel drive to meet the horses. Conker follows at his heels.

Jane remains at the entrance to the house with Georgy straddled on her hip and Ted's sweaty palm gripped in her hand. Hopefully, Fanny can be trusted not to get herself crushed beneath the carriage wheels.

Henry flings open the door and leaps out before the vehicle has come to a standstill. He looks taller and broader than when Jane last saw him, and more dashing than ever in his captain's uniform. He grips Neddy by the upper arm, the brothers examining each other for signs of ageing and laughing raucously, as if their mortality is the greatest entertainment. When Neddy finally releases him, Henry stands to attention and announces, in a voice of great solemnity, 'My dearest brother and sisters, please allow me to present Mrs Henry Austen.'

His obvious pride and delight in his new wife tugs at Jane's heart. She prays it will not be diminished when she breaks the news to her most sensitive brother that the woman who refused this position is on her way to join them. His lady, her face covered by a wide-brimmed bonnet, pokes her head out from within. She wears a gold velvet spencer. The vibrant shade complements the epaulettes of Henry's scarlet coat perfectly. As she takes his hand, she kicks one foot free of her creamy muslin skirts and places it on the first rung of the ladder. A silver buckle, sparkling with jewels, adorns her elegant court shoe.

Jane falters. Georgy almost slips out of her grasp.

Seeing her face, Neddy throws back his head and lets out a huge, belly-rumbling laugh. 'What sport!'

For a moment, Jane thinks she's caught hold of the worst end of the staff. This familiar creature must have travelled to Rowling *with* Henry and his wife.

'I think you mean Mrs *Elizabeth* Austen, dear.' Eliza places both feet on the ground. Henry stands even taller as he beams down at her, chest puffed like a cockerel. 'I've told you. I don't care how unconventional it is, I won't be referred to by your Christian name.'

Jane gasps. 'You never did?'

Eliza bites the tip of her glove between her small white teeth. She tugs it off slowly, revealing a simple gold band on the ring finger of her left hand. 'Oh, but we did!'

Elizabeth claps her hands together, as she does when one of the children performs a clever trick. 'Naughty, Uncle Henry! You should have told us.'

'We thought we'd surprise you.' Henry shoots Elizabeth a rueful smile. 'You don't mind, do you?' Elizabeth shakes her head as she reaches over her bump to receive their kisses, making a good show of being delighted with her new sister-in-law.

But Jane minds. She minds very much.

Typical Henry not to consider the extra work his sport might incur for his hostess. And Jane, who has lain awake all night feeling as sick as if she had eaten an entire roast pig. She'd wager Miss Pearson minds too. Does the poor girl even know she's been thrown over? What was Eliza thinking? She swore she would never trade the liberty of widowhood for the comforts of marriage. Didn't she?

Jane's ire is quashed by the sight of Eliza's twelve-year-old son, Hastings, gingerly climbing down from the carriage. Henry and Eliza may be radiant – but Hastings has shrunk. His health has never been robust, but the last time Jane saw him he was plump and pretty. Now he is thin and frail with a papery complexion. He suffers from a similar phlegmatic complaint to her brother Georgy. The family prayed that, like the elder Georgy, Hastings's suffering would decline with age. Instead, it only increases. She pats his head, relishing the feel of his silken curls as she brushes past.

Once the rest of the family have retreated into the house, and Eliza has taken Little Georgy from her arms, Jane remains on the steps with Henry. He clasps his hands behind his back and shifts his weight from foot to foot. Jane jabs his chest with one finger. 'You, sir, are a shameless rogue.' She twists her mouth, fighting to contain her smile. 'And I am so very glad for you.'

He leans forward, strong arms enveloping her waist. She presses her nose to his shoulder. The cloying scent of Eliza's French perfume mingles with his familiar, brotherly smell. He squeezes her too tightly, crushing the air from her lungs as he lifts her from the ground. She's missed him. Only now he is before her does she dare to admit to herself how much.

He will know how best to save Agnes, she's sure of it. Of all Jane's brothers, Henry is the one she relies on most. If she must share him with another woman, at least Eliza will be up to the task.

'Put me down, you blockhead,' Jane wheezes, tears gathering in her eyes.

'I'm sorry.' His boyish grin illuminates his handsome features. Eliza is all he has ever wanted. As distasteful as it is to acknowledge, he has followed her around like a doting lamb ever since he was an eight-year-old schoolboy, and she a sophisticated debutante of eighteen. 'I really am so happy. I didn't even know it was possible.'

'What about Miss Pearson? I don't suppose she's partaking in the celebrations for your recent nuptials.'

'Ah, Miss Pearson.' Henry scratches his clean-shaven jaw. 'I promise I let her down as gently as I could. That reminds me. Could you pay her a visit on your way back to Hampshire and return her letters to me?'

'You want *me* to do your dirty work?'

'I can't keep them. It would be most ungentlemanly. Besides, Eliza and I aren't going back through London. Once we've concluded our visit here, we're planning on residing at Margate for the rest of my leave.'

Jane squeezes her hands into tight fists to prevent herself from whacking him about the head. 'You're leaving me stranded in Kent, as well as asking me to clean up after you? May I remind you that you were meant to be escorting me back to Steventon? How am I supposed to get home now?'

'Can't James fetch you?'

'No, he can't. Mary's leash does not extend this far.'

Henry tips his head to one side. 'I'm sorry to let you down, but I may not have long to enjoy my newly married state. There's talk of the Oxfordshires being asked to volunteer overseas.'

'Overseas? But you're the militia.'

'Ireland,' he continues. 'Circumstances there are even worse for the poor than they are here. The rebels are openly courting the assistance of the French to overthrow the Crown. And if Bonaparte gets a foothold across the Irish Sea, it will be only a matter of time before Britain is overrun.' Jane remembers Agnes relaying her story at Crundale. How desperate her mother must have been to sacrifice one of her children to save the others. 'And besides that, Eliza says the sea bathing at Margate is excellent. It'll be good for Hastings.'

Jane's shoulders drop from around her ears. Henry doesn't even have the grace to allow her to be vexed with him. 'You scoundrel. You know I'd do anything for you, don't you?' She looks towards the open front door. 'How is Hastings, really? I swear he was much stouter the last time I saw him.'

'Let's not talk of that now.' A shadow passes over Henry's features as he ushers her inside. It is as Jane suspected: the little boy is fading. She must not begrudge Henry and Eliza this short lease on happiness. Eliza is destined to endure yet more tragedy. But, thank God, Henry will be there to comfort her if – or, rather, when – the worst happens, and Eliza's heart is irrevocably broken by the untimely death of her beloved son.

Later that evening, Jane settles Hastings to sleep on a truckle bed in her room. The newly-weds deserve their privacy, but she would rather Hastings did not pass the night alone in case he suffers a fit. He sucks his thumb and stares up at her with doleful eyes as she recounts *The Adventures of Robinson Crusoe*. Every time his eyelids droop, she considers making a dash for the door so that she may gain a private audience with his mother. After Jane let Henry shepherd her inside, he became conjoined with Neddy: the two of them growing merrier and trading increasingly raffish insults with each glass of wine. Eliza will have to be Jane's confidante. She may appear untouched by her suffering, but as an émigré of revolutionary France, Eliza has witnessed the very worst humanity is capable of. She will counsel Jane wisely on what she must do. But every time Jane stops reading and tries to leave, Hastings lifts his head and says, 'And then, cousin?'

When he finally nods off, his thumb slipping from his mouth as his eyes flicker behind their lids, Jane kisses his damp forehead and makes her escape. As she emerges onto the landing, the jolly cries of her brothers, carried on clouds of pungent tobacco smoke, drift upwards through the house. The door to the newly-weds' chamber is open. By candlelight, Eliza's face is serious as she contemplates the contents of her valise resting on the four-poster bed. She senses Jane's presence and speaks without pausing in her task. 'How's my darling boy?'

Jane slides inside the room, closing the door after herself. 'Downstairs, puffing a cheroot, judging by the stench of it.'

'I meant my son – *not* my husband.'

'Fast asleep. I'll ask one of the maids to sit with him, until I retire.'

'Tell me, are you pleased with your new sister-in-law?'

'Very much so. I thank Heaven you're here. I've never felt so alone as I have these last few weeks.'

Eliza frowns. 'You haven't been alone. You were with your family.'

'Yes, but ...' Jane hesitates. The knowledge of Neddy's transgression and her fears for Agnes's safety have been hanging on her mind for so long without her being at liberty to speak of either topic that she cannot fathom where to begin. Once she denounces Neddy, relations within her family will never be the same again.

'I expect you're missing Cassandra?'

Jane chokes on a sob. She has been in Kent for almost a month without receiving a single letter in her sister's hand. When they were little, her father used to tease that Jane was so devoted to her elder sister that if Cassandra was to have her head cut off, Jane would go too. It is true, she would. For it is inconceivable that there could ever be a Jane if there was no Cassandra. Her face must reveal the true extent of her distress, as Eliza rushes towards her, arms open.

'My poor darling, you mustn't worry. James and Mary will be taking good care of her.'

Jane lets herself be folded into her cousin's embrace. 'Speaking of my new sisters-in-law, I believe I know why you haven't been invited to visit Deane.'

Eliza flinches, as if she has been caught helping herself to the wine cabinet. 'Dear Mary, such a sensible choice. You'll never hear me say a word against her.'

'Is that your own particular style of revenge?' Jane cannot help but laugh. 'And was it before or after Henry pledged his troth to Miss Pearson that you decided you would accept him, after all?'

'We have only one life, Jane. And I could not, in all good conscience, sacrifice *my* happiness in favour of someone else's.' Eliza wriggles her shoulders, all innocence. 'I didn't know if I would ever marry again. But, as it turns out, there's only so long a woman can resist being happy.'

'Do you love him?' Jane would hate to think Eliza chose Henry out of convenience. As her first cousin, he is a prudent choice. She knows him well enough to trust he would never mistreat her, and she has always exhibited a sense of ownership over him. But being unable to bear the idea of him falling in love with someone else is not the same as being in love with him.

'Oh, *ma chérie*, you know better than to ask that of me, for I am immune to love!' Eliza's eyes dance with the light of a thousand candles. Even the most highly paid actress could not falsify this much delight. 'But enough of my escapades. Why are you crying? Things can't really be so dire. Can they?'

'Oh, but they are. Almost as soon as I arrived I overheard –'

'Everything in order?' Elizabeth swings open the door, balancing a bundle of folded towels above her protruding belly. 'We gave it a good airing for you, and I laid out my best linens.' Jane springs out of Eliza's arms and turns away to wipe her tears. She cannot let Elizabeth see her upset. The poor woman has enough to worry about without stumbling across Jane gossiping about Neddy's indiscretions. She must wait until Elizabeth retires before continuing her story.

Eliza takes the towels, placing them on the bed beside her valise. 'What shall we call each other, now that we're sisters? We can't both be Elizabeth Austen.'

Elizabeth frowns. 'But I will be Elizabeth Knight.'

Eliza's lips purse with amusement. 'And so you will, dear.'

Jane bites back a laugh. Elizabeth is the daughter of a baronet, and is married to the elder, richer brother, but Henry's star is in its ascent, and Eliza remains the *ci-devant* Comtesse de Feuillide. Her sisters-in-law are circling each other, vying for superiority. She hopes they settle the matter swiftly, so that she may conclude her conversation with Eliza.

But as Elizabeth turns to leave, she gasps – bending from the waist and clutching one corner of the four-poster bed. An almighty popping sound erupts – startling Jane.

'Will you look at that?' Eliza nods to the puddle forming at Elizabeth's feet. Her waters have broken. 'It's as if she was waiting for the cavalry to arrive.'

Jane grabs a towel from the bed. '*I'm* supposed to be the cavalry.' She kneels beside her sister-in-law, attempting to mop up the leakage before it ruins Elizabeth's slippers and runs through the floorboards.

'Oh, no, don't use those. They're my finest,' Elizabeth cries, lifting each of her soggy feet in turn. 'Fetch the old ones I left in the garret. Make haste, will you?'

As she rises, Jane cannot help but flick her gaze at Eliza. The new Mrs Austen smirks. She knows exactly who the inferior linens in the garret were earmarked for.

Chapter Twenty-six

Several weeks later, Jane stands beside the washstand in Neddy and Elizabeth's bedroom, folding and refolding squares of muslin to be used as clouts. At least, it *feels* as if it is several weeks later. According to Eliza's timepiece, only ninety minutes have passed. Already Jane is desperate to escape the cloying room. Despite the mild summer night, all the windows are closed and the velvet curtains are drawn tight. The fire burns as furiously as a blacksmith's forge, catching motes of dust and transforming them into crackling flashes of light. In preparation for expelling the baby, Elizabeth's body has been expunging every other substance it contains. Consequently, the air is thick with pungent odours. Jane faces the wall, catching only glimpses of the action in the reflection of the looking glass above Elizabeth's dressing-table.

The expectant mother is stripped to her shift, resting face down on her elbows and knees on the mattress of the

four-poster bed. She has been very vocal, shouting directions and asking questions. Now she is quiet, apart from
the occasional wail. The midwife, a local woman with large
hands and muscular forearms, is not overly concerned that
the baby appears to be arriving more than a fortnight before
it was anticipated. Between her, Elizabeth and Eliza, they
have agreed not to call for Dr Wilmot if they can avoid
doing so. His interventions are far from welcome and, as
Elizabeth protested, she managed perfectly well with the
assistance of the midwife alone on the previous three occasions she gave birth. Jane dares not point out that Elizabeth's
pregnancy has already proved so much more trying this
time. The others will know what they are about. This is not,
and Jane hopes never will be, her domain.

Elizabeth grows very still and begins emitting a low
humming sound. Her dark hair is slick against her forehead
and her cheeks are red as she pants into the pillow. It is as
if she has entered a trance, utterly consumed by pain. She is
barely recognizable as Jane's proud, dignified sister-in-law.
Eliza sits on a stool beside the bed, dipping a cloth into a
pail of iced water and using it to dab Elizabeth's forehead.
The midwife stands guard over her lower extremities. Occasionally, she climbs onto the bed and lifts Elizabeth's shift,
kneeling behind her to get a better look at proceedings.

Jane sorely regrets failing to make explicit enquiries to
Cassandra as to what exactly she was supposed to do at this
moment. In fact, she bitterly regrets volunteering to come at

all. It might have benefited Cassandra to be forced to continue with her commitments. Occupation is the best cure for melancholia. If she'd been denied the liberty to nourish her grief, it might not have consumed her so completely. Or it might not have made a jot of difference. Right now, Jane does not care. She would feed her beloved sister piece by piece to a pack of hungry wolves if it meant she could get out of this veritable torture chamber. If Elizabeth was in her right mind, there is no way she would want Jane, of all people, to witness her debasement. She crams herself further into the corner, attempting to remove herself, body and mind from the action.

'I could fit ten fingers up there,' says the midwife, proudly. 'Won't be long now.'

Jane's shoulders jerk forward as she cups both hands over her mouth.

Eliza wrings a damp cloth between both hands. 'Go and fetch some brandy, will you, Jane?'

Light-headed, Jane dashes for the door. 'Will a glass do, or should I bring the bottle?'

'I don't know.' Eliza appraises her coolly. 'How much will it take for you to regain command of yourself, and provide some actual assistance?'

Despite the offence, Jane flees without hesitation. She thumps downstairs, giddy at being excused. She is so faint that her knees threaten to buckle. She pictures herself sliding to a heap at the bottom of the staircase in her haste to put as much distance as possible between herself and the birthing room.

In the hall, thick blue clouds of smoke waft from the cracks around the door to Neddy's study. From within, her brothers let out twin guffaws, reawakening Jane's dormant fury. To the devil with Elizabeth's proclamation that she must not intrude on a gentleman's private space. Jane does not even bother to knock before she flings open the door. Her vision takes a moment to adjust. In the gloom, Neddy reclines behind his desk with his chair tipped back at a perilous angle as he balances one booted foot on the leather-topped surface. Henry, with more respect for the opulent furniture, lounges on a small sofa beside the fire. Both men peer at her quizzically through bloodshot eyes. They are as drunk as a pair of His Majesty's tars granted shore leave for the night.

'Oh, I see.' Jane casts a disdainful eye over them both. 'It's all very well for you two, making merry while we women get on with the unpleasant business.'

'Has the little fellow arrived?' Neddy sweeps his foot to the floor.

'Not yet.'

'But Beth's well? Things are progressing as expected?'

'Yes.' Jane grips the back of the sofa, leaning all her weight on it. 'According to the midwife, things are coming along swimmingly.'

'Then why are you down here?' Henry removes the cheroot from his lips and puffs out a great cloud of smoke.

Jane wafts away the fumes as she perches on the arm of the sofa. 'Eliza sent me to fetch some brandy.'

Neddy jumps up and rushes towards the mahogany cabinet. The key is still in the lock. He grabs a dusty bottle and pours a generous measure into a tumbler, before handing it to Jane. 'Beth usually prefers port.'

'It's not for her.' Jane swings a foot back and forth as she swallows the brandy in one gulp.

'So we see.' Henry raises an eyebrow.

'By God, it's a barbaric business.' She wipes her mouth with the back of her hand as she holds out the glass for a refill. 'How can you stand to put her through it, Ned? How can anyone stand it?'

'It'll be worth it. You'll see.' Neddy takes the glass obediently.

'What do Mother and Father always say? There's no greater blessing.' Henry pats Jane's knee. From his doe-eyed expression, it's clear he's savouring the prospect of having his own children. With Eliza. What formidable beings they will be, imbued with both Henry and Eliza's charm. Will the world ever be ready for such a terrifying breed of creatures?

Neddy places a fresh glass of brandy in Jane's palm, closing her hands around it to prevent her from smashing his best crystal. She tries to sip it slowly, hoping the taste of apples and dried oak rolling across her tongue will still it from voicing what is really on her mind. Her nerves are screaming at her to challenge Neddy on his reckless behaviour once and for all. 'What were you up to, before I burst in on you?'

'Merely attempting to keep ourselves occupied.' Neddy shrugs. 'Don't go thinking it's not an ordeal for the father too, Jane.'

Her fingers squeeze the glass. How dare Neddy describe waiting as an 'ordeal' compared to the torment Elizabeth is submitting herself to?

'Perhaps you could read to us?' says Henry.

'I'm so agitated I couldn't apply my mind to a list of laundry.' Besides, Neddy has declined to hear Jane's work so many times that the prospect of forcing it on him now is humiliating. The only people who are prepared to listen to her stories in East Kent are Mrs Knight and Agnes. And even then she is never sure if Mrs Knight has made it to the end of the first sentence before dropping off.

'Has she read *Catherine* for you yet?' asks Henry. 'I'm convinced she modelled the hero after me.'

'Only his most irritating attributes,' replies Jane.

'Is *Catherine* the one with the dreadful American lady?' Neddy scratches the back of his head. Trust him to find Mrs Johnson's colonial roots more offensive than Lady Susan's scandalous antics.

'No, she's come a long way since then. Father esteemed *First Impressions* so highly that he submitted it to the bookseller Thomas Cadell.'

Jane almost slides off the arm of the sofa. As far as she knows, *First Impressions* has never left her side. 'He did not.'

'He did.' Henry grins. 'He put it in the post as soon as he waved you adieu at Dartford.'

'But I have it here, with me.'

'Do you? Or do you have the title page and a sheaf of fresh paper?'

Jane runs to the parlour, where *First Impressions* remains propped up against the sideboard. She tears at the ribbon, flicking through the subsequent pages, they are all blank. Her heart beats furiously at the prospect of a crowd of stuffy old men in London poring over her work. She did not write it with them in mind. She doubts they will understand her characters, let alone sympathize with their actions. And yet ... She holds it to her chest as she races back to Henry. 'Has Father heard back? Is Cadell going to publish it?'

'It was a no, I'm afraid. It wasn't that he didn't like it, he didn't even read it. He sent it back by return of post.'

'Oh.' Jane slumps onto the sofa beside him, confused as to whether she's more relieved or disappointed that Thomas Cadell, the famously selective bookseller, will not be reading her manuscript. It was kind of her father to believe her work worthy of his notice, yet she is mortified by Mr Austen's audacity. Fancy having the nerve to offer *First Impressions* to Frances Burney's publisher. 'Why didn't Papa tell me he was planning to submit it?'

Henry rests an arm on the back of the sofa. 'He probably

didn't want you to get your hopes up, in case of having them dashed.'

'Then why are you telling her?' asks Neddy.

'Because I think she should raise them even higher.'

'It's not even finished yet. I'm confident I can improve it.' As with all her compositions, Jane had laboured hard over *First Impressions*, and was well satisfied with the draft before she put it aside. But with time, her previous work is losing its lustre. Especially as lately she has wished to toy with an entirely new style. As Agnes believed was already the case, she resolves to use this fresh supply of paper to immerse herself within her characters, committing their every thought and feeling to the page. Not having to rely solely on letters will carry the added advantage of allowing her to reunite the sisters. Contriving excuses to separate them so that they could correspond was becoming tiresome, as they so clearly belong together.

'That's the spirit. You mustn't lose heart.' Henry tickles the soft flesh above her knee with his finger and thumb. 'We'll make an authoress of you yet. You've always been the clever one.'

Jane stares into the bottom of her glass, looking for trouble. 'No, I'm not. James is the clever one.'

'Ah, no. You're mistaken there. James is the firstborn. He doesn't have to be clever because Mother and Father believe all that he does is perfect regardless.'

A smile tugs at Jane's lips. It's a blessed relief to have Henry back at her side. 'Cassandra is the kind one.'

Henry shoots her a rueful grin. 'I'm the naughty one.'

Neddy's features turn dour. 'And *I*'m the one they sold.'

Jane's blood roars in her ears. 'How dare you, of all people, say that?'

'It's true, isn't it?' Neddy tips his port down his throat. 'They sent me packing at the first opportunity. Run along, Ned. Take care to make yourself agreeable. Don't ever forget that the hopes and dreams of your entire family rest upon your shoulders.'

Jane has fought so hard not to let this anger overtake her. But now every muscle in her body quivers with indignation. She cannot sit back and listen to Neddy describe himself as a victim. Not while Elizabeth is labouring in agony, and Agnes's peace is irrevocably shattered. 'Our parents saw an opportunity for their son to get on in life. As much as it pained them, they did it for *you*, Ned. You, who received every advantage. So how can you, of all people, have the gall to compare your adoption by the gentle, kind-hearted Knights to ... to ...'

'To what?' Neddy's eyes widen with every furious word she utters. Meanwhile, Henry's attention switches between his brother and sister, with the horrified expression of a man watching two bare-knuckle pugilists trade blows.

The room is silent and still as several awful seconds pass. If Jane reveals what she knows, everything will change. She risks banishing herself from Neddy and his family for ever. Even her own parents could disown her for exposing him.

And yet there is a rage inside Jane that cannot be quashed. 'To the way you bought and sold Agnes?'

Henry draws a sharp breath while Neddy blinks, his face as inscrutable as one of her blank pages.

'It's no use playing the innocent with me.' Jane jabs a finger in the air. Neddy does not even have the integrity to own his sins. 'I overheard you talking to her bully.'

'Jane.' Neddy's cheroot is sticking to his lower lip. 'What in God's name are you speaking of?'

'Don't you dare try to refute it. I heard everything you said to that despicable man. It was a few days after I arrived. You were in the lane, at the back of the garden.'

All the colour drains from Neddy's cheeks. 'You did?'

Jane stands tall. She has said her piece now. She may as well press her point. 'Feeling sorry for yourself, because you could no longer *use* the *Infanta*.'

'What's going on?' Henry's voice is low and tense.

'The *Infanta*. That's what Agnes, the poor wretch Mrs Knight has taken pity on, calls herself.'

'God's bollocks, Jane.' Neddy shoots up so quickly, his chair topples over. 'What are you talking about? The *Infanta* is a ship. The *Infanta de Castilla*.'

Jane sways, caught off guard. 'A ship.'

'Yes. A bloody ship. Went down off the coast of Harty, almost a month ago.'

This cannot be right. Every word of Neddy and Fairbairn's

conversation is singed on Jane's brain. She cannot have mis-construed him. 'You said she was a perfect beauty?'

'She was ... A fifty-five-foot cutter. Room for twelve or fourteen guns. Frank or Charles would have been proud to command her, I'm sure.'

Jane replays every line of the conversation in her head. Neither of the men mentioned a ship, not once. What was it that had made her so certain they were referring to Agnes? 'But you told that villain he must recover her. You can't recover a ship, not after it has sunk in open water.'

'I know. But I was so desperate I didn't care if it was impossible or not. She was carrying my cargo. I've never laid a finger on Agnes. I never even saw her before Mother took her in. The closest I've ever been to her was when we met her at Crundale. Why on earth would you think I was referring to her?'

Despite all her previous conviction, Jane is fast shrinking into the Turkey rug. 'La Infanta de Castilla is how Eleanor introduced herself. "*Infanta*" is akin to princess in Spanish.'

'Is it?' Neddy creases his brow. 'I thought it meant "child"? You know, like infant?'

Jane shakes her head in disbelief. 'No. Besides, La Infanta de Castilla was Queen Eleanor. She married King Edward I. Did you really not make the connection?' She looks to Henry for reassurance, but his bemused features tell her he is just as lost on the path of her tenuous reasoning.

'No, Jane.' Neddy's voice ricochets off the walls. 'I know you were always clamouring to get into Father's school-room, but *I* was desperate to get out.'

'B-but you said losing her must be your punishment for straying.' She stamps one foot as her voice turns into a whine.

Neddy scrapes his palm over his face. 'From the *law*, not my wife. I attempted to use the *Infanta* to send a portion of my wool to the Continent to avoid paying excise duty. But the damned ship sank and now I'm worse off than ever.'

'Your wool?'

'Yes, Jane. My wool. I do run a sheep farm here, in case you haven't noticed. These new taxes are ridiculous. I know we have a responsibility to contribute to the war chest, but how is an honest man meant to make a living when Parliament insists on skimming off every bit of profit and more besides?'

Jane and Henry exchange a glance of mutual horror. Neddy, the Austens' most revered child and magistrate for the county, is a common smuggler.

'Don't you dare look at me like that, either of you.' Neddy's countenance turns puce. 'I've a growing family to support. And you never concerned yourself with where the money would come from when I offered to pay Georgy's legal fees. Did you?'

Chastened, Jane's cheeks blaze with shame. He is right. The Austens are so used to taking handouts from Neddy, they never think twice about whether he can afford them. He takes a sip of port, slamming the glass on the desk and wiping his mouth. 'I'd already committed to taking the extra acreage from Sir William. I thought I'd reserved enough in savings for the first year's rent but, after settling the final bill from that bloodsucking lawyer, there wasn't enough left. I needed to find a way to cover the discrepancy quickly. And you honestly thought I was being unfaithful to Beth? Jesus Christ, Jane. What kind of man do you think I am?'

At that very moment Jane's guardian angel, in the form of Eliza, pokes her head around the door, saving her from having to answer. 'Goodness me, what's going on in here? I thought your new son had a pair of lungs on him. It's clear where he gets them from.'

In an instant, all the tension in Neddy's taut frame evaporates and his usual colour is restored. 'My – my new son? I have another son?'

'Yes.' Eliza beams. 'Would you like to meet him? Mother and baby are ready to receive you now.'

Neddy bounds for the door. As he passes Jane, he shoots her the darkest of looks, causing her to tremble. 'We'll discuss this matter later.'

Chapter Twenty-seven

Upstairs in her boudoir, Elizabeth is resurrected. She reclines gracefully, eyes bright and features placid, on a bank of snow-white pillows. The midwife must have helped her change into a crisp cap and dressing-gown, and her hair is neatly brushed away from her face, plaited in a long dark coil. Cradled in her arms is the most beautiful, vulnerable and terrifying creature Jane has ever laid eyes on. A tiny cherub, with a squashed round face, pink cheeks and enormous blue-grey eyes, which seem to take in everything and nothing all at once. The baby yawns, exhausted from the effort of battling his way into the world. As he does, he stretches his wrinkled hands. His tiny fingernails look as soft as butter.

Neddy perches beside Elizabeth, one arm slung around her shoulders in a proprietary manner as they gaze down at their newborn son. Henry and Eliza sit at the bedside, hands clasped as they occasionally break from admiring each other to glance in the baby's general direction. Jane hovers at the foot of the bed, unsure of her place in this rejuvenated family. How will Neddy ever find it in himself to forgive her? Her heart sags at the thought that this new nephew may never lisp her name. Who will teach him how to make a paper ship if Jane is barred from Rowling? Cassandra's efforts always sink. What if, after news of her ghastly accusation arrives at Steventon, Jane is expelled from the rectory? Where would she go? No one will marry her now, not even Dr Storer. She has severed the one connection who guaranteed her security. She will have to become a governess – forced to labour day and night to improve the stubborn minds of children she is not even related to. How will she bear it? Maybe she should find herself a bawd instead.

She must not jest. Not even inside her own head. Her jokes are unfunny and vile. And, like everything else she does, bound to expose her to contempt and ridicule. What did she think she was doing? She should have had faith in her brother from the start, not allowed her suspicion to fester until it turned into a canker. She thought she was being prudent in keeping her theories to herself. Instead, she has been misled by the arrogance of her own convictions. Mrs Knight is right – she is nothing but a foolish young lady of little experience and no consequence. Nobody appointed *her* as Agnes's saviour. Why would they, when Jane does not even have the means to take command of her own life?

Henry leans towards the bed, placing one hand on Elizabeth's arm. 'You'll have to find a name for the little fellow.'

'We've already discussed it,' Elizabeth murmurs, without taking her eyes off the babe. 'With your permission, we'd like to call him Henry.'

'After me?' Henry sits taller, beaming at Eliza. She squeezes his hand, her own eyes glittering with pride.

Jane presses her palms flat against her abdomen to prevent herself from making a display of her distress. How many girls would Elizabeth have to birth before one was baptized 'Jane'? After what she's just done, it would take an infinite number. Why would anyone want to curse their offspring by naming them after her? Forget her needlework, her turn on the pianoforte, or even her compositions, Jane's major accomplishment is taking a bad situation and making it a thousand times worse. Mrs Knight commanded her to act as a friend to Agnes, no more. Has she even done that? Biddy has not replied to her note, and Jane is no closer to helping her to safety. After Neddy's revelation, she feels further away from the truth than ever. Jane travelled to Rowling to act as envoy from the Steventon Austens. Instead, she's created an irreparable rift in the family, and done everything she can to heap scorn upon her own head by accusing everyone's favourite brother of whoring.

Yet she was justified in her belief that Neddy was hiding something. Jane may have been wildly mistaken in what it was, but some veracity was buried among her awful suspicions. Neddy has been overly secretive these last few weeks, lying to his wife and under the power of an unscrupulous villain. Jane must persevere – force him to confess what he knows and atone for his crimes by arresting the captain. If Neddy merely dealt with Fairbairn to transport his wool, he will not know about his connection to Agnes. Neither can he know that the reason the *Infanta* sank, and all of her crew, plus the other women and girls on board, lost their lives, was the captain's recklessness. Jane prays she has not left it too late to tell him and enlist his help. Every day she hesitated she has made it less likely that the authorities will be able to trace the old man from the inn to stand as witness. She drifts away from the bed, towards the window, determined not to ruin the tender moment by breaking down into sobs at what a fool she has been in thinking she could manage this situation alone.

From outside, horses' hoofs clatter and carriage wheels turn over the gravel. Jane hooks a finger around the velvet curtain, lifting it from the glass. It is past midnight, well beyond the hour for receiving visitors. Yet Mrs Knight's distinctive coach is parked in the drive. Armand barks a few words to Roger and the man goes running towards the stables.

Jane's stomach tightens. Why is Mrs Knight here? She has never deigned to visit Rowling in all the time Jane has been in Kent. Armand opens the carriage door, and hands down his mistress with another woman. Jane presses her face to the window, hoping to see Agnes. Perhaps the girl will have returned to herself long enough to give Neddy a first-hand account of the shipwreck and he will arrest Captain Fairbairn immediately. But Jane can tell from the second woman's dress and demeanour that it is Grace, not Agnes, who is Mrs Knight's companion. Armand shepherds both women inside the house, without waiting for any third female to appear. Jane drops the curtain and steps backwards, colliding with Henry. He frowns at her, as if Jane might be able to provide an explanation as to why the notoriously reclusive widow is making house calls in the early hours of the morning.

Footsteps thump up the stairs and Alice pokes her head around the door. 'I'm so sorry to disturb you, sir.' She pants, breathless from the sudden exertion. 'But Mrs Knight has arrived.'

Neddy peers at her, as if not fully comprehending. 'Mother? At Rowling?'

Alice only nods.

'She's probably heard about little Henry.' Neddy presses a kiss to Elizabeth's temple before he stands. 'Come to congratulate us. You sleep now, darling.'

But Jane knows full well the baby's arrival cannot be the reason Mrs Knight is here. Like any sensible woman, Mrs Knight gave clear instructions that she was not to be notified of Elizabeth's lying-in until the event was over, mother and baby out of danger. Enough time has not passed for a messenger to make his way from Rowling to Godmersham and back.

The midwife takes the tightly swaddled bundle from his mother's arms. Elizabeth yawns, almost as widely as her new son. 'I am rather tired.'

Eliza pats her hand. 'Would you like me to remain? I could fetch us some caudle.'

'No, no. You go. You can all go now.' Elizabeth closes her eyes. 'Thank you for your assistance, Eliza.'

She does not thank Jane. And why should she? Jane is as useless as a left-footed spinster at a public assembly. She follows Neddy down the stairs, eager to find out what's occurred but wanting to fade into the background so that her brother might forget she is there. In the entrance hall, Mrs Knight wrings her hands. She and Grace are still in their bonnets and capes, anxiously standing beside the dying fire rather than allowing themselves to be shown into the parlour. Armand lurks in the shadowy alcove, blunderbuss glinting in the candlelight.

'Neddy,' Mrs Knight rushes to him, collapsing into his arms, 'I'm so sorry to trouble you.'

'Not at all, Mother.' He steers her towards the wooden bench, but she does not sit. 'How did you know Elizabeth had been brought to bed already?'

'I didn't. Are she and the baby well?'

'Perfectly so. But why are you here?'

'It's Agnes.' Mrs Knight sobs. 'The man claiming to be

her guardian came to the house, demanding she be returned to him. And the poor lamb . . . She was so frightened. She ran away before I could stop her.'

'Agnes's guardian had the audacity to present himself at Godmersham?' Neddy lowers his brow, seeming as incredulous as he is furious. 'Uninvited?'

'It's worse than that, Ned.' Mrs Knight grips one of his big hands between both of hers. 'He's armed and accompanied by a whole gang of brigands. They're scouring the park, intent on capturing her!'

Jane falters, reaching for the newel post for support, while Eliza dashes towards Neddy's study. Jane cannot blame her for wishing to flee. She lost her first husband to the Terror in France and almost lost her own life in the Mount Street Riot. The prospect of mob violence following her here, to Kent, must be terrifying. Henry chases after her.

Mrs Knight presses her eyes closed, drawing a ragged breath. 'Forgive me, I didn't want to burden you with this. Not now, when Elizabeth needs you. But Agnes's guardian is a dastardly villain. He's known all around these parts.'

Neddy's face turns hard as flint. 'What's his name, Mother?'

'It's Mr Spooner. He's one of those ruffians from the Sea Salter Company.' As Jane suspected, Fairbairn has used an alias to claim Agnes. 'I can't let him take her, Neddy. He's already subjected her to the most despicable form of abuse.'

Neddy's eyes flick to Jane. Clearly he is only now realizing the enormity of her accusations against him. She stumbles backwards, overwhelmed with guilt and shame at her stupidity. If she had confessed everything she had learnt in Whitstable and asked for Neddy's help sooner, Mrs Knight would have been spared this invasion and Agnes would be safe.

'I swear, Mother.' Neddy sets his mouth in a thin line. 'He'll rue the day.'

Armand steps forward. 'I took the liberty of rousing your men, sir.' If Armand was colluding with Fairbairn, he would not have come to seek help. Unless he is deliberately leading her brother into danger.

Grace clings to her mistress. 'Mr Penlington is attempting to secure the house. But if they try to enter, he won't be able to hold them off for long.'

Neddy takes a sharp breath. 'I'll fetch my guns.'

'Here.' Eliza stands in the doorway to Neddy's study, grasping the enormous rifles, previously displayed above the fireplace. The barrels are so long they reach her earlobes. Jane underestimated Eliza. She went to raid the arsenal, not cower in fear. Behind her, Henry has attired himself in his full militia uniform, complete with sabre, and is loading shot into a satchel.

Neddy throws on a hunting jacket and takes the rifles from Eliza. 'Let's away.'

'Stop!' Jane screams, her panic getting the better of her. She will not let Neddy go into battle against a horde of blackguards without being party to the full extent of their wickedness. 'Spooner is more determined than you know. He's been harassing Mrs Knight by letter, using the name Captain Fairbairn and vowing to kill anyone who stands between him and Agnes. He must have an accomplice familiar with the park.'

'Is this true, Mother?'

Mrs Knight places a hand to her throat. 'I have received some vile notes, but I had no notion they were connected to the man claiming to be Agnes's guardian.'

'It's him, I'm sure of it. He's a cold-blooded killer. It's his fault the *Infanta* sank. An old man I met in Dartford witnessed the tragedy. It was the captain's negligence, not an act of God, that caused the ship to capsize. Agnes is the only other survivor. That's why he's so desperate to snatch her. Her testimony would see him hanged.'

'And you're telling me this *now*?' Neddy shakes his head, incredulous at her idiocy.

'We should call in the dragoons,' says Henry. 'There's a garrison at Canterbury.'

Neddy gives a curt nod. 'Send a groom with a message, certainly, but I'll not wait for them.'

Eliza grabs Henry's hand as he passes. 'Come back to me,' she says, voice breathy. He pauses to kiss her full on the mouth before the three men spill out into the night. Once they have left, Eliza takes Mrs Knight's free arm. 'Let's get you settled by the fire, ma'am. You've had a terrible shock.'

Mrs Knight grips her wrist. 'Tell me about the baby . . .'

'Little Henry? He's a poppet.'

'Another boy? Oh, we are blessed. And what a charming name.'

'Yes, I certainly think so . . .'

Between Grace and Eliza, Mrs Knight is led into the parlour. But instead of joining them, Jane walks in the opposite direction through the open door. The cries of working men and horses' hoofs are calling her out into the moonlight. A dozen boys and men run to and fro across the gravel driveway, preparing to defend Godmersham Park. Neddy's carriage horses look far too dainty to enter the fray, yet they are saddled alongside the commonest draught horse in his stable. All of the riders, Jane is sickened to see, are armed with pistols or clubs tied to their belts. Armand piles pitchforks inside the coach and orders Neddy's shepherds onto the rumble seat. Even in this chaos, he will not risk spoiling the upholstery. Roger holds two enormous hunters steady for her brothers. Neddy climbs onto his but as Henry is about to do the same his gaze meets Jane's. He rushes towards her, resting his hands on her shoulders and bearing his weight down on her. 'Stay here,' he says, in a peremptory tone she imagines he usually reserves for his lesser soldiers.

'Where else would I go?' Jane lays a hand across her chest. Her heart is beating to a gallop. She could hardly grab a rifle and leap into the saddle to help save Agnes, however much she wants to.

'Nowhere.' Henry's lip twitches. 'That's what I said, stay

here. Where you're safe and can't get yourself into any further trouble.'

Perplexed as to why he should think it necessary to compel her to remain, Jane stands paralysed as Henry dashes for his horse. All of the men leave in a cloud of dust and enraged masculinity. Conker brushes past her skirts and darts out onto the road, barking furiously at being left behind. Despite wearing only her slippers, Jane sprints after him, yelling for the stupid dog to return. The animal's misguided loyalty will get him killed if he tries to keep in step with the horses all the way to Godmersham. A hundred yards along the drive, she catches up with him, as he howls to the waning moon at the indignity of being left behind when there's a hunt afoot. She crouches beside him, rubbing both hands over his velvet ears and nuzzling his neck for comfort. The night is still, and bright, and Jane has never felt more insignificant, both she and the dog deemed utterly unfit for this fight. And yet the very fact that Henry warned her to 'stay there' implies there might be somewhere she could go to assist in preserving Agnes. If only Jane could intuit where it is.

Chapter Twenty-eight

R ather than return to the house, Jane paces the garden, hoping the scent of lavender will calm her jangled nerves. Bereft of his master, Conker shadows her every move. Riding hard over the fields, Jane calculates the men could reach Godmersham within the hour. Will Agnes be able to evade the gang until then? That is, if Fairbairn has not seized her already? She prays the girl has found somewhere safe to hide. Neddy is an excellent shot, and he has the assistance of two trained soldiers – but he is used to hunting game, not villains, and who knows if Armand is really to be trusted? Henry was right to send for the dragoons, but how long will it take them to provide reinforcements? Given Mr Bridges' warnings about the villainous Sea Salter Company and Mr Skeete's threat to cut out Molly's tongue, Jane dreads to think what motley crew Captain Fairbairn has assembled.

Unable to find peace, she perches on the edge of the wooden bench in the arbour and worries the skin around her thumb with her teeth. Conker stretches out at her feet, resting his despondent head on her slipper. Even if Neddy is successful in rounding up the captain and his gang, Agnes may still be lost to them. Now that she knows the mansion is not safe, she may never return. She's left before – Mrs Knight said she disappeared once for hours. Has she ever wandered out of the park into the surrounding countryside? She may have gone out in the same way Fairbairn has been entering – presumably through the breach in the perimeter wall. Jane's throat tightens at the thought of Agnes alone in this brutal world. The girl has no rank, no wealth. Worse, she has no kindly family and no friends, other than Jane and Mrs Knight, who will seek to protect her.

'Where are you, Agnes?' Jane whispers to the stars. 'Where can you have run to?' The night is so clear that Jane can identify all the familiar constellations floating above Kent. Orion, the warrior, wears his belt proudly while Virgo shimmers in the darkness. Libra, the scales, is just out of her reach. Beneath these giants of the night sky, Jane is a tiny, inconsequential being. Compared to the heavens, her life is short, and narrow, and completely devoid of any significance. But stargazing is a distraction.

Think, Jane. Think.

If Agnes has left Godmersham Park, where would she go?

Nowhere. When faced with horrors she cannot abide, Agnes leaves herself behind. It took Mrs Knight's gentle ministrations for her to return. The question then becomes not *where* is Agnes but *who* is Agnes? Would Biddy have the gumption to run? Not likely: she is fixed on her childish games, taking comfort in the repetition of her movements. Poor Nessa would scurry under the furniture in fear. Even Agnes said not to mind her – *She wouldn't dare be so bold if you were a real threat.* She cannot be Eleanor. The princess would remain poised, daring any intruder to interfere with her. Besides, nobody has professed to having seen Mrs Knight's foreign princess roaming the countryside. But travellers along the road to Canterbury have reported someone even more incongruous . . .

Suddenly the answer to where Agnes goes when she absconds from Godmersham Park is so obvious that Jane laughs.

But it is miles away. Jane cannot make it there on foot and Neddy has not left a single horse in his stable. She has no choice but to ask for help. Jane stands and turns her head towards Goodnestone. Is it her imagination or are the faint clouds of smoke rising from the chimney stacks of the elegant house visible in the distance? There are no guarantees Jane's plan will work, but she must try. Agnes's very life may depend upon it. She grabs Conker by the collar and, using the silk sash of her gown, ties the whimpering dog to the arbour so he may not follow her on this foolhardy mission.

Chapter Twenty-nine

By the time Jane jogs up the drive, she is breathless and doubled over with an agonizing stitch. As tempting as it was to take the shortcut through the copse from Rowling, the prospect of triggering a giant steel mantrap in the darkness keeps her on the well-trodden path. Her stupid house slippers do nothing but impede her journey. She dared not go back inside to change into her walking boots in case Eliza or Mrs Knight discovered her intentions and admonished her to wait until help could be summoned. If Jane is to save Agnes, there is not a moment to spare, and the only 'help' who is not already employed in defending Godmersham Park is here at Good-nestone. At least, she prays he's still here. She clutches her side as she limps past the stable block.

On the ground floor of the great house, all the windows are shuttered, and the doors are bolted. She must not rouse the servants. If Neddy wanted Sir William's help in dis-arming Captain Fairbairn, he would have sent for it. Jane cannot give her brother any more reasons to disown her. He already has far too many available to him. What she needs, therefore, is a discreet method of alerting Mr Bridges to her presence. She has no clue which of the many windows belongs to his chamber. Goodnestone is a mansion. There are at least twenty sash windows on the upper two floors to choose from. But only one is aglow with candles. And only a profligate, like Mr Bridges, would burn through the baronet's cash in reading by the light of so many at this ungodly hour.

Jane grabs a chunk of gravel and flings it at the window. It grazes the wall, almost hitting her in the face as it ricochets back towards her. She forces down an expletive, then pokes around in the shrubbery for a better stone. With the window fixed in her sights, she hurls it with all her might.

The inevitable tinkling of smashed glass follows.

Capital. Now Neddy can add vandalizing his brother-in-law's property to his list of reasons to despise her.

The empty sash slides upwards and an aggrieved Mr Bridges sticks his head out. 'What's afoot down there?' When his eye alights on Jane, standing in the shrubbery without cloak or bonnet, his expression switches from out-rage to wolfish curiosity. She places one finger over her lips and beckons him to join her. He nods, disappears inside and brings down the sash with a thump. Fragments of loose glass fall to the ground. Her initial triumph at having successfully alerted him to her presence fades to trepidation as to how he might react to her plea for assistance. By his own account, the man is a coward. She must impress upon him how dire the situation is.

Mr Bridges comes running from the direction of a side entrance, dressed only in his shirtsleeves. He has not even paused to tie his cravat. 'Jane?'

'Oh, Mr Bridges.' She rushes to him. He places his hands on her shoulders, while she grips the sinuous strength of his forearms. 'All the men are gone, and I need you.'

He cups her cheek with his warm hand. 'Sweet girl.' He smiles benignly down at her. 'I know it must feel like that, with so many gentlemen having been called away to fight, and I'm very flattered, but we really haven't known each other long. Besides, your brother is bound to challenge me in defence of your honour, and I already know for certain he's a much better shot than I am.'

She thrusts both fists up through his arms, breaking his hold on her. 'Not like *that*, you idiot.'

Mr Bridges continues as if he has not heard her: 'This is my fault. I led you on. I am so terribly fond of you, and I thought a little frisson might lift your spirits after your disappointment with the young Irish fellow.'

Of all the mortifying conversations Tom Lefroy has wormed his way into since he fled Hampshire, Jane was unprepared for this to be one of them. Her toes curl in her slippers as she fights to keep her voice from shaking. 'And, pray tell me, how do *you* know about my Irish friend?'

'You told me.'

'I most certainly did not.'

'Um ...' Mr Bridges shifts his weight from one booted foot to the other. 'In that case, my sister might have mentioned it.'

Of course Elizabeth would have no compunction in sharing the news of Jane's humiliation far and wide. She is determined to see Jane married and off Neddy's hands. Whether she achieves this by advertising her charms or her desperate availability is neither here nor there. 'Did she tell you to flirt with me outrageously too?'

'No, I assure you. That was entirely of my own volition.' He edges away from her, like a hound that knows it is in for a whipping.

'Allow me to clarify matters.' Jane draws a deep breath. 'All the men of Rowling Farm have gone to Godmersham Park to ward off Spooner and his gang of vicious thugs. He was captain of the shipwreck Mr Skeete was so anxious to conceal, and Agnes, Mrs Knight's foreign princess, is the only other survivor. Spooner wants to murder her before she can bear witness to his crimes. Understandably, the terrified girl has absconded. What I need is for you to convey me to where I believe she is hiding. Do you think you could manage that?'

'I see.' Mr Bridges tiptoes backwards, looking as mortified as Jane hitherto felt. 'I'll, erm, run to the stables. Shall I?'

'If it's not too inconvenient.'

'Wait here. I won't be long!' He spins on his heel and goes
dashing off with even more alacrity than Jane could have
wished for.

A short while later, Mr Bridges reappears, riding an enormous bay stallion. 'Where are we off to?'

'St Augustine's Abbey, in search of the "bloody nun". As
Mr Blackall said, several people have witnessed the phe-
nomenon, but you and I know new ghosts don't just pop
up and start haunting places after lying peacefully for hundreds of years.' To his credit, Mr Bridges nods along to Jane's
every word, as if she was making perfect sense. Which at
this point in proceedings, even Jane is not convinced is the
case. However, it may well have been Mrs Knight's house
guest, rather than one of her servants, who left the kitchen
door unbolted after she escaped on a midnight jaunt to the
abbey. 'It *must* be Agnes. But ...' Jane points the vacant
space behind the horse's tail '... where is your gig?'

He frowns. 'It's the middle of the night. I can't very well
disturb the coachman. Not unless you want everyone to
know about this. Which I presume you don't. Otherwise,
you'd have banged on the front door, like a civilized person.'
He reaches a hand down to help her mount. He is still in
his shirtsleeves, and is not wearing gloves. But, then, neither

is Jane. 'William is bound to take the cost of replacing that pane of glass out of my allowance, you know.'

'I do apologize. As we've already established, I was *desperate* for you.' Mr Bridges has the courtesy to look rueful. The animal whinnies, and prances sideways. Jane eyes it warily. Sensing her trepidation, Mr Bridges points to a mounting block beside the front step. She climbs it, reaching for his forearm and lifting one foot to rest on his boot. 'Why do these matters always have to involve a horse?'

'We're in the English countryside. How else do you propose to get abroad?' He hoists her onto the saddle with surprising strength.

'I'm ready. Walk on.' Jane perches sideways behind him, one leg crossed over the other.

'Not like that you're not.' His profile is silhouetted by the moon, so close to Jane her lips almost touch the evening shadow on his cheek. 'You'll slip off and break your neck. Sit properly.'

'Astride? But it's unladylike.' Jane is already mortified to have exposed half an inch of white thigh above her garter as he hoisted her into the saddle. 'What if someone sees us?'

'My dear Jane, whether you're sitting astride or not, if anyone catches us cavorting around alone in the dead of night, both our reputations will be in tatters. We'll have no option but to marry.'

'Good Lord, I hadn't thought of that.' She shudders. All

her previous reserve abandoned, Jane wraps her arms tightly around his trim waist. 'This operation is even more perilous than I imagined.'

'Exactly.' He tightens his jaw. 'So, throw your leg over and hold on tight.'

Chapter Thirty

St Augustine's Abbey lies in darkness. Jane and Mr Bridges did not pass a single other traveller on their race to reach the ruin. In the black of night, the tower is far eerier than Jane remembers. Moonlight reflects from the yellow stone, highlighting the fallen pillars. Strange noises drift from the fields beyond and dark shapes move as shadows all around them. They are merely cattle, grazing on Sir Edward Hale's rich pasture. Jane refuses to let her nerves get the better of her as she dismounts and begins calling, 'Agnes.'

'We could ride on to the inn and ask to borrow a lantern?' Mr Bridges glances towards the irregular outline of Canterbury's rooftops in the distance.

'There's no time. We must find her.' Jane sets off, stumbling over the loose bits of rubble concealed in the grass. 'Perhaps we should separate? She could be hiding anywhere.'

'For someone whose intelligence is so highly lauded, you

say some very silly things.' Mr Bridges secures the horse to a branch of a sprawling oak.

'What's the matter? Are you afraid the monks will serenade you?' Jane does not slow down to wait for him.

'Is there a more terrifying sound than vespers?' He grabs her hand, pulling her to an abrupt standstill. 'Wait!'

'What is it?'

'Look, there.' He gestures towards the remains of the small chapel. 'You were right.' A few yards away, on the marble slab of the altarpiece, a woman's body is stretched out. Her features denote a resigned peace, and her skin is luminous. Not a nun in a white habit with blood running from a head wound, but Agnes in her nightdress, her red hair fanned out around her pale face.

'Agnes!' Jane's heart constricts as she races towards her. At the arched entrance, she hesitates, burying her face in Mr Bridges' chest. Agnes is too calm, too still. She does not stir at the sound of Jane's voice. Her eyes are closed. Deep shadows cut into the hollows of her cheeks. A memory surfaces of another young woman laid out in a borrowed nightdress – one whom Jane could not save. 'She's dead.'

'No, she can't be . . .' He wraps his arms around Jane.

Beside them, the body emits a long, pitiful keening, echoing around the stone chamber. Jane rushes to kneel beside the altar, where Agnes lies as still as a stone effigy atop a tomb. 'Agnes, what's the matter? Are you hurt?'

'Agnes is gone.' She answers without opening her eyes,

her monotone voice betraying only the slightest hint of an Irish accent.

Jane looks to Mr Bridges, who stares down at her with equal consternation. She wants to ask him to lift Agnes in his arms and forcibly carry her to safety, but Jane knows that would alarm her even further. Instead she pushes her hand along the altar, until their fingers are almost touching. 'Where has Agnes gone? Can you tell me?'

'To the devil.'

The words send an icy shiver through Jane's soul. Agnes's body is here, talking to her, and yet this is not Agnes. It is possible that Agnes is so terrified, so damaged, that she may never surface again. 'Then who, may I ask, are you?'

'Derdriu.' Derdriu's eyes flicker open, but she stares at the heavens rather than at Jane.

'Derdriu, listen to me. You must come with us. I know you have been terribly frightened, with that horrid man intent on hurting you. But my brothers have set out to arrest him, and Mrs Knight is most anxious for your return. We must take you back to her, so that she can keep you safe.'

Derdriu does not flinch. Instead, she stares, unseeing, at the night sky. 'I'm not frightened. I'm not anything. Agnes was the one who was always so afraid. Nothing can hurt me for I am made of stone.'

Jane meets the tip of Derdriu's index finger with her own. It is so cold, she must have been lying here for some time. Is this how Agnes has endured, by becoming impassive when subjected to the captain's abuse? 'You are not stone. You are someone and you matter. You must cease this talk at once and allow me to take you, and Agnes, to safety.'

Still, Derdriu refuses to move. Her breathing is slow, her body listless. 'You cannot save Agnes. She is beyond salvation.'

'No, Derdriu,' Jane protests, thinking that Derdriu must hold Agnes responsible for the vile depravities to which Captain Fairbairn exposed her. 'None of it was Agnes's fault. She was just a child.'

'I keep finding her here, begging for absolution. But this is not the Lord's house. It's crumbling rock and emptiness, like me.'

Jane recalls Agnes's words when she refused to enter the church in Crundale. *I can't confess. He'll smite me for what I've done.* What sin is weighing on her conscience? If Jane can draw it out of Derdriu, Agnes may return. As horrific as it was to bear witness to Agnes's pain, Derdriu's resignation is even worse. 'What terrible deed did Agnes commit? Why does she require forgiveness? Tell me, Derdriu, so that I may understand.'

'The *Infanta.*'

'The princess?' Jane asks.

'The ship. Agnes sank it. She killed all those men, and the other girls.'

'But Agnes couldn't sink a ship.'

'Yes, she did. She sank the ship, and she drowned everyone on board. She would have slain herself, too.'

'No.' Jane places her hand over Derdriu's, hoping to suffuse her with some warmth of her own. 'It was the captain's fault. He attempted to turn the boat in a mighty gale without readying the sails. There was a witness – an old man was watching from the Isle of Sheppey. We'll find him and he'll swear to it, I promise.'

'The Lord is the only true witness, and He knows.'

Jane looks at Mr Bridges. He remains beside her, one hand resting on her shoulder in reassurance. 'What does he know?' Jane asks.

Derdriu's fingers remain limp. 'As the storm hit, Agnes was praying for death. And then, when the wave washed over, she didn't hold on. She could have, but she didn't.'

'She was swept overboard?'

'She *let* herself be taken. She believed even Hell would be a blessed release from this torment. But he ... he wouldn't let her go. So long as there is breath in his body, he'll never let her go. And, in his haste, they were all tipped screaming into the swell.'

'Oh, Derdriu.' Jane swallows, picturing the dreadful scene. *Tossed and turned like it was no more than a toy. Mast broke first. Snapped in two like a blade of straw. We could hear the sailors' screams. But we can't do nothing, not when the sea decides she's going to make you hers.* 'That is horrifying. But it's not Agnes's fault. She's just a girl. She could no more control the actions of that despicable man any more than she could the sea, or the wind.'

'They all died because of her, and now she is doomed for all eternity.'

'No, she is not. I won't let her be.' Jane turns to Mr Bridges in desperation. 'Do something.'

'Like what?' He stares down at her, wide-eyed.

'You intend to be a clergyman, forgive her.'

'In the Anglican Church, Jane. I won't hear confession. I'm not even ordained.'

Derdriu lifts her head. 'Jane?'

Is it possible that Derdriu is so closed off from Agnes's other parts that she had not recognized Jane before now? 'That's right. I'm Jane.'

'You wrote to us.' Derdriu places one hand flat against the slab and pushes herself upright.

'I did, yes.' Neither Biddy nor Agnes responded to Jane's note; she was not certain either of them read it. But now, as the girl withdraws a familiar square of yellowed paper from beneath her nightgown, Jane can see she must have. The frayed edges attest to its having been unfolded and refolded a thousand times, and the singed corners prove it has been scrutinized by candlelight. Derdriu sits cross-legged on the altar, holding the letter aloft as her eyes scan the words. She blinks. The note wavers as her hands shake. In an instant, her entire demeanour switches. She gazes around the ruined chapel with large, fearful eyes, lips trembling.

'Agnes?' Jane can hardly dare to believe she has returned.

'Miss Jane.' Agnes reaches for Jane's hand, clasping it tight. 'Why do I keep waking here? Where is Mrs Knight? You said I would be safe if I stayed where she could see me. I must get back to her.'

'Yes, you must.' Jane's heart lifts. Despite all the odds, she has recovered Agnes. 'She's at Rowling. Let me take you to her immediately.'

Agnes unfolds her legs and jumps down from the altar. Jane holds her hand as she leads her hastily over the grass towards the horse. The one horse, which Mr Bridges thought adequate to carry out their rescue operation. Jane throws him a chagrined look.

'I . . . er . . . I suppose we'll have to separate.' He frees the reins, tossing them to Jane. 'You know the route. Even if you don't, just set off along the high road, and the horse will make his own way back to Goodnestone.'

'But what about you? We can't leave you stranded.'

'You mustn't worry about me, Jane. I'm a man.' He places one hand on his hip. 'I'll walk to Canterbury and hire a mount. It's not that far. I might even catch up with you on the road.'

'It's just . . .' Jane chews the inside of her cheek. She's going to have to admit how utterly useless she is. 'I'm not a particularly skilled horsewoman. I'm not certain I can command such an enormous beast.'

Mr Bridges tips his face upwards. 'Well, luckily for you, it would appear your companion is.'

Jane follows his gaze. Agnes has mounted the animal. She sits astride, face placid as she holds the reins in one hand and pats the horse's neck with the other. With her hair hastily swept under a felt hat and her nightgown tucked into a pair of breeches, she sits as confident in the saddle as any of Jane's brothers. She does not even bother using the stirrups. Rather, as Frank was wont to do when he fancied a hack but was too lazy to tack up, she presses her bare feet into the horse's girth.

'Up you go.' Mr Bridges laces his fingers together and crouches before Jane. She places her foot in his makeshift cradle. This is it. The last leg of her journey to save Agnes. Then, God willing, she will never have to ride on horseback again for as long as she lives. She grips the polished leather and hoists herself up, but as soon as Mr Bridges removes his support she slides down again. The horse prances sideways, and her stomach roils. She is not even on the monstrous beast, and already she is falling off. Mr Bridges places a hand on the back of her right thigh and shoves her back on. Of all the indignities! Agnes remains poised. The girl's body is uncharacteristically tense – spine straight and shoulders back. Jane reaches her arms around her waist but does not press tightly, as she did with Mr Bridges. She can sense a detached air emanating from Agnes, and the last thing she would want is to intrude on her person. 'All set?' Mr Bridges grins up at them.

'Quite.' Jane shoots him a vexed look. The rascal is enjoying her discomfort. 'And, Mr Bridges . . .'

'Yes?'

'Watch out for those singing monks, won't you? Gah!' She screams as he slaps the horse on the rump, sending them racing off into the night.

Chapter Thirty-one

They make it as far as the winding lane between Rowling and Goodnestone before the horse slows to a limp. Jane tries to ignore the uneven roll of his movements, telling herself he will pick up again in just a few moments and carry them to safety. But when he comes to a complete halt, refusing to budge no matter how hard Agnes digs her heels into his solid girth, neither can deny the problem any longer. Agnes slides to the ground and leads the animal towards the chestnut fence surrounding the cornfield. Without uttering a word, she runs a palm down each of his forelegs, lifting them in turn to examine his hoofs.

'What's wrong?' asks Jane.

'Damn beast is lame.' Agnes loops the reins around the stile. 'Must have thrown a shoe, back on the high road.'

Perhaps it is not a disaster. Mr Bridges said the horse would return to Goodnestone of its own accord, but, from here, Jane and Agnes can walk to Rowling. Above the treetops, moonlight bounces off the manor's slate-tiled roof. Even on foot it will take less than half an hour. By now, Eliza is bound to have discovered Jane is missing and be distressed at her unexplained absence. Likewise, both Agnes and her benefactress will be highly agitated until they are reunited. Jane uses the stile to aid her dismount. 'Don't despair, we've almost reached my brother's home, where Mrs Knight is waiting. She'll be so relieved to see you unharmed, and I expect your spirits will be so much calm—'

'Quiet,' Agnes says, in a growl. She walks out into the middle of the lane and stands, hands planted on her hips and grim-faced. From the distance comes the ominous rumble of horses. Could it be Mr Bridges following them from Canterbury? No, the sound is continuous: there is more than one rider. Jane prays it is Neddy and Henry returning from Godmersham after having secured the park, rather than Spooner and his gang fleeing the site of a massacre. But if her brothers were on their way home, why would they be riding so hard?

A cold, damp cape of fear curls around Jane's shoulders. She sets off towards Rowling, willing Agnes to join her. But there is something wrong with Agnes. She does not follow. Instead, she remains motionless, eyes trained on the bend where the path meets the main road. 'Come, Agnes. Look, you can see the house through the trees. If we hurry, we'll be there in no time –'

'I said QUIET, bitch.'

Jane stops dead. The words came from the girl's mouth, but it was distinctly *not* Agnes's voice. She turns to see her standing in the open, as if waiting for the riders in the distance. There is something oddly familiar about her stance. She stands with her knees soft, and her feet turned out. Frank does it, as does Charles. They call it their 'sea legs'. Agnes has transformed herself, but not into any of the alternative personae that Jane has met before. This character is too vulgar, too masculine, too malicious. 'Oh, my God. You're him. *You*'re Captain Fairbairn!'

'What? Did you mistake me for that pathetic whelp, Agnes?' the captain sneers, as the sinister noise of hoofs beating the ground grows ever louder.

Jane clamps both hands over her mouth. 'You can't be. Agnes is so afraid of you. She said you'd take her away. This makes no sense.' And yet it makes perfect sense. The devil Agnes is most afraid of is the one who lurks beneath her own breast. Spooner is not Captain Fairbairn. Agnes is. Jane remembers Biddy's warning: *You mustn't speak of him. You mustn't even think of him, or he'll find a way in.* Not into the park, as Jane feared, but worse: into Agnes's very mind. 'Why would you write such nasty things about yourself? Why try to persuade Mrs Knight to turn you out?'

'Because Agnes *has* to go back to Spooner. I must take her back to him.'

'No.' Jane reaches out, clutching the captain's arm. It is no wonder none of the servants at the park had spotted an intruder if Agnes, as Fairbairn, was leaving the vile notes. His paper matched Neddy's as he likely stole it from Mrs Knight who probably frequents the same stationer as her son in Canterbury. Jane tries dragging him away from the road, but he is as immovable as Mr Bridges' horse. 'We can't let Spooner or his gang find you. You did so well to escape, you must never go back.'

But the captain remains adamant. 'Didn't you listen to Derdriu? Spooner won't ever stop looking for her. If she runs, it'll only inflame his ire.' The clattering grows louder. A shot rings out, followed by heated cries. The riders will round the bend in just a few moments. 'That's Spooner. He's coming.'

'It can't be.' Jane tugs on the captain's elbow, desperately trying to lead him towards the bank. 'My brothers went to Godmersham with a small army to defeat him.'

'Spooner will have found a way to slip their net. He always does. And he won't stop, not until Agnes is dead. She belongs to him, see? The only reason he turned that ship around was so he could pluck her from the waves and smite her himself.'

'No.' Jane leans all her weight into the captain in an attempt to push him away. 'Agnes doesn't belong to anyone but herself. I will not let you surrender her to that vile man. She doesn't deserve to be betrayed again. Especially not by you.'

'Betrayed?' He stares back, wide-eyed, with genuine

confusion. 'I'm not betraying her, I'm *protecting* her. Who do you think swam to shore after the ship capsized? Not Agnes, she'd have gone under willingly.' He jabs a finger to his breast. 'It was me. It's always me who must do whatever's necessary to keep her alive. Without me, she'd have had her throat slit and been tossed overboard, like all his other useless whores.'

Finally, Jane releases the captain, scrabbling towards the bank to save herself. They have run out of time. Even if they set off along the lane now, the riders would spot them from the road. She will have to risk the copse instead. 'Please, Agnes, Captain Fairbairn, we can hide in the woods until they pass by.'

'I can't.' The captain balls his fists, standing rigid. 'He'll find her. Agnes has gone too far by involving your family. He really will kill her this time.'

'No. We must away, now!' Jane climbs backwards up the slope and towards the dense woodland. Under the trees' canopy, the footpath is only just visible. She casts her eyes deeper into the wilderness, trying to remember the steps she trod with Neddy. It is a gamble, but one she cannot avoid.

The captain lifts his head. 'Unless he takes you.'

A lone rider rounds the bend. Jane holds her breath as she prays for the familiar shape of Mr Bridges or one of her brothers, even Armand with his frightful blunderbuss. Instead, a wiry figure in a knitted hat is mounted on the horse. The captain is right, Spooner has found them.

'It's too late. He'll take you!' Captain Fairbairn lunges towards Jane.

But Jane is already running, faster than she has ever run in her life. Faster than she ever thought possible. Green leaves slap her face, and branches crack against her body. Her lungs burn, her slippers fly from her feet, and yet still she runs. The captain is so close, Jane can hear his ragged breath. Who was pursuing Spooner? Was it her brothers and the dragoons, or is he accompanied by his own band of villains? How long will it be before he reaches her? Could Jane make it all the way back to Rowling with the captain on her tail?

'Agnes!' a man's voice cries. 'I saw yer. Get back here, girl.'

The copse is too dense for anyone to have followed them on horseback. If Spooner is in the woods, he must have pursued them on foot. The captain is right: Spooner will never let Agnes go, no matter the cost. But Agnes, as Fairbairn, is only a few paces behind and Jane is not ready to give up on her yet.

Jane's stockinged feet pound into the dirt. She fixes on the footpath, trying to make out the safest route through the dense foliage. She must steer clear of the trap. Her eyes scan the trees for a reference point. An ugly, bleeding canker against pale green bark is lit by the silver moon. A horrid thought occurs. No, she must not – it is too risky. But what if taking that risk is the only way to save Agnes *and* herself? The captain is treading on Jane's heels. She reaches behind, grabbing his wrist and forcing him to follow as they veer off the beaten path, skirting the alder. Footsteps crash after them.

Snap!

A spring catches, and two giant rings of steel collide. Flesh crunches against bone. It is like the sound of her mother wringing the neck of a chicken, only a thousand times more sickening. Pain shoots along the side of Jane's shin, as her ankle twists and she spirals out of control. She lands on her hands, grit scraping the skin from her palms. Beside her, Agnes – for Jane can already tell, from the girl's terrified expression, that Agnes has returned – tumbles to the ground. From behind them comes the ear-splitting scream of a man in agony.

Jane and Agnes are free, while Spooner is caught in the deathly jaws of Sir William's mantrap.

Chapter Thirty-two

'**J**ane!' Eliza's face is a portrait of fury as she stands at the door of Rowling Manor in the gentle glow of firelight. 'Where in God's name have you been? One moment you were there, the next you'd disappeared off the face of the earth, and all that was left of you was your sash tied around the execrable dog. I feared you'd been kidnapped!'

'*Excusez-moi, madame.*'

Jane is shielded from her new sister-in-law's wrath by the gruff interjection of her saviour, Armand, who has carried her like a babe all the way home from the copse as she berated herself for having doubted his fidelity. 'I must put Miss Austen somewhere she can raise her leg.'

Thankfully, Jane's prayers did not go unheeded and it was Neddy, closely followed by Armand and several of the men from Rowling, who had been pursuing Spooner along the main road. Neddy was horrified to stumble across his youngest sister sitting among the undergrowth in her house gown and stockinged feet in the early hours. Perhaps even more horrified than he had been when he followed Spooner's agonized cries to discover him with his mangled knee caught tight between the steel teeth of the baronet's trap.

'A cold compress, if you please?' Armand looks to the small crowd of women as he places Jane on the oak bench in the hall. Kitty and Alice dash off towards the kitchen, while Eliza, Mrs Knight and Grace remain. Jane's left ankle has swollen to a thick trunk, twice the size of the other. She cannot look at it without her stomach turning. However, Armand has prodded at the throbbing joint and assured her it is not broken, and the graceful turn of her calf will return in just a few days.

'Agnes?' Mrs Knight rushes towards the figure lurking in the doorway.

'Mistress.' Agnes's voice catches. 'I'm so sorry, I meant to bide with you. I really did.'

'Oh, you poor child, I'm not angry. I'm just so relieved to see you're unhurt.' Mrs Knight takes the girl by her hand and pulls her inside, towards the fire. 'Where did you get to? We scoured the house looking for you.'

'I . . . I can't explain.' Agnes's face crumples, and Jane aches at the sight of her obvious fear and confusion. 'I was at the empty church, and then I was in the woods with Miss Jane.'

Mrs Knight turns to Jane. '*You* found her?'

'I did, yes. Haunting St Augustine's Abbey.' Jane winces as Alice returns two steps ahead of Kitty and presses a damp cloth to her ankle. Conker, sensing Jane's discomfort, rests his snout in her lap. The dog's nature is far more forgiving than her own. She is glad. The feel of his velvet ears, beneath her fingers, is exactly what she needs to restore her equilibrium.

'Godmersham is preserved, madame.' Armand bows to Mrs Knight, like a warrior returned from battle to lay his victory at his queen's feet. 'The invaders put up little resistance, after we fired a few warning shots at their heads. Captain Austen has the gang secure until the dragoons arrive. Their leader escaped the park, but your son tracked him here.'

'Spooner must have spotted Agnes and me on our way out of Canterbury and risked capture to pursue us.' Jane shudders: she and Agnes were also being hunted.

Mrs Knight clutches her throat. 'But you caught the villain? He's secured now?'

'As secure as a man can be.' The coachman shoots Jane an admiring glance. 'He is caught in a six-stone trap with his leg half off.'

'No!' the women, apart from Jane, exclaim at once.

'*C'est vrai*. We have despatched one of the men to fetch a surgeon, and Mr Austen remains to guard the prisoner. But I do not think Spooner capable of going anywhere, unless it is to Hell.' Armand shrugs, with his usual air of Gallic nonchalance. 'Miss Austen displayed enormous courage in leading him towards the trap.'

'Enormous stupidity, more like.' Eliza has taken over the

cold compress and is pressing it earnestly to Jane's ankle while picking dead leaves out of her stockings. 'Really, Jane. Couldn't you have told *me* where you were going?'

'Hush now, cousin,' says Mrs Knight, in her most commanding tone. 'You heard my coachman. Miss Austen displayed enormous courage in apprehending the villain. And Armand would know. He's a veteran of the attack on the Tuileries. Aren't you, Armand?'

'*Oui*. And now I must bid you adieu.' He lets out a heavy sigh as he heads for the door. 'I expect the surgeon will want to move Spooner, but I will not have that man's blood all over my coach. He can go in a wheelbarrow, for all I care.'

Chapter Thirty-three

Agnes, Godmersham Park

'Sleep while you can, for dawn is almost upon us.' Grace pulls the gold quilt to Agnes's chin as she lies, heart racing, limbs stiff, in the centre of the four-poster bed. After Armand had conveyed the three women from Rowling to Godmersham, Grace insisted on wiping the tears from Agnes's face, and even bathed her hands and feet in warm, soapy water. Yet Agnes fears she will dirty the pristine linen if she moves so much as an inch. Mrs Knight may have reinstated her in one of her many fine chambers, but Agnes knows she is an interloper, polluting everything she touches. The maid turns to leave, stooping to pick up Agnes's precious breeches, traded for a plume of peacock feathers from the gardener's boy. As she does so, the candlelight throws a monstrous shadow of her slight form onto the papered wall behind her, and Agnes must steel herself not to cry out. Is it really Grace, or

Spooner and his men come to grab her? 'I'll take these down to the laundry, shall I?' Grace smiles, unaware of the horrifying apparition behind her.

'No.' Agnes sits upright, reaching for her belongings but caught from the waist down between the tightly wound sheets. 'Leave them be. I'll need them on the morrow.'

'There now, miss.' Grace tuts, as if she can sense Agnes's furtive intentions. 'We'll not have you slipping out in disguise again. What would the mistress say?'

'But I must go ...' In Kent, Agnes has met with more kindness than she thought possible. In return, she has brought nothing but trouble to all those who befriended her: poor Mrs Wilmot tended Agnes's wounds, only to suffer her husband's wrath when Nessa would not be made pliant; gentle Mrs Knight welcomed Agnes into her home, but was forced to flee in fear of her life when Agnes's past caught up with them both; and Miss Jane gave Agnes hope that she was not alone in her affliction. Yet Agnes could tell, when she came to in the woods as Spooner lay injured, how truly terrified of Captain Fairbairn Jane had been. The memory of her new friends' goodness must be enough to sustain Agnes. She cannot risk embroiling them any further in her troubles, and she could not bear to remain as their sympathy turned to scorn.

At first light, to preserve her resolve, she'll quit the mansion without taking her leave. If she heads west, towards London and away from the sea, she will put even more distance between herself and the years of misery she spent imprisoned in Spooner's wooden world. Once a kindly sailor asked Agnes why she returned to the *Infanta* when, in a city or even a busy port, a girl like her might lose herself among the crowd. At first, she was too afraid even to repeat the words in her head. Then, when she did, she held the prospect of escape to her chest as a secret morsel of hope to sustain herself. But as Agnes has discovered, no matter how far she runs, she can never escape her torment.

'You'll feel better after some rest. You always do.' Grace places a hand lightly on Agnes's shoulder, causing her to flinch as she is recalled to the present. 'I'll lay out a clean gown, ready for the morning.' The maid bustles around the room arranging the fine stockings and petticoats that Mrs Knight procured. Agnes ignores her, staring mutely at the single candle flickering on the stand beside her bed until Grace is done with fussing.

Finally alone, Agnes presses her face to the cool pillow and a scalding teardrop slides down her cheek. She wishes she could be one of the others. Eleanor has no qualms about accepting Mrs Knight's hospitality, while Agnes fears even a pallet on the floor of the servants' quarters would be too good for her. She squeezes her eyes shut and calls for the princess. Try as she might, Eleanor will not come. None of them does as they are bade. Rather, they come and go inside her mind at liberty – sometimes permitting Agnes to remain, trapped in a waking nightmare as she watches herself speak and act as another. More often than not, they snuff her out and the memory of what she has endured, especially as Derdriu, does not resurface until days, weeks, sometimes years afterwards. As frightening as it is not to recall events, there are things about her life that Agnes would rather not be party to.

When Fairbairn takes hold, it is as if Agnes ceases to exist. The first she heard of the captain was after she awoke, confused as to why she was back on board the *Infanta* after summoning all her courage and dashing through the streets of Roscoff. She assumed Spooner must have caught up with her and could not fathom why she had been spared the lash, until Derdriu revealed the captain had forced her to return before Spooner noticed she was missing. Undeterred, Agnes tried again in Cherbourg and in Ostend, only for the same pattern to repeat itself. Just as freedom was within her grasp, the captain compelled her back to the ship. Those times she did not escape unpunished. As she lay, trying to block out the pain, the others began whispering their recriminations. They say it is Agnes's fault the captain surfaces. They are as terrified of him as she is, for he has threatened to murder every one of them in his fight for supremacy. But, they say, if Agnes did not provoke Fairbairn, he would not come at all. She must try harder to submit. It is only when she tries to flee, that the captain chokes the rest of them.

Agnes cannot remember a time when she was whole, one girl inside one body. She suspects she must have been, back in Ireland, when she lived in the one-room cottage over-looking the blustery bay with her mammy, her brother and sisters, those short years of hunger and petty squabbles as they eked a living from the earth, before Pa died and Agnes sailed away to learn what it was to be truly afraid. Surely she must have been granted a short period of being alone in her own mind. Yet she knows Biddy says she came first, and there are probably others who claim that right too. All the voices clamouring to be heard believe Agnes's body is theirs. But when Agnes catches her reflection in the mirror, she is the only one whose insides match her outside. That must mean this tired, wretched person belongs to her, must it not?

For a long time, Agnes wondered why she alone had been cursed so. People can be terrifying in their changeability, but nobody else seemed forced to share. Until she met Miss Jane, with her many voices and letters to her various parts. Agnes would never have guessed such an elegant young lady could be afflicted in a manner so similar to herself. She dreads to think what terrible thing happened to cause Jane to shatter. She tried to enquire, yet Jane denied it. She is probably ashamed, frightened of what may happen if anyone finds out about her other selves. Agnes has always been afraid and with good reason. When she attempted to account for the princess to Dr Storer, he declared her a lunatic and, although she prays for the Lord's help, Mr Blackall claimed a demon lurked inside her. Mrs Knight was the first to remain unperturbed by the sudden inexplicable shifts in Agnes's character.

'What's all this?' The widow stands at the door to her chamber in a silk banyan and nightcap, as if Agnes has summoned her soothing presence. 'Grace tells me you're talking of leaving again. Be assured, my dear, you will go nowhere until we've had the chance to discuss your future.'

Agnes sits upright. 'But what if he comes back?'

'Mr Spooner?' Mrs Knight sets down her candle as she perches on the side of Agnes's bed. 'That's impossible. He was gravely injured and my son, the magistrate, arrested him. Think hard, try to remember.'

'Not him, Captain Fairbairn.' Agnes's lip trembles as she repeats the name of her greatest foe.

'Why would he? You told Miss Austen the captain emerged because, if Mr Spooner found you'd escaped, the consequences would be more severe than if you'd remained. But now Mr Spooner and his associates are in the custody of the authorities, there is nowhere the captain could take you. Is there?'

Agnes can hardly dare to hope that Mrs Knight is right. If Captain Fairbairn was to remain buried, her mind, though never quiet, might be in harmony. She pictures Spooner, caught in the mantrap as if an iron devil had reached through the earth to claim him. Mrs Knight is correct: he ought not to be able to recover from his horrific injuries or to evade the law. But Agnes made the mistake of believing she was free once before, when she awoke on the beach at Whitstable and realized the ship was lost. After that, Spooner rose from the dead to pursue her. 'I don't belong in this house, in this world. It would be better for everyone if I wasn't here at all.'

Mrs Knight places her palm over Agnes's trembling fingers, the scent of lavender water emanating from her clean skin. 'My dear, there was a time when I believed the same. After I was married, when I failed to produce the heir my husband so desperately wanted, I feared it was my fault – a punishment for sins I had committed, for sins that had been inflicted on me. I believed Thomas would be so disgusted if he knew the truth of my past that he would despise me for my failings. Yet we must live, Agnes. It is our duty to live. Each of us must carve out a place to do so, and the Lord has a way of providing what we truly need. As Thomas proved my protector, I will protect you.'

Agnes stares at the faint freckles on the back of Mrs Knight's hand, wishing she could prove worthy of her kindness. 'There can be no place for a creature as wicked and forlorn as myself.'

'I have a sanctuary in mind, you wait and see. But you need time to recover from your ordeal and I have some arrangements yet to make. Sleep now. Say your prayers and, remember, the Lord *is* forgiveness.' Mrs Knight extinguishes Agnes's light, then retrieves her own.

Agnes nods in tired acquiescence before collapsing onto

the pillow. Perhaps she will stay, just a while longer, until she can formulate a better plan than walking aimlessly towards a city she has never been to and that can guarantee her no friendly welcome. As Mrs Knight departs, she stumbles over the Lord's Prayer. Would that Agnes could find solace in religion, but the words do not fit easily on her tongue. Instead, she reaches for the frayed note tucked inside the sleeve of her nightgown. The paper is soft with wear and its edges are blackened from reading late at night, too close to the flame. In the current gloom, with her eyes adjusting to the lack of the candle, Agnes can only just make out the lines. But, by now, she has learnt the words by rote and it is the familiar shape of the small, neat handwriting that serves as an anchor to her wandering spirit.

Dear Agnes, Biddy, Eleanor (or whoever you may be as you read this),

Whenever you are tempted to fear yourself most afflicted and alone, please take this letter as my sincere assurance that, even in your darkest hour, there is another being who is thinking of you. I see how you have suffered and, though it is not within my power to undo the past, I may remain with you in the present – if you will only allow me the privilege of doing so. For the promotion of your health and happiness, and indeed your very safety, I beg

you never to depart from the sight of your dear friends,
among whose number I am blessed to count myself.

Yours most truly,
Jane

Agnes's heartbeat slows and her body falls limp. The note slips from her hand onto the quilt. It doesn't matter how many times she reads it, or who she is when she does so, Jane's words remain the same.

Chapter Thirty-four

Jane wakes to a sharp stab of pain as Neddy gently lifts her feet onto his lap and sits down beside her on the sofa. Blinding sunlight slices through the gap between the curtains of his study, illuminating the two enormous rifles propped up beside the fireplace. She must have been snoozing for hours, waiting for him to return. 'I'm so sorry, Ned.'

'Don't be.' Neddy is still wearing his sports coat and boots and looks decidedly exhausted after his night of battle. Conker is stretched out on the rug, as if he, too, is worn out after all the excitement. 'Spooner was trespassing, and you were only trying to save yourself and Agnes. It was very brave of you to seek to protect her.'

'Are you sure you don't mean reckless?' Jane had been bracing herself for a severe reprimand from her brother. She is not sure Eliza will ever forgive her for sneaking off alone. Or for ruining such a fine pair of silk stockings.

'I admit it was most imprudent. Anything might have

happened. Mother would never have forgiven me if you'd come to disaster under my watch. But . . .'

'But?' Jane asks, wondering which mother Neddy is referring to. Mrs Knight is certainly pleased with her for retrieving Agnes but, if Jane's plan had failed and both she and Agnes had fallen victim to Spooner, she expects the widow would have attributed their downfall to Jane's impudence.

'I'm not sure one can be brave without being reckless. Look at our brothers, Frank and Charles. Neither could have risen through the ranks of the navy without risking their lives.' Neddy's eyes twinkle with grudging respect. 'I was very close behind Spooner, but I cannot say for certain I'd have caught up with him if you hadn't intervened. It's not your fault he fell prey to Sir William's trap. You've no need to ask my forgiveness on his account.'

'Oh, I didn't mean to apologize for injuring that scoundrel.'

'You didn't?'

'No. It would never have happened if he hadn't behaved so abominably towards Agnes and Heaven only knows how many other girls. I meant I was sorry for presuming the worst of you, Ned. I accused you of the most heinous crime, and I never even gave you the chance to defend yourself.'

'Ah.' Neddy rests back against the cushions, exhaling loudly. 'Again, that's not entirely your fault . . . I suspected you'd overheard my confrontation with Spooner that day.

I should have dealt with it by clarifying matters.' He considers for a long moment. 'But I couldn't bear to provoke your disgust. You'd only just arrived, and I was intent on restoring myself in your affections after so many years apart. It's as you said. I've been blessed to receive every advantage and I dread to think I might disappoint our family.'

Jane lays a hand on his forearm. 'Are your affairs really so dire?'

'Not so bad as to justify my actions. I regret what I did bitterly, and I swear I shall never attempt anything like it again.' He stares at her, his features contorted with misery.

'It's not as if anyone pays the duty on tea.' Jane tries to comfort him, but even to herself her voice sounds hollow. If Neddy objects to the new taxes, he should be using his privileged position to lobby Parliament, not seeking ways to circumvent the law.

'Yes, but where does one draw the line?' He places his hand over hers. 'My interactions with the Sea Salter Company may have begun innocuously, with purchasing a few cheap crates of Bordeaux. Then, before I knew it, I was smuggling my wool to the Continent and unwittingly contributing to the abuse of Agnes. Corruption is a disease, Jane. One must purge even the smallest instance before it rots the whole. Can you believe our Riding Officer, Mr Skeete, was among the villains rounded up at Godmersham?'

While Jane has confessed to Neddy her midnight dash

to save Agnes, she does not think it politic for him to know every detail of her adventure in Whitstable with Mr Bridges. 'You won't be ruined, then?'

'No, but I need to find the means to pay Sir William. I'll begin by being honest with Beth about what we can and cannot afford. She expects us to live as if I've already come into my fortune, but my income is more akin to that of a tenant farmer than a grand gentleman. That's all I amount to presently. I may have vastly more acreage at my disposal than Father, but I face all the same challenges. It's high time Beth and I began living in a style more befitting our circum-stances. We'll need to retrench. I might even have to ...' Neddy swallows. 'No, there must be another way around it. I'll think of something.'

'What is it?' Jane straightens, thinking of all the things her mother and father rely on Neddy's assistance to pay for. Her brother Georgy's welfare is first and foremost in her mind.

'I might have to sell the phaeton and swap the carriage mares for an ordinary pair of draught horses.'

'Is that all?' She laughs.

'You don't sound very sympathetic.'

'Oh, Neddy, I assure you I'm mortified on your behalf. Imagine, the ignominy of being seen driving through Kent, day after day, in nothing more luxurious than a rickety old chaise pulled by ... I can't even say the words.' She pauses, placing the back of her hand to her forehead for effect.

'An *ordinary* pair of draught horses. It's just too ghastly to contemplate.'

'All right, Jane. That's enough of your biting wit.' Neddy takes her hand in his. 'I know you were still in leading strings when I left Steventon.'

'I wasn't that little.'

'You were five, and I was fourteen. Almost a man, and old enough to know my loyalty will always remain with my family. Both my families.' He squeezes her fingers a little too tightly, crushing her knuckles. 'Trust me when I say you may ever rely on me in times of distress.'

'Thank you, Neddy. And I promise we don't love you for your fortune alone.' Jane rests her head on his shoulder. 'Although it certainly helps.' His chest rumbles with laughter. 'What *will* happen to Mr Spooner and his gang?'

'At present, the scoundrels are sleeping off their criminal exertions in Canterbury County Gaol. But pretty soon they'll be up in front of the bench for trespass. If found guilty, they'll either be hanged or, if the magistrate is inclined to show mercy, despatched to a penal colony for fourteen years.'

'Aren't you the magistrate?'

'I am, yes,' he says, as if only just remembering this. 'And while, in this moment, I could cheerfully string up the lot of them for frightening Mother, I hope to recover myself in time to pass judgement with a cool head.'

'I'm sure you'll do the right thing.' Jane sighs. That her

brother is already contemplating showing Spooner's gang clemency is a sure sign he will. She is so very glad their father managed to instil his merciful temperament in his son, who is responsible for administering justice.

'As for Spooner . . .' Neddy sucks the air through his teeth '. . . if he survives, which, between ourselves, I'm not at all certain he will . . .'

'No? I thought it was just his leg that was broken.' When Jane left the copse, Spooner remained impaled, but the variety of his curses and the strength with which they were delivered led her to believe his injuries were not life-threatening.

'Yes, but the last time I saw him, Dr Storer was about to remove the offending limb with a new invention he's keen to patent called the "automatic amputator".'

Jane is hit with a sudden desire to vomit. 'Please don't tell Dr Storer about my ankle. I've only turned it. It'll be perfectly restored in a couple of days, so long as I rest. I really don't require any medical attention.'

'What? You don't want to try his contraption for yourself? It sounds very impressive. He claimed it would take Spooner's leg off in just one blow.' Neddy makes a chopping motion just below Jane's knee. 'Apparently, it relies on a very sharp blade being dropped from a great height, like a humane version of the guillotine.'

'Actually, Neddy, I think the guillotine *was* invented to serve as a more humane means of despatch.'

'Only a mind as brilliant and twisted as yours could contemplate such a thing, Jane.'

'It's true!' She laughs. 'It lops everyone's heads off equally, you see? From prince to pauper.'

'Indeed. Well, if Spooner survives, he, too, will be tried for trespass. And in that instance, given what you and Mother have told me about his other crimes, I should say it's incredibly unlikely I'd be disposed to show any mercy at all.' Neddy's features turn grave. Jane has no sympathy for Spooner, but even she can understand it is an unenviable task to be called on to decide whether another man mounts the scaffold or not. 'So, you can see why I'm hoping Dr Storer might save me a job.'

'Aren't you afraid Spooner will accuse you of smuggling in return?'

'It would hardly help his cause to blacken my name. And if he did, who would be minded to believe him over me? All the evidence, including the tubs of wool and the logbook, sank with the *Infanta*.'

'Then let us pray Dr Storer does his best – or should I say his worst? – to save his patient.'

Neddy smiles, placing a hand on her throbbing ankle. 'Are you sure you don't like the good doctor? If any of his inventions prove popular, he stands to make an enormous amount of money.'

'I've already told you, I don't like him at all.' The one thing Jane's adventure with Mr Bridges has shown her is the benefit of having a helpmate who will follow her commands without question. If a husband could be relied upon to act accordingly, marriage might prove a more enticing prospect.

'Pity. You'd make a formidable duo.'

'We most certainly would not.'

'No? But we couldn't help noticing how much you enjoyed midwifery.' Neddy's lips quirk into a half-smile. 'Beth wants to know if you'll be joining us for the arrival of all our children from now on. She says it was a comfort to find she was not the most distressed person in the birthing room.'

'Stop it.'

'What do you call that shade of green your face is? Only it's rather fetching, and I'm thinking of having the parlour repainted soon.' Neddy laughs as Jane whacks his shoulder. If he is teasing her so much, he must have forgiven her. 'I'll leave you to get some rest, but before I do, you should know that a letter arrived for you from Steventon.'

'You may place it on the mantel. My eyes are too sore to read at present,' she says. How typical of her mother to reply with a detailed account of the old man's travelling plans at the precise moment Jane no longer needs them.

'Oh, but I suspect you'll want to read this one immediately.' Neddy extracts a neat square of paper from his breast pocket. One glance and Jane is forced to bite back a sob of relief. It is not Mrs Austen's hand that greets her, but Cassandra's.

7. *Letter to Cassandra Austen*

Rowling Farm, Saturday, 1 July 1797

My dearest Cassandra,

Of course it is not too much to ask. Now that Elizabeth is safely delivered of her baby, I will deliver myself to you.

Pray endure until my arrival,

J.A.

Miss Austen
Steventon
Overton
Hants

Chapter Thirty-five

Jane is packing, haphazardly winding items of clothing into tight balls and shoving them into her trunk. The volume of her luggage has expanded since she arrived in Kent, so that she must make use of every available square inch. She would happily abandon the new gowns as she doesn't anticipate many opportunities to parade around looking fashionable once she has returned to Steventon. Perhaps Neddy could pawn them to help maintain the carriage horses. But she would not want Elizabeth to think her ungrateful, so she continues to wrinkle the fabric, hoping this will enable the lid to shut.

Henry and Eliza have removed to Margate. They very generously offered to take Jane with them, probably so she could mind Hastings while they remained tête-à-tête. But Jane is determined to get back to the rectory and has begged Mrs Knight's assistance to convey her thither. It will never be easy for someone as proud as Jane to ask for help but, she has discovered, if she is brave enough to do so occasionally the reward is worth the risk of refusal. And Jane really must get home because Cassandra has finally written. Forget Mary's cold souse, the one thing her beloved sister has declared might ease her grief is Jane's company, and there is nothing on God's green earth that will prevent Jane from reaching her. Least of all her own pride.

As she busies herself with pairing stockings and tossing them into her trunk, the door of her bedroom opens, just a crack, and a piece of paper, wrapped around a small object and tied with string, bounces across the carpet. Her first thought is that Fanny and Ted are playing a trick on their departing aunt. But when Jane unties the string, she finds an oddly familiar pebble and a note written in the exquisite hand of a gentleman with an artist's touch.

Meet me at the arbour.

BEB

Jane complies immediately, grateful for the opportunity to thank Mr Bridges for his part in Agnes's salvation. She could never have retrieved the girl without his assistance, and she shudders to imagine what the consequences would have been if Spooner had spotted Derdriu alone at the abbey. From the reckless manner in which he sacrificed the *Infanta* to pursue her across the waves, Jane is certain he would have risked capture to inflict on her one last lethal punishment.

A few moments later, Jane finds Mr Bridges pacing up and down beside the clematis, handsomer than ever in his travelling clothes. His gig rests in the lane behind the house. 'Have you been to call on your sister?' she asks. Elizabeth is recovering well from her lying-in and has expressed a warm desire to receive all her relations. She is so good-tempered, Jane wonders if Kitty was right in her assertion that her sister-in-law's ill nature was brought about by anxiety over the impending birth of her child. Now that baby Henry has been safely delivered, Jane has every hope that Elizabeth's health will be fully restored and that she will retain her more cheerful disposition. Until the next time she conceives, that is.

'I did wait on Beth, yes,' Mr Bridges replies, eyes shining at the sight of Jane.

'Is Hen with you?'

'Oh, no, I came alone.' He removes his tall-crowned hat, running his fingers through his dark hair. 'Hen is avoiding our dear sister. She and Blackall are officially engaged. They're hoping to have the whole thing sewn up before Beth is churched, so she can't object.'

Clever Henrietta, waiting for her sister to be indisposed before securing her future. 'And Sir William has given them his blessing?'

'Well, he took a bit of convincing – but apparently Mr Blackall's collection of sermons is most profitable. And he received a capital advance for the new treatise he's writing.'

'That's wonderful news.' Jane forces out the words,

schooling herself that Mr Blackall's literary success does not make hers any less likely. 'Tell me, what did you make of Little Henry?'

'He's an angel.'

'Isn't he? Were you hoping for a Little Brook?'

'Goodness, no. There are more than enough Brooks in the world already.'

'There are?'

'Yes, we're all called Brook,' he says, as if Jane should know this. 'It's a family name. My father was Brook, William is Brook-William, then there's Brook-Henry and I'm Brook-Edward. On it goes. None of us goes by 'Brook', it would be too confusing. Don't you have a family name?'

'Yes, it's Austen.' Jane frowns. 'But I don't understand, why did you tell me to call you Brook if nobody else does?'

'Because Edward is your brother's name, and the last thing I wanted was for you to think of me as a brother.' He steps closer, towering over her while looking like a nervous schoolboy. 'I wanted to speak to you alone as Beth said you were leaving.'

'That's right. This afternoon, in fact.' Something strange is happening inside Jane's abdomen. It's as if his nerves are contagious.

He twists his hat in his hands. 'Me too.'

She waits, but he says no more. Instead he just looks at her with an intensity that makes her want to run and hide. 'Well, then, Godspeed.' She moves to leave.

He steps into her path, impeding her progress. 'It's as I predicted. William has had his fill of my antics and finds he can suddenly afford whatever sum it might take to send me on my way. Thank you kindly for your assistance in hastening his generosity.'

'Me?' She lays a hand on her breast. 'I'm so sorry. Was it the window?'

'Goodness, he doesn't even know about that yet. I colluded with the housekeeper to replace the pane before he noticed. No, no. As discreet as we were, he somehow discovered our midnight jaunt and is convinced we came across Agnes while trying to elope.' Mr Bridges laughs softly while familiar flames of mortification lick Jane's cheeks. 'He thought it would be prudent to separate us before we had another chance.'

'Did he now?'

'Come, it is amusing. As if we'd be fool enough to set off for Gretna Green on just the one horse.'

'I'm so glad I was able to provide such sport for you and your relations. I came into Kent for no other purpose.'

'Don't be offended. It's not that William has any objection to you. It's me. He doesn't think I'm mature enough to make such an important decision. He says if I can't settle on a profession I'm not ready for a wife.'

Jane raises a palm, in hopes it will put an end to this torment. 'Mr Bridges, I assure you, there is no need to explain. I'm quite familiar with the steps of this dance.'

'And we're so young. I am anyway. You're what?'

'One-and-twenty,' she answers, through gritted teeth.

'Exactly. Not that young for a lady of your rank, is it? I expect you'll be looking to make your choice sooner rather than later?'

'Do you ever know when to desist in speaking?' Unfortunately, it seems Jane and Mr Bridges really do have a lot in common.

'If I opt for the Church, it will take me several years to achieve ordination. And even then I wouldn't be fully independent. I'd have to wait for the present incumbent to die before I take over the living of Goodnestone,' he continues, and Jane is struck with the notion they are having two separate conversations – like a pair of actors, treading the same boards but reading from two different plays. Again, she tries to leave, but Mr Bridges grabs her hand. 'But, Jane . . .' he peers at her with an earnestness she is not at all used to from him '. . . it won't be this way for ever. As you said, I'm a young man of good family. I'm bound to fall on my feet eventually. And then . . .' He steps closer, leaning his tall frame down to hers.

And then? She will not ask. He leaves the remainder of the sentence hanging in the lavender-scented air between them.

Rather than saying anything further at all, he snakes an arm around her waist. Their eyes meet. Jane tips her head backwards, a mere fraction, in invitation – and his lips, when they meet hers, are irresistible. She lets her lids sink closed and abandons herself to the blissful sensation of his kiss. For once, he does not smell of snuff. In fact, he tastes suspiciously of peppermint. When they eventually break apart, noses bumping, Mr Bridges offers her a bashful smile and from somewhere deep, in what Jane believed to be the empty chrysalis of her heart, the faintest fluttering stirs.

'I apologize if this is untoward,' he colours, 'but may I write to you?'

'Yes. Yes, you may,' she replies, shocked at the breathy rasp of her own voice. 'But make it worth the postage, won't you? Remember, if I want to read a travelogue, I can borrow one from the circulating library.'

He leans in to give her one last kiss before letting her go. Dazed, she follows him into the lane. He mounts his gig and doffs his hat before taking the reins.

'Brook!' Jane calls after him.

He glances over his shoulder, beaming at the sound of his Christian name on her lips.

'You're not a coward.' Jane meets his brilliant smile with her own.

'No, I really don't think I am!' He laughs and, with a final salute, departs. The horse's hoofs and the gig's wheels stir up a great cloud of dust. Jane lingers until he is completely out of sight, with the thrill of a gambler who, in the instant before they are about to fold, discovers they have everything to play for.

*

Later that afternoon, Jane and Mrs Knight travel to Briar Farm with Agnes on the first stage of Jane's journey back to Hampshire. The lady abbess is leaning on her stick among the hollyhocks going to seed in the drive as the coach draws near. At the sight of her, Agnes's posture relaxes as if she recognizes the old woman. After the coach rolls to a halt, she alights and skips up the path, towards the makeshift nunnery where she has been accepted as a lay sister. 'Wait, Agnes. I have a parting gift for you.' Jane climbs out, brandishing the pretty pocketbook she bought in Canterbury. She is so glad she resisted the urge to write in it. With the help of Alice, she has pressed the pages smooth and it is as good as new. 'I thought it might help if you kept a journal. It might prevent you from becoming so confused.'

Agnes's eyes cloud at the offering. 'I can read a little, but I never learnt to make my letters.'

Jane frowns, confused at how Agnes could have written to her and Mrs Knight in the guise of another when she claims to be illiterate. 'But Biddy did?'

'Yes, Biddy did.' Agnes smiles proudly. 'She went to Sunday school.'

'Oh.' Yet again Jane is forced to reappraise Agnes. She assumed *she* was the original girl, trapped beneath the terror of her ordeal. But maybe that is Biddy. Or, perhaps, Eleanor, Agnes, Biddy, Nessa, Derdriu, and even the terrible Captain Fairbairn, are all as vital as each other. 'In that case, do you think you could pass this on to Biddy for me?'

'Certainly.' Agnes retrieves the book from Jane's hands, clutching it to her chest. 'I expect she'll like it here.'

'I hope you all will.' If Agnes cannot be cured of her affliction, Jane prays that living in this quiet community of women will afford her the solace she deserves.

'I'm so sorry again, for anything the captain may have done or said.' Agnes's forehead crumples. For the first time that day, she looks afraid.

'Agnes, really, there's no need.'

'He never meant any harm to you or to my mistress. It was always me he wanted to silence. Those nasty notes were all aimed at driving out the others so that he could smother me. And even then, he was only trying to –'

'Protect you, I know. But you won't need that kind of protection ever again. There's no way Mr Spooner can hurt you now.' Miraculously, Spooner had survived his initial amputation, but infection soon set into the wound and Dr Storer admits his patient's chances of recuperation are nil. Even the maggots do not seem to be aiding his recovery. Agnes's abuser is destined to die in excruciating agony. 'Just promise me you'll stay here, where the lady abbess can take care of you.'

'I'll try, I swear to it. Thank you, Miss Jane. Thank you, Miss Dashwood. Thank you, Miss Marianne.' Agnes throws an arm around Jane, kissing her cheek.

Jane does not correct her to say that she is 'merely Jane'. There are no impermeable divisions in Jane's mind. She can slip in and out of her characters as easily as changing into a new gown. Jane is distinctly *not* her heroines, yet none would exist without her, and Jane would not be Jane if it wasn't for Catherine, Lizzy, Miss Dashwood, and even the diabolical Lady Susan. Agnes has taught her this.

'Thank you, mistress,' Agnes calls over Jane's shoulder, before running off towards the heavenly sound of the female choir drifting from inside the farmhouse. The lady abbess nods to Mrs Knight in a gesture that Jane knows is designed to reassure her that her former charge will be safe in her care. Still, Mrs Knight looks forlorn at the way Agnes abandoned her so readily.

Jane hastens her step to join the widow, threading her arm through Mrs Knight's as they make their way back towards the coach. 'It was very kind of you to accommodate Agnes at Godmersham Park for so long. But she'll flourish here, I'm sure of it.'

'I know, but I shall miss her. If there's one thing the last few weeks have confirmed, it's that I've shut myself away from society for far too long.' Mrs Knight fingers the mourning brooch pinned to her breast. The sunlight warms the pearls surrounding it and Jane sees that Mrs Knight's black silk pelisse is shot through with regal purple. Perhaps there was a point in her visit to her dressmaker, after all. 'I'll never cease to grieve for my dear husband, but I've come to a resolution. It's time for me to start living in the world once again.'

'That sounds commendable.' Jane pats her hand. As they

saunter down the path towards the coach, she eyes the gallant Armand. He cannot be more than a decade younger than his mistress. Now that Jane is no longer so afraid of him, she can see – with his aquiline nose and proud features – he is actually very handsome. 'You intend to remarry!' she gasps. This really could be a disaster for Neddy. Even if Mrs Knight is too old to bear children, her new husband will surely have a claim to her wealth.

'Remarry?' Mrs Knight stops short, wrinkling her nose. 'Miss Austen! Where do you get these ridiculous notions from?'

'I'm sorry, I just thought ...'

'Why would a woman in my enviable position do that?'

'For love?' Jane asks, bracing herself for the scolding she's bound to receive in return.

'Pah, as if I'd be so foolish! No, I've made arrangements to sign my estate over to Neddy. He's ready to be of full use to the neighbourhood. And, really, what's the point in waiting until my death? The mansion is far too big for me, and it would bring me great pleasure to see my grandchildren enjoying it. You needn't pretend surprise. We both know you were listening at the door when I broached the matter with my solicitor.'

'I ... I was.' Belatedly, Jane realizes this was the subject of the private conversation she overheard in Canterbury. Mrs Knight never once considered transferring her estate to Agnes. It was always intended for Neddy – but she is going against her husband's wishes in handing it to him *before* she dies.

'Indeed you were. As you will have noted, Mr Furley took some persuading to draw up the papers. But he's finally agreed on the condition I maintain one of my smaller properties, a little house called White Friars in Canterbury, and withdraw a modest sum from the income annually. Barring that, my entire estate shall be transferred to Neddy in a manner that cannot be reversed.'

'How modest a sum?' Jane cannot resist enquiring.

'Two thousand pounds. Mr Furley was most anxious I did not impoverish myself, but I'm confident I can live according to my means.'

'I'm sure you are,' says Jane, thinking that only someone as accustomed to great wealth as Mrs Knight could describe an annual income of two thousand pounds as 'modest'.

'I'd like to inform Neddy and vacate immediately. You don't think it will be too much for him and Elizabeth to absorb so soon after the arrival of baby Henry, do you?'

'No, they'll be delighted.' And more than a little relieved, Jane imagines. 'Is that why you were waiting to discuss the matter with Neddy?'

'That, and tying things up with Briar Farm. The freehold remains part of Godmersham, but I've given the lease of the farmhouse and the surrounding acreage to the order for the next thousand years. It's what my ancestor Dame Lucy would have wanted.'

'That really is so very generous of you.' Neddy was right about his mother. Despite her grandiose demeanour, she is the most tender-hearted woman Jane has ever met.

'It's my privilege. And, in return, the sisters will care for Agnes. They know all about her affliction and have promised to treat her with the utmost compassion. She will no longer require any special patronage from me.' Mrs Knight fixes her steely eyes on Jane. 'But it strikes me, dear, that perhaps you do.'

Jane's step falters. 'Me?'

'Yes. If it's acceptable to you, I'd like to award you a regular allowance. It won't be enough to make you independent.' She flicks her wrist loftily. 'But it would mean you won't have to go cap in hand to your father or one of your brothers every time you want to furnish yourself with a pocketbook or a new gown.'

'I couldn't possibly accept your charity, not when you've done so much for my family already.'

'It's not charity, Miss Austen. I expect you to labour for it.'

'Labour for it?' Jane asks, picturing herself in the distinctive purple and black livery of Godmersham Park. She is not sanguine it will flatter her complexion.

'Yes, through your compositions.'

Jane halts, her heart beating faster. 'You're offering to give me an allowance so that I may pursue my *writing*? I thought you were not listening when I read my work aloud.'

'Not listening? How could I not listen? Dear girl, your words have a way of piercing one's soul.'

'They do?'

'They really do.' Mrs Knight reaches out to take Jane's arm. 'But I could tell you were making progress with Agnes, and I didn't want to interfere.'

'I – I don't know what to say.' Jane swallows, trying to dislodge the awkward lump in her throat. Her eyes sting and her vision is blurred. To think that she might receive something even more valuable than praise according to the merit of her work.

'Don't say anything. Just write. You're far better at that.'

'Thank you, Mrs Knight.' Jane wipes a tear from her cheek. 'Sincerely, thank you.'

Mrs Knight walks on, not caring to witness Jane's uncharacteristic show of sentimentality. 'I demand the first reading of all new manuscripts before they're circulated any wider than your Steventon family. You must send me the one your father was so enamoured of. What's it called again?'

'*First Impressions.*'

'Well, that's no good.'

'Is it not?' Jane is disappointed to discover having a patron will necessarily involve exposing herself to all manner of helpful hints.

'No, I must have read two novels by that title already.' Mrs Knight frowns. 'I command you to come up with something more original. Tell me, have you read any Frances Burney?'

'Why, she's my particular favourite.'

'Mine, too. What a coincidence. Oh, are you sure I can't

persuade you to remain in Kent a few days longer? We could visit my little pied-à-terre in Canterbury.'

'No. I'm dreadfully sorry, but I've absented myself for far too long already. Cassandra is not adjusting to the death of her fiancé. I need to get back to her as soon as I can.' Jane's spirit rises at the thought of home. Even if, as Mary writes, Cassandra is so altered she must prepare herself for the worst. 'It pains me to hear that she is so distressed. I must put aside my selfishness and help her endure. She requested my presence herself.'

'Poor child, the agony of grief is something I know all too well.' Mrs Knight offers Jane a sad smile. Armand steps forward to hand his mistress into the carriage. Jane follows her inside, taking a seat on the bench beside her. 'You know the plan. I'll travel with you as far as Sittingbourne. We'll stay with some old friends, whom I have long since neglected. Then I shall return with my footman, but Armand will hire a post-chaise and escort you to the Pearsons' address in Town. You'll spend the night with them and, in the morning, Captain Pearson will put you in the mail coach to Deane. Don't be daunted. It will do you good to exercise some independence.'

Jane nods, committing to mind each leg of her intended journey for the hundredth time. Despite the misunderstanding between her and Neddy, she is glad they have had this opportunity to renew their familial bond, and she flatters herself that her niece and nephews will remember her at least until she has journeyed so far as Sittingbourne. While she may not have found her sister-in-law any more amiable, she does have a greater degree of sympathy for Elizabeth's predicament, and spending time with Agnes has shown Jane that embracing one's most abominable qualities can sometimes prove necessary to one's very survival. Jane is not looking forward to visiting the jilted Miss Pearson, or returning her letters to Henry, but the family's generous offer of accommodation means there will be only a few days until Jane and her beloved sister are reunited. Her heart aches at the bitter-sweet prospect. Cassandra may be diminished for ever by this blow, but her happiness remains vital to Jane's own. Between them, the sisters must find a way to preserve each other.

To be continued . . .

Author's Note

A Fortune Most Fatal is a work of fiction: in composing it, I've altered the dates of several historical events to fit within my timeline and borrowed liberally from the life stories of Jane Austen and her acquaintances. Jane Austen first visited Edward Austen (later Knight) at Rowling in 1794. Francis Austen joined the *Triton* in 1796. I've aged Sir Brook-William Bridges, and Henrietta Bridges is entirely fictional. Elizabeth Austen (née Bridges), rather than her mother, died suddenly a fortnight after birthing her eleventh living child, in 1808. Edward and Elizabeth's son, Henry, was born in May 1797. Henry Austen married Eliza de Feuillide in December 1797. Jane Austen commenced *Elinor and Marianne* (later *Sense and Sensibility*) in 1795, *First Impressions* (later *Pride and Prejudice*) in 1796 and *Susan* (not *Catherine*, later *Northanger Abbey*) in 1798. I have my Jane writing an early draft of *Sense and Sensibility* here because this is my tribute to that novel. Catherine Knight awarded Jane Austen a small annual allowance, making her Austen's only patron during her lifetime.

Dissociative identity disorder (DID) can be triggered by severe and complex trauma, including sexual abuse, in childhood. Agnes and her alternative identities are based on first-hand accounts from people with this condition who often describe it as a protection mechanism, whereby every alternative identity emerges to shield the child from the reality of their suffering or to help them process what has happened. While I have certainly dramatized Agnes's story, I have done my utmost to do this sensitively by listening to the criticism those with DID have voiced about portrayals of their condition in the media, and by drawing on my own experience of suffering from post-traumatic stress disorder.

Along with Jane Austen's friends and family, two other real historical figures inspired this novel. In 1817, a former servant girl, Mary Baker (née Willcocks), persuaded a Gloucester magistrate and his wife she was Princess Caraboo of the fictional island of Javasu in the Indian Ocean, and that she had been captured by pirates and escaped by jumping overboard in the Bristol Channel, then swimming ashore. Her ruse was eventually discovered but, rather than prosecute, Mary's benefactress gave her some money to start afresh in America. Everyone who knew Mary said she loved to tell stories. It made me wonder, if Mary had been born into the class of women who were fortunate enough to receive an education, would she be remembered as another Jane Austen?

In the nineteenth century, Robert Fairbairn, my direct ancestor, commanded the *Princess Victoria* steam-vessel on the Thames. He was tried at the Old Bailey in 1835 and again in 1840 for unlawful killing and was acquitted both times but, to misquote Oscar Wilde, to be tried once for manslaughter may be regarded as a misfortune; to be tried twice looks like carelessness. I was initially horrified that research into our family tree had brought to light such a villain. However, when I read the transcripts of his trials, I realized that, like Agnes's alternative identity, the real Captain Fairbairn was forced to make some very difficult decisions to preserve the lives of those under his care.

Acknowledgements

Whenever I meet another devoted Janeite, I find we have something in common: Austen's works have provided solace through a particularly painful time in our lives. It is this ability to reflect our distress back to us in a way that offers support which makes Austen such a beloved writer, and that I have attempted to pay tribute to in *A Fortune Most Fatal*.

In bringing Austen's story to the page, I am blessed with the support of . . .

My extremely dedicated agent, Juliet Mushens, and everyone at Mushens Entertainment, who make me feel as if they are there to champion my work, hold my hand and answer my questions at any time of the day or night.

My fabulous team at Penguin Michael Joseph in the UK, including my editor Grace Long (who wisely pointed out that Agnes deserved her own voice), Phillipa Walker and Nick Lowndes (editorial), Hazel Orme (copy-editor), Stephen Ryan and Sarah Davies (proofreaders), Ciara Berry and Lily Evans (publicity), Courtney Barclay (marketing), Nina Elstad (design), Serena Nazareth (production) and Kelly Mason (sales).

My fantastic agent in the US, Jenny Bent, and my wonderful team at Union Square & Co, including Claire Wachtel and Juliana Nador (editorial), Erik Jacobsen (jacket design), Kevin Ullrich (interior design), Kristin Mandaglio (project editor) and Sandy Noman (production manager).

As well as the incredible team of co-agents, publishers and translators around the world who have made *Miss Austen Investigates* available to readers across an amazing nineteen territories (and counting!).

Elizabeth Welke (Felicity George) and Suzy Vadori who encouraged me to tell the story I needed to rather than what I felt might have been expected in a follow-up to the first *Miss Austen Investigates*. My fellow debuts and crime writers who have supported me in this journey and helped to demystify the publishing world.

The Austen biographers, scholars and historians whose work has proved invaluable to me: Deirdre Le Faye, Susannah Fullerton, Claire Tomalin, Lucy Worsley, Helena Kelly, Devoney Looser, Paula Byrne, John Mullen, Brian Southam, Mary Waugh and Jenny Uglow.

Everyone who has helped me track down random facts about Austen and her family, and get a sense of the locations where this novel is set, especially: Martin Caddick from Chawton House, Hampshire Record Office, Tess Plumptre of Goodnestone Park, Godmersham Park Heritage Centre and the National Garden Scheme.

Phoebe Judge and Lauren Spohrer of the podcast *Criminal* for igniting my fascination with Princess Caraboo (episode #185 'The Princess', featuring Meg Russet). Those with Dissociative Identity Disorder who have shown tremendous courage in voicing their experiences, as well as their concerns about how this condition is represented in the media, especially Emma and her system from the *System Speak* podcast.

Every English teacher I ever had, but especially Mrs Daniels (Charles Edward Brooke, London), who in 1992 swapped my Sweet Valley High books for Alice Walker's *The Color Purple*. My mum, dad, and sister, Kelly, for making me feel like writing stories was the thing I was always meant to do. My husband, Stephen, and our daughters, Eliza and Rosina, for accompanying me on my quest to visit every single house Jane Austen ever stepped over the threshold of. My dog Toby, who reminded me to take screen breaks and occasionally leave the house.

Finally, my readers – it is a joy to share the comfort I find in Jane Austen with you.